One

Lady Winwood being denied, the morning caller inquired with some anxiety for Miss Winwood, or, in fact, for any of the young ladies. In face of the rumour which had come to her ears it would be too provoking if all the Winwood ladies were to withhold themselves. But the porter held the door fully open and said that Miss Winwood was at home.

Directing the coachman of her extremely smart town carriage to wait for her, Mrs Maulfrey stepped into the dim hall, and said briskly: 'Where is Miss Winwood? You need not be at the trouble of announcing me.'

All the young ladies, it seemed, were in the small saloon. Mrs Maulfrey nodded, and walked across the hall with a click of her high heels. As she ascended the stairs her armazine skirts, spread over very large *paniers à coudes*, brushed the banisters on either side of her. She reflected, not for the first time, that the stairway was too narrow, and the carpet positively shabby. She would be ashamed for her part of such oldfashioned furnishings; but although she claimed cousinship, she was not, she admitted to herself, a Winwood of Winwood.

The small saloon, by which name the porter designated a back sitting-room given over to the use of the young ladies, lay up one pair of stairs, and was well known to Mrs Maulfrey. She tapped with her gloved hand on one of the panels of the door, and entered on the echo of her knock.

The three Misses Winwood were grouped by the window,

presenting an artless and agreeable picture. Upon a faded yellow satin sopha sat Miss Winwood and Miss Charlotte, their arms entwined about each other's waists. They were much alike, but Miss Winwood was held to be the greater beauty. Her classic profile was turned to the door, but upon Mrs Maulfrey's rustling entrance she looked round and displayed to the visitor a pair of melting blue eyes and a sweet, arched mouth that formed at the moment an O of mild surprise. A quantity of fair curls dressed without powder and threaded by a blue riband framed her face and tumbled on to her shoulders in several ordered locks.

Miss Charlotte was not seen to advantage beside the Beauty of the Family, but she was a true Winwood, with the famous straight nose and the same blue eyes. Her curls, not quite so fair as her sisters, owed their existence to hot irons, her eyes were of a shallower blue, and her colouring inclined towards the sallow; but she was allowed to be a very well-looking young lady.

Miss Horatia, the youngest of the three, had nothing that declared her lineage except her nose. Her hair was dark, her eyes a profound grey, and her brows, nearly black and rather thick, were quite straight, and gave her a serious, almost frowning, expression. No amount of careful training would induce an arch in them. She was quite half a head shorter than her sisters, and, at the age of seventeen, was obliged regretfully to admit that she was not likely to grow any taller.

When Mrs Maulfrey came into the room Horatia was seated on a low stool by the sopha, propping her chin in her hands, and scowling dreadfully. Or perhaps, thought Mrs Maulfrey, that was just a trick of those preposterous eyebrows.

All three sisters wore morning toilets of worked muslin over slight hoops, with tiffany sashes round their waists. Countrified, thought Mrs Maulfrey, giving her fringed silk mantle a satisfied twitch.

'My dears!' she exclaimed. 'I came the instant I heard! Tell me at once, is it true? Has Rule offered?'

Miss Winwood, who had risen gracefully to receive her

The Convenient Marriage

Author of over fifty books, Georgette Heyer is one of the best-known and best-loved of all historical novelists, making the Regency period her own. Her first novel, *The Black Moth*, published in 1921, was written at the age of seventeen to amuse her convalescent brother; her last was *My Lord John*. Although most famous for her historical novels, she also wrote twelve detective stories. Georgette Heyer died in 1974 at the age of seventy-one.

The Convenient Marriage

Georgette Heyer

arrow books

Reissued by Arrow Books in 2013

2 4 6 8 10 9 7 5 3 1

First published in the United Kingdom in 1934 by William Heinemann

Arrow Books
Random House, 20 Vauxhall Bridge Road,
London SW1V 2SA

www.randomhouse.co.uk

Addresses for companies within The Random House Group Limited can be found at:
www.randomhouse.co.uk/offices.htm

The Random House Group Limited Reg. No. 954009

A CIP catalogue record for this book
is available from the British Library

ISBN 9780099585558

The Random House Group Limited supports the Forest Stewardship
Council® (FSC®), the leading international forest-certification organisation.
Our books carrying the FSC label are printed on FSC®-certified paper. FSC is
the only forest-certification scheme supported by the leading environmental
organisations, including Greenpeace. Our paper procurement policy can
be found at: www.randomhouse.co.uk/environment

Typeset by SX Composing DTP, Rayleigh, Essex
Printed and bound in Great Britain by Clays Ltd, St Ives PLC

cousin, seemed to droop and to grow pale. 'Yes,' she said faintly. 'Alas, it is quite true, Theresa.'

Mrs Maulfrey's eyes grew round with respect. 'Oh, Lizzie!' she breathed. 'Rule! A Countess! Twenty thousand a year, I have heard, and I daresay it may be found to be more!'

Miss Charlotte set a chair for her, observing with a reproving note in her voice: 'We believe Lord Rule to be a most eligible gentleman. Though no one,' she added, clasping Miss Winwood's hand tenderly, 'however genteel, could be worthy of our dearest Lizzie!'

'Lord, Charlotte!' said Mrs Maulfrey tartly, 'Rule's the biggest prize in the market, and you know it. It is the most amazing piece of good fortune ever I heard. Though I will say, Lizzie, you deserve it. Yes, you do, and I am quite enchanted for you. Only to think of the Settlements!'

'I find the thought of Settlements particularly indelicate, Theresa,' said Miss Charlotte. 'Mama will no doubt arrange with Lord Rule, but Lizzie cannot be supposed to concern herself with such sordid questions as the size of Lord Rule's fortune.'

The youngest Miss Winwood, who all the time had continued to sit with her chin in her hands, suddenly raised her head and delivered herself of one shattering word. 'S-stuff!' she said, in a deep little voice that just quivered on a stammer.

Miss Charlotte looked pained; Miss Winwood gave a rather wan smile. 'Indeed, I fear Horry is in the right,' she said sadly. 'It is just the Fortune.' She sank on to the sopha again, and gazed fixedly out of the window.

Mrs Maulfrey became aware that the steady blue eyes were swimming in tears. 'Why, Lizzie!' she said. 'One would think you had had dark tidings instead of a splendid Offer!'

'Theresa!' intoned Miss Charlotte, putting both arms about her sister. 'Is this worthy of you? Can it be that you have forgotten Mr Heron?'

Mrs Maulfrey had forgotten Mr Heron. Her jaw dropped slightly, but she recovered in a moment. 'To be sure: Mr Heron,' she said. 'It is very afflicting, but – Rule, you know! I don't say poor Mr Heron is not a very estimable creature, but a mere lieutenant, dearest Lizzie, and I daresay will soon have to go back to that horrid war in America – it's not to be thought of, my love!'

'No,' said Elizabeth in a suffocated voice. 'Not to be thought of.'

Horatia's dark gaze dwelled broodingly on her second sister. 'I think it would be a very good thing if Charlotte were to have R-Rule,' she pronounced.

'Horry!' gasped Charlotte.

'Lord, my dear, what things you say!' remarked Mrs Maulfrey indulgently. 'It's Elizabeth Rule wants.'

Horatia shook her head vehemently. 'No. Only a Winwood,' she said in the tense way she had. 'All arranged years ago. I d-don't believe he's set eyes on L-Lizzie upwards of half a d-dozen times. It can't signify.'

Miss Charlotte released her sister's hand, and said palpitatingly: 'Nothing – *nothing* would induce me to marry Lord Rule, even if he had offered for me! The very notion of Matrimony is repugnant to me. I have long made up my mind to be a Prop to Mama.' She drew a breath. 'If ever any gentleman could induce me to contemplate the Married State, I assure you, my dear Horry, it would be one far other than Lord Rule.'

Mrs Maulfrey had no difficulty in interpreting this announcement. 'For my part, I like a rake,' she observed. 'And Rule is so extremely handsome!'

'I think,' said Horatia obstinately, 'that M-Mama might have suggested Charlotte.'

Elizabeth turned her head: 'You don't understand, Horry dear. Mama could not do such an odd thing.'

'Does my Aunt force you to it, Lizzie?' inquired Mrs Maulfrey, pleasantly intrigued.

'Oh no, no!' Elizabeth replied earnestly. 'You know Mama's tenderness. She is all consideration, all sensibility! It is only my own consciousness of my Duty to the Family that leads me to take a step so – so disastrous to my happiness.'

4

'M-mortgages,' said Horatia cryptically.

'Pelham, I suppose?' said Mrs Maulfrey.

'Of course it is Pelham,' replied Charlotte with a touch of bitterness. 'Everything is his fault. Ruin stares us in the face.'

'Poor Pelham!' Elizabeth said, with a sigh for her absent brother. 'I am afraid he is very extravagant.'

'It's his gambling debts, I take it,' opined Mrs Maulfrey. 'My Aunt seemed to think that even your Portions . . .' She left the sentence delicately unfinished.

Elizabeth flushed, but Horatia said: 'You can't blame P-Pel. It's in the blood. One of us must m-marry Rule. Lizzie's the eldest and the p-prettiest, but Charlotte would do very well. Lizzie's promised to Edward Heron.'

'Not "promised", dearest,' Elizabeth said in a low voice. 'We only – hoped, if he could but get his Captaincy, perhaps Mama would consent.'

'Even supposing it, my love,' said Mrs Maulfrey with great good sense, 'what – what, I ask of you, is a Captain of a Line Regiment when compared with the Earl of Rule? And from all I hear the young man has the most meagre of fortunes, and who, pray, is to buy his promotion?'

Horatia said, quite undaunted: 'Edward t-told me that if he had the good fortune to be in another engagement there might be a ch-chance.'

Miss Winwood gave a slight shudder, and lifted one hand to her cheek. 'Don't, Horry!' she begged.

'It doesn't signify,' Mrs Maulfrey declared. 'I know you will say I am unfeeling, my dear Lizzie, but it would not do at all. Why, how would you contrive on the young man's pay? It is all horribly sad, but only think of the position you will fill, the jewels you will have!'

The prospect appeared to affect Miss Winwood with revulsion, but she said nothing. It was left to Horatia to express the sentiments of all three sisters. 'Vulgar!' she said. 'You are, you know, Theresa.'

Mrs Maulfrey blushed, and made a business of arranging her

stiff skirts. 'Of course I know *that* would not weigh with Lizzie, but you can't deny it is a brilliant match. What does my Aunt feel?'

'Deeply thankful,' said Charlotte. 'As indeed we must all be, when we consider the straits Pelham has placed us in.'

'Where is Pelham?' demanded Mrs Maulfrey.

'We are not quite certain,' answered Elizabeth. 'We think perhaps in Rome now. Poor Pel is but an indifferent correspondent. But I feel sure we shall hear from him quite soon.'

'Well, he will have to come home for your wedding, I suppose,' said Mrs Maulfrey. 'But, Lizzie, you must tell me! Has Rule paid his addresses? I had not the least idea of anything of the kind, though, naturally, I had heard that it was in a way arranged. But he has been so very –' She apparently thought better of what she had been about to say, and broke off. 'But that's neither here nor there, and I daresay he will be a charming husband. Have you given him your answer, Lizzie?'

'Not yet,' said Elizabeth almost inaudibly. ' I – I too had no notion of it, Theresa. I have met him, of course. He stood up with me for the first two dances at the subscription-ball at Almack's, when Pelham was at home. He was – he has always been – all that is amiable, but that he intended offering for my hand I never dreamed. He waited on Mama yesterday only to – to solicit her permission to pay his addresses to me. There is nothing announced yet, you must understand.'

'Everything of the most correct!' approved Mrs Maulfrey. 'Oh, my love, I cannot help it if you say I have no sensibility, but only conceive of having Rule paying his addresses to one! I declare I would give my eyes – or, I would have,' she corrected herself, 'had I not married Mr Maulfrey. And so,' she added, 'would every other young lady in town! Why, my dears, you would not believe the caps that have been set at him!'

'Theresa, I must, I must request you not to talk in that odious way!' said Charlotte.

Horatia was looking at her cousin with interest. 'Why do you

6

say "only c-conceive of Rule paying his addresses to one"? I thought he was quite old.'

'Old?' said Mrs Maulfrey. 'Rule? Nothing of the sort, my dear! Not a day above thirty-five, I'll stake my reputation. And what a leg! What an air! The most engaging smile!'

'I c-call that old,' said Horatia calmly. 'Edward is only t-twenty-two.'

There did not seem to be much to say after that. Mrs Maulfrey, perceiving that she had culled all the news that her cousins could at this present impart, began to think of taking her leave of them. Though sorry for Elizabeth's evident distress at the magnificent prospect ahead of her she could not in the least understand it, and considered that the sooner Lieutenant Heron was posted back to his regiment the better it would be. Therefore, when the door opened to admit a spare female of uncertain age, who informed Elizabeth with a flutter in her voice that Mr Heron was below and begged the favour of a word with her, she pursed her lips, and looked as disapproving as she could.

Elizabeth's colour fluctuated, but she rose up from the sopha, and said quietly: 'Thank you, Laney.'

Miss Lane seemed to share a little of Mrs Maulfrey's disapproval. She regarded Elizabeth in a deprecating way, and suggested: 'My dear Miss Winwood, do you think you should? Do you think your Mama would like it?'

Elizabeth replied with her gentle air of dignity: 'I have Mama's permission, dear Laney, to – to tell Mr Heron of the approaching change in my estate. Theresa, you won't I know, speak of Lord Rule's obliging offer until – until it is formally announced.'

'Too noble creature!' Charlotte sighed, as the door closed softly behind Miss Winwood. 'How very lowering it is to reflect upon the trials that afflict the Female Sex!'

'Edward is afflicted too,' said Horatia practically. Her penetrating eyes rested on her cousin. 'Theresa, if you ch-chatter about this you will be sorry. Something must be d-done.'

7

'What can be done, when our sweetest Lizzie goes a Willing Sacrifice to the Altar?' said Charlotte in a hollow voice.

'Trials! Sacrifice!' exclaimed Mrs Maulfrey. 'Lord, one would think Rule an ogre to listen to you! You put me out of all patience, Charlotte. A house in Grosvenor Square, and Meering, which I am told is quite superb, the park seven miles about, and three lodge-gates!'

'It will be a great position,' said the little governess in her breathless way. 'But who should fill it better than dear Miss Winwood? One has always felt that she was destined for a high place.'

'Pho!' said Horatia scornfully, and snapped her fingers. '*That* for Rule's great p-position!'

'Miss Horatia, I beg of you, not that ungenteel gesture!'

Charlotte came to the support of her sister. 'You should not snap your fingers, Horry, but you are quite in the right. Lord Rule does very very well for himself in getting a Winwood for his bride.'

Meanwhile Miss Winwood, pausing only for a moment on the staircase to calm the agitation which the news of Mr Heron's arrival had induced, went down to the library on the ground floor of the house.

Here there awaited her a young man in a state of greater agitation than her own.

Mr Edward Heron, of the 10th Foot, at present in America, was stationed in England on Recruiting Service. He had been wounded at the Battle of Bunker's Hill, and sent home shortly afterwards, his wound being of a serious enough nature to preclude his taking further part – for a time at least – in the hostilities abroad. Upon his recovery gazetted, greatly to his chagrin, for Home Service.

The acquaintance between himself and Miss Winwood was of long standing. The younger son of a country gentleman whose estates marched with Viscount Winwood's, he had known the Misses Winwood almost from the hour of his birth. He was of excellent if impoverished family, and had he been the possessor

8

of a rather large fortune might have been deemed an eligible though not brilliant match for Elizabeth.

When Miss Winwood entered the library he arose from a seat by the window, and came towards her with an anxious look of inquiry upon his countenance. He was a personable young man, and looked very well in his scarlet regimentals. He had height, and good shoulders, and a frank, open countenance, rather pale still from prolonged suffering. He carried his left arm a little stiffly, but declared himself to be in perfect health, and very ready to rejoin his regiment.

A glance at Miss Winwood's face informed him that the anxiety occasioned by her brief note had not been misplaced. Taking her hands in a strong clasp he said urgently: 'What has occurred? Elizabeth! Something terrible?'

Her lips quivered. She drew her hands away, and put one of them out to grasp a chairback. 'Oh, Edward, the worst!' she whispered.

He grew paler. 'Your note alarmed me. Good God, what is it?'

Miss Winwood pressed her handkerchief to her mouth. 'Lord Rule was with Mama yesterday – in this very room.' She raised her eyes imploringly to his face. 'Edward, it is all at an end. Lord Rule has offered for my hand.'

A dreadful stillness fell in the shadowed room. Miss Winwood stood with bowed head before Mr Heron, leaning a little on the chair-back.

Mr Heron did not move, but presently he said rather hoarsely: 'And you said – ?' But it was hardly a question; he spoke it mechanically, knowing what she must have said.

She made a hopeless gesture. 'What can I say? You know so well how it is with us.'

He took a step away from her, and began to pace up and down the room. 'Rule!' he said. 'Is he very rich?'

'Very rich,' Elizabeth desolately.

Words crowded in Mr Heron's throat, hurt, angry, passionate words, yet not one of them could he utter. Life had dealt him her cruellest blow, and all that he could find to say, and that in a numb voice which did not seem to belong to him, was: 'I see.' He perceived that Elizabeth was silently weeping, and at once came to her, and took her hands, and drew her to a couch. 'Oh, my love, don't cry!' he said, a catch in his own voice. 'Perhaps it is not too late: we can contrive something – we must contrive something!' But he spoke without conviction, for he knew that he would never have anything to set against Rule's fortune. He put his arms round Elizabeth, and laid his cheek against her curls while her tears fell on his gay scarlet coat.

After a little while she drew herself away. 'I am making you unhappy too,' she said.

At that he went down on his knee beside her, and hid his face in her hands. She did not make any effort to pull them away, but said only: 'Mama has been so kind. I am permitted to tell you myself. It is – it must be goodbye, Edward. I have not strength to continue seeing you. Oh, is it wrong of me to say that I shall have you in my heart always – always?'

'I cannot let you go!' he said with suppressed violence. 'All our hopes – our plans – Elizabeth, Elizabeth!'

She did not speak, and presently he raised his face, flushed now and haggard. 'What can I do? Is there nothing?'

She touched the couch beside her. 'Do you think I have not tried to think of something?' she said sadly. 'Alas, did we not feel always that ours was nothing but a dream, impossible to realise?'

He sat down again, leaning his arm on his knee, and looking down at his own neat boot. 'It's your brother,' he said. 'Debts.'

She nodded. 'Mama told me so much that I did not know. It is worse than I imagined. Everything is mortgaged, and there are Charlotte and Horatia to think for. Pelham has lost five thousand guineas at a sitting in Paris.'

'Does Pelham never win?' demanded Mr Heron despairingly.

'I don't know,' she replied. 'He says he is very unlucky.'

He looked up. 'Elizabeth, if it hurts you I am sorry, but that you should be sacrificed to Pelham's selfish, thoughtless –'

'Oh, hush!' she begged. 'You know the Fatal Tendency in us

Winwoods. Pelham cannot help it. My father even! When Pelham came into his inheritance he found it already wasted. Mama explained it all to me. She is so very sorry, Edward. We have mingled our tears. But she thinks, and how can I not feel the truth of it, that it is my Duty to the Family to accept of Lord Rule's offer.'

'Rule!' he said bitterly. 'A man fifteen years your senior! a man of his reputation. He has only to throw his glove at your feet, and you – Oh God, I cannot bear to think of it!' His writhing fingers created havoc amongst his pomaded curls. 'Why must his choice light upon you?' he groaned. 'Are there not others enough?'

'I think,' she said diffidently, 'that he wishes to ally himself with our Family. They say he is very proud, and our name is – is also a proud one.' She hesitated, and said, colouring: 'It is to be a marriage of convenience, such as are the fashion in France. Lord Rule does not – cannot pretend to love me, nor I him.' She glanced up, as the gilt time-piece on the mantelshelf chimed the hour. 'I must say goodbye to you,' she said, with desperate calm. 'I promised Mama – only half an hour. Edward –' She shrank suddenly into his embrace – 'Oh, my love, remember me!' she sobbed.

Three minutes later the library door slammed, and Mr Heron strode across the hall towards the front door, his hair in disorder, his gloves and cocked hat clenched in his hand.

'Edward!' The thrilling whisper came from the stairhead. He glanced up, heedless of his ravaged face and wild appearance.

The youngest Miss Winwood leaned over the balustrade, and laid a finger on her lips. 'Edward, c-come up! I must speak to you!'

He hesitated, but an imperious gesture from Horatia brought him to the foot of the stairs. 'What is it?' he asked curtly.

'Come up!' repeated Horatia impatiently.

He slowly mounted the stairs. His hand was seized, and he was whisked into the big withdrawing-room that overlooked the street.

Horatia shut the door. 'D-don't speak too loud! Mama's bedroom is next door. What did she say?'

'I have not seen Lady Winwood,' Mr Heron answered heavily.

'Stupid! L-Lizzie!'

He said tightly: 'Only goodbye.'

'It shan't be!' said Horatia, with determination. 'L-listen, Edward! I have a p-plan!'

He looked down at her, a gleam of hope in his eyes. 'I'll do anything!' he said. 'Only tell me!'

'It isn't anything for you to do,' said Horatia. 'I am g-going to do it!'

'You?' he said doubtfully. 'But what can you do?'

'I d-don't know, but I'm g-going to try. M-mind, I can't be sure that it will succeed, but I think perhaps it m-might.'

'But what is it?' he persisted.

'I shan't say. I only told you because you looked so very m-miserable. You had better trust me, Edward.'

'I do,' he assured her. 'But –'

Horatia pulled him to stand in front of the mirror over the fireplace. 'Then straighten your hair,' she said severely. 'J-just look at it. You've crushed your hat too. There! Now, g-go away, Edward, before Mama hears you.'

Mr Heron found himself pushed to the door. He turned, and grasped Horatia's hand. 'Horry, I don't see what you can do, but if you can save Elizabeth from this match –'

Two dimples leapt into being; the grey eyes twinkled. 'I know. You w-will be my m-most obliged servant. Well, I will!'

'More than that!' he said earnestly.

'Hush, Mama will hear!' whispered Horatia, and thrust him out of the room.

TWO

r Arnold Gisborne, lately of Queens' College, Cambridge, was thought by his relatives to have been very fortunate to have acquired the post of secretary to the Earl of Rule. He was tolerably satisfied himself, employment in a noble house was a fair stepping-stone to a Public Career, but he would have preferred, since he was a serious young man, the service of one more nearly concerned with the Affairs of the Nation. My Lord of Rule, when he could be moved thereto, occasionally took his seat in the Upper House, and had been known to raise his pleasant, lazy voice in support of a Motion, but he had no place in the Ministry, and he displayed not the smallest desire to occupy himself with Politicks. If he spoke, Mr Gisborne was requested to prepare his speech, which Mr Gisborne did with energy and enthusiasm, hearing in his imagination the words delivered in his own crisp voice. My lord would glance over the sheets of fine handwriting, and say: 'Admirable, my dear Arnold, quite admirable. But not quite in my mode, do you think?' And Mr Gisborne would have sadly to watch my lord's well-kept hand driving a quill through his most cherished periods. My lord, aware of his chagrin, would look up and say with his rather charming smile: 'I feel for you, Arnold, believe me. But I am such a very frippery fellow, you know. It would shock the Lords to hear me utter such energetic sentiments. It would not do at all.'

'My lord, may I say that you like to be thought a frippery fellow?' asked Mr Gisborne with severity tempered by respect.

13

'By all means, Arnold. You may say just what you like,' replied his lordship amiably.

But in spite of this permission Mr Gisborne did not say anything more. It would have been a waste of time. My lord could give one a set-down, though always with that faint look of amusement in his bored grey eyes, and always in the pleasantest manner. Mr Gisborne contented himself with dreaming of his own future, and in the meantime managed his patron's affairs with conscientious thoroughness. The Earl's mode of life he could not approve, for he was the son of a Dean, and strictly reared. My lord's preoccupation with such wanton pieces of pretty femininity as La Fanciola, of the Opera House, or a certain Lady Massey filled him with a disapproval that made him at first scornful, and later, when he had been my lord's secretary for a twelve-month, regretful.

He had not imagined, upon his first setting eyes on the Earl, that he could learn to like, or even to tolerate, this lazy, faintly mocking exquisite, but he had not, after all, experienced the least difficulty in doing both. At the end of a month he had discovered that just as his lordship's laced and scented coats concealed an extremely powerful frame, so his weary eyelids drooped over eyes that could become as keen as the brain behind.

Yielding to my lord's charm, he accepted his vagaries if not with approval at least with tolerance.

The Earl's intention to enter the married state took him by surprise. He had no notion of such a scheme until a morning two days after his lordship had visited Lady Winwood in South Street. Then, as he sat at his desk in the library, Rule strolled in after a late breakfast, and perceiving the pen in his hand, complained: 'You are always so damnably busy, Arnold. Do I give you so much work?'

Mr Gisborne got up from his seat at the desk. 'No, sir, not enough.'

'You are insatiable, my dear boy.' He observed some papers in Mr Gisborne's grasp, and sighed. 'What is it now?' he asked with resignation.

14

'I thought, sir, you might wish to see these accounts from Meering,' suggested Mr Gisborne.

'Not in the least,' replied his lordship, leaning his big shoulders against the mantelpiece.

'Very well, sir.' Mr Gisborne laid the papers down, and said tentatively: 'You won't have forgotten that there is a Debate in the House to-day which you will like to take part in?'

His lordship's attention had wandered; he was scrutinizing his own top-boot (for he was dressed for riding) through a long-handled quizzing-glass, but he said in a mildly surprised voice: 'Which I shall what, Arnold?'

'I made sure you would attend it, my lord,' said Mr Gisborne defensively.

'I am afraid you were in your cups, my dear fellow. Now tell me, do my eyes deceive me, or is there a suggestion – the merest hint – of a – really, I fear I must call it a bagginess about the ankle?'

Mr Gisborne glanced perfunctorily down at his lordship's shining boot. 'I don't observe it, sir.'

'Come, come, Arnold!' the Earl said gently. 'Give me your attention, I beg of you!'

Mr Gisborne met the quizzical gleam in my lord's eyes, and grinned in spite of himself. 'Sir, I believe you should go. It is of some moment, in the Lower House –'

'I felt uneasy at the time,' mused the Earl, still contemplating his legs. 'I shall have to change my bootmaker again.' He let his glass fall on the end of its long riband, and turned to arrange his cravat in the mirror. 'Ah! Remind me, Arnold, that I am to wait on Lady Winwood at three. It is really quite important.'

Mr Gisborne stared. 'Yes, sir?'

'Yes, quite important. I think the new habit, the coat *dos de puce* – or is that a thought sombre for the errand? I believe the blue velvet will be more fitting. And the *perruque à bourse*? You prefer the Catogan wig, perhaps, but you are wrong, my dear boy, I am convinced you are wrong. The arrangement of curls in the front gives an impression of heaviness. I feel sure you would not wish me to be heavy.' He gave one of the lace ruffles that fell over his hand a flick. 'Oh, I have not told you, have I? You must know that I am contemplating matrimony, Arnold.'

Mr Gisborne's astonishment was plain to be seen. 'You, sir?' he said, quite dumbfounded.

'But why not?' inquired his lordship. 'Do you object?'

'Object, sir! I? I am only surprised.'

'My sister,' explained his lordship, 'considers that it is time I took a wife.'

Mr Gisborne had a great respect for the Earl's sister, but he had yet to learn that her advice carried any weight with his lordship. 'Indeed, sir,' he said, and added diffidently: 'It is Miss Winwood?'

'Miss Winwood,' agreed the Earl. 'You perceive how important it is that I should not forget to present myself in South Street at – did I say three o'clock?'

'I will put you in mind of it, sir,' said Mr Gisborne dryly.

The door opened to admit a footman in blue livery. 'My lord, a lady has called,' he said hesitatingly.

Mr Gisborne turned to stare, for whatever Rule's amusements abroad might be, his inamoratas did not wait upon him in Grosvenor Square.

The Earl raised his brows. 'I am afraid – I am very much afraid – that you are – shall we say – a little stupid, my friend,' he said. 'But perhaps you have already denied me?'

The lackey looked flustered, and answered: 'The lady bade me tell your lordship that Miss Winwood begs the favour of a word with you.'

There was a moment's silence. Mr Gisborne had with difficulty checked the exclamation that rose to his lips, and now affected to arrange the papers on his desk.

The Earl's eyes, which had narrowed suddenly, to his servant's discomfiture, were once more bland and expressionless. 'I see,' he remarked. 'Where is Miss Winwood?'

'In the smaller saloon, my lord.'

'Very well,' said his lordship. 'You need not wait.'

The lackey bowed, and went out. My lord's gaze rested thoughtfully on Mr Gisborne's profile. 'Arnold,' he said softly. Mr Gisborne looked up. 'Are you very discreet, Arnold?' said his lordship.

Mr Gisborne met his look full. 'Yes, sir. Of course.'

'I am sure you are,' said his lordship. 'Perhaps even – a little deaf?'

Mr Gisborne's lips twitched. 'Upon occasion, amazingly deaf, sir.'

'I need not have asked,' said the Earl. 'You are a prince of secretaries, my dear fellow.'

'As to that, sir, you are very obliging. But certainly you need not have asked.'

'My maladroitness,' murmured his lordship, and went out.

He crossed the wide marble paved hall, observing as he passed a young woman, obviously an abigail, seated on the edge of a straight chair, and clutching her reticule in a frightened manner. Miss Winwood, then, had not come quite unattended.

One of the lackeys sprang to throw open the massive mahogany door that led into the small saloon, and my lord went in.

A lady, not so tall as he had expected to see, was standing with her back to the door, apparently inspecting an oil painting that hung on the far wall. She turned quickly as he came in, and showed him a face that certainly did not belong to Miss Winwood. He checked for a moment, looking down at her in some surprise.

The face under the simple straw hat also showed surprise. 'Are you L-Lord Rule?' demanded the lady.

He was amused. 'I have always believed so,' he replied.

'Why, I th-thought you were quite old!' she informed him ingenuously.

'That,' said his lordship with perfect gravity, 'was unkind in you. Did you come to see me in order to – er – satisfy yourself as to my appearance?'

She blushed fierily. 'P-please forgive m-me!' she begged,

stammering dreadfully. 'It w-was very r-rude of m-me, only you s-see I was surprised just for the m-moment.'

'If you were surprised, ma'am, what can I be but deeply flattered?' said the Earl. 'But if you did not come to look me over, do you think you could tell me what it is I am to have the honour of doing for you?'

The bright eyes looked resolutely into his. 'Of c-course, you don't know who I am,' said the visitor. 'I'm afraid I d-deceived you a little. I was afraid if you knew it was not L-Lizzie you might not receive me. But it was not quite a lie to say I was Miss W-Winwood,' she added anxiously. 'B-because I am, you know. I'm Horry Winwood.'

'Horry?' he repeated.

'Horatia,' she explained. 'It is an odious name, isn't it? I was given it on account of Mr W-Walpole. He is my godfather, you understand.'

'Perfectly,' bowed his lordship. 'You must forgive me for being so dull-witted, but would you believe it? – I am still quite in the dark.'

Horatia's gaze faltered. 'It is – it is very difficult to explain it to you,' she said. 'And I expect you are horridly shocked. But I did bring my m-maid, sir.'

'That makes it far less shocking,' said his lordship reassuringly. 'But would it not be much easier to explain this very difficult matter to me if you were to sit down? Will you let me take your cloak?'

'Th-thank you,' said Horatia, relinquishing it. She bestowed a friendly smile upon her host. 'It is not anything n-near so difficult as I thought it would be. Before you came in my spirits quite f-failed. You see, my M-mama has not the smallest n-notion of my being here. But I couldn't think of anything else to do.' She gripped her hands together, and drew a deep breath. 'It is because of L-Lizzie – my sister. You have offered for her, haven't you?'

Slightly taken aback, the Earl bowed. Horatia said in a rush: 'C-could you – would you m-mind very much – having m-me instead?'

The Earl was seated in a chair opposite to her, absently swinging his eyeglass, his gaze fixed on her face in an expression of courteous interest. The eyeglass stopped swinging suddenly, and was allowed to fall. Horatia, looking anxiously across at him, saw a rather startled frown in his eyes, and hurried on: 'Of c-course I know it ought to be Charlotte, for she is the elder, but she said nothing would induce her to m-marry you.'

His lips quivered. 'In that case,' he said, 'it is fortunate that I did not solicit the honour of Miss Charlotte's hand in marriage.'

'Yes,' agreed Horatia. 'I am sorry to have to say it, but I am afraid Charlotte shrinks from the idea of m-making such a sacrifice, even for L-Lizzie's sake.' Rule's shoulders shook slightly. 'Have I said s-something I shouldn't?' inquired Horatia doubtfully.

'On the contrary,' he replied. 'Your conversation is most salutary, Miss Winwood.'

'You are laughing at me,' said Horatia accusingly. 'I d-daresay you think I am very stupid, sir, but indeed, it is most serious.'

'I think you are delightful,' said Rule. 'But there seems to be some misapprehension. I was under the impression that Miss Winwood was – er – willing to receive my addresses.'

'Yes,' concurred Horatia. 'She is w-willing, of course, but it makes her dreadfully unhappy. Th-that's why I came. I hope you don't m-mind.'

'Not at all,' said his lordship. 'But may I know whether I appear to all the members of your family in this disagreeable light?'

'Oh no!' said Horatia earnestly. 'M-mama is excessively pleased with you, and I myself d-don't find you disagreeable in the least. And if only you would be so v-very obliging as to offer for m-me instead of Lizzie I should like you very well.'

'But why,' asked Rule, 'do you want me to offer for you?'

Horatia's brows drew close over the bridge of her nose. 'It must sound very odd,' she admitted. 'You see, Lizzie must m-marry Edward Heron. Perhaps you do not know him?'

'I believe I have not the pleasure,' said the Earl.

'W-well, he is a very particular friend of ours, and he loves L-Lizzie. Only you know how it is with younger sons, and poor Edward is not even a Captain yet.'

'I am to understand that Mr Heron is in the Army?' inquired the Earl.

'Oh, yes, the T-tenth Foot. And if you had not offered for L-Lizzie I feel sure M-mama would have consented to him being contracted to her.'

'It was most lamentable of me,' said Rule gravely. 'But at least I can remedy the error.'

Horatia said eagerly: 'Oh, you will take m-me instead?'

'No,' said Rule, with a faint smile. 'I won't do that. But I will engage not to marry your sister. It's not necessary to offer me an exchange, my poor child.'

'B-but it is!' said Horatia vigorously. 'One of us m-must marry you!'

The Earl looked at her for a moment. Then he got up in his leisurely way, and stood leaning on the back of a chair.

'I think you must explain it all to me,' he said. 'I seem to be more than ordinarily dull this morning.'

Horatia knit her brows. 'Well, I'll t-try," she said. 'You see, we're so shockingly poor. Charlotte says it is all P-Pelham's fault, and I dare say it may be, but it is no use blaming him, b-because he cannot help it. G-gambling, you know. Do you gamble?'

'Sometimes,' answered his lordship.

The grey eyes sparkled. 'So do I,' declared Horatia un-expectedly. 'N-not really, of course, but with Pelham. He taught me. Charlotte says it is wrong. She is l-like that, you know, and it makes her very impatient with poor P-Pel. And I m-must say I feel a little impatient myself when Lizzie has to be sacrificed. Mama is sorry too, b-but she says we must all feel d-deeply thankful.' She coloured, and said rather gruffly: 'It's v-vulgar to care about Settlements, but you are very rich, are you not?'

'Very,' said his lordship, preserving his calm.

'Yes,' nodded Horatia. 'W-well – you see!'

'I see,' agreed Rule. 'You are going to be the Sacrifice.'

She looked up at him rather shyly. 'It c-can't signify to you, can it? Except that I know I'm not a Beauty, like L-Lizzie. But I have got the Nose, sir.'

Rule surveyed the Nose. 'Undoubtedly, you have the Nose,' he said.

Horatia seemed determined to make a clean breast of her blemishes. 'And p-perhaps you could become used to my eyebrows?'

The smile lurked at the back of Rule's eyes. 'I think, quite easily.'

She said sadly: 'They won't arch, you know. And I ought to t-tell you that we have quite given up hope of my g-growing any taller.'

'It would certainly be a pity if you did,' said his lordship.

'D-do you think so?' Horatia was surprised. 'It is a great trial to me, I can assure you.' She took a breath, and added, with difficulty: 'You m-may have n-noticed that I have a – a stammer.'

'Yes, I had noticed,' the Earl answered gently.

'If you f-feel you c-can't bear it, sir, I shall quite understand,' Horatia said in a small, anxious voice.

'I like it,' said the Earl.

'It is very odd of you,' marvelled Horatia. 'But p-perhaps you said that to p-put me at my ease?'

'No,' said the Earl. 'I said it because it was true. Will you tell me how old you are?'

'D-does it matter?' Horatia inquired forebodingly.

'Yes, I think it does, said his lordship.

'I was afraid it m-might,' she said. 'I am t-turned seventeen.'

'Turned seventeen!' repeated his lordship. 'My dear, I couldn't do it.'

'I'm too young?'

'Much too young, child.'

Horatia swallowed valiantly. 'I shall grow older,' she ventured. 'I d-don't want to p-press you, but I am thought to be quite sensible.'

'Do you know how old I am?' asked the Earl.

'N-no, but my cousin, Mrs M-Maulfrey, says you are not a d-day above thirty-five.'

'Does not that seem a little old to you?' he suggested.

'Well, it is rather old, perhaps, b-but no one would think you were as much,' said Horatia kindly.

At that a laugh escaped him. 'Thank you,' he bowed. 'But I think that thirty-five makes a poor husband for seventeen.'

'P-pray do not give that a thought, sir!' said Horatia earnestly. 'I assure you, for my p-part I do not regard it at all. In f-fact, I think I should quite like to marry you.'

'Would you?' he said. 'You do me great honour, ma'am.' He came towards her, and she got up. He took her hand, and raised it to his lips a moment. 'Now what is it you want me to do?'

'There is one very particular thing,' Horatia confided. 'I should not c-care to ask it of you, only that we are m-making a bargain, are we not?'

'Are we?' said his lordship.

'But you know w-we are!' Horatia said. 'You w-want to marry into m-my Family, don't you?'

'I am beginning to think that I do,' remarked his lordship.

Horatia frowned. 'I quite understood that that was why you offered for L-Lizzie.'

'It was,' he assured her.

She seemed satisfied. 'And you do not w-want a wife to interfere with you. Well, I p-promise I won't.'

His lordship looked down at her rather enigmatically. 'And in return?'

She drew closer. 'C-could you do something for Edward?' she begged. 'I have d-decided that there is only one thing for him, and that is a P-patron!'

'And – er – am I to be the Patron?' asked his lordship.

'Would you m-mind very m-much?'

A muscle at the corner of the Earl's mouth twitched, but he answered with only the suspicion of a tremor in his voice: 'I shall be happy to oblige you, ma'am, to the best of my poor endeavour.'

'Thank you very m-much,' said Horatia seriously. 'Then he and Lizzie can be m-married, you see. And you will tell Mama that you would just as soon have me, won't you?'

'I may not phrase it quite like that,' said the Earl, 'but I will endeavour to make the matter plain to her. But I do not entirely see how I am to propose this exchange without divulging your visit to me.'

'Oh, you need not m-mind that!' said Horatia cheerfully. 'I shall tell her m-myself. I think I had b-better go now. No one knows where I am, and perhaps they m-may wonder.'

'We will drink to our bargain first, do you not think?' said the Earl, and picked up a small gilt handbell, and rang it.

A lackey came in answer to the bell. 'You will bring me – ' the Earl glanced at Horatia – 'ratafia, and two glasses,' he said. 'And my coach will be at the door within ten minutes.'

'If – if the c-coach is for me,' said Horatia, 'it is only a step to South Street, sir.'

'But I would rather that you permitted me to convey you,' said his lordship.

The butler brought the ratafia himself, and set the heavy silver tray down on a table. He was dismissed with a nod, and went regretfully. He would have liked to see with his own eyes my lord drink a glass of ratafia.

The Earl poured two glasses, and gave one to Horatia. 'The bargain!' he said, and drank heroically.

Horatia's eyes twinkled merrily. 'I f-feel sure we shall deal f-famously together!' she declared, and raised the glass to her lips.

Five minutes later his lordship walked into the library again. 'Ah – Arnold,' he said. 'I have found something for you to do.'

'Yes, sir?' said Mr Gisborne, rising.

'You must get me a Captaincy,' said Rule. 'A Captaincy in the – in the 10th Foot, I think, but I am sure you will find out.'

'A Captaincy in the 10th Foot?' repeated Mr Gisborne. 'For whom, sir?'

'Now, what was the name?' wondered his lordship. 'Hawk –

23

Hernshaw – Heron. I rather think it was Heron. For a Mr Edward Heron. Do you know a Mr Edward Heron?'

'No, sir, I don't.'

'No,' sighed Rule. 'Nor do I. It makes it very awkward for us, but I have great faith in you, Arnold. You will find out all about this Edward Heron.'

'I'll try, sir,' replied Mr Gisborne.

'I am afraid I give you a deal of trouble,' apologized his lordship, preparing to depart. At the door he looked back. 'By the way, Arnold, I think you may be under some slight misapprehension. It is the youngest Miss Winwood who does me the honour of accepting my hand.'

Mr Gisborne was startled. 'Miss Charlotte Winwood, sir? The youngest Miss Winwood, I believe, is scarcely out of the schoolroom.'

'Certainly not Miss Charlotte Winwood,' said the Earl. 'I have it on excellent authority that nothing would induce Miss Charlotte to marry me.'

'Good God, my lord!' said Mr Gisborne blankly.

'Thank you, Arnold. You comfort me,' said his lordship, and went out.

Three

The youngest Miss Winwood's return to South Street was witnessed by both her sisters from the windows of the withdrawing-room. Her absence had certainly been remarked but since the porter was able to inform the rather agitated governess that Miss Horatia had gone out attended by her maid, no great concern was felt. It was odd of Horatia, and very wayward, but no doubt she had only stolen out to buy the coquelicot ribbons she had coveted in a milliner's window, or a chintz patch for a gown. This was Elizabeth's theory, delivered in her soft, peaceable voice, and it satisfied Lady Winwood, lying upon the sopha with her vinaigrette to hand.

The appearance of a town coach, drawn by perfectly matched bays with glittering harness, did not occasion more than a fleeting interest until it became apparent that this opulent equipage was going to draw up at the door of No. 20.

Charlotte exclaimed: 'Lord, who can it be? Mama, a caller!' She pressed her face against the window, and said: 'There is a crest on the panel, but I cannot distinguish – Lizzie, I believe it is Lord Rule!'

'Oh no!' Elizabeth fluttered, pressing a hand to her heart.

By this time the footman had sprung down, and opened the coach door. Charlotte grew pop-eyed. 'It's Horry!' she gasped.

Lady Winwood clutched the vinaigrette. 'Charlotte, my nerves!' she said in a fading voice.

'But, Mama, it is!' insisted Charlotte.

Elizabeth had a premonition. 'Oh, what can she have been

doing?' she said, sinking into a chair, and growing quite pale. 'I hope nothing – nothing dreadful!'

Impetuous footsteps were heard on the stairs; the door was opened urgently, and Horatia stood before them, flushed and bright-eyed, and swinging her hat by its ribbon.

Lady Winwood's hands fumbled with her Medici scarf. 'Dearest, the draught!' she moaned. 'My poor head!'

'Pray, Horry, shut the door!' said Charlotte. 'How can you bounce so when you know how shattered Mama's nerves are?'

'Oh, I am sorry!' Horatia said, and carefully shut the door. 'I forgot. L-Lizzie, everything is settled, and you *shall* m-marry Edward!'

Lady Winwood was moved to sit up. 'Good God, the child's raving! Horatia, what – *what* have you been doing?'

Horatia tossed the cloak aside, and plumped down on the stool beside her mother's sopha. 'I've b-been to see Lord Rule!' she announced.

'I knew it!' said Elizabeth, in the voice of Cassandra.

Lady Winwood sank back upon her cushions with closed eyes. Charlotte, observing her alarming rigidity, shrieked: 'Unnatural girl! Have you no consideration for our dearest Mama? Lizzie, hartshorn!'

The hartshorn, the vinaigrette, and some Hungary Water applied to the temples restored the afflicted Lady Winwood to life. She opened her eyes and found just strength to utter: 'What did the child say?'

Charlotte, fondly clasping her mother's frail hand, said: 'Mama, do not agitate yourself, I beg of you!'

'You n-need not be agitated, M-mama,' Horatia told her penitently. 'It is quite true that I've b-been to see Lord Rule, but –'

'Then all is at an end!' said Lady Winwood fatalistically. 'We may as well prepare to enter the Debtors' Prison. I am sure I do not mind for myself, for my Days are Numbered, but my beautiful Lizzie, my sweetest Charlotte –'

'M-mama, if only you w-would listen to me!' broke in Horatia. 'I have explained everything to L-Lord Rule, and –'

'Merciful heavens!' said Elizabeth. 'Not – not Edward?'

'Yes, Edward. Of course I told him about Edward. And he is n-not going to marry you, Lizzie, but he p-promised he would be Edward's P-patron instead –'

Lady Winwood had recourse to the vinaigrette again, and desired feebly to be told what she had ever done to deserve such calamity.

'And I explained how n-nothing would induce Charlotte to m-marry him, and he did not seem to m-mind that.'

'I shall die,' said Charlotte with resolution, 'of Mortification!'

'Oh, Horry dear!' sighed Elizabeth, between tears and laughter.

'And I asked him,' concluded Horatia triumphantly, 'if he would marry m-me instead. And he is g-going to!'

Her relatives were bereft of speech. Even Lady Winwood apparently considered that the situation had gone beyond the powers of her vinaigrette to mend, for she allowed it to slip from her hand to the floor while she stared in a bemused way at her youngest-born.

It was Charlotte who found her voice first. 'Horatia, do you say that you had the Indelicacy, the Impropriety, the – the Forwardness, to ask Lord Rule to marry you?'

'Yes,' said Horatia staunchly. 'I had to.'

'And – and –' Charlotte groped for words – 'he consented to – to marry you in place of *Lizzie*?'

Horatia nodded.

'He cannot,' said Charlotte, 'have noticed the Stammer.'

Horatia put up her chin. 'I s-spoke to him about the S-stammer, and he said he l-liked it!'

Elizabeth rose up from her chair and clasped Horatia in her arms. 'Oh, why should he not? Dearest, dearest, never could I permit you to sacrifice yourself for me!'

Horatia suffered the embrace. 'Well, to tell you the truth, Lizzie, I would like to m-marry him. But I c-can't help wondering whether you are quite sure you d-don't want to?' She searched her sister's face. 'D-do you really like Edward better?'

'Oh, my love!'

'Well, I c-can't understand it,' said Horatia.

'It is not to be supposed,' stated Charlotte flatly, 'that Lord Rule was in earnest. Depend upon it, he thinks Horry a Mere Child.'

'N-no, he does not!' said Horatia, firing up. 'He w-was in earnest, and he is c-coming to tell M-mama at three this afternoon.'

'I beg that no one will expect me to face Lord Rule!' said Lady Winwood. 'I am ready to sink into the ground!'

'Will he come?' demanded Charlotte. 'What irremediable harm may not Horry's impropriety have wrought? We must ask ourselves, will Lord Rule desire to ally himself with a Family one of whose members has shown herself so dead to all feelings of Modesty and Female Reserve?'

'Charlotte, you shall not say that!' said Elizabeth with unwonted stringency. 'What should he think but that our dearest is but an impulsive child?'

'We must hope it,' Charlotte said heavily. 'But if she has divulged your attachment to Edward Heron I fear that all is at an end. We who know and value dear Horry do not notice her blemishes, but what gentleman would engage to marry her in place of the Beauty of the Family?'

'I thought of that myself,' admitted Horatia. 'He s-says he thinks he will grow used to my horrid eyebrows quite easily. And I will t-tell you something, Charlotte! He said it would be a p-pity if I became any taller.'

'How mortifying it is to reflect that Lord Rule may have been amusing himself at the expense of a Winwood!' said Charlotte.

But it seemed that Lord Rule had not been amusing himself. At three o'clock he walked up the steps of No. 20 South Street, and inquired for Lady Winwood.

In spite of her dramatic refusal to face the Earl, Lady Winwood had been induced to await him in the withdrawing-room, fortified by smelling-salts, and a new polonaise with tobine

28

stripes which had arrived from her dressmaker's just in time to avert a nervous collapse.

Her interview with his lordship lasted for half an hour, at the end of which time the footman was despatched to inform Miss Horatia that her presence in the withdrawing-room was desired.

'Aha!' cried Horatia, shooting a wicked glance at Charlotte, and springing to her feet.

Elizabeth caught her hands. 'Horry, it is not too late! If this arrangement is repugnant to you, for Heaven's sake speak, and I will throw myself upon Lord Rule's generosity!'

'Repugnant? S-stuff!' said Horatia, and danced out.

'Horry, Horry, at least let me straighten your sash!' shrieked Charlotte.

'Too late,' Elizabeth said. She clasped her hands to her breast. 'If I could be assured that this is no Immolation upon the Altar of Sisterly Love!'

'If you wish to know what I think,' said Charlotte, 'Horry is very well pleased with herself.'

Horatia, opening the door into the withdrawing-room, found her mother actually upon her feet, the smelling-salts lying forgotten on an ormolu table by the fire. In the middle of the room Rule was standing, watching the door, one hand, with a great square sapphire glowing on it, resting on a chairback.

He looked very much more magnificent and unapproachable in blue velvet and gold lacing than he had seemed in his riding habit, and for a moment Horatia surveyed him rather doubtfully. Then she saw him smile and was reassured.

Lady Winwood swam towards her and embraced her. 'My dearest!' she said, apparently overcome. 'My lord, let my treasured child answer you with her own lips. Horatia love, Lord Rule has done you the honour to request your hand in marriage.'

'I t-told you he was going to, M-mama!' said Horatia incorrigibly.

'Horatia – I beg of you!' implored the long-suffering lady. 'Your curtsy, my love!'

Horatia sank obediently into a curtsy. The Earl took her

hand, as she rose, and bowed deeply over it. He said, looking down at her with a laugh in his eyes: 'Madam, may I keep this little hand?'

Lady Winwood heaved a tremulous sigh, and wiped away a sympathetic tear with her handkerchief.

'P-pretty!' approved Horatia. 'Indeed you m-may, sir. It is very handsome of you to give me the p-pleasure of having you p-propose for me.'

Lady Winwood looked round apprehensively for her salts, but perceiving that his lordship was laughing, changed her mind. 'My baby . . . !' She said indulgently: 'As you see, my lord, she is all unspoiled.'

She did not leave the newly-plighted pair alone, and the Earl presently took his leave with equal correctness. The front door had barely closed behind him before Lady Winwood had clasped Horatia in a fond embrace. 'Dearest child!' she said. 'You are very, very fortunate! So personable a man! Such delicacy!'

Charlotte put her head round the door. 'May we come in, Mama? Has he really offered for Horry?'

Lady Winwood dabbed at her eyes again. 'He is everything that I could wish for! Such refinement! Such *ton!*' Elizabeth had taken Horatia's hand, but Charlotte said practically: 'Well, for my part, I think he must be doting. And repulsive as the thought is, I suppose the Settlements . . . ?'

'He is all that is generous!' sighed Lady Winwood.

'Then I'm sure I wish you joy, Horry,' said Charlotte. 'Though I must say that I consider you far too young and heedless to become the wife of any gentleman. And I only pray that Theresa Maulfrey will have enough proper feeling to refrain from chattering about this awkward business.'

It did not seem at first as though Mrs Maulfrey would be able to hold her tongue. Upon the announcement of the betrothal she came to South Street, just as her cousins knew she would, all agog to hear the whole story. She was palpably dissatisfied with Elizabeth's careful tale of 'a mistake', and demanded to know the truth. Lady Winwood, rising for once to the occasion, announced that the matter had been arranged by herself and his lordship, who had met Horatia and been straightway captivated by her.

With this Mrs Maulfrey had to be content, and after condoling with Elizabeth on having lost an Earl only to get a lieutenant in exchange, and with Charlotte on being left a spinster while a chit from the schoolroom made the match of the season, she departed, leaving a sense of relief behind her, and a strong odour of violet scent.

Charlotte opined darkly that no good would come of Horatia's scandalously contrived marriage.

But Charlotte was alone in her pessimism. A radiant Mr Heron, fervently grasping both Horatia's hands, thanked her from the heart, and wished her happiness. Mr Heron had had the honour of meeting Lord Rule at an extremely select soirée in South Street, and his lordship had roused himself to take the young man aside and talk to him of his future. Mr Heron had no hesitation in declaring the Earl to be a very good sort of a man indeed, and no further remarks concerning his reputation or his advanced years were heard to pass his lips. Elizabeth, too, who had been forced to nerve herself to meet her erstwhile suitor, found the ordeal shorn of its terrors. My lord kissed her hand, and as he released it said with his slight, not unpleasing drawl: 'May I hope, Miss Winwood, that I am no longer an ogre?'

Elizabeth blushed, and hung her head. 'Oh – Horry!' she sighed, a smile trembling on her lips. 'Indeed, my lord, you were never that.'

'But I owe you an apology, ma'am,' he said solemnly, 'for I made you "dreadfully unhappy".'

'If we are to talk of apologies, sir – ! You, who have been all kindness!' She lifted her eyes to his face, and tried to thank him for what he would do for Mr Heron.

Apparently he did not choose to be thanked; he put it aside with his lazy laugh, and somehow she could not go on. He stayed by her for a few minutes, and she had leisure to observe him.

Later she told Mr Heron seriously that she thought Horry might be very happy.

'Horry is happy,' replied Mr Heron, with a chuckle.

'Ah yes, but you see, dearest, Horry is only a child. I feel – I feel anxiety, I won't conceal from you. Lord Rule is not a child.' She puckered her brow. 'Horry does such things! If he will only be gentle with her, and patient!'

'Why, love,' said Mr Heron, humouring her, 'I don't think you need to put yourself about. His lordship is all gentleness, and I don't doubt will have patience enough.'

'All gentleness,' she repeated. 'Indeed he is, and yet – do you know, Edward, I think I might be afraid of him? Sometimes, if you do but notice, he has a trick of closing his lips that gives to the whole face an air of – I must say inflexibility, quite foreign to what one knows of him. But if he will only come to love Horry!'

No one but Miss Winwood was inclined to indulge in such questionings, least of all Lady Winwood basking in the envy of her acquaintance. Everyone was anxious to felicitate her; everyone knew what a triumph was hers. Even Mr Walpole, who was staying in Arlington Street at the time, came to pay her a morning visit, and to glean a few details. Mr Walpole's face wore an approving smile, though he regretted that his god-daughter should be marrying a Tory. But then Mr Walpole was so very earnest a Whig, and even he seemed to think that Lady Winwood was right to disregard Rule's political opinions. He set the tips of his fingers together, crossing one dove-silk stockinged leg over the other, and listened with his well-bred air to all Lady Winwood had to say. She had a great value for Mr Walpole, whom she had known for many years, but she was careful in what she told him. No one had a kinder heart than this thin, percipient gentleman, but he had a sharp nose for a morsel of scandal, and a satiric pen. Let him but get wind of Horatia's escapade, and my Lady Ossory and my Lady Aylesbury would have the story by the next post.

Fortunately, the rumour of Rule's offer for Elizabeth had not reached Twickenham, and beyond wondering that Lady

Winwood should care to see Horatia married before the divine Elizabeth (who was quite his favourite), he said nothing to put an anxious mother on her guard. So Lady Winwood told him confidentially that, although nothing was yet to be declared, Elizabeth too was to leave the nest. Mr Walpole was all interest, but pursed his lips a little when he heard about Mr Edward Heron. To be sure, of good family (trust Mr Walpole to know that!), but he could have wished for someone of greater consequence for his little Lizzie. Mr Walpole did so like to see his young friends make good matches. Indeed, his satisfaction at Horatia's betrothal made him forget a certain disastrous day at Twickenham when Horatia had shown herself quite unworthy of having the glories of his little Gothic Castle exhibited to her, and he patted her hand, and said that she must come and drink a syllabub at Strawberry quite soon. Horatia, under oath not to be *farouche* ('for he may be rising sixty, my love, and live secluded, but there's no one whose good opinion counts for more'), thanked him demurely, and hoped that she would not be expected to admire and fondle his horrid little dog, Rosette, who was odiously spoiled, and yapped at one's heels.

Mr Walpole said that she was very young to contemplate matrimony, and Lady Winwood sighed that alas, it was true: she was losing her darling before she had even been to Court.

That was an unwise remark, because it gave Mr Walpole an opportunity for recounting, as he was very fond of doing, how his father had taken him to kiss George the First's hand when he was a child. Horatia slipped out while he was in the middle of his anecdote, leaving her Mama to assume an expression of spurious interest.

In quite another quarter, though topographically hardly a stone's throw from South Street, the news of Rule's betrothal created different sensations. There was a slim house in Hertford Street where a handsome widow held her court, but it was not at all the sort of establishment that Lady Winwood visited. Caroline Massey, relict of a wealthy tradesman, had achieved her position in the Polite World by dint of burying the late Sir Thomas' connection with the City in decent oblivion, and relying upon her own respectable birth and very considerable good looks. Sir Thomas' fortune, though so discreditably acquired, was also useful. It enabled his widow to live in a very pretty house in the best part of town, to entertain in a lavish and agreeable fashion, and to procure the sponsorship of a Patroness who was easygoing enough to introduce her into Society. The offices of this Patroness had long ceased to be necessary to Lady Massey. In some way, best known (said various indignant ladies) to herself, she had contrived to become a Personage. One was for ever meeting her, and if a few doors remained obstinately closed against her, she had a sufficient following for this not to signify. That the following consisted largely of men was not likely to trouble her; she was not a woman who craved female companionship, though a faded and resigned lady, who was believed to be her cousin, constantly resided with her. Miss Janet's presence was a sop thrown to the conventions. Yet, to do them justice, it was not Lady Massey's morals that stuck in the gullets of certain aristocratic dames. Everyone had their own *affaires*, and if gossip whispered of intimacies between the fair Massey and Lord Rule, as long as the lady conducted her amorous passages with discretion only such rigid moralists as Lady Winwood would throw up hands of horror. It was the fatal taint of the City that would always exclude Lady Massey from the innermost circle of Fashion. She was not *bon ton*. It was said without rancour, even with a pitying shrug of well-bred shoulders, but it was damning. Lady Massey, aware of it, never betrayed by word or look that she was conscious of that almost indefinable bar, and not even the resigned cousin knew that to become one of the Select was almost an obsession with her.

There was only one person who guessed, and he seemed to derive a certain sardonic amusement from it. Robert, Baron Lethbridge, could usually derive amusement from the frailty of his fellows.

Upon an evening two days after the Earl of Rule's second visit to the Winwood establishment, Lady Massey held a card-party

34

in Hertford Street. These parties were always well attended, for one might be sure of deep play, and a charming hostess, whose cellar (thanks to the ungenteel but knowledgeable Sir Thomas) was excellently stocked.

The saloon upon the first floor was a charming apartment, and set off its mistress to advantage. She had lately purchased some very pretty pieces of gilt furniture in Paris, and had had all her old hangings pulled down, and new ones of straw-coloured silk put in their place, so that the room, which had before been rose-pink, now glowed palely yellow. She herself wore a gown of silk brocade with great panniers, and an underskirt looped with embroidered garlands. Her hair was dressed high in a *pouf au sentiment*, with curled feathers for which she had paid fifty louis apiece at Bertin's, and scented roses, placed artlessly here and there in the powdered erection. This coiffure had been the object of several aspiring ladies' envy, and had put Mrs Montague-Damer quite out of countenance. She too had acquired a French fashion, and had expected to have it much admired. But the exquisite *pouf au sentiment* made her own *chien couchant* look rather ridiculous, and quite spoiled her evening's enjoyment.

The gathering in the saloon was a modish one; dowdy persons had no place in Lady Massey's house, though she could welcome such freaks as the Lady Amelia Pridham, that grossly fat and free-spoken dame in the blonde satin who was even now arranging her rouleaus in front of her. There were those who wondered that the Lady Amelia should care to visit in Hertford Street, but the Lady Amelia, besides being of an extreme good nature, would go to any house where she could be sure of deep basset.

Basset was the game of the evening, and some fifteen people were seated at the big round table. It was when Lord Lethbridge held the bank that he chose to make his startling announcement. As he paid on the *couch* he said with a faintly malicious note in his voice: 'I don't see Rule to-night. No doubt the bridegroom-elect dances attendance in South Street.'

Opposite him, Lady Massey quickly looked up from the cards in front of her, but she did not say anything.

A Macaroni, with an enormous ladder-toupet covered in blue hair-powder, and a thin, unhealthily sallow countenance, cried out: 'What's that?'

Lord Lethbridge's hard hazel eyes lingered for a moment on Lady Massey's face. Then he turned slightly to look at the startled Macaroni. He said smilingly: 'Do you tell me I am before you with the news, Crosby? I thought you of all people must have known.' His satin-clad arm lay on the table, the pack of cards clasped in his white hand. The light of the candles in the huge chandelier over the table caught the jewels in the lace at his throat, and made his eyes glitter queerly.

'What are you talking about?' demanded the Macaroni, half rising from his seat.

'But Rule, my dear Crosby!' said Lethbridge. 'Your cousin Rule, you know.'

'What of Rule?' inquired the Lady Amelia, regretfully pushing one of her rouleaus across the table.

Lethbridge's glance flickered to Lady Massey's face again. 'Why, only that he is about to enter the married state,' he replied.

There was a stir of interest. Someone said: 'Good God, I thought he was safe to stay single! Well, upon my soul! Who's the fortunate fair one, Lethbridge?'

'The fortunate fair one is the youngest Miss Winwood,' said Lethbridge. 'A romance, you perceive. I believe she is not out of the schoolroom.'

The Macaroni, Mr Crosby Drelincourt, mechanically straightened the preposterous bow he wore in place of a cravat. 'Pho, it is a tale!' he said uneasily. 'Where had you it?'

Lethbridge raised his thin, rather slanting brows. 'Oh, I had it from the little Maulfrey. It will be in the *Gazette* by to-morrow.'

'Well, it's very interesting,' said a portly gentleman in claret velvet, 'but the game, Lethbridge, the game!'

'The game,' bowed his lordship, and sent a glance round at the cards on the table.

Lady Massey, who had won the *couch*, suddenly put out her

hand and nicked the corner of the Queen that lay before her. 'Paroli!' she said in a quick, unsteady voice.

Lethbridge turned up two cards, and sent her a mocking look. 'Ace wins, Queen loses,' he said. 'Your luck is quite out, my lady.'

She gave a little laugh. 'I assure you I don't regard it. Lose to-night, win to-morrow. It goes up and down.'

The game proceeded. It was not until later when the company stood about in little chatting groups, partaking of very excellent refreshments, that Rule's betrothal was remembered. It was Lady Amelia, rolling up to Lethbridge, with a glass of hot negus in one hand and a sweet biscuit in the other, who said in her downright way: 'You're a dog, Lethbridge. What possessed you to hop out with that, man?'

'Why not?' said his lordship coolly. 'I thought you would all be interested.'

Lady Amelia finished her negus, and looked across the room towards her hostess. 'Diverting,' she commented. 'Did she think to get Rule?'

Lethbridge shrugged. 'Why do you ask me? I'm not in the lady's confidence.'

'H'm! You've a trick of knowing things, Lethbridge. Silly creature. Rule's not such a fool.' Her cynical eye wandered in search of Mr Drelincourt, and presently found him, standing apart, and pulling at his underlip. She chuckled. 'Took it badly, eh?'

Lord Lethbridge followed the direction of her gaze. 'Confess, I've afforded you some amusement, my lady.'

'Lord, you're like a gnat, my dear man.' She became aware of little Mr Paget inquisitively at her elbow, and dug at his ribs with her fan. 'What do you give for Crosby's chances now?'

Mr Paget tittered. 'Or our fair hostess's, ma'am!'

She gave a shrug of her large white shoulders. 'Oh, if you want to pry into the silly woman's affairs – !' she said, and moved away.

Mr Paget transferred his attention to Lord Lethbridge.

''Pon my soul, my lord, I'll swear she went white under the

rouge!' Lethbridge took snuff. 'Cruel of you, my lord, 'pon my soul it was!'

'Do you think so?' said his lordship with almost dulcet sweetness.

'Oh, positively, sir, positively! Not a doubt she had hopes of Rule. But it would never do, you know. I believe his lordship to be excessively proud.'

'Excessively,' said Lethbridge, with so much dryness in his voice that Mr Paget had an uncomfortable feeling that he had said something inopportune.

He was so obsessed by this notion that he presently confided the interchange to Sir Marmaduke Hoban, who gave a snort of laughter and said: 'Damned inopportune!' and walked off to replenish his glass.

Mr Crosby Drelincourt, cousin and heir-presumptive to my Lord of Rule, seemed disinclined to discuss the news. He left the party early, and went home to his lodging in Jermyn Street, a prey to the gloomiest forebodings.

He passed an indifferent night, and awoke finally at an uncommonly early hour, and demanded the *London Gazette*. His valet brought it with the cup of chocolate with which it was Mr Drelincourt's habit to regale himself on first waking. Mr Drelincourt seized the journal and spread it open with agitated fingers. The announcement glared at him in incontrovertible print.

Mr Drelincourt looked at it in a kind of daze, his night-cap over one eye.

'Your chocolate, sir,' said his valet disinterestedly.

Mr Drelincourt was roused out of his momentary stupor. 'Take the damned stuff away!' he shouted, and flung the *Gazette* down. 'I am getting up!'

'Yes, sir. Will you wear the blue morning habit?'

Mr Drelincourt swore at him.

The valet, accustomed to Mr Drelincourt's temper, remained unmoved, but found an opportunity while his master was pulling on his stockings to peep into the *Gazette*. What he saw brought a faint, sour smile to his lips. He went away to prepare a razor with which to shave Mr Drelincourt.

The news had shocked Mr Drelincourt deeply, but habit was strong, and by the time he had been shaved he had recovered sufficient mastery over himself to take an interest in the all-important question of his dress. The result of the care he bestowed upon his person was certainly startling. When he was at last ready to sally forth into the street he wore a blue coat with long tails and enormous silver buttons, over a very short waistcoat, and a pair of striped breeches clipped at the knee with rosettes. A bow served him for cravat, his stockings were of silk, his shoes had silver buckles and heels so high that he was obliged to mince along; his wig was brushed up *en hérisson* to a point in the front, curled in pigeons' wings over the ears, and brought down at the back into a queue confined in a black silk bag. A little round hat surmounted this structure, and to complete his toilet he had a number of fobs and seals, and carried a long, clouded cane embellished with tassels.

Although the morning was a fine one Mr Drelincourt hailed a chair, and gave the address of his cousin's house in Grosvenor Square. He entered the sedan carefully, bending his head to avoid brushing his toupet against the roof; the men picked up the poles, and set off northwards with their exquisite burden.

Upon his arrival in Grosvenor Square Mr Drelincourt paid off the chairmen and tripped up the steps to the great door of Rule's house. He was admitted by the porter, who looked as though he would have liked to have shut the door in the visitor's painted face. Mr Drelincourt was no favourite with Rule's household, but being in some sort a privileged person he came and went very much as he pleased. The porter told him that my lord was still at breakfast, but Mr Drelincourt waved this piece of information aside with an airy gesture of one lily-white hand. The porter handed him over to a footman, and reflected with satisfaction that that was a nose put well out of joint.

Mr Drelincourt rarely waited upon his cousin without letting his gaze rest appreciatively on the fine proportions of his rooms, and the elegance of their appointments. He had come to regard Rule's possessions in some sort as his own, and he could never enter his house without thinking of the day when it would belong to him. To-day, however, he was easily able to refrain from the indulgence of this dream, and he followed the footman to a small breakfast-room at the back of the house with nothing in his head but a sense of deep injury.

My lord, in a dressing-gown of brocaded silk, was seated at the table with a tankard and a sirloin before him. His secretary was also present, apparently attempting to cope with a number of invitations for his lordship, for as Mr Drelincourt strutted in he said despairingly: 'But, sir, you must surely remember that you are promised to her Grace of Bedford to-night!'

'I wish,' said Rule plaintively, 'that you would rid yourself of that notion, my dear Arnold. I cannot imagine where you had it. I never remember anything disagreeable. Good-morning, Crosby.' He put up his glass the better to observe the letters in Mr Gisborne's hand. 'The one on the pink paper, Arnold. I have a great predilection for the one writ on pink paper. What is it?'

'A card-party at Mrs Wallchester's, sir,' said Mr Gisborne in a voice of disapproval.

'My instinct is never at fault,' said his lordship. 'The pink one it shall be. Crosby, really there is no need for you to stand. Have you come to breakfast? Oh, don't go, Arnold, don't go.'

'If you please, Rule, I wish to be private with you,' said Mr Drelincourt, who had favoured the secretary with the smallest of bows.

'Don't be shy, Crosby,' said his lordship kindly. 'If it's money Arnold is bound to know all about it.'

'It is not,' said Mr Drelincourt, much annoyed.

'Permit me, sir,' said Mr Gisborne, moving to the door.

Mr Drelincourt put down his hat and his cane, and drew out a chair from the table. 'Not breakfast, no!' he said a little peevishly.

The Earl surveyed him patiently. 'Well, what is it now, Crosby?' he inquired.

'I came to,' said Mr Drelincourt, 'I came to speak to you about this – this betrothal.'

'There's nothing private about that,' observed Rule, addressing himself to the cold roast beef.

'No, indeed!' said Crosby with a hint of indignation in his voice. 'I suppose it is true?'

'Oh, quite true,' said his lordship. 'You may safely felicitate me, my dear Crosby.'

'As to that – why, certainly! Certainly, I wish you very happy,' said Crosby, put out. 'But you never spoke a word of it to me. It takes me quite by surprise. I must think it extremely odd, cousin, considering the singular nature of our relationship.'

'The – ?' My lord seemed puzzled.

'Come, Rule, come! As your heir I might be supposed to have some claim to be apprised of your intentions.'

'Accept my apologies,' said his lordship. 'Are you sure you won't have some breakfast, Crosby? You do not look at all the thing, my dear fellow. In fact, I should almost feel inclined to recommend another hairpowder than this blue you affect. A charming tint, Crosby: you must not think I don't admire it, but its reflected pallor upon your countenance –'

'If I seem pale, cousin, you should rather blame the extraordinary announcement in to-day's *Gazette*. It has given me a shock; I shan't deny it has given me a shock.'

'But, Crosby,' said his lordship plaintively, 'were you really sure that you would outlive me?'

'In the course of nature I might expect to,' replied Mr Drelincourt, too much absorbed in his disappointment to consider his words. 'I can give you ten years, you must remember.'

Rule shook his head. 'I don't think you should build on it,' he said. 'I come of distressingly healthy stock, you know.'

'Very true,' agreed Mr Drelincourt. 'It is a happiness to all your relatives.'

'I see it is,' said his lordship gravely.

'Pray don't mistake me, Marcus!' besought his cousin. 'You must not suppose that your demise could occasion in me

41

anything but a sense of the deepest bereavement, but you'll allow a man must look to the future.'

'Such a remote future!' said his lordship. 'It makes me feel positively melancholy, my dear Crosby.'

'We must all hope it may be remote,' said Crosby, 'but you cannot fail to have observed how uncertain is human life. Only to think of young Frittenham, cut off in the very flower of his youth by the overturning of his curricle! Broke his neck, you know, and all for a wager.'

The Earl laid down his knife and fork, and regarded his relative with some amusement. 'Only to think of it!' he repeated. 'I confess, Crosby, what you say will add – er – piquancy to my next race. I begin to see that your succession to my shoes – by the way, cousin, you are such a judge of these matters, do, I beg of you, tell me how you like them?' He stretched one leg for Mr Drelincourt to look at.

Mr Drelincourt said unerringly: '*A la d'Artois*, from Joubert's. I don't favour them myself, but they are very well – very well indeed.'

'It's a pity you don't,' said his lordship, 'for I perceive that you may be called upon to step into them at any time.'

'Oh, hardly that, Rule! Hardly that!' protested Mr Drelincourt handsomely.

'But consider how uncertain is human life, Crosby! You yourself said it a moment back. I might at any moment be thrown from a curricle.'

'I am sure I did not in the least mean –'

'Or,' continued Rule pensively, 'fall a victim to one of the cut-throat thieves with which I am told the town abounds.'

'Certainly,' said Mr Drelincourt a little stiffly. 'But I don't anticipate –'

'Highwaymen too,' mused his lordship. 'Think of poor Layton with a bullet in his shoulder on Hounslow Heath not a month ago. It might have been me, Crosby. It may still be me.'

Mr Drelincourt rose in a huff. 'I see you are determined to make a jest of it. Good God, I don't desire your death! I should be excessively sorry to hear of it. But this sudden resolve to marry when everyone had quite given up all idea of it, takes me aback, upon my soul it does! And quite a young lady, I apprehend.'

'My dear Crosby, why not say a very young lady? I feel sure you know her age.'

Mr Drelincourt sniffed. 'I scarcely credited it, cousin, I confess. A schoolroom miss, and you well above thirty! I wish you may not live to regret it.'

'Are you sure,' said his lordship, 'that you won't have some of this excellent beef?'

An artistic shudder ran through his cousin. 'I never – positively never – eat flesh at this hour of the morning!' said Mr Drelincourt emphatically. 'It is of all things the most repugnant to me. Of course you must know how people will laugh at this odd marriage. Seventeen and thirty-five! Upon my honour, I should not care to appear so ridiculous!' He gave an angry titter, and added venomously: 'To be sure, no one need wonder at the young lady's part in it! We all know how it is with the Winwoods. She does very well for herself, very well indeed!'

The Earl leaned back in his chair, one hand in his breeches pocket, the other quite idly playing with his quizzing-glass. 'Crosby,' he said gently, 'if ever you repeat that remark I am afraid – I am very much afraid – that you will quite certainly predecease me.'

There was an uncomfortable silence. Mr Drelincourt looked down at his cousin and saw that under the heavy lids those bored eyes had entirely lost their smile. They held a very unpleasant glint. Mr Drelincourt cleared his throat, and said, his voice jumping a little: 'My dear Marcus – ! I assure I meant nothing in the world! How you do take one up!'

'You must forgive me,' said his lordship, still with that alarming grimness about his mouth.

'Oh, certainly! I don't give it a thought,' said Mr Drelincourt. 'Consider it forgotten, cousin, and as for the cause, you have me wrong, quite wrong, you know.'

The Earl continued to regard him for a moment; then the grimness left his face, and he suddenly laughed.

Mr Drelincourt picked up his hat and cane, and was about to take his leave when the door opened briskly, and a lady came in. She was of middle height, dressed in a gown of apple-green cambric with white stripes, in the style known as *vive bergère,* and had a very becoming straw hat with ribands perched upon her head. A scarf caught over one arm, and a sunshade with a long handle completed her toilet, and in her hand she carried, as Mr Drelincourt saw at a glance, a copy of the *London Gazette.*

She was an extremely handsome woman, with most speaking eyes, at once needle-sharp, and warmly smiling, and she bore a striking resemblance to the Earl.

On the threshold she checked, her quick gaze taking in Mr Drelincourt. 'Oh – Crosby!' she said, with unveiled dissatisfaction.

Rule got up, and took her hand. 'My dear Louisa, have you also come to breakfast?' he inquired.

She kissed him in a sisterly fashion, and replied with energy: 'I breakfasted two hours ago, but you may give me some coffee. I see you are just going, Crosby. Pray don't let me keep you. Dear me, why will you wear those very odd clothes, my good creature? And that absurd wig don't become you, take my word for it!'

Mr Drelincourt, feeling unable to cope adequately with his cousin, merely bowed, and wished her good morning. No sooner had he minced out of the room than Lady Louisa Quain flung down her copy of the *Gazette* before Rule. 'No need to ask why that odious little toad came,' she remarked. 'But, my dear Marcus, it is too provoking! There is the most nonsensical mistake made! Have you seen it?'

Rule began to pour coffee into his own unused cup. 'Dear Louisa, do you realise that it is not yet eleven o'clock, and I have already had Crosby with me? What time can I have had to read the *Gazette?*'

She took the cup from him, observing that she could not conceive how he should care to go on drinking ale with his breakfast. 'You will have to put in a second advertisement,' she

44

informed him. 'I can't imagine how they came to make such a stupid mistake. My dear, they have confused the names of the sisters! Here it is! You may read for yourself: "The Honourable Horatia Winwood, youngest daughter of —" Really, if it were not so vexing it would be diverting! But how in the world came they to put "Horatia" for "Elizabeth"?'

'You see,' said Rule apologetically, 'Arnold sent the advertisement to the *Gazette.*'

'Well, I never would have believed Mr Gisborne to be so big a fool!' declared her ladyship.

'But perhaps I ought to explain, my dear Louisa, that he had my authority,' said Rule still more apologetically.

Lady Louisa, who had been studying the advertisement with a mixture of disgust and amusement, let the *Gazette* drop, and twisted round in her chair to stare up at her brother in astonishment. 'Lord, Rule, what can you possibly mean?' she demanded. 'You're not going to marry Horatia Winwood!'

'But I am,' said his lordship calmly.

'Rule, have you gone mad? You told me positively you had offered for Elizabeth!'

'My shocking memory for names!' mourned his lordship.

Lady Louisa brought her open hand down on the table. 'Nonsense!' she said. 'Your memory's as good as mine!'

'My dear, I should not like to think that,' said the Earl. 'Your memory is sometimes too good.'

'Oh!' said the lady critically surveying him. 'Well, you had best make a clean breast of it. Do you really mean to marry that child?'

'Well, she certainly means to marry me,' said his lordship.

'What?' gasped Lady Louisa.

'You see,' explained the Earl, resuming his seat, 'though it ought to be Charlotte, she has no mind to make such a sacrifice, even for Elizabeth's sake.'

'Either you are out of your senses, or I am!' declared Lady Louisa with resignation. 'I don't know what you're talking about, and how you can mean to marry Horatia, who must be still in the schoolroom, for I'm sure I have never clapped eyes on her – in place of that divinely beautiful Elizabeth –'

'Ah, but I am going to grow used to the eyebrows,' interrupted Rule. 'And she has the Nose.'

'Rule,' said her ladyship with dangerous quiet, 'do not goad me too far! Where have you seen this child?'

He regarded her with a smile hovering round his mouth. 'If I told you, Louisa, you would probably refuse to believe me.'

She cast up her eyes. 'When did you have this notion of marrying her?' she asked.

'Oh, I didn't,' replied the Earl. 'It was not my notion at all.'

'Whose, then?'

'Horatia's, my dear. I thought I had explained.'

'Do you tell me, Marcus, the girl asked you to marry her?' said Lady Louisa sarcastically.

'Instead of Elizabeth,' nodded his lordship. 'Elizabeth, you see, is going to marry Mr Heron.'

'Who in the world is Mr Heron?' cried Lady Louisa. 'I declare, I never heard such a farrago! Confess, you are trying to take me in.'

'Not at all, Louisa. You don't understand the situation at all. One of them must marry me.'

'That I can believe,' she said dryly. 'But this nonsense about Horatia? What is the truth of it?'

'Only that Horatia offered herself to me in her sister's place. And that – but I need not tell you – is quite for your ears alone.'

Lady Louisa was not in the habit of giving way to amazement, and she did not now indulge in fruitless ejaculations. 'Marcus, is the girl a minx?' she asked.

'No,' he answered. 'She is not, Louisa. I am not at all sure that she is not a heroine.'

'Don't she wish to marry you?'

The Earl's eyes gleamed. 'Well, I am rather old, you know, though no one would think it to look at me. But she assures me she would quite like to marry me. If my memory serves me, she prophesied that we should deal famously together.'

46

Lady Louisa, watching him, said abruptly: 'Rule, is this a love-match?'

His brows rose; he looked faintly amused. 'My dear Louisa! At my age?'

'Then marry the Beauty,' she said. 'That one would understand better.'

'You are mistaken, my dear. Horatia understands perfectly. She engages not to interfere with me.'

'At seventeen! It's folly, Marcus.' She got up, drawing her scarf around her. 'I'll see her for myself.'

'Do,' he said cordially. 'I think – but I may be prejudiced – you will find her adorable.'

' If you find her so,' she said, her eyes softening, 'I shall love her – even though she has a squint!'

'Not a squint,' said his lordship. 'A stammer.'

Four

The question Lady Louisa Quain longed to ask yet did not ask was: 'What of Caroline Massey?' Her brother's relations with the fair Massey were perfectly well known to her, nor was she, in the general way, afraid of plain speaking. She told herself that nothing she could say would be likely to have any effect on his conduct, but admitted that she lacked the moral courage to broach the subject. She believed that she enjoyed a good deal of Rule's confidence, but he had never discussed his amorous adventures with her, and would be capable of delivering an extremely unpleasant snub if she trespassed on forbidden ground.

Although she did not flatter herself that her influence had had very much to do with it, it was she who had urged him to marry. She said that if there was one thing she found herself unable to bear it was the prospect of seeing Crosby in Rule's shoes. It was she who had indicated Miss Winwood as a suitable bride. She liked Elizabeth, and was quick to value not only her celestial good looks, but the sweetness of her disposition as well. Surely the possession of so charming a wife would wean Rule from his odious connection with the Massey. But now it did not seem as though Rule cared whom he married and that augured very ill for his bride's future influence over him. A chit of seventeen too! It could not be more unpromising.

She waited on Lady Winwood and met Horatia. She left South Street later in quite another frame of mind. That black-browed child was no simpering miss from the schoolroom. Lord!

thought her ladyship, what a dance she would lead him! It was better, far better than she had planned. Elizabeth's docility would not have answered the purpose near so well as Horatia's turbulence. Why, she told herself, he'll have not a moment's peace and no time at all for that odious Massey creature!

That Rule foresaw the unquiet future that so delighted his sister seemed improbable. He continued to visit in Hertford Street, and no hint of parting crossed his lips.

Lady Massey received him in her rose and silver boudoir two days after the announcement of his betrothal. She was dressed in a négligée of lace and satin, and reclined on a brocaded sopha. No servant announced him; he came into the room as one who had the right, and as he shut the door, remarked humorously: 'Dear Caroline, you've a new porter. Did you tell him to shut the door in my face?'

She held her hand to him. 'Did he do so, Marcus?'

'No,' said his lordship. 'No. That ignominious fate has not yet been mine.' He took her hand and raised it to his lips. Her fingers clasped his, and drew him down to her. 'I thought we were being very formal,' he said, smiling, and kissed her.

She retained her hold on his hand, but said half quizzically, half mournfully: 'Perhaps we should be formal – now, my lord.'

'So you did tell the porter to shut the door in my face?' sighed his lordship.

'I did not. But you are to be married, are you not, Marcus?'

'Yes,' admitted Rule. 'Not just at this moment, you know.'

She smiled, but fleetingly. 'You might have told me,' she said.

He opened his snuff-box and dipped in his finger and thumb. 'I might, of course,' he said, possessing himself of her hand. 'A new blend, my dear,' he said, and dropped the pinch on to her white wrist, and sniffed.

She pulled her hand away. 'Could you not have told me?' she repeated.

He shut his snuff-box and glanced down at her, still good-humoured, but with something at the back of his eyes which gave her pause. A little anger shook her; she understood quite well: he would not discuss his marriage with her. She said, trying to make her voice light: 'You will say it is not my business, I suppose.'

'I am never rude, Caroline,' objected his lordship mildly.

She felt herself foiled, but smiled. 'No indeed. I've heard it said you're the smoothest-spoken man in England.' She studied her rings, moving her hand to catch the light. 'But I didn't know you thought of marriage.' She flashed a look up at him. 'You see,' she said, mock-solemn, 'I thought you loved me – only me!'

'What in the world,' inquired his lordship, 'has that to do with my marriage? I am entirely at your feet, my dear. Quite the prettiest feet I ever remember to have seen.'

'And you've seen many, I apprehend,' she said with a certain dryness.

'Dozens,' said his lordship cheerfully.

She did not mean to say it, but the words slipped out before she could guard her tongue. 'But for all that you are at my feet, Marcus, you have offered for another woman.'

The Earl had put up his glass to inspect a Dresden harlequin upon the mantelpiece. 'If you bought that for a Kändler, my love, I am much afraid that you have been imposed upon,' he remarked.

'It was given me,' she said impatiently.

'How shocking!' said his lordship. 'I will send you a very pretty pair of dancing figures in its place.'

'You are extremely obliging, Marcus, but we were speaking of your marriage,' she said, nettled.

'You were speaking of it,' he corrected. 'I was trying to – er – turn the subject.'

She got up from the sopha and took an impatient step towards him.

'I suppose,' she said breathlessly, 'you did not think the fair Massey worthy of so signal an honour?'

'To tell you the truth, my dear, my modesty forbade me to suppose that the fair Massey would – er – contemplate marriage with me.'

'Perhaps I would not,' she replied. 'But I think that was not your reason.'

'Marriage,' said his lordship pensively, 'is such a very dull affair, you know.'

'Is it, my lord? Even marriage with the noble Earl of Rule?'

'Even with me,' agreed Rule. He looked down at her, a curious expression that was not quite a smile in his eyes. 'You see, my dear, to use your own words, you would have to love me – only me.'

She was startled. Under her powder a faint flush crept into her cheeks. She turned away with a little laugh and began to arrange the roses in one of her bowls. 'That would certainly be very dull,' she said. She glanced sideways at him. 'Are you perhaps jealous, my lord?'

'Not in the least,' said the Earl placidly.

'But you think that were I your wife you might be?'

'You are so charming, my dear, that I feel sure I should have to be,' said his lordship bowing.

She was too clever a woman to press her point. She thought she had gone too far already, and however angry she might be at his marriage she had no wish to alienate him. At one time she had held high hopes of becoming the Countess of Rule, though she was perfectly aware that such an alliance would be deemed a shocking one by the Polite World. She knew now that Rule had baffled her. She had caught a glimpse of steel, and realised that there was something hidden under that easy-going exterior that was as incalculable as it was unexpected. She had imagined that she could twist him round her finger; for the first time she was shaken by doubt, and knew that she must tread warily if she did not wish to lose him.

This she certainly did not want to do. The late Sir Thomas had, in his disagreeable way, tied up his capital so fast that his widow found herself for ever in most unpleasant straits. Sir Thomas had had no sympathy with females who doted on pharaoh and deep basset. Happily the Earl of Rule was not afflicted by the same scruples, and he had not the smallest

51

objection to assisting pecuniarily a distressed lady. He never asked uncomfortable questions on the vice of gambling, and his purse was a fat one.

He had startled her to-day. She had not thought that he dreamed of a rival; now it appeared that he knew very well, probably had known from the first. She would have to be careful; trust her to know how matters lay between him and Robert Lethbridge!

No one ever spoke of it, no one could tell how the story got about, but any number of people knew that once Robert Lethbridge had aspired to the hand of Lady Louisa Drelincourt. Louisa was now the wife of Sir Humphrey Quain, with no breath of scandal attaching to her name, but there had been a day, in her mad teens, when the town hummed with gossip about her. No one knew the whole story, but everyone knew that Lethbridge had been head over ears in love with her and had proposed for her hand, and been rejected, not by the lady herself but by her brother. That had surprised everybody, because although it was true that Lethbridge had a dreadful reputation ('the wildest rake in town, my love!'), no one could have supposed that Rule of all people would put his foot down. Yet he had certainly done so. That was common knowledge. Just what had happened next no one exactly knew, though everyone had his or her version to propound. It had all been so carefully hushed up, but a whisper of Abduction started in Polite Circles. Some said it was no abduction but a willing flight north to Gretna, across the Border. It may have been so, but the runaways never reached Gretna Green. The Earl of Rule drove such fleet horses.

Some held that the two men had fought a duel somewhere on the Great North Road; others spread a tale that Rule carried not a sword but a horse-whip, but this was generally allowed to be improbable, for Lethbridge, however infamous his behaviour, was not a lackey. It was a pity that no one had the true version of the affair, for it was all delightfully scandalous. But none of the three actors in the drama ever spoke of it and if Lady Louisa was reported to have eloped with Lethbridge one night, she was known twenty-four hours later to be visiting relatives in the neighbourhood of Grantham. It was quite true that Robert Lethbridge disappeared from society for several weeks, but he reappeared in due course without wearing any of the symptoms of the baffled lover. The town was agog to see how he and Rule would comport themselves when they met, as they were bound to meet, but once again disappointment awaited the scandal-mongers.

Neither showed any sign of enmity. They exchanged several remarks on different subjects, and if it had not been for Mr Harry Crewe, who had actually seen Rule drive his racing curricle out of town at the extremely odd hour of ten in the evening, even the most inveterate gossip-mongers would have been inclined to have believed the whole tale a mere fabrication.

Lady Massey knew better than that. She was well acquainted with Lord Lethbridge and would have wagered her very fine diamonds that the sentiments he cherished towards the Earl of Rule were tinged with something more than a habitual maliciousness.

As for Rule, he betrayed nothing, but she was not inclined to run the risk of losing him by encouraging too openly the advances of Robert Lethbridge.

She finished the arrangement of her flowers and turned, a gleam of rueful humour in her fine eyes.

'Marcus, my dear,' she said helplessly, 'something much more important! Five hundred guineas at loo, and that odious Celestine dunning me! What am I to do?'

'Don't let it worry you, my dear Caroline,' said his lordship. 'A trifling loan, and the matter is settled.'

She was moved to exclaim: 'Ah, how good you are! I wish – I wish you were not to be married, Marcus. We have dealt extremely, you and I, and I have a notion that it will all be changed now.'

If she referred to their pecuniary relations she might have been thought to have reason for this speech. Lord Rule was likely to find himself with new demands on his purse in the very near future. Viscount Winwood was on his way home to England.

The Viscount, having received in Rome the intelligence of his youngest sister's betrothal, was moved to comply with his parent's desire for his immediate return, and set forward upon the journey with all possible speed. Merely halting a few days in Florence, where he happened to chance upon two friends, and spending a week in Paris upon business not unconnected with the gaming-tables, he made the best of his way home, and would have arrived in London not more than three days later than his fond mother expected him had he not met Sir Jasper Middleton at Breteuil. Sir Jasper, being on his way to the Capital, was putting up at the Hôtel St Nicholas for the night, and was in the midst of a solitary dinner when the Viscount walked in. Nothing could have been more providential, for Sir Jasper was heartily bored with his own company, and had been yearning this many a day to have his revenge on Pelham for a certain game of piquet played in London some months before.

The Viscount was delighted to oblige him; they sat up all night over the cards and in the morning the Viscount, absent-minded no doubt through lack of sleep, embarked in Sir Jasper's post-chaise and was so borne back to Paris. The game of piquet being continued in the chaise, he noticed nothing amiss until they arrived at Clermont, and since by that time there were only some seven or eight posts to go before they reached Paris, it needed no great persuasion to induce him to continue the journey.

He arrived eventually in London to find the preparations for Horatia's nuptials in full swing; and he expressed himself extremely well satisfied with the contract, cast a knowing eye over the Marriage Settlements, congratulated Horatia on her good fortune, and went off to pay his respects to the Earl of Rule.

They were naturally not strangers to each other, but since Pelham was some ten years the Earl's junior they moved in different circles and their acquaintanceship was slight. This circumstance did not weigh with the lively Viscount in the least; he greeted Rule with all the casual bonhomie he used towards his cronies and proceeded, by way of making him feel one of the family, to borrow money from him.

'For I don't mind telling you, my dear fellow,' he said frankly, 'that if I'm to appear the thing at this wedding of yours I must give my tailor a trifle on account. Won't do if I come in rags, you know. Girls won't like it.'

The Viscount was not exactly a fop, but anything less ragged than his slim person would have been hard to find. It did not require the efforts of two stout men to coax him into his coats, and he had a way of arranging his cravat askew, but his clothes were made by the first tailor in town, and of the finest stuffs, embellished with any quantity of heavy gold lacing. At the moment he sat in one of Rule's chairs with his legs stretched out in front of him, and his hands thrust into the pockets of a pair of fawn breeches. His velvet coat hung open to display a waistcoat embroidered in a design of exotic flowers and humming birds. A fine sapphire pin was stuck in the cascade of lace at his throat and his stockings, which represented a dead loss of twenty-five guineas to his hosier, were of silk with large clocks.

The Viscount nobly upheld the Winwood tradition of good looks. He had a reasonable height, and a slender build, and bore a resemblance to his sister Elizabeth. Both had golden locks, and deep blue eyes, straight and beautiful noses, and delicately curved lips. There the likeness ended. Elizabeth's celestial calm was quite lacking in her brother. The Viscount's mobile face was already rather lined, and his eye was a roving one. He looked to be very good-natured, which indeed he was, and appeared to survey the world with a youthful air of cynicism.

Rule received with equanimity the suggestion that he should pay for his prospective brother-in-law's wedding clothes. He glanced down at his guest with some amusement, and said in his bored way: 'Certainly, Pelham.'

The Viscount looked him over with approval. 'I'd a notion we should deal famously,' he remarked. 'Not that I'm in the habit of borrowing from my friends, y'know, but I count you one of the family, Rule.'

'And admit me to its privileges,' said the Earl gravely. 'Admit me still further and let me have a list of your debts.'

The Viscount was momentarily startled. 'Hey? What, all of 'em?' He shook his head. 'Devilish handsome of you, Rule, but can't be done.'

'You alarm me,' said Rule. 'Are they beyond my resources?'

'The trouble is,' said the Viscount confidentially, 'I don't know what they are.'

'My resources, or your debts?'

'Lord, man, the debts! Can't remember the half of 'em. No, it's no use arguing. I've tried to add 'em up a score of times. You think you've done it and then some damned bill you forgot years ago crops up. Never come to the end of it. Wiser to leave it alone. Pay as you go, that's my motto.'

'Is it?' said Rule, mildly surprised. 'I shouldn't have thought it.'

'What I mean,' explained the Viscount, 'is, when a fellow puts the bailiffs on to you, so to speak, then it's time to settle with him. But as for paying all my bills – damme, I never heard of such a thing! Wouldn't do at all.'

'Nevertheless,' said Rule, moving over to his desk, 'I believe you must oblige me in this. Your arrest for debt, perhaps even in the act of bestowing your sister's hand on me in marriage, would quite unnerve me.'

The Viscount grinned. 'Would it so? Well, they can't clap up a peer yet, y'know. Just as you please, of course, but I warn you, I'm in pretty deep.'

Rule dipped a quill in the standish. 'If I were to give you a draft on my bankers for five thousand? Or shall we say ten, as a rounder sum?'

The Viscount was moved to sit up. 'Five,' he said firmly. 'Since you're making a point of it, I don't mind settling up to five thousand, but give away ten thousand pounds to a lot of tradesmen I can't and I won't do. Damme, flesh and blood won't stand it!'

He watched Rule's quill move across the paper, and shook his head. 'Seems wicked to me,' he said. 'I've nothing to say against spending money, but blister it, I don't like to see it thrown away!' He sighed. 'You know, I could put it to better use, Rule,' he suggested.

Rule shook the sand off the paper and handed it to him. 'But somehow I feel sure you won't, Pelham,' he said.

The Viscount cocked an eyebrow intelligently. 'Like that, is it?' he said. 'Oh, very well! But I don't like it. I don't like it at all.'

Nor did his sisters like it when they heard of it. 'Given you five thousand pounds to pay your debts?' cried Charlotte. 'I never heard of such a thing!'

'No more did I,' agreed Pelham. 'Thought for a moment the man was queer in his head, but he don't seem to be.'

'Pel, I do think perhaps you might have waited,' Elizabeth said rather reproachfully. 'It seems almost – almost indecent.'

'And it will all go on gaming,' said Charlotte.

'Devil a penny of it, miss, so that's all you know,' replied the Viscount without rancour.

'Why n-not?' inquired Horatia bluntly. 'It usually d-does.'

Her brother threw her a look of scorn. 'Lord, Horry, if a man trusts you with a cool five thousand to pay your debts, there's no more to be said.'

'I suppose,' said Charlotte waspishly, 'Lord Rule requires to see your accounts.'

'I'll tell you what it is, Charlotte,' the Viscount informed her, 'if you don't sweeten that tongue of yours you'll never get a husband.'

Elizabeth intervened rather hastily. 'Will it meet them all, Pel?'

'It'll keep the blood-suckers quiet for a while,' replied his lordship. He nodded to Horatia. 'He'll make you a devilish good husband, I daresay, but you'd best be careful how you deal with him, Horry!'

'Oh,' said Horatia, 'you don't understand, P-Pel! We are not going to interfere with each other at all! It is j-just like a French marriage of c-convenience.'

'I'm not saying it ain't convenient,' said the Viscount, glancing at Rule's draft, 'but if you take my advice you won't play your tricks on Rule. I've a strong notion you might regret it.'

'I have felt that too,' Elizabeth said, an anxious note in her voice.

'S-stuff!' pronounced Horatia, unimpressed.

Five

The wedding of the Earl of Rule to Miss Horatia Winwood passed off without any unseemly fracas, such as the arrest of the bride's brother for debt or a scene created by the bridegroom's mistress (an event not entirely unexpected by the hopeful), occurring to mar its propriety. The Earl arrived punctually, which surprised everyone, including his harassed secretary; and the bride seemed to be in excellent spirits. Indeed, there were those who considered her spirits too excellent for so solemn an occasion. She was not observed to shed a single tear. However, this lack of sensibility was more than made up for by the demeanour of Lady Winwood. Nothing could have been more proper than that lady's whole bearing. She was supported by her brother, and wept silently throughout the ceremony. Miss Winwood and Miss Charlotte as bridesmaids looked beautiful and behaved becomingly; Mr Walpole's sharp eyes took in everything; Lady Louisa Quain bore up very well, but had recourse to her handkerchief when my lord took Horatia's hand in his; Mr Drelincourt wore a new wig, and a look of saintly resignation; and the Viscount performed his part with careless grace.

It was understood that after a few days spent in the country, the bride and groom were bound for Paris, the choice of destination having been left to the bride. Elizabeth thought it an odd place for a honeymoon, but 'Pho!' said Horatia. 'We are not like you and Edward, w-wanting to make love all d-day long! I want to see things, and go to V-Versailles, and b-buy smarter clothes than Theresa Maulfrey's!'

This part at least of her programme was faithfully carried out. At the end of six weeks the noble pair returned to London, the bride's luggage, so it was rumoured, occupying an entire coach.

The nuptials of her youngest-born had proved to be too much for Lady Winwood's delicate constitution. The varied emotions she had sustained were productive of a fit of the vapours, and the intelligence that her son had signalized his sister's wedding-day by betting fifty pounds on a race between two geese in Hyde Park set the seal to her collapse. She withdrew with her two remaining daughters (one, alas, so soon to be reft from her) to the fastness of Winwood, and there built up her shattered nervous system on a diet of eggs and cream and paregoric draughts, and the contemplation of the Marriage Settlements.

Charlotte, who had thus early in life perceived the Hollowness of Worldly Pleasures professed herself very well pleased with the arrangement, but Elizabeth, though she would not have dreamed of urging Poor Dear Mama, would have preferred to be in London for Horry's home-coming. And this in despite of the fact that Mr Heron found it easily compatible with his not very arduous duties to spend a considerable portion of his time at his home, not two miles distant from Winwood.

Of course Horry journeyed into Hampshire to visit them, but she came without the Earl, a circumstance that distressed Elizabeth. She arrived in her own chaise, a high-sprung affair with huge wheels and the most luxurious blue velvet upholstery; was attended by her abigail, two postilions, and a couple of grooms riding behind the chaise. At first glance she seemed to her sisters to have changed out of all recognition.

Evidently the day of demure muslins and chip hats was done, for the vision in the chaise wore a gown of tobine stripes over a large hoop, and the hat perched on top of curls dressed *à la capricieuse* bore several waving plumes.

'Good gracious, it cannot be Horry!' gasped Charlotte, falling back a step.

But it was soon seen that the change in Horatia went no deeper than her clothes. She could hardly wait for the steps of the chaise to be let down before she sprang into Elizabeth's arms, and she paid not the slightest heed to the crushing of her stiff silk gown or the tilting of that preposterous hat. From Elizabeth she flew to Charlotte, words bubbling off her tongue. Oh, yes, it was the same Horry: no doubt of that.

She stayed one night only at Winwood, which, said Charlotte, was just as well for her Mama, whose state of health was still too precarious to enable her to bear so much chatter and excitement.

Had she enjoyed her honeymoon? Oh, she had had a famous time! Only fancy, she had been to Versailles and spoken with the Queen, and it was perfectly true, the Queen was the most ravishingly beautiful creature and so elegant that she set all the fashions. See, she herself was wearing shoes *cheveux à la Reine*! Whom else had she met! Why, everyone in the world! Such routs, such soirées, and oh, the fireworks at the Tuileries ball!

It was not until they had retired to bed that Elizabeth had any opportunity for a *tête-à-tête*. But no sooner did Horatia set eyes on her sister than she sent her maid away, and curled up on the sopha with Elizabeth beside her. 'I'm so g-glad you came, L-Lizzie,' she said confidingly. 'Charlotte disapproves d-dreadfully of me, doesn't she?'

Elizabeth smiled. 'I am sure you don't care a rap for her disapproval, Horry.'

'Of c-course I don't. I do so hope you will be m-married very soon, L-Lizzie. You have no n-notion how agreeable it is.'

'Quite soon now, we hope. But with Mama so poorly I don't think of it. Are you – are you very happy, dearest?'

Horatia nodded vigorously. 'Oh, yes! Only that I can't help f-feeling sometimes that I stole M-Marcus from you, Lizzie. But you do still prefer Edward, don't you?'

'Always,' Elizabeth answered, laughing. 'Is it very bad taste in me?'

'Well, I m-must say I can't understand it,' said Horatia candidly. 'But perhaps it is b-because you aren't horribly worldly, like m-me. L-Lizzie, even if it is odious of m-me, I must say it is delightful to have just what one wants, and to d-do as one pleases.'

'Yes,' agreed Miss Winwood rather doubtfully, 'I suppose it is.' She stole a glance at Horatia's profile. 'Lord Rule – could not accompany you on this visit?'

'As a m-matter of fact,' admitted Horatia, 'he would have come, only I w-wanted to have you all to m-myself, so he gave up the notion.'

'I see,' said Elizabeth. 'Don't you think, love, that you should have come together, perhaps?'

'Oh, no,' Horatia assured her. 'He quite understood, you know. I find too that fashionable p-people hardly ever do things together.'

'Horry dear,' said Miss Winwood with difficulty, 'I do not want to sound like Charlotte, but I have heard that when – when their wives are so very fashionable – gentlemen do sometimes look elsewhere for entertainment.'

'I know,' said Horatia sapiently. 'But you see I p-promised I wouldn't interfere with Rule.'

It was all very disturbing, Elizabeth felt, but she said no more. Horatia returned to town next day, and the Winwoods heard of her thereafter through the medium of the post and the *Gazette*. Her letters were not very illuminating, but it was apparent that she was enjoying a life full of social engagements.

Elizabeth heard more direct tidings of her from Mr Heron upon the occasion of his next visit into the country.

'Horry?' said Mr Heron. 'Well, yes, I have seen her, but not quite lately, my love. She sent me a card for her drum Tuesday se'nnight. It was a very brilliant affair, but you know I am not in the way of going out a great deal. Still, I did go there,' he added. 'Horry was in spirits, I thought.'

'Happy?' Elizabeth said anxiously.

'Oh, certainly! My lord too was all amiability.'

'Did he seem – could you tell whether he seemed fond of her?' Elizabeth asked.

'Well,' said Mr Heron reasonably, 'you would not expect him

to display his affection in public, dearest. He was just as he always is. A little amused, I thought. You see, Horry seems to have become quite the rage.'

'Oh, dear!' said Miss Winwood, with deep foreboding. 'If only she does not do anything shocking!' A glance at Mr Heron's face made her cry out: 'Edward, you have heard something! I beg you will tell me at once!'

Mr Heron made haste to reassure her. 'No, no, nothing in the world, my love. Merely that Horry seems to have inherited the Fatal Tendency to gamble. But nearly everyone plays nowadays, you know,' he added soothingly.

Miss Winwood was not soothed, nor did an unexpected visit a week later from Mrs Maulfrey do anything to alleviate her alarms.

Mrs Maulfrey was staying at Basingstoke with her Mama-in-law, and drove over to Winwood to pay a morning call on her cousins. She was far more explicit than had been Mr Heron. She sat in a *bergère* chair in the saloon, facing Lady Winwood's couch, and, as Charlotte afterwards remarked, that that afflicted lady did not suffer an immediate relapse was due to her own fortitude rather than to any consideration shown her by her guest.

It was quite obvious that Mrs Maulfrey had not come on any charitable errand. Charlotte, always just, said: 'Depend upon it, Theresa tried to patronize Horry. You know her encroaching way. And really, I cannot altogether blame Horry for snubbing her, though I hope I am far from excusing Horry's excesses.'

Horry, it seemed, was becoming the talk of the Town. Lady Winwood, receiving this piece of news, was moved to recall with complacency a day when she herself had been a reigning toast.

'A Toast!' said Mrs Maulfrey. 'Yes, aunt, and I am sure no one need wonder at it, but Horry is not a Beauty, and if she is a Toast, which I never yet heard, it is certainly not on that account.'

'We ourselves think dear Horry very pretty, Theresa,' said Miss Winwood gently.

'Yes, my dear, but you are partial, as indeed I am too. No one is fonder of Horry than I am, and I put her behaviour down to her childishness, I assure you.'

'We are aware,' said Charlotte, sitting very straight and stiff in her chair; 'that Horry is little more than a child, but we should find it hard to believe that the behaviour of a Winwood could be such as to call for that or any other excuse.'

Slightly quelled by that stern gaze, Mrs Maulfrey fidgeted with the strings of her reticule, and said with a light laugh: 'Oh, certainly, my dear! But I saw with my own eyes Horry strip one of the bracelets off her wrist at Lady Dollabey's card-party – pearls and diamond chips, my love! the most ravishing thing! – and throw it on to the table as her stake because she had lost all her money. You may imagine the scene: gentlemen are so thoughtless, and of course several must needs encourage her, staking rings and hair-buckles against her bracelet, and such nonsense.'

'Perhaps it was not very wise of Horry,' said Elizabeth. 'But not, I think, such a very great matter.'

'I am bound to say,' remarked Charlotte, 'that I hold gaming in any form in the utmost abhorrence.'

Lady Winwood unexpectedly entered the lists. 'Gaming has always been a passion with the Winwoods,' she observed. 'Your Papa was greatly addicted to every form of it. I myself, when my health permits it, am excessively fond of cards. I remember some very pleasant evenings at Gunnersbury, playing at silver pharaoh with the dear Princess. Mr Walpole too! I wonder that you can talk so, Charlotte: it is quite disloyal to Papa's memory, let me tell you. Gaming is quite in the mode; I do not disapprove of it. But I must say I cannot approve of the Winwood luck. Do not tell me my little Horatia has inherited that, Theresa! Did she lose the bracelet?'

'Well, as to that,' said Mrs Maulfrey reluctantly, 'it was not staked in the end. Rule came into the card-room.'

Elizabeth looked quickly across at her. 'Yes?' she said. 'He stopped it?'

'N-no,' said Mrs Maulfrey, with dissatisfaction. 'Hardly that.

He said in his quiet way that it might be difficult to assess the worth of a trinket, and picked up the bracelet, and put it back on Horry's wrist, and set a rouleau of guineas down in its place. I did not wait to see any more.'

'Oh, that was well done of him!' Elizabeth cried, her cheeks glowing.

'Certainly one may say that he behaved with dignity and propriety,' conceded Charlotte. 'And if that is all you have to tell us of Horry's behaviour, my dear Theresa, I must confess I feel you have wasted your time.'

'Pray do not be thinking that I am a mere mischief-maker, Charlotte!' besought her cousin. 'And it is not by any means all. I have it on the best of authority that she had the – yes, positively I must call it the audacity – to drive young Dashwood's gig up St James's for a bet! Right under the windows of White's, my dear! Now don't mistake me: I am sure no one thinks anything but that she's a madcap child – indeed, I understand she takes extremely, and people think her exploits vastly diverting, but I put it to you, is this conduct befitting the Countess of Rule?'

'If it befits a Winwood – which, however, I do not maintain,' said Charlotte with hauteur, 'it may certainly befit a Drelincourt!'

This crushing rejoinder put Mrs Maulfrey so much out of countenance that she found herself with very little more to say, and presently took her leave of the Winwood ladies. She left behind her a feeling of uneasiness which culminated in a suggestion, put tentatively forward by Elizabeth, that Lady Winwood should think of returning to South Street. Lady Winwood said in a failing voice that no one had the least regard for the frailty of her poor nerves, and if ever good had come of interfering between man and wife she had yet to hear of it.

However, the business was settled in the end by a letter from Mr Heron. Mr Heron had got his Captaincy, and was to go into the West Country in the further execution of his duties. He desired to make Elizabeth his wife without any more delay, and proposed an immediate wedding.

65

Elizabeth would have liked to be married quietly at Winwood, but her Mama, having no notion of allowing her triumph in getting two daughters respectably married within three months to pass unnoticed, arose tottering from her couch and announced that never should it be said that she had Failed in her Duty towards her loved ones.

The wedding was naturally not so brilliant an affair as Horatia's, but it passed off very well, and if the bride appeared pale she was allowed to be in great beauty for all that. The bridegroom looked extremely handsome in his regimentals, and the ceremony was graced by the presence of the Earl and Countess of Rule, the Countess wearing for the occasion a gown that made every other lady blink with envy.

Elizabeth, in all the bustle of hurried preparation, had had few opportunites of being private with Horatia, and on the only occasion when she found herself alone with her sister she had realized with a sinking heart that Horatia was on her guard against too intimate a conversation. She could only hope to have more opportunity later in the year, when Horatia promised to come to Bath, which watering-place Captain Heron was to make his headquarters.

Six

'*W*ell, if you wish to know what I think,' said Lady Louisa stringently – 'though I make not the smallest doubt that you don't – you're a fool, Rule!'

The Earl, who was still glancing over some papers brought to him by Mr Gisborne a few moments before his sister's arrival, said absently: 'I know. But you must not let it distress you, my dear.'

'What,' demanded her ladyship, disregarding this flippancy, 'are those papers? You need not put yourself to the trouble of telling me. I know the look of a bill, trust me!'

The Earl put them into his pocket. 'If only more people understood me so well!' he sighed. 'And respected my – er – constitutional dislike of answering questions.'

'The chit will ruin you,' said his sister. 'And you do nothing – nothing to avert calamity!'

'Believe me,' said Rule, 'I hope to have enough energy to avert that particular calamity, Louisa.'

'I wish I may see it!' she replied. 'I like Horry. Yes, I do like her, and I did from the start, but if you'd one grain of sense, Marcus, you would take a stick and beat her!'

'But think how fatiguing!' objected the Earl.

She looked scornfully across at him. 'I wanted her to lead you a dance,' she said candidly. 'I thought it would be very good for you. But I never dreamed she would make herself the talk of the town while you stood by and watched.'

'You see, I hardly ever dance,' Rule excused himself.

Lady Louisa might have replied with some asperity had not a light footstep sounded at that moment in the hall, and the door opened to admit Horatia herself.

She was dressed for the street, but carried her hat in her hand, as though she had just taken it off. She threw it on to a chair, and dutifully embraced her sister-in-law. 'I am sorry I was out, L-Louisa. I have been to see M-Mama. She is feeling very low, because of having l-lost Lizzie. And Sir P-Peter Mason, whom she quite thought was g-going to offer for Charlotte because he doesn't like L-levity in a Female, is promised to Miss Lupton after all. M-Marcus, do you think Arnold might like to m-marry Charlotte?'

'For heaven's sake, Horry,' cried Lady Louisa with foreboding, 'don't ask him!'

Horatia's straight brows drew together. 'N-no, of course not. But I m-might throw them together, I think.'

'Not, I beg of you,' said his lordship, 'in this house.'

The grey eyes surveyed him questioningly. 'N-not if you would rather I didn't,' said Horatia obligingly. 'I am not set on it, you understand.'

'I am so glad,' said his lordship. 'Consider the blow to my self-esteem if Charlotte were to accept Arnold's hand in marriage.'

Horatia twinkled. 'Well, you n-need not put yourself about, sir, for Charlotte says she is going to D-dedicate her Life to M-mama. Oh, are you going already, Louisa?'

Lady Louisa had risen, drawing her scarf round her shoulders. 'My dear, I have been here this age. I came only for a word with Marcus.'

Horatia stiffened slightly. 'I see,' she said. 'It was a p-pity I came in, perhaps.'

'Horry, you're a silly child,' said Lady Louisa, tapping her cheek. 'I have been telling Rule he should beat you. I doubt he is too lazy.'

Horatia swept a polite curtsy, and closed her lips firmly together.

The Earl escorted his sister out of the room, and across the hall. 'You are not always very wise, are you, Louisa?' he said.

'I never was,' she answered ruefully.

Having seen his sister into her carriage the Earl returned rather thoughtfully to the library. Horatia, swinging her hat defiantly, was already crossing the hall towards the stairs, but she paused as Rule spoke to her. 'Do you think you could spare me a moment of your time, Horry?'

The scowl still lingered on her brow. 'I'm g-going to luncheon with Lady M-Mallory,' she informed him.

'It is not yet time for luncheon,' he replied.

'No, but I have to change my g-gown.'

'That is naturally important,' agreed the Earl.

'Well, it is,' she insisted.

The Earl held the door into the library open. Up went Horatia's chin. 'I m-may as well tell you, my lord, that I'm feeling c-cross, and when I'm cross I don't talk to p-people.'

Across the wide stretch of hall the Earl's eyes met and held hers. 'Horry,' he said pleasantly, 'you know how much I dislike exertion. Don't put me to the trouble of fetching you.'

The chin came down a little, and the smouldering eyes showed a certain speculative interest. 'C-carry me, do you m-mean? I wonder if you would?'

The gravity of Rule's expression was dispelled by slight look of amusement. 'And I wonder whether you really think that I would not?' he said.

A door at the end of the hall, leading to the servants' quarters, opened, and a footman came out. Horatia shot a triumphant glance at the Earl, set one foot on the bottom stair, hesitated, and then swung round and walked back into the library.

The Earl closed the door. 'You play fair, Horry, at all events,' he remarked.

'Of c-course,' said Horatia, seating herself on the arm of a chair and once more tossing her ill-used hat aside. 'I did not m-mean to be disobliging, but when you talk me over with your sister it makes me f-furious.'

'Are you not rather leaping to conclusions?' suggested Rule.

'Well, anyway, she said she had been t-telling you that you ought to beat me,' said Horatia, kicking her heel against the chair-leg.

'She is full of good advice,' agreed his lordship. 'But I haven't beaten you yet, Horry, in spite of it.'

Slightly mollified, the bride remarked: 'No, b-but I think when she says things about m-me you might defend m-me, sir.'

'You see, Horry,' said his lordship with a certain deliberation, 'you make that rather difficult.'

There was an uncomfortable pause. Horatia flushed to the roots of her hair, and said, stammering painfully: 'I'm s-sorry. I d-don't m-mean to behave outrageously. W-what have I done n-now?'

'Oh, nothing really very desperate, my dear,' Rule said non-committally. 'But do you think you could refrain from intro-ducing a wild animal into Polite Circles?'

A giggle, hastily choked, escaped her. 'I was afraid you'd hear about that,' she confessed. 'B-but it was quite an accident, I assure you, and – and very diverting.'

'I haven't the least doubt of that,' Rule replied.

'Well, it truly was, M-Marcus. It jumped on to Crosby's shoulder and p-pulled his wig off. But nobody m-minded at all, except Crosby. I'm afraid it isn't a very well-trained monkey.'

'I'm afraid it can't be,' said Rule. 'Some such suspicion did cross my mind when I found it had – er – visited the breakfast-table before me the other morning.'

'Oh dear!' Horatia said contritely. 'I am very sorry. Only Sophia Colehampton has one, and it goes everywhere with her, so I thought I would have one too. However, I d-don't really like it m-much, so I think I won't keep it. Is that all?'

He smiled. 'Alas, Horry, it is only the beginning. I think – yes, really I think you must explain some of these.' He drew the sheaf of bills out of his pocket and gave them to her.

On the top lay a sheet of paper covered with Mr Gisborne's neat figures. Horatia gazed in dismay at the alarming total. 'Are they – all mine?' she faltered.

'All yours,' said his lordship calmly.

Horatia swallowed. 'I d-didn't mean to spend as m-much as that. Indeed I c-can't imagine how it can have come about.'

The Earl took the bills from her, and began to turn them over. 'No,' he agreed, 'I have often thought it very odd how bills mount up. And one must dress, after all.'

'Yes,' nodded Horatia, more hopefully. 'You do understand that, d-don't you, Marcus?'

'Perfectly. But – forgive my curiosity, Horry – do you invariably pay a hundred and twenty guineas for a pair of shoes?'

'What?' shrieked Horatia. The Earl showed her the bill. She stared at it with dawning consternation. 'Oh!' she said. 'I – I remember now. You s-see, Marcus, they – they have heels studded with emeralds.'

'Then the matter becomes comprehensible,' said his lordship.

'Yes. I wore them at the Subscription-ball at Almack's. They are called *venez-y-voir*, you know.'

'That would account, no doubt,' remarked Rule, 'for the presence of the three young gentlemen whom I found – er – assisting at your toilet that evening.'

'B-but there is nothing in that, Rule!' objected Horatia, lifting her downcast head. 'It is quite the thing for gentlemen to be admitted as soon as the under-dress is on. I know it is, b-because Lady Stokes d-does it. They advise one how to p-place one's p-patches, and where to bestow one's flowers, and what p-perfume to use.'

If the Earl of Rule found anything amusing in being instructed by his bride in the art of dalliance the only sign he gave of it was the very faintest quiver of the lips. 'Ah!' he said. 'And yet –' he looked down at her, half-smiling – 'And yet I believe I might advise you in these matters to even better purpose.'

'B-but you're my husband,' Horatia pointed out.

He turned back to the bills. 'That is undoubtedly a handicap,' he admitted.

Horatia appeared to consider the subject closed. She peered

over his arm. 'Have you f-found anything else dreadful?' she inquired.

'My dear, are we not agreed that one must dress? I don't question your expenditure – though I confess I succumbed to curiosity over the shoes. What – shall we say – puzzles me a trifle –'

'I know,' she interrupted, sedulously regarding her feet. 'You w-want to know w-why I haven't paid them myself.'

'My inquisitive disposition,' murmured his lordship.

'I c-couldn't,' said Horatia gruffly. 'That's w-why!'

'A very adequate reason,' said that placid voice. 'But I thought I had made provision. My lamentable memory must be at fault again.'

Horatia set her teeth. 'I m-may deserve it, sir, but p-please don't be odious. You know you m-made provision.'

He laid the bills down. 'Pharaoh, Horry?'

'Oh n-no, not all of it!' she said eagerly, glad to be able to produce an extenuating circumstance. 'B-Basset!'

'I see.'

The note of amusement had left his voice; she ventured to raise her eyes, and saw something very like a frown on his face. 'Are you d-dreadfully angry?' she blurted out.

The frown cleared. 'Anger is too fatiguing an emotion, my dear. I was wondering how best to cure you.'

'C-cure me? You can't. It's in the b-blood,' said Horatia frankly. 'And even Mama don't disapprove of gaming. I didn't understand it quite p-perfectly at first, and I d-daresay that is why I lost.'

'Quite possibly,' assented Rule. 'Madam Wife, I am constrained to tell you – in my character of indignant husband – that I cannot countenance excessive gaming.'

'Don't, oh *don't*,' implored Horatia, 'm-make me promise to p-play only whist and silver pharaoh! I c-couldn't keep it! I will be m-more careful, and I'm sorry about those shocking bills! – Oh gracious, only look at the time! I must go, I p-positively must go!'

'Don't distress yourself, Horry,' recommended the Earl. 'To be the last arrival is always effective.' But he spoke to space. Horatia had gone.

His wife's gyrations, however much perturbation they might occasion Lady Louisa, were watched by others with very different feelings. Mr Crosby Drelincourt, whose world had assumed a uniformly dun hue from the moment of his cousin's betrothal, began to observe a ray of light breaking through the gloom, and Lady Massey, taking note of the young Countess's every exploit and extravagance, patiently bided her time. Rule's visits to Hertford Street had become more infrequent, but she was far too clever to reproach him, and took care to be her most charming self whenever she saw him. She was already acquainted with Horatia – a circumstance she owed to the kind offices of Mr Drelincourt, who made it his business to present her to the Countess at a ball – but beyond exchanging curtsies and polite greetings with Horatia whenever they chanced to meet she had not sought to increase the friendship. Rule had a way of seeing more than he appeared to, and it was unlikely that he would permit an intimacy between his wife and his mistress to grow up without interference.

It seemed to be Mr Drelincourt's self-appointed duty to make presentations to his new cousin. He even presented Robert Lethbridge to her, at a drum at Richmond. His lordship had been out of town when the Earl and Countess of Rule returned from their honeymoon and by the time he first clapped eyes on the bride she had already – as young Mr Dashwood so brilliantly phrased it – Taken the Town by Storm.

Lord Lethbridge saw her first at the drum, dressed in satin *soupir étouffe*, with a coiffure *en diadème*. A patch called the Gallant was set in the middle of her cheek, and she fluttered ribbons *à l'attention*. She certainly took the eye, which may have been the reason for Lord Lethbridge's absorption.

He stood against one wall of the long saloon, and his eyes rested on the bride with a curious expression in them, hard to read. Mr Drelincourt, observing him from a distance, ranged alongside, and said with a titter: 'You are admiring my new cousin, my lord?'

'Profoundly,' said Lethbridge.

'For my part,' shrugged Mr Drelincourt, never one to conceal his feelings, 'I find those eyebrows positively grotesque. I do not call her a beauty. Decidedly I do not.'

Lethbridge's glance flickered to his face; his lips curled imperceptibly. 'You ought to be delighted with her, Crosby,' he said.

'Pray allow me to present you to the Paragon!' said Mr Drelincourt crossly. 'But I warn you, she stammers hideously.'

'And gambles, and drives gigs up St James's,' said his lordship. 'I never hoped for better.'

Mr Drelincourt looked sharply round at him. 'Why – why.'

'What a fool you are, Crosby!' said Lethbridge. 'Present me!'

'Really, my lord, really! Pray how am I to take that?'

'I had not the least intention of being enigmatic, believe me,' replied Lethbridge acidly. 'Make me known to this excellent bride.'

'You are in a devilish humour, my lord, I protest,' complained Crosby, but he moved towards the group about Horatia. 'Cousin, permit me! May I present one who is all eagerness to meet you?'

Horatia had very little desire to meet any crony of Mr Drelincourt's whom she cordially despised, and she turned with obvious reluctance. But the man who stood before her was not at all like Crosby's usual companions. None of the absurdities of the Macaroni marred the elegance of his person. He was dressed with magnificence, and he seemed to be considerably older than Mr Drelincourt.

'Lord Lethbridge, my Lady Rule!' said Crosby. 'You perceive him quite agog to meet the lady about whom the whole town is talking, dear cousin.'

Horatia, spreading her skirts in a curtsy, flushed a little for Mr Drelincourt's words stung. She arose swimmingly and extended her hand. Lord Lethbridge received it on his wrist and bent with incomparable grace to salute it. A flicker of interest awoke in Horatia's eyes: his lordship had an air.

'Our poor Crosby has always such a happy turn of phrase,' murmured Lethbridge, and won a glimpse of dimple. 'Ah, precisely! Let me lead you to that couch, madam.'

She took his arm and went with him across the saloon. 'C-Crosby detests me,' she confided.

'But of course,' said his lordship.

She frowned, rather puzzled. 'That isn't very c-civil, sir. Why should he?'

His brows rose in momentary surprise; he looked critically at her, and laughed. 'Oh – because he has such execrable taste, ma'am!'

It did not seem to Horatia as though this was the reason he really had in mind, and she was about to inquire deeper into the matter when he changed the subject. 'I need hardly ask, ma'am, whether you are *ennuyée* to the point of extinction with such affairs as these?' he said, indicating with a wave of his hand the rest of the company.

'N-no, I am not,' replied Horatia. 'I l-like it.'

'Delightful!' smiled his lordship. 'You infect even such jaded spirits as mine with enthusiasm.'

She looked a little doubtful. What he said was excessively polite, but the tone he used held a tinge of light mockery which baffled while it intrigued her. 'J-jaded spirits usually seek the c-card-room, sir,' she remarked.

He was gently fanning her with the cabriolet-fan he had taken from her hand, but he paused, and said with a quizzical look: 'Ah – and so sometimes do enthusiastic ones, do they not?'

'S-sometimes,' admitted Horatia. 'You have heard all about m-me.'

'By no means, ma'am. But when I learn of a lady who never refuses a wager, why, I desire to know more of her.'

'I am certainly very p-partial to games of chance, sir,' said Horatia wistfully.

'One day you shall play your cards against me,' said Lethbridge, 'if you will.'

A voice spoke immediately behind them. 'Do not play with Lord Lethbridge, ma'am, if you are wise!'

Horatia looked over her shoulder. Lady Massey had entered the saloon through a curtained archway, and was standing leaning her hand lightly on the back of the couch. 'Oh?' Horatia said, glancing at Lethbridge with new interest. 'Will he f-fleece me?'

Lady Massey laughed: 'Why, ma'am, am I to tell you that you are talking to the most hardened gamester of our times? Be warned, I implore you?'

'Are you?' inquired Horatia, regarding Lethbridge, who had risen at Lady Massey's approach, and was watching her with an indefinable smile. 'Then I should l-like very m-much to play with you, I assure you!'

'You will need iron nerves, ma'am,' Lady Massey said banteringly. 'If he were not here I might tell you some shocking tales about him.'

At that moment Lord Winwood, who was strolling towards the doorway, caught sight of the group by the couch, and promptly bore down upon his sister. He executed a bow in Lady Massey's direction, and bestowed a nod on Lethbridge. 'You're very obedient, ma'am. Servant, Lethbridge. I've been looking all over for you, Horry. Promised to present a fellow to you.'

Horatia got up. 'Well, b-but – '

The Viscount took her hand to draw it through his arm, and as he did so pinched her fingers significantly. Understanding this brotherly nip to mean that he had something of importance to say to her, Horatia sketched a curtsy to Lady Massey, and prepared to walk away with the Viscount, only pausing to say seriously: 'P-perhaps we shall try a throw against each other some day, my lord.'

'Perhaps,' Lethbridge bowed.

The Viscount led her firmly out of earshot. 'Good God,

76

Horry, what's all this?' he demanded, with pious intention but a complete absence of tact. 'Keep away from Lethbridge: he's dangerous. Damme, was there ever such a one for getting into the wrong company?'

'I sh-shan't keep away from him,' declared Horatia. 'Lady M-Massey says he is a hardened g-gamester!'

'So he is,' said the ill-advised Viscount. 'And you're no pigeon for his plucking, Horatia, let me tell you.'

Horatia pulled her hand away, her eyes flashing. 'And I-let me tell you, P-Pel, that I'm a m-married lady now, and I w-won't be ordered about by you!'

'Married! Ay, so you are, and you've only to let Rule get wind of this and there'll be the devil to pay. The Massey too! 'Pon my soul, if ever I met another to equal you!'

'W-well, and what have you against Lady M-Massey?' said Horatia.

'What have I – ? Oh Lord!' The Viscount tugged ruefully at his solitaire. 'I suppose you don't – no, exactly. Now don't plague me with a lot of silly questions, there's a good girl. Come and drink a glass of negus.'

Still standing by the couch, Lord Lethbridge watched the departure of the brother and sister, and turned his head to observe Lady Massey. 'Thank you, my dear Caroline,' he said sweetly. 'That was vastly kind of you. Did you know it?'

'Do you think me a fool?' she retorted. 'When that plum drops into your hand, remember then to thank me.'

'And the egregious Winwood, I fancy,' remarked his lordship, helping himself to a pinch of snuff. 'Do you want that plum to fall into my hand, dear lady?'

The look that passed between them was eloquent enough. 'We need not fence,' Lady Massey said crisply. 'You have your own ends to serve; maybe I can guess what they are. My ends I daresay you know.'

'I am quite sure that I do,' grinned Lethbridge. 'Do forgive me, my dear, but though I have a reasonable hope of achieving mine, I'm willing to lay you any odds you don't achieve yours.

Now is not that outspoken? You did say we need not fence, did you not?'

She stiffened. 'What am I to understand by that, if you please?'

'Just this,' said Lethbridge, shutting his enamelled snuff-box with a snap. 'I don't need your assistance, my love. I play my cards to suit myself, neither to oblige you nor Crosby.'

'I imagine,' she said dryly, 'we all of us desire the same thing.'

'But my motive,' replied his lordship, 'is by far the purest.'

Seven

*L*ady Massey, accepting Lethbridge's snub with tolerable equanimity, had no difficulty in interpreting his last cryptic speech. Her momentary anger gave place immediately to a somewhat cynical amusement. She herself was hardly of the stuff that could plan the undoing of a bride for no more personal reason than a desire for revenge on the groom, but she was able to appreciate the artistry of such a scheme, while the cold-bloodedness of it, though rather shocking, could not but entertain her. There was something a little devilish in it, and it was the devil in Lethbridge that had always attracted her. Nevertheless, had Horatia been any other man's wife than Rule's she would have thought shame to lend herself even passively to so inhuman a piece of mischief. But Lady Massey, prepared before she set eyes on Horatia to resign herself to the inevitable, had changed her mind. She flattered herself that she knew Rule, and who knowing him could think for a moment that this ill-assorted union could end in anything but disaster? He had married for an heir, for a gracious châtelaine, certainly not for the alarums and excursions that must occur wherever Horatia went.

Something he had once said to her remained significantly in her memory. His wife must care for him – only for him. She had caught then a glimpse of steel, implacable as it was unexpected.

Rule, for all his easy going, would be no complaisant husband and if this loveless marriage of convenience went awry, why then, divorce was not so rare in these days. If a Duchess could suffer it, so too might a Countess. Once free of his tempestuous wife, with her hoydenish flights and her gaming excesses, he would turn with relief to one who created no scenes and knew to a nicety how to please a man.

It suited Lady Massey very well to permit Lethbridge to work his mischief; she wanted to have no hand in it; it was an ugly business after all, and her provocative words to Horatia had been the malicious prompting of the moment rather than a concerted attempt to throw her into Lethbridge's arms. Yet finding herself beside Horatia at Vauxhall Gardens a week later, and seeing Lethbridge answer a beckoning gesture from a fair beauty in one of the boxes only with a wave of his hand, she could not resist the impulse to say: 'Alas, poor Maria! What a fruitless task to attempt Robert Lethbridge's enslavement! As though we had not all tried – and failed!'

Horatia said nothing, but her eyes followed Lethbridge with a speculative gleam in them.

It did not need Lady Massey's words to spur up her interest. Lethbridge, with his hawk-eyes and his air of practised ease, had at the outset attracted her, already a trifle bored by the adulation of younger sparks. He was very much the man-of-the-world, and to add to his fascination he was held to be dangerous. At the first meeting it had seemed as though he admired her; had he shown admiration more plainly at the second his charm might have dwindled. He did not. He let half the evening pass before he approached her and then he exchanged but the barest civilities and passed on. They met at the card table at Mrs Delaney's house. He held the bank at pharaoh and she won against the bank. He complimented her, but still with that note of mockery as though he refused to take her seriously. Yet, when she walked in the Park with Mrs Maulfrey two days later and he rode past, he reined in and sprang lightly down from the saddle and came towards her, leading his mount, and walked beside her a considerable distance, as though he were delighted to have come upon her.

'La, child!' cried Mrs Maulfrey, when at last he took his leave of them. 'You'd best have a care – he's a wicked rake, my dear! Don't fall in love with him, I beg of you!'

'F-fall in love!' said Horatia scornfully. 'I want to play c-cards with him!'

He was at the Duchess of Queensberry's ball, and did not once approach her. She was piqued, and never thought to blame Rule's presence for his defection. Yet when she visited the Pantheon in Lady Amelia Pridham's party, Lethbridge, arriving solitary midway through the evening, singled her out and was so assiduous in his attentions that he led her to suppose that at last they were becoming intimate. But upon a young gentleman's approaching to claim Horatia's attention his lordship relinquished her with a perfectly good grace and very soon afterwards withdrew to the card-room. It was really most provoking, quite enough to make any lady determined to plan his downfall, and it did much to spoil her enjoyment of the party. Indeed, the evening was not a success. The Pantheon, so bright and new, was very fine, of course, with its pillars and its stucco ceilings and its great glazed dome, but Lady Amelia, most perversely, did not want to play cards, and in one of the country dances Mr Laxby, awkward creature, trod on the edge of her gown of diaphanous Jouy cambric just come from Paris, and tore the hem past repair. Then, too, she was obliged to decline going for a picnic out to Ewell on the following day on the score of having promised to drive to Kensington (of all stuffy places!) to visit her old governess, who was living there with a widowed sister. She had half a notion that Lethbridge was to be at the picnic and was seriously tempted to bury Miss Lane in oblivion. However, the thought of poor Laney's disappointment prevented her from taking this extreme step, and she resolutely withstood all the entreaties of her friends.

The afternoon dutifully spent in Kensington proved to be just as dull as she had feared it would be and Laney, so anxious to know all she had been doing, so full of tiresome gossip, made it impossible for her to leave as soon as she would have liked to have done. It was very nearly half-past four before she entered her coach, but fortunately she was to dine at home that evening before going with Rule to the Opera, so that it did not greatly signify that she was bound to be late. But she felt that she had spent an odious day, the only ray of consolation – and that, she admitted, a horridly selfish one – being that the weather, which had promised so well in the morning, had become extremely inclement, quite unsuitable for picnics, the sky being overcast by lunch-time, and some thunderous clouds gathering which made the light very bad as early as four o'clock. A threatening rumble sounded as she stepped into the coach, and Miss Lane at once desired her to remain on until the storm had passed. Luckily the coachman was confident that it would hold off for some time yet, so that Horatia was not obliged to accept this invitation. The coachman was somewhat startled at receiving a command from her ladyship to spring his horses, as she was monstrously late. He touched his hat in a reluctant assent and wondered what the Earl would say if it came to his ears that his wife was driven into town at the gallop.

It was, accordingly, at a spanking pace that the coach headed eastwards, but a flash of lightning making one of the leaders shy badly across the road, the coachman soon steadied the pace, which, indeed, he had had some trouble in maintaining, both his wheelers being good holders and quite unused to so headlong a method of progression.

The rain still held off, but lightning quivered frequently and the noise of thunder afar became practically continuous, while the heavy clouds overhead obscured the daylight very considerably and made the coachman anxious to pass the Knightsbridge toll-gate as soon as possible.

A short distance beyond the Halfway House, an inn mid-way between Knightsbridge and Kensington, a group of some three or four horsemen, imperfectly concealed by a clump of trees just off the road, most unpleasantly assailed the vision of both the men on the box. They were some way ahead, and it was difficult in the uncertain light to observe them very particularly. Some heavy drops of rain had begun to fall, and it was conceivable that the horsemen were merely seeking shelter from the imminent downpour. But the locality had a bad reputation, and although the hour was too early for highwaymen to be abroad the coachman whipped up his horses with the intention of passing the dangerous point at the gallop, and recommended the groom beside him to be ready with the blunderbuss.

That worthy, peering uneasily ahead, disclosed the fact that he had not thought proper to bring this weapon, the expedition hardly being of a nature to render such a precaution necessary. The coachman, keeping to the crown of the road, tried to assure himself that no highwaymen would dare to venture forth in broad daylight. 'Sheltering from the rain, that's all,' he grunted, adding rather inconsequently: 'Saw a couple of men hanged at Tyburn once. Robbing the Portsmouth Mail. Desperate rogues, they was.'

They were now come within hailing distance of the mysterious riders, and to both men's dismay the group disintegrated and the three horsemen spread themselves across the road in a manner leaving no room for doubt of their intentions.

The coachman cursed under his breath, but being a stout-hearted fellow lashed his horses to a still wilder pace in the hope of charging through the chain across the road. A shot, whistling alarmingly by his head, made him flinch involuntarily, and at the same moment the groom, quite pale with fright, grabbed at the reins and hauled on them with all his strength. A second shot set the horses swerving and plunging, and while the coachman and groom fought for possession of the reins a couple of the frieze-clad ruffians rode up and seized the leaders' bridles, and so brought the whole equipage to a standstill.

The third man, a big fellow with a mask covering his entire face, pressed up to the coach, shouting: 'Stand and deliver!' and leaning from the saddle wrenched open the door.

Horatia, startled, but as yet unalarmed, found herself confronted by a large horse-pistol, held in a grimy hand. Her astonished gaze travelled upwards to the curtain-mask and she cried out: 'Gracious! F-foot-pads!'

A laugh greeted this exclamation and the man holding the barker said in a beery voice: 'Bridle culls, my pretty! We bain't no foot-scamperers! Hand over the gewgaws and hand 'em quick, see?'

'I shan't!' said Horatia, grasping her reticule firmly.

It seemed as though the highwayman was rather at a loss, but while he hesitated a second masked rider jostled him out of the way and made a snatch at the reticule. 'Ho-ho, there's a fat truss!' he gloated, wresting it from her, 'and a rum fam on your finger too! Now softly, softly!'

Horatia, far more angry than she was frightened at having her purse wrenched from her, tried to pull her hand away, and failing, dealt her assailant a ringing slap.

'How dare you, you odious p-person!' she raged.

This was productive only of another coarse guffaw, and she was beginning to feel really rather alarmed when a voice suddenly shouted: 'Lope off! Lope off! or we'll be snabbled! Coves on the road!'

Almost at the same moment a shot sounded, and hooves could be heard thundering down the road. The highwayman released Horatia in a twinkling; another shot exploded; there was a great deal of shouting and stamping and the highwaymen galloped off into the dusk. The next instant a rider on a fine bay dashed up to the coach and reined in his horse, rearing and plunging. 'Madam!' the newcomer said sharply, and then in tones of the utmost surprise: 'My Lady Rule! Good God, ma'am, are you hurt?'

'W-why, it's you!' cried Horatia. 'No, I'm n-not in the least hurt.'

Lord Lethbridge swung himself out of the saddle and stepped lightly up on to the step of the coach, taking Horatia's hand in his. 'Thank God I chanced to be at hand!' he said. 'There is nothing to frighten you now, ma'am. The rogues are fled.'

Horatia, an unsatisfactory heroine, replied gaily: 'Oh, I w-wasn't frightened, sir! It is the m-most exciting thing that has ever happened to m-me! But I must say I think they were very cowardly robbers to run away from one m-man.'

A soundless laugh shook his lordship. 'Perhaps they ran away from my pistols,' he suggested. 'So long as they have not harmed you –'

'Oh, n-no! But how came you on this road my l-lord?'

'I have been visiting friends out at Brentford,' he explained.

'I thought you were going to the p-picnic at Ewell?' she said.

He looked directly into her eyes. 'I was,' he answered. 'But my Lady Rule did not join the party.'

She came aware that her hand was still reposing in his and drew it away. 'I d-didn't think you c-cared a rap for that,' she said.

'Didn't you? But I did care.'

She looked at him for a moment and then said shyly: 'P-please will you d-drive back with m-me?'

He appeared to hesitate, that queer twisted smile hovering round his mouth.

'Why n-not?' Horatia asked.

'No reason in the world, ma'am,' he replied. 'If you wish it of course I will drive with you.' He stepped down into the road again, and summoned up the groom, telling him to mount the bay horse. The groom, who was looking shame-faced from his late encounter with the coachman, hastened to obey him. Lord Lethbridge again climbed into the coach; the door was shut; and within a few minutes the vehicle began to move forward in the direction of London.

Inside it Horatia said with the frankness her family considered disastrous: 'I quite thought you d-did not like m-me very much, you know.'

'Did you? But that would have been very bad taste on my part,' said his lordship.

'W-well, but you p-positively avoid me when we meet,' Horatia pointed out. 'You know you d-do!'

'Ah!' said his lordship. 'But that is not because I do not like you, ma'am.'

'W-why, then?' asked Horatia bluntly.

He turned his head. 'Has no one warned you that Robert Lethbridge is too dangerous for you to know?'

Her eyes twinkled. 'Yes, any number of people. Did you g-guess that?'

'Of course I did. I believe Mamas all warn their daughters against my wicked wiles. I am a very desperate character, you know.'

She laughed. 'W-well, if I don't m-mind, why should you?'

'That is rather different,' Lethbridge replied. 'You see, you are – if you will let me say so – very young.'

'D-do you mean that I am too young to b-be a friend of yours?'

'No, that is not what I mean. You are too young to be allowed to do – unwise things, my dear.'

She looked inquiring. 'W-would it be unwise of me to know you?'

'In the eyes of the world, certainly it would.'

'I d-don't give a fig for the world!' declared Horatia roundly.

He stretched out his hand to take hers, and kissed her fingers. 'You are – a very charming lady,' he said. 'But were you and I to call friends, ma'am, the world would talk, and the world must not talk about my Lady Rule.'

'Why should people think odious things about you?' asked Horatia, indignation in her voice.

A sigh escaped him. 'Unfortunately, ma'am, I have made for myself a most shocking reputation and once one has done that there is no being rid of it. Now I feel quite sure that your excellent brother told you to have naught to do with Lethbridge. Am I right?'

She coloured. 'Oh, n-no one pays the least heed to P-Pel!' she assured him. 'And if you will l-let me be a friend of yours I w-will be whatever anyone says!'

Again he seemed to hesitate. A warm hand once more clasped his. 'P-please let m-me!' Horatia begged.

His fingers closed round hers. 'Why?' he asked. 'Is it because

86

you want to gamble with me? Is that why you offer me your friendship?'

'N-no, though that w-was what I wanted, to begin with,' Horatia admitted. 'But now that you've told me all this I feel quite d-differently and I *won't* be one of those horrid p-people who believe the worst.'

'Ah!' he said, 'but I am afraid Rule would have something to say to that, my dear. I must tell you that he is not precisely one of my well-wishers. And husbands, you know, have to be obeyed.'

It was on the tip of her tongue to retort that she did not care a fig for Rule either, when it occurred to her that this was scarcely a proper sentiment, and she replied instead: 'I assure you, sir, Rule d-does not interfere with my f-friendships.'

They had come by this time to the Hercules Pillars Inn by Hyde Park, and only a comparatively short distance remained between them and Grosvenor Square. The rain, which was now coming down in good earnest, beat against the windows of the coach, and the daylight had almost vanished. Horatia could no longer distinguish his lordship with any clarity, but she pressed his hand and said: 'So that is quite decided, isn't it?'

'Quite decided,' said his lordship.

She withdrew her hand. 'And I will be v-very friendly and set you down at your house, sir, for it is raining much too hard for you to ride your horse. P-please tell my coachman your direction.'

Ten minutes later the coach drew up in Half-Moon Street. Horatia beckoned up her groom and bade him ride his lordship's horse on to its stable. 'And I n-never thanked you, my lord, for rescuing me!' she said. 'I am truly very much obliged.'

Lethbridge replied: 'And so am I, ma'am, for having been granted the opportunity.' He bowed over her hand. 'Till our next meeting,' he said, and stepped down on to the streaming pavement.

The coach moved forward. Lethbridge stood for a moment in the rain, watching it sway up the road towards Curzon Street and then turned with the faintest shrug of his shoulders and walked up the steps of his house.

The door was held for him by the porter. He said respectfully: 'A wet evening, my lord.'

'Very,' said Lethbridge curtly.

'I should tell your lordship that a – a person has called. He arrived but a short time ahead of your lordship, and I have him downstairs, keeping an eye on him.'

'Send him up,' Lethbridge said, and went into the room that overlooked the street.

Here he was joined in a few moments by his visitor, who was ushered into the room by the disapproving porter. He was a burly individual, dressed in a frieze coat, with a slouch hat grasped in one dirty hand. He grinned when he saw Lethbridge and touched his finger to his forelock, 'Hoping all's bowman, your honour, and the leddy none the worse.'

Lethbridge did not reply, but taking a key from his pocket unlocked one of the drawers of his desk and drew out a purse. This he tossed across the room to his guest, saying briefly: 'Take it, and be off with you. And remember, my friend, to keep your mouth shut.'

'God love yer, may I shove the tumbler if ever I was one to squeak!' said the frieze-clad gentleman indignantly. He shook the contents of the purse out on to the table and began to tell over the coins.

Lethbridge's lip curled. 'You can spare yourself the pains. I pay what I promised.'

The man grinned more knowingly than ever. 'Ah, you're a peevy cull, you are. And when I works with a flash, why, I'm careful, see?' He told over the rest of the money, scooped it all up in one capacious paw, and bestowed it in his pocket. 'Right it is,' he observed genially, 'and easy earned. I'll let myself out of the jigger.'

Lethbridge followed him into the narrow hall. 'No doubt,' he said. 'But I will give myself the pleasure of seeing you off the premises.'

'God love yer, do you take me for a mill ken?' demanded the visitor, affronted. 'Lordy, them as is on the rattling lay don't take to slumming kens!' With which lofty but somewhat obscure remark he took himself off down the steps of the house and slouched away towards Piccadilly.

Lord Lethbridge shut the door and stood for a moment in frowning silence. He was aroused from his abstraction by the approach of his valet, who came up the stairs from the basement to attend him and remarked with concern that the rain had wetted his lordship's coat.

The frown cleared. 'So I perceive,' Lethbridge said. 'But it was undoubtedly worth it.'

Eight

*I*t was past five o'clock when Horatia arrived in Grosvenor Square, and upon hearing the time from the porter, she gave a small shriek of dismay, and fled upstairs. In the upper hall she almost collided with Rule, already dressed for the opera. 'Oh, my l-lord, such an adventure!' she said, breathlessly. 'I am horribly l-late, or I would tell you now. Do p-pray forgive me! I w-won't be above a moment!'

Rule watched her vanish into her own room, and proceeded on his way downstairs. Apparently having very little dependence on his wife's notions of time, he sent a message to the kitchens that dinner was to be set back half an hour, and strolled into one of the saloons to await Horatia's reappearance. The fact that the opera began at seven did not seem to worry him in the least, and not even when the hands of the gilt clock on the mantelpiece stood at a quarter to six did he betray any sign of impatience. Below stairs the cook, hovering anxiously between a couple of fat turkey poults on the spits and a dish of buttered crab, called down uncouth curses on the heads of all women.

But by five minutes to six the Countess, a vision of gauze, lace, and plumes, took her seat at the dinner-table opposite her husband, and announced with a winning smile that she was not so very late after all. 'And if it is G-Gluck, I d-don't mind m-missing some of it,' she remarked. 'But I m-must tell you about my adventure. Only fancy, M-Marcus, I have been held up by highwaymen!'

'Held up by highwaymen?' repeated the Earl, somewhat surprised.

Horatia, her mouth full of buttered crab, nodded vigorously.

'My dear child, when and where?'

'Oh, by the Halfway House when I was c-coming home from Laney's. It was f-full daylight too and they t-took my purse. But there wasn't much in it.'

'That was fortunate,' said the Earl. 'But I don't think I entirely understand. Was this daring robbery effected without any opposition being offered by my heroic servants?'

'W-well, Jeffries had not brought his p-pistols, you see. The coachman explained it all to me afterwards.'

'Ah!' said the Earl. 'Then no doubt he will carry his goodness far enough to explain it all to me as well.'

Horatia, who was in the act of serving herself from a dish of artichokes, looked up quickly at that, and said: 'P-please don't be disagreeable about it, Rule. It was m-my fault for staying so long with L-Laney. And I don't think Jeffries could have d-done anything even with a b-blunderbuss because there were a n-number of them, and they all shot pistols!'

'Oh!' said Rule, his eyes narrowing a little. 'How many, in fact?'

'W-well, three.'

His lordship's brows rose. 'You begin to interest me rather profoundly, Horry. You were held up by three men –'

'Yes, and they were all m-masked.'

'I thought perhaps they might be,' said his lordship. 'But do you tell me that the only thing you lost to these – er – desperadoes – was your purse?'

'Yes, but one of them t-tried to pull a ring off my finger. I d-dare say they would have taken everything I had only that in the very n-nick of time I was rescued. W-was not that romantic, sir?'

'It was certainly fortunate,' said the Earl. 'May I ask who they were who performed this gallant deed?'

'It was Lord L-Lethbridge!' replied Horatia, bringing out the name with a slightly defiant ring.

For a moment the Earl did not say anything at all. Then he reached out his hand for the decanter of claret, and refilled his glass. 'I see,' he said. 'So he too was in Knightsbridge? What a singular coincidence!'

'Yes, w-wasn't it?' agreed Horatia, glad to find that her announcement had not provoked any signs of violent disapproval.

'Quite – er – providential,' said his lordship. 'And did he put all these armed men to flight single-handed?'

'Yes, quite. He c-came g-galloping up, and the highwaymen ran away.'

The Earl inclined his head with an expression of courteous interest. 'And then?' he said gently.

'Oh, th-then I asked him if he would d-drive home with me, and I must tell you, Rule, he was not at all inclined to at f-first, but I insisted, so he d-did.' She drew a breath. 'And p-perhaps I ought to tell you, also, that he and I have d-decided to be friends.'

Across the table the Earl's calm eyes met hers. 'I am of course honoured by this confidence, my dear. Am I expected to make any remark?'

Horatia blurted out: 'W-well, Lord Lethbridge t-told me you would not l-like it.'

'Ah, did he indeed?' murmured his lordship. 'And did he give any reason for my supposed dislike?'

'N-no, but he told m-me that he was not a p-proper person for me to know, and that m-made me excessively sorry for him, and I said I did not c-care what the world said, and I would know him.'

The Earl touched his lips with his napkin. 'I see. And if – let us suppose – I were to take exception to this friendship – ?'

Horatia prepared for battle. 'W-why should you, sir?'

'I imagine that his lordship's rare foresight prompted him to tell you my reasons,' replied Rule a little dryly.

'They seem to m-me very stupid and – yes, unkind!' declared Horatia.

'I was afraid they might,' said Rule.

'And,' said Horatia with spirit, 'it is no g-good telling me I m-mustn't know Lord L-Lethbridge, because I shall!'

'Would it be any good, I wonder, if I were to request you – quite mildly, you understand – not to make a friend of Lethbridge?'

'No,' said Horatia. 'I l-like him, and I won't be ruled by odious p-prejudice.'

'Then if you have finished your dinner, my love, let us start for the opera,' said Rule tranquilly.

Horatia got up from the table feeling that the wind had been taken out of her sails.

The work being performed at the Italian Opera House, of which his lordship was one of the patrons, was *Iphigénie en Aulide*, a composition that had enjoyed a considerable success in Paris, where it was first produced. The Earl and Countess of Rule arrived midway through the first act, and took their seats in one of the green boxes. The house was a blaze of light, and crowded with persons of fashion who, while having no particular taste for music, all flocked to the King's Theatre, some with the mere intention of being in the mode, others for the purpose of displaying expensive toilets, and a few, like the Earl of March, who sat with his glass levelled at the stage, in the hope of discovering some new dancer of surpassing attractions. Amongst this frippery throng were also to be seen the *virtuosi*, of whom Mr Walpole, comfortably ensconced in Lady Hervey's box, was of the most notable. In the pit a number of young gentlemen congregated, who spent the greater part of their time in ogling the ladies in the boxes. The Macaronis were represented by Mr Fox, looking heavy-eyed, as well he might, having sat till three in the afternoon playing hazard at Almack's; by my Lord Carlisle, whose round youthful countenance was astonishingly embellished by a patch cut in the form of a cabriolet; and of course by Mr Crosby Drelincourt, with a huge nosegay stuck in his coat, and a spy-glass set in the head of his long cane. The Macaronis, mincing, simpering, sniffing at crystal scent-bottles, formed a startling contrast to the Bucks, the young sparks who, in defiance of their affected contemporaries, had flown to another extreme of fashion. No extravagance of costume distinguished these gentlemen, unless a studied slovenliness could be called such, and their amusements were of a violent nature, quite at variance with your true Macaroni's notions of entertainment. These Bloods were to be found at any prize-fight, or cockfight, and when these diversions palled could always while away an evening in masquerading abroad in the guise of footpads, to the terror of all honest townsfolk. Lord Winwood, who was engrossed throughout the first act of the opera in a heated argument respecting the chances of his pet bruiser, the Fairy, against Mr Farnaby's protégé, the Bloomsbury Tiger, at Broughton's Amphitheatre next evening, was himself something of a Blood, and had spent the previous night in the Roundhouse, having been moved to join a party of light-hearted gentlemen at the sport of Boxing the Watch. As a result of this strenuous pastime his lordship had an interesting bruise over one eye, a circumstance that induced Mr Drelincourt to utter a squeak of horror on sight of him.

When the curtain presently fell on the first act the real business of the evening might be said to begin. Ladies beckoned from boxes, gentlemen in the pit went to pay their court to them, and a positive buzz of conversation arose.

Rule's box was very soon full of Horatia's friends, and his lordship, ousted from his wife's side by the ardent Mr Dashwood, suppressed a yawn and strolled away in search of more congenial company. He was presently to be seen in the parterre, chuckling at something Mr Selwyn seemed to have sighed wearily into his ear, and just as he was about to move towards a group of men who had hailed him, he chanced to look up at the boxes, and saw something that apparently made him change his mind. Three minutes later he entered Lady Massey's box.

Since his marriage he had not singled Lady Massey out in public, so that it was with triumph mixed with surprise that she held out her hand to him. 'My lord! – You know Sir Willoughby, I believe? And Miss Cloke, of course,' she said, indicating two of

94

her companions. 'How do you like the *Iphigénie*, sir? Lord Lethbridge and I are agreed that Marinozza is sadly out of voice. What do you say?'

'To tell you the truth,' he replied, 'I only arrived in time to see her exit.' He turned. 'Ah, Lethbridge!' he said in his soft, sleepy way. 'What a fortunate *rencontre*! I apprehend that I stand in your debt, do I not?'

Lady Massey looked sharply round, but the Earl had moved to where Lethbridge stood at the back of the box, and Sir Willoughby Monk's stout form obscured her view of him.

Lethbridge bowed deeply. 'I should be happy indeed to think so, my lord,' he said with exquisite politeness.

'Oh, but surely!' insisted Rule, gently twirling his eyeglass. 'I have been held quite spell-bound by the recountal of your – what shall I call it? – your knight-errantry this very afternoon.'

Lethbridge's teeth gleamed in a smile. 'That, my lord? A mere nothing, believe me.'

'But I am quite lost in admiration, I assure you,' said Rule. 'To tackle three – it was three, was it not? Ah yes! – to tackle three desperate villains single-handed argues an intrepidity – or should I say a daring? – you were always daring, were you not, my dear Lethbridge? – a daring, then, that positively takes one's breath away.'

'To have succeeded,' said Lethbridge, still smiling, 'in depriving your lordship of breath is a triumph in itself.'

'Ah!' sighed the Earl. 'But you will make me emulative, my dear Lethbridge. More of these deeds of daring and I shall really have to see if I cannot – er – deprive you of breath.'

Lethbridge moved his hand as though to lay it on his sword-hilt. No sword hung at his side, but the Earl, watching this movement through his glass, said in the most friendly way imaginable: 'Precisely, Lethbridge! How well we understand each other!'

'Nevertheless, my lord,' Lethbridge replied, 'you must permit me to say that you might find that task a difficult one.'

'But somehow I feel – not entirely beyond my power,' said his lordship, and turned back to pay his respects to Lady Massey.

In the box opposite the crowd had begun to grow thinner, only Lady Amelia Pridham, Mr Dashwood, and Viscount Winwood remaining. Mr Dashwood having borne the Viscount company on his adventures of the previous night, Lady Amelia was scolding them both for their folly when Mr Drelincourt entered the box.

Mr Drelincourt wanted to speak with his cousin Rule, and was quite put out to find him absent. Nor was his annoyance assuaged by the naughty behaviour of my Lady Rule, who, feeling that she had a score to pay off, chanted softly:

> *'The Muse in prancing up and down*
> *Has found out something pretty,*
> *With little hat, and hair dressed high —'*

Mr Drelincourt, reddening under his paint, interrupted this popular ditty. 'I came to see my cousin, ma'am!'

'He isn't here,' said Horatia. 'C-Crosby, your wig is l-like the last verse of the song. You know, it runs like this: *Five pounds of hair they wear behind, the ladies to delight, O!* – only it doesn't delight us at all.'

'Vastly diverting, ma'am,' said Mr Drelincourt, a little shrilly. 'I quite thought I had seen Rule beside you in this box.'

'Yes, b-but he has walked out for a while,' replied Horatia. 'Oh, and you c-carry a fan! Lady Amelia, only see! Mr Drelincourt has a fan m-much prettier than mine!'

Mr Drelincourt shut the fan with a snap. 'Walked out, has he? Upon my word, you are monstrously used, cousin, and you a bride!' He peered through the glass in the head of his cane at the boxes opposite, and uttered a titter. 'What fair charmer can have lured him – Good God, the Massey! Oh, I beg pardon, cousin – I should not have spoken! A jest – the merest jest, I assure you! I had not the least intention – la, do but observe the creature in the puce satin over there!'

Viscount Winwood, who had caught something of this interchange, started up out of his chair with a black scowl on his face, but was restrained by Lady Amelia, who grasped the skirts of his coat without ceremony and gave them an admonitory tug. She got up ponderously, and surged forward. 'So it's you, is it, Crosby? You may give me your arm back to my box, if it's strong enough to support me.'

'With the greatest pleasure on earth, ma'am!' Mr Drelincourt bowed, and tittupped out with her.

Mr Dashwood, observing the bride's expression of puzzled inquiry, coughed, exchanged a rueful glance with the Viscount, and took his leave.

Horatia, her brows knit, turned to her brother. 'What did he m-mean, P-Pel?' she asked.

'Mean? Who?' said the Viscount.

'Why, C-Crosby! Didn't you hear him?'

'That little worm! Lord, nothing! What should he mean?'

Horatia looked across at the box opposite. 'He said he should not have spoken. And *you* said – only the other d-day – about Lady M-Massey –'

'I didn't!' said the Viscount hastily. 'Now don't for God's sake ask a lot of silly questions, Horry!'

Horatia said, with a flash of her eyes: 'Tell me P-Pelham!'

'Ain't nothing to tell,' replied the Viscount, wriggling nobly. 'Except that the Massey's reputation don't bear probing into; but what of that?'

'V-very well,' said Horatia, a singularly dogged look about her mouth. 'I shall ask Rule.'

The Viscount was seriously alarmed by this threat, and said rashly: 'No, don't do that! Damme, there's nothing to ask, I tell you!'

'P-perhaps Crosby will explain it then,' said Horatia. 'I will ask him.'

'Don't you ask that viper anything!' ordered the Viscount. 'You'll get nothing but a pack of scandal-mongering lies from him. Leave well alone, that's my advice.'

The candid grey eyes lifted to his face. 'Is R-Rule in love with Lady M-Massey?' Horatia asked bluntly.

'Oh, nothing like that!' the Viscount assured her. 'These little affairs don't mean being in love, y'know. Burn it, Horry, Rule's a man of the world! There's nothing in it, my dear gal – everyone has 'em!'

Horatia glanced across at Lady Massey's box again, but the Earl had disappeared. She swallowed before replying: 'I kn-know. P-please don't think that I m-mind, because I d-don't. Only I think I m-might have been told.'

'Well, to tell you the truth, I thought you must know,' said Pelham. 'It's common knowledge, and it ain't as though you married Rule for love, after all.'

'N-no,' agreed Horatia, rather forlornly.

Nine

*I*t was not a difficult matter for Lord Lethbridge and Lady Rule to pursue their newly declared friendship. Both being of the *haut ton* they visited the same houses, met, quite by chance, at Vauxhall, at Marylebone, even at Astley's Amphitheatre, whither Horatia dragged the unwilling Miss Charlotte Winwood to see the still new wonder of the circus.

'But,' said Charlotte, 'I must confess that I can discover nothing to entertain or elevate the mind in the spectacle of noble horses performing the steps of a minuet, and I cannot conceal from you, Horatia, that I find something singularly repugnant in the notion that the Brute Creation should be obliged to imitate the actions of Humanity.'

Mr Arnold Gisborne, their chosen escort, appeared to be much struck by this exposition, and warmly felicitated Miss Winwood on her good sense.

At which moment Lord Lethbridge, who had quite by accident taken it into his head to visit the Amphitheatre on this particular evening, entered the box, and after a brief interchange of civilities with Miss Winwood and Mr Gisborne, took the vacant chair beside Horatia and proceeded to engage her in conversation.

Under cover of the trumpets which heralded the entrance into the ring of a performer who was advertised on the bill to jump over a garter fifteen feet from the ground at the same time firing off two pistols, Horatia said reproachfully: 'I sent you a c-card for it, but you did not come to my hurricane-party, sir. That was not very friendly of you, now w-was it?'

He smiled. 'I do not think my Lord Rule would exactly welcome my presence in his house, ma'am.'

Her face hardened at that, but she replied lightly enough: 'Oh, you n-need not put yourself about for that, sir. My lord does not interfere with m-me, or – or I with him. Shall you be at the ball at Almack's Rooms on Friday? I have promised M-Mama I will take Charlotte.'

'Happy Charlotte!' said his lordship.

Almost any right-minded young female would have echoed his words, but Miss Winwood was at that very moment confiding to Mr Gisborne her dislike of such frivolous amusements.

'I own,' agreed Mr Gisborne, 'that this present rage for dancing is excessive, yet I believe Almack's to be a very genteel club, the balls not in the least exceptionable, such as those held at Ranelagh and Vauxhall Gardens. Indeed, I believe that since Carlisle House was given up the general *ton* of these entertainments is much raised above what it was.'

'I have heard,' said Charlotte with a blush, 'of masquerades and ridottos from which all Refinement and Decorum – but I will not say more.'

Happily for Miss Winwood no ball at Almack's Rooms was ever sullied by any absence of propriety. The club, which was situated in King Street, was in some sort an off-shoot of Almack's in Pall Mall. It was so exclusive that no one hovering hopefully on the fringe of Society could ever hope for admittance. It had been founded by a *coterie* of ladies headed by Mrs Fitzroy and Lady Pembroke, and for the sum of ten guineas, a very modest subscription, a ball and a supper were given once a week there for three months of the year. Almack himself, with his Scotch accent and his bag-wig, waited at supper, while Mrs Almack, dressed in her best saque, made tea for the noble company. The club had come to be known as the Marriage Mart, a circumstance which induced Lady Winwood to persuade Charlotte into accepting her sister's invitation. Her own indifferent health made it impossible for her to chaperone Charlotte herself at all the places of entertainment where a young lady making her début ought to be seen, so she was once more extremely thankful that Horatia was suitably married.

Lord Winwood and his friend Sir Roland Pommeroy, a very fine young buck, were chosen by Horatia as escorts to the ball. Sir Roland expressed himself to be all happiness, but the Viscount was less polite. 'Hang you, Horry, I hate dancing!' he objected. 'You've a score of beaux, all of 'em falling over themselves for chance of leading you out. Why the plague d'you want me?'

But it seemed that Horatia for some reason best known to herself did want him. Warning her that he had no notion of dancing through the night and would probably end in the card-room, the Viscount gave way. Horatia said, with truth, that she had not the least objection to him playing cards, since no doubt she would find partners enough without him. Had the Viscount realized what particular partner she had in mind he might not have yielded so easily.

As it was, he escorted both his sisters to King Street and performed his duties to his own satisfaction by leading Horatia out for the opening minuet, and going down one of the country dances with Charlotte. After that, seeing his sisters comfortably bestowed in the middle of Horatia's usual court, he departed in search of liquid refreshment and more congenial entertainment. Not that he expected to derive much enjoyment even in the card-room, for dancing and not gaming being the object of the club stakes would be low, and the company probably unskilled. However, he had caught sight of his friend Geoffrey Kingston when he first arrived, and had no doubt that Mr Kingston would be happy to sit down to a quiet game of piquet.

It was some time before Lord Lethbridge appeared in the ballroom, but he came at last, very handsome in blue satin, and Miss Winwood, who happened to catch sight of him first, instantly recognized the saturnine gentleman who had joined them at Astley's. When he presently approached Horatia, and

Miss Winwood observed the friendly, not to say intimate, terms they seemed to be on, misgiving seized her, and she began to fear that Horatia's frivolity was not confined to the extravagance of her dress, whose great hoop and multitude of ribbons and laces she had already deplored. She contrived to catch Horatia's eye in a reproving fashion, just as her sister was going off for the second time on Lord Lethbridge's arm to join the dance.

Horatia chose to ignore this look, but it had not escaped Lethbridge, who said, raising his brows: 'Have I offended your sister? I surprised a most unloving light in her eye.'

'W-well,' said Horatia seriously, 'it was not very polite in you not to ask her to d-dance this time.'

'But I never dance,' said Lethbridge, leading her into the set.

'S-silly! you are dancing,' Horatia pointed out.

'Ah, with you,' he replied. 'That is different.'

They became separated by the movement of the dance, but not before Lethbridge had marked with satisfaction the blush that mounted to Horatia's cheeks.

She was certainly not displeased. It was quite true that Lethbridge hardly ever danced, and she knew it. She had seen one or two envious glances follow her progress on the floor and she was far too young not to feel conscious of triumph. Rule might prefer the riper attractions of Caroline Massey, but my Lady Rule would show him and the rest of the Polite World that she could capture a very rare prize on her own account. Quite apart from mere liking, which she undoubtedly felt towards Lethbridge, he was the very man for her present purpose. Such easy conquests as Mr Dashwood, or young Pommeroy, would not answer at all. Lethbridge, with his singed reputation, his faint air of haughtiness, and his supposed heart of marble, was a captive well worth displaying. And if Rule disliked it – why, so much the better!

Lethbridge, perfectly aware of these dark schemes, was playing his cards very skilfully. Far too clever to show an ardency which he guessed would frighten Horatia, he treated her with admiration savoured with the mockery he knew she found tantalizing. His manner was always that of a man many years her senior; he teased her, as in his continued refusal to play cards with her; he would pique her being unaware of her presence for half an evening, and devoting himself to some other gratified lady.

As they came together again, he said with his bewildering abruptness: 'My lady, that patch!'

Her finger stole to the tiny square of black silk at the corner of her eye. 'W-why, what, sir?'

'No,' he said, shaking his head. 'Not the Murderous, I beg of you! It won't do.'

Her eyes twinkled merrily. As she prepared to go down the dance again, she said over her shoulder: 'Which then, p-please?'

'The Roguish!' Lethbridge answered.

When the dance ended, and she would have rejoined Charlotte and Sir Roland, he drew her hand through his arm and led her towards the room where the refreshments were laid.

'Does Pommeroy amuse you? He does not me.'

'N-no, but there is Charlotte, and perhaps –'

'Forgive me,' said Lethbridge crisply, 'but neither does Charlotte amuse me – Let me fetch you a glass of ratafia.'

He was back in a moment, and handed her a small glass. He stood beside her chair sipping his own claret and looking straight ahead of him in one of his abstracted fits.

Horatia looked up at him, wondering, as she so often did, why he should all at once have lost interest in her.

'Why the Roguish, my lord?'

He glanced down. 'The Roguish?'

'You said I must wear the Roguish p-patch.'

'So I did. I was thinking of something else.'

'Oh!' said Horatia, snubbed.

His sudden smile lit his eyes. 'I was wondering when you would cease to call me so primly "my lord",' he said.

'Oh!' said Horatia, reviving. 'B-but indeed, sir –'

'But indeed, ma'am!'

'W-well, but what should I c-call you?' she asked doubtfully.

'I have a name, my dear. So too have you – a little name that I am going to use, with your leave.'

'I d-don't believe you c-care whether you have my l-leave or not!' said Horatia.

'Not very much,' admitted his lordship. 'Come, shake hands on the bargain, Horry.'

She hesitated, saw him laughing and dimpled responsively. 'Oh, very well, R-Robert!'

Lethbridge bent and kissed the hand she had put into his. 'I protest I never knew how charming my poor name could sound until this moment,' he said.

'Pho!' said Horatia. 'I am very sure any number of ladies have b-been before me with it.'

'But they none of them called me R-Robert,' explained his lordship.

Meanwhile, the Viscount, emerging briefly from the card-room, was obliged to answer a beckoning signal from Miss Winwood. He strolled across the room to her, and asked casually: 'Well, Charlotte, what's to do?'

Charlotte took his arm and made him walk with her towards one of the window embrasures. 'Pelham, I wish you won't go back to the card-room. I am uneasy on Horry's account.'

'Why, what's the little hussy about now?' inquired the Viscount, unimpressed.

'I do not say that it is anything but the thoughtlessness that we, alas, know so well,' said Charlotte earnestly, 'but to dance twice in succession with one gentleman and to go out on his arm gives her an air of singularity which I know dear Mama, or indeed Lord Rule, would deprecate.'

'Rule ain't so strait-laced. Whom has Horry gone off with?'

'With the gentleman whom we met at Astley's the other evening, I think,' said Charlotte. 'His name is Lord Lethbridge.'

'What?' exclaimed the Viscount. 'That fellow here? Odd rot him!'

Miss Winwood clasped both hands on his arm. 'Then my fears are not groundless? I should not wish to speak ill of one who is indeed scarcely known to me, yet from the moment I set eyes on his lordship I conceived a mistrust of him which his conduct to-night has done nothing to diminish.'

The Viscount scowled darkly. 'You did, eh? Well, it ain't my business, and I've warned Horry, but if Rule don't put his foot down mighty soon he's not the man I think him, and so you may tell Horry.'

Miss Winwood blinked. 'But is that all you mean to do, Pelham?'

'Well, what can I do?' demanded the Viscount. 'Do you suppose I'm going to go and snatch Horry from Lethbridge at the sword's point?'

'But –'

'I'm not,' said the Viscount definitely. 'He's too good a swordsman.' With which unsatisfactory speech he walked off, leaving Miss Winwood greatly disturbed, and not a little indignant.

The Viscount might seem to his sister to treat the matter with callousness, but he was moved to broach the subject to his brother-in-law in what he considered to be a very delicate manner.

Coming out of the card-room at White's he nearly walked into Rule, and said with great cheerfulness: 'Burn it, that's fortunate. The very man I want!'

'How much, Pelham?' inquired his lordship wearily.

'As a matter of fact I was looking for someone who might lend me some money,' said the Viscount. 'But how you rumbled it beats me!'

'Intuition, Pelham, just intuition.'

'Well, lend me fifty pounds and you shall have it back tomorrow. My luck's going to turn.'

'What makes you think so?' Rule asked, handing over a bill.

The Viscount pocketed it. 'Much obliged to you. I'll swear you're a good fellow. Why, I've been throwing out for the last hour, and a man can't go on throwing out for ever. Which reminds me, Rule, I've something to say to you. Nothing of moment, you understand, but you know what women are, rabbit 'em!'

'None better,' said his lordship 'So you may safely leave the matter in my hands, my dear Pelham.'

'Blister it, you seem to know what I'm going to say before I've said it!' complained the Viscount. 'Mind you, I warned Horry he was dangerous at the outset. But then, women are such fools!'

'Not only women,' murmured Rule. 'Will you do me a favour, Pelham?'

'Anything in the world!' replied the Viscount promptly. 'Pleasure!'

'It is quite a small thing,' Rule said. 'But I shall stand greatly in your debt if you would refrain in future from – er – warning Horry.'

The Viscount stared. 'Just as you say, of course, but I don't care to see that fellow Lethbridge dancing attendance on my sister, and so I tell you!'

'Ah, Pelham!' The Viscount, who had turned to go back into the card-room, checked, and looked over his shoulder. 'Nor do I,' said Rule pensively.

'Oh!' said the Viscount. He had flash of insight. 'Don't want me to meddle, eh?'

'You see, my dear boy,' said his lordship apologetically, 'I am not really such a fool as you think me.'

The Viscount grinned, promised that there should be no meddling and went back to make up for lost time in the card-room. True to his word, he arrived in Grosvenor Square next morning and impressively planked fifty pounds in bills down on the table before Rule. His luck, it seemed, had turned.

Never one to neglect opportunity, he spent a week riotously following his rare good fortune. No less than five bets of his making were entered in the book at White's; he won four thousand in a night at pharaoh, lost six at quinze on Wednesday, recovered and arose a winner on Thursday, on Friday walked into the hazard-room at Almack's and took his seat at the fifty-guinea table.

'What, Pel, I thought you was done up!' exclaimed Sir Roland Pommeroy, who had been present on the disastrous Wednesday.

'Done up? Devil a bit!' replied the Viscount. 'My luck's in.' He proceeded to fix two pieces of leather round his wrist to protect his ruffles. 'Laid Finch a pony on Tuesday Sally Danvers would be the lighter of a boy by Monday.'

'Ecod, you're mad, Pel!' said Mr Fox. 'She's had four girls already!'

'Mad be damned!' quoth the Viscount. 'I had the news on the way here. I've won.'

'What, she's never given Danvers an heir at last?' cried Mr Boulby.

'An heir?' said the Viscount scornfully. 'Two of 'em! She's had twins!'

After this amazing intelligence no one could doubt that the signs were extremely propitious for the Viscount. In fact, one cautious gentleman removed himself to the quinze room, where a number of gamesters sat round tables in silence, with masks on their faces to conceal any betraying emotion, and rouleaus of guineas in front of them.

As the night wore on the Viscount's luck, which had begun by fluctuating in an uncertain fashion, steadied down. He started the evening by twice throwing out three times in succession, a circumstance which induced Mr Fox to remark that the gull-gropers, or money-lenders, who waited in what he called the Jerusalem chamber for him to rise, would find instead a client in his lordship. However, the Viscount soon remedied this set-back by stripping off his coat and putting it on again inside out, a change that answered splendidly, for no sooner was it made than he recklessly pushed three rouleaus into the centre of the table, called a main of five, and nicked it. By midnight his winnings, in the form of rouleaus, bills and several vowels, or notes of hand, fairly littered the stand at his elbow, and Mr Fox, a heavy loser, called for his third bottle.

There were two tables in the hazard-room, both round, and large enough to accommodate upwards of twenty persons. At the one every player was bound by rule to keep not less than fifty guineas before him, at the other the amount was fixed more moderately at twenty guineas. A small stand stood beside each player with a large rim to hold his glass or his teacup and a wooden bowl for the rouleaus. The room was lit by candles in pendent chandeliers, and so bright was the glare that quite a number of gamesters, the Viscount amongst them, wore leather guards bound round their foreheads to protect their eyes. Others, notably Mr Drelincourt, who was feverishly laying and staking odds at the twenty-guinea table, affected straw hats with very broad brims, which served the double purpose of shading their eyes and preventing their wigs from becoming tumbled. Mr Drelincourt's hat was adorned with flowers and ribands and was held by several other Macaronis to be a vastly pretty affair. He had put on a frieze greatcoat in place of his own blue creation, and presented an astonishing picture as he sat alternately sipping his tea and casting the dice. However, as it was quite the thing to wear frieze coats and straw hats at the gaming table, not even his severest critics found anything in his appearance worthy of remark.

For the most part silence broken only by the rattle of the dice and the monotonous drone of the groom-porters' voices calling the odds brooded over the room, but from time to time snatches of desultory talk broke out. Shortly after one o'clock quite a burst of conversation proceeded from the twenty-guinea table, one of the gamesters having taken it into his head to call the dice in the hope of changing his luck. Someone, while they waited for a fresh bale, had started an interesting topic of scandal and a shout of laughter most unpleasantly assailing the ears of Lord Cheston, a rather nervous gambler, caused him to deliver the dice at the other table with a jerk that upset his luck.

'Five-to-seven, and three-to-two against!' intoned the groom-porter dispassionately.

The laying and staking of bets shut out the noise of the other table, but as silence fell again and Lord Cheston picked up the box, Mr Drelincourt's voice floated over to the fifty-guinea table with disastrous clarity.

'Oh, my lord, I protest; for my part I would lay you odds rather on my Lord Lethbridge's success with my cousin's stammering bride!' said Mr Drelincourt with a giggle.

The Viscount, already somewhat flushed with wine, was in the act of raising his glass to his lips when this unfortunate remark was wafted to his ears. His cerulean blue eyes, slightly clouded but remarkably intelligent still, flamed with the light of murder, and with a spluttered growl of 'Hell and damnation!' he lunged up out of his chair before anyone could stop him.

Sir Roland Pommeroy made a grab at his arm. 'Pel, I say, Pel! Steady!'

'Lord, he's three parts drunk!' said Mr Boulby. 'Here's a pretty scandal! Pelham, for God's sake think what you're doing!'

But the Viscount, having shaken Pommeroy off, was already striding purposefully over to the other table, and seemed to have not the least doubt of what he was doing. Mr Drelincourt, looking round, startled to see who was bearing down upon him, let his jaw drop in ludicrous dismay, and received the contents of his lordship's glass full in his face. 'You damned little rat, take that!' roared the Viscount.

There was a moment's shocked silence, while Mr Drelincourt sat with the wine dripping off the end of his nose, and staring at the incensed Viscount as one bemused.

Mr Fox, coming over from the other table, grasped Lord Winwood by the elbow, and addressed Mr Drelincourt with severity. 'You'd best apologize, Crosby,' he said. 'Pelham, do recollect! This won't do, really it won't!'

'Recollect?' said the Viscount fiercely. 'You heard what he said, Charles! D'you think I'll sit by and let a foul-mouthed –'

'My lord!' interrupted Mr Drelincourt, rising and dabbing at his face with a rather unsteady hand. 'I – I apprehend the cause of your annoyance. I assure your lordship you have me wrong! If I said anything that – that seemed –'

Mr Fox whispered urgently: 'Let it alone now, Pel! You can't fight over your sister's name without starting a scandal.'

'Be damned to you, Charles!' said the Viscount. 'I'll manage it my way. I don't like the fellow's hat!'

Mr Drelincourt fell back a pace; someone gave a snort of laughter, and Sir Roland said wisely: 'That's reasonable enough. You don't like his hat. That's devilish neat, 'pon my soul it is! Now you come to mention it, ecod, I don't like it either!'

'No, I don't like it!' declared the Viscount, rolling a fiery eye at the offending structure. 'Pink roses, egad, above that complexion! Damme, it offends me, so it does!'

Mr Drelincourt's bosom swelled. 'Sirs, I take you all to witness that his lordship is in his cups!'

'Hanging back, are you?' said the Viscount, thrusting Mr Fox aside. 'Well, you won't wear that hat again!' With which he plucked the straw confection from Mr Drelincourt's head and casting it on the floor ground his heel in it.

Mr Drelincourt, who had borne with tolerable composure the insult of a glass of wine thrown in his face, gave a shriek of rage, and clapped his hands to his head. 'My wig! My hat! My God, it passes all bounds! You'll meet me for this, my lord! I say you shall meet me for this!'

'Be sure I will!' promised the Viscount, rocking on the balls of his feet, his hands in his pockets. 'When you like, where you like, swords or pistols!'

Mr Drelincourt, pale and shaking with fury, besought his lordship to name his friends. The Viscount cocked an eyebrow at Sir Roland Pommeroy. 'Pom? Cheston?'

The two gentlemen indicated expressed their willingness to serve him.

Mr Drelincourt informed them that his seconds would wait upon them in the morning, and with a somewhat jerky bow withdrew from the room. The Viscount, his rage at the insult to Horatia slightly assuaged by the satisfactory outcome of the disturbance, returned to his table and continued there in the highest fettle until eight in the morning.

Somewhere about noon, when he was still in bed and asleep, Sir Roland Pommeroy visited his lodging in Pall Mall and, disregarding the valet's expostulations, pushed his way into my lord's room and rudely awakened him. The Viscount sat up, yawning, rolled a blear-eye upon his friend, and demanded to know what the devil was amiss.

'Nothing's amiss,' replied Sir Roland, seating himself on the edge of the bed. 'We have it all fixed, snug as you please.'

The Viscount pushed his nightcap to the back of his head and strove to collect his scattered wits. 'What's fixed?' he said thickly.

'Lord, man, your meeting!' said Sir Roland, shocked.

'Meeting?' The Viscount brightened. 'Have I called someone out? Well, by all that's famous!'

Sir Roland, casting a dispassionate and expert eye over his principal, got up and went over to the wash-basin and dipped one of his lordship's towels in cold water. This he wrung out and silently handed to the Viscount, who took it gratefully and bound it round his aching brow. It seemed to assist him to clear his brain, for presently he said: 'Quarrelled with someone, did I? Damme, my head's like to split! Devilish stuff, that burgundy.'

'More likely the brandy,' said Sir Roland gloomily. 'You drank a deal of it.'

'Did I so? You know, there was something about a hat – a damned thing with pink roses. It's coming back to me.' He clasped his head in his hands, while Sir Roland sat and picked his teeth in meditative patience. 'By God, I have it! I've called Crosby out!' suddenly exclaimed the Viscount.

'No, you haven't,' corrected Sir Roland. 'He called you. You wiped your feet on his hat, Pel.'

'Ay, so I did, but that wasn't it,' said the Viscount, his brow darkening.

Sir Roland removed the gold toothpick from his mouth, and said succinctly: 'Tell you what, Pel, it had best be the hat.'

The Viscount nodded. 'It's the devil's own business,' he said ruefully. 'Ought to have stopped me.'

'Stop you!' echoed Sir Roland. 'You flung a glass of wine in the fellow's face before anyone knew what you was about.'

The Viscount brooded, and presently sat up again with a jerk. 'By God, I'm glad I did it! You heard what he said, Pom?'

'Drunk, belike,' offered Sir Roland.

'There's not a word of truth in it,' said the Viscount with grim meaning. 'Not a word, Pom, d'you take me?'

'Lord, Pel, no one ever thought there was! Ain't one fight enough for you?'

The Viscount grinned rather sheepishly and leaned back against the bed-head. 'What's it to be? Swords or pistols?'

'Swords,' replied Sir Roland. 'We don't want to make it a killing matter. Fixed it all up for you out at Barn Elms, Monday at six.'

The Viscount nodded, but seemed a trifle abstracted. He discarded the wet towel and looked wisely across at his friend. 'I was drunk, Pom, that's the tale.'

Sir Roland, who had resumed the use of his toothpick, let it fall in his surprise, and gasped: 'You're never going to back out of it, Pel?'

'Back out of it?' said the Viscount. 'Back out of a fight? Burn it, if I don't know you for a fool, Pom, I'd thrust that down your gullet, so I would!'

Sir Roland accepted this shamefacedly, and begged pardon.

'I was drunk,' said the Viscount, 'and I took a dislike to Crosby's hat – Damn it, what's he want with pink roses in his hat? Answer me that!'

'Just what I said myself,' agreed Sir Roland. 'Fellow can wear a hat at Almack's if he likes. Do it myself sometimes. But pink roses – no.'

'Well, that's all there is to it,' said the Viscount with finality. 'You put it about I was in my cups. That's the tale.'

Sir Roland agreed that ought certainly to be the tale and picked up his hat and cane. The Viscount prepared to resume his interrupted slumber, but upon Sir Roland's opening the door, opened one eye and adjured him on no account to forget to order breakfast at Barn Elms.

Monday dawned very fair, a cool lifting mist giving promise of a fine day to come. Mr Drelincourt, accompanied in a coach by his seconds, Mr Francis Puckleton and Captain Forde, arrived at Barn Elms some time before six, this excessive punctuality being accounted for by the irregularity of the Captain's watch. 'But it's no matter,' said the Captain. 'Drink a bumper of cognac and take a look at the ground, hey, Crosby?'

Mr Drelincourt assented with rather a wan smile.

It was his first fight, for though he delighted in the delivery of waspish speeches he had never until that fatal Friday felt the least desire to cross swords with anyone. When he had seen the Viscount stalking towards him at Almack's he had been quite aghast, and would have been perfectly willing to eat the rash words that had caused all the bother had not the Viscount committed that shocking rape upon his hat and wig. Mr Drelincourt was so much in the habit of considering his appearance above anything else that this brutal action had roused him to a really heroic rage. At that moment he had quite genuinely wanted to spit the Viscount on the end of a small-sword, and if only they could have engaged there and then he had no doubt that he would have acquitted himself very well. Unfortunately etiquette did not permit of so irregular a proceeding, and he had been forced to kick his heels for two interminable days. When his rage had died down it must be confessed that he began to look forward with apprehension to Monday's meeting. He spent a great deal of the weekend perusing Angelo's *Ecole d'Armes*, a work that made his blood run quite cold. He had, of course, learned the art of fencing, but he had a shrewd notion that a buttoned foil presented a very different appearance from a naked duelling sword. Captain Forde congratulated him on having hit upon a worthy opponent in the Viscount, who, he said, though he was perhaps a trifle reckless, was no mean swordsman. He had already fought two duels, but one had been with pistols, with which weapon he was considered to be very dangerous. Mr Drelincourt could only be thankful that Sir Roland had chosen swords.

Captain Forde, who seemed to take a gruesome delight in the

affair, recommended his principal to go early to bed on Sunday night and on no account to drink deep. Mr Drelincourt obeyed him implicitly, but passed an indifferent night. As he tossed and turned, wild ideas of inducing his seconds to settle for him crossed his brain. He wondered how the Viscount was spending the night and entertained a desperate hope that he might be drinking himself under the table. If only some accident or illness would befall him! Or perhaps he himself could be smitten by a sudden indisposition? But in the cold light of dawn he was forced to abandon this scheme. He was not a very brave man, but he had his pride: one could not draw back from an engagement.

Mr Puckleton was the first of his seconds to arrive in the morning, and while Crosby dressed he sat astride a chair sucking the knob of his tall cane and regarding his friend with a melancholy and not unadmiring eye.

'Forde's bringing the weapons,' he said. 'How do you feel, Crosby?'

There was an odd sensation in the pit of Mr Drelincourt's stomach, but he replied: 'Oh, never better! Never better, I assure you.'

'For myself,' said Mr Puckleton, 'I shall leave it all to Forde. To tell you the truth, Crosby, I've never acted for a man before. Wouldn't do it for anyone but you. I can't stand the sight of blood, you know. But I have my vinaigrette with me.'

Then Captain Forde arrived with a long flat case under his arm. Lord Cheston, he said, had engaged to bring a doctor with him, and Crosby had better make haste, for it was time they were starting.

The morning air struck a chill into Mr Drelincourt's bones; he huddled himself into his greatcoat and sat in a corner of the coach listening to the macabre conversation of his two companions. Not that either the Captain or Mr Puckleton talked about the duel; in fact, they chatted on the most mild subjects such as the beauty of the day, the quietness of the streets, and the Duchess of Devonshire's *al fresco* party. Mr Drelincourt found himself hating them for their apparent callousness, yet when the

Captain did mention the duel, reminding him to meet so dashing a fighter as the Viscount with steadiness and caution, he turned a sickly hue and did not answer.

Arrived at Barn Elms they drew up at an inn adjacent to the meeting place, and there the Captain discovered that his watch was considerably in advance of the correct time. Casting a knowing glance at his pallid principal, he then made his suggestion they should drink a glass of cognac, for, said he in Mr Puckleton's ear: 'We'll never get our man on the ground by the looks of it.'

The brandy did little to restore Mr Drelincourt's failing spirits, but he drank it, and with an assumption of nonchalance accompanied his seconds out of the back of the inn and across a field to the ground, which was pleasantly situated in a sort of spinney. Captain Forde said that he could not have a better place for fighting. 'Upon my word, I envy you, Crosby!' he said heartily.

After that they walked back to the inn, to find that a second coach had driven up, containing Lord Cheston and a neat little man in black who clasped a case of instruments, and bowed very deeply to everybody. At first he mistook Captain Forde for Mr Drelincourt, but this was soon put right, and he bowed again to Crosby and begged pardon.

'Let me assure you, sir, that if it should chance that you are to be my patient you need have no alarms, none at all. A clean sword wound is a very different affair from a bullet wound, oh, very different!'

Lord Cheston offered his snuff-box to Mr Puckleton. 'Attended a score of these affairs, haven't you, Parvey?'

'Dear me, yes, my lord!' replied the surgeon, rubbing his hands together. 'Why, I was present when young Mr Ffolliot was fatally wounded in Hyde Park. Ah, before your time, that would be, my lord. A sad business – nothing to be done. Dead on the instant. Dreadful!'

'Dead on the instant?' echoed Mr Puckleton, turning pale. 'Oh, I trust nothing of that sort – really I wish I had not consented to act!'

The Captain gave a scornful snort and turned his shoulder, addressing Cheston. 'Where's Sir Roland, my lord?' he asked.

'Oh, he's coming with Winwood,' replied Cheston, shaking some specks of snuff out of his lace ruffle. 'Daresay they'll drive straight to the ground. Thought Pom had best go and make sure Winwood don't over-sleep. The very devil to wake up is Pel, you know.'

A faint, last hope flashed into Mr Drelincourt's soul that perhaps Sir Roland would fail to bring his principal to the meeting place in time.

'Well,' said the Captain, glancing at his watch, 'may as well go on to the ground, eh, gentlemen?'

The little procession started out once more, the Captain striding ahead with Lord Cheston, Mr Drelincourt following with his friend Puckleton and the doctor bringing up the rear.

Dr Parvey hummed a little tune to himself as he trod over the grass; Cheston and the Captain were talking casually of the improvements at Ranelagh. Mr Drelincourt cleared his throat once or twice and at last said: 'If – if the fellow offers me an apology I think I should let it rest at that, d-don't you, Francis?'

'Oh, yes, pray do!' agreed Mr Puckleton with a shudder. 'I know I shall feel devilish queasy if there is much blood.'

'He was drunk, you know,' Crosby said eagerly. 'Perhaps I should not have heeded him. I daresay he will be sorry by now: I don't – I don't object to him being asked if he cares to apologize.'

Mr Puckleton shook his head. 'He'd never do it,' he opined. 'He's fought two duels already, so I'm told.'

Mr Drelincourt gave a laugh that quivered uncertainly in the middle. 'Well, I hope he mayn't have sat up over the bottle last night.'

Mr Puckleton was inclined to think that even such a mad young buck as Winwood would not do that.

By this time they had reached the ground and Captain Forde had opened that sinister case. Reposing in a bed of velvet lay two shining swords, their blades gleaming wickedly in the pale sunlight.

'It still wants a few minutes to six,' observed the Captain. 'I take it your man won't be late?'

Mr Drelincourt stepped forward. 'Late? I give you my word I don't intend to wait upon his lordship's convenience! If he does not come by six I shall assume he does not mean to meet me, and go back to town.'

Lord Cheston looked him over with a certain haughtiness. 'Don't put yourself about, sir: he'll be here.'

From the edge of the clearing a view of the road could be obtained. Mr Drelincourt watched it in an agony of suspense, and as the moments dragged past began to feel almost hopeful.

But just as he was about to ask Puckleton the time (for he felt sure it must now be well over the hour), a gig came into sight, bowling at a fine rate down the road. It drew up at the gate which stood open on to the meadow and turned in.

'Ah, here's your man!' said Captain Forde. 'And six of the clock exactly!'

Any hopes that Mr Drelincourt still nursed were put to flight. The Viscount, with Sir Roland Pommeroy beside him, was driving the gig himself, and from the way in which he was handling a restive horse it was evident that he was not in the least fuddled by drink. He drew up on the edge of the clearing, and sprang down from the high perch.

'Not late, am I?' he said. 'Servant, Puckleton, servant, Forde. Never saw such a perfect morning in my life.'

'Well, you don't see many of 'em, Pel,' remarked Cheston, with a grin.

The Viscount laughed. His laughter sounded fiendish to Mr Drelincourt.

Sir Roland had picked the swords out of their velvet bed and was glancing down the blades.

'Nothing to choose between 'em,' said Cheston, strolling over to him.

The Captain tapped Mr Drelincourt on the shoulder. 'Ready, sir? I'll take your coat and wig.'

Mr Drelincourt was stripped of his coat and saw that the

Viscount, already in his shirt-sleeves, had sat down on a tree-stump and was pulling off his top boots.

'Take a drop of cognac, Pel?' inquired Sir Roland, producing a flask. 'Keep the cold out.'

The Viscount's reply was clearly wafted to Mr Drelincourt's ears. 'Never touch spirit before a fight, my dear fellow. Puts your eye out.' He stood up in his stockinged feet and began to roll up his sleeves. Mr Drelincourt, handing his wig to Mr Puckleton's tender care, wondered why he had never before realized what sinewy arms the Viscount had. He found that Lord Cheston was presenting two identical swords to him. He gulped, and took one of them in a damp grasp.

The Viscount received the other, made a pass as though to test its flexibility, and stood waiting, the point lightly resting on the ground.

Mr Drelincourt was led to his place, the seconds stepped back. He was alone, facing the Viscount, who had undergone some sort of transformation. The careless good humour had left his handsome face, his roving eye look remarkably keen and steady, his mouth appallingly grim.

'Ready, gentlemen?' Captain Forde called. 'On guard!'

Mr Drelincourt saw the Viscount's sword flash to the salute, and setting his teeth went through the same motions.

The Viscount opened with a dangerous thrust in prime, which Mr Drelincourt parried, but failed to take advantage of. Now that the assault was begun his jumping nerves became steadier; he remembered Captain Forde's advice, and tried to keep a good guard. As for luring his opponent on, he was kept too busy keeping a proper measure to think of it. An opportunity offering he delivered a thrust in tierce which ought to have ended the affair. But the Viscount parried it by yielding the foible, and countered so quickly that Mr Drelincourt's heart leapt into his mouth as in the very nick of time he recovered his guard.

The sweat was rolling off his brow and his breath came in exhausted gasps. All at once he thought he saw an opening and lunged wildly. Something icily cold pierced his shoulder, and as he reeled the second's sword struck his wavering blade upwards. It flew out of his hand, and he sank back into the arms of Mr Puckleton, who cried out: 'My God, is he killed? Crosby! Oh, there is blood! I positively cannot bear it!'

'Killed? Lord, no!' said Cheston scornfully. 'Here, Parvey, neatly pinked through the shoulder. I take it you are satisfied, Forde?'

'I suppose so,' grunted the Captain. 'Damme, if I ever saw a tamer fight!' He looked disgustedly down at the prostrate form of his principal, and inquired of Dr Parvey whether it was a dangerous wound.

The doctor glanced up from his work and beamingly replied: 'Dangerous, sir? Why, not in the least! A little blood lost, and no harm done. A beautifully clean wound!'

The Viscount, struggling into his coat, said: 'Well, I'm for breakfast. Pom, did you bespeak breakfast?'

Sir Roland, who was conferring with Captain Forde, looked over his shoulder. 'Now, Pel, would I forget a thing like that? I'm asking Forde here if he cares to join us.'

'Oh, by all means!' said the Viscount, shaking out his ruffles. 'Well, if you're ready, I am, Pom. I'm devilish hungry.'

With which he linked his arm in Sir Roland's and strolled off to tell his groom to drive the gig round to the inn.

Mr Drelincourt, his shoulder bandaged and his arm put into a sling, was assisted to his feet by the cheerful doctor, and assured that he had merely received a scratch. His surprise at finding himself still alive held him silent for a few moments, but he presently realized that the dreadful affair was at an end, and that his wig lay on the ground beside his shoes.

'My toupet!' he said faintly. 'How could you, Francis? Give it to me at once!'

Ten

For several days after his encounter with the Viscount Mr Drelincourt kept his bed, a pale and interesting invalid. Having conceived a dislike of Dr Parvey, he rejected all that Member of the Faculty's offers to attend to him to his lodging, and drove home with only the faithful but shaken Mr Puckleton to support him. They shared the vinaigrette, and upon arrival in Jermyn Street Mr Drelincourt was supported upstairs to his bed-chamber, while Mr Puckleton sent the valet running to fetch the fashionable Dr Hawkins. Dr Hawkins took a suitably grave view of the wound and not only blooded Mr Drelincourt, but bade him lie up for a day or two, and sent off the valet once more to Graham's, the apothecary's for some of the famous Dr James' powders.

Mr Puckleton had been so much upset by the fury of the Viscount's sword-play, so thankful that he had not stood in his friend's shoes, that he was inclined to look upon Mr Drelincourt as something of a hero, and said so often that he wondered how Crosby should have challenged Winwood so coolly, that Mr Drelincourt began to feel that he had indeed behaved with great intrepidity. He no less than Mr Puckleton had been impressed by the skill the Viscount displayed, and by dint of dwelling on his lordship's two previous encounters he soon talked himself into believing that he had been pinked by a hardened and expert duellist.

These agreeable reflections were put to flight by the appearance of the Earl of Rule, who came to visit his afflicted relative on the following morning.

Mr Drelincourt had not the smallest desire to meet Rule at the moment, and he sent a hasty message downstairs that he was unable to receive anyone. Congratulating himself on having acted with considerable presence of mind, he composed himself against a bank of pillows, and resumed his study of the *Morning Chronicle*.

He was interrupted by his cousin's pleasant voice. 'I am sorry you are too ill to receive me, Crosby,' said the Earl, walking into the room.

Mr Drelincourt gave prodigious start, and let the *Morning Chronicle* fall. His eyes goggled at Rule, and he said between alarm and indignation: 'I told my man I could not see visitors!'

'I know you did,' replied the Earl, laying his hat and cane on a chair. 'He delivered your message quite properly. Short of laying hands on me there was no stopping me, no stopping me at all, my dear Crosby.'

'I'm sure I don't know why you was so anxious to see me,' said Mr Drelincourt, wondering how much his lordship had heard.

The Earl looked rather surprised. 'But how would it be otherwise, Crosby? My heir desperately wounded, and I not at his side? Come come, my dear fellow, you must not believe me so heartless!'

'You are very obliging, Marcus, but I find myself still too weak to converse,' said Mr Drelincourt.

'It must have been a deadly wound, Crosby,' said his lordship sympathetically.

'Oh, as to that, Dr Hawkins does not consider my case desperate. A deep thrust, and I have lost a monstrous amount of blood, and had a deal of fever, but the lung is unharmed.'

'You relieve me, Crosby. I feared that I might be called upon to arrange your obsequies. A melancholy thought!'

'Vastly!' said Mr Drelincourt, eyeing him with resentment.

The Earl pulled a chair forward and sat down. 'You see, I had the felicity of meeting your friend Puckleton,' he explained. 'His account of your condition quite alarmed me. My stupid gullibility, of course. Upon reflection I perceive that I should have guessed from his description of Pelham's swordplay that he was prone to exaggerate.'

'Oh,' said Mr Drelincourt, with a self-conscious laugh, 'I don't profess to be Winwood's match with swords!'

'My dear Crosby, I did not suppose you a master, but this is surely over-modesty?'

Mr Drelincourt said stiffly: 'My Lord Winwood is known to be no mean exponent of the art, I believe.'

'Well, no,' replied the Earl, considering the point. 'I don't think I should call him mean. That is being too severe, perhaps. Let us say a moderate swordsman.'

Mr Drelincourt gathered the scattered sheets of the *Morning Chronicle* together with one shaking hand. 'Very well, my lord, very well, and is that all you have to say? I am ordered to rest, you know.'

'Now you put me in mind of it,' said the Earl, 'I remember there was something else. Ah yes, I have it! Do tell me Crosby – if you are not too exhausted by this tiresome visit of mine, of course – why did you call Pelham out? I am quite consumed by curiosity.'

Mr Drelincourt shot a quick look at him. 'Oh, you might well ask! Indeed, I believe I should have made allowance for his lordship's condition. Drunk, you know, amazingly drunk!'

'You distress me. But continue, dear cousin, pray continue!'

'It was absurd – a drunken fit of spleen, I am persuaded. His lordship took exception to the hat I wear at cards. His behaviour was most violent. In short, before I could know what he would be at he had torn the hat from my head. I could do no less than demand satisfaction, you'll agree.'

'Certainly,' agreed Rule. 'Er – I trust you are satisfied, Crosby?' Mr Drelincourt glared at him. His lordship crossed one leg over the other. 'Strange how misinformed one may be!' he mused. 'I was told – on what I thought credible authority – that Pelham threw a glass of wine in your face.'

There was an uncomfortable pause. 'Well, as to that – his lordship was quite out of his senses, not accountable, you know.'

'So he did throw his wine in your face, Crosby?'

'Yes, oh yes! I have said, he was most violent, quite out of his senses.'

'One might almost suppose him to have been forcing a quarrel on you, might not one?' suggested Rule.

'I daresay, cousin. He was bent on picking a quarrel,' muttered Mr Drelincourt, fidgeting with his sling. 'Had you been present you would know there was no doing anything with him.'

'My dear Crosby, had I been present,' said Rule softly, 'my well-meaning but misguided young relative would not have committed any of these assaults upon your person.'

'N-no, c-cousin?' stammered Mr Drelincourt.

'No,' said Rule, rising, and picking up his hat and stick. 'He would have left the matter in my hands. And I, Crosby, should have used a cane, not a small-sword.'

Mr Drelincourt seemed to shrink into his pillows. 'I – I am at a loss to understand you, Marcus!'

'Would you like me to make my meaning even clearer?' inquired his lordship.

'Really, I – really, Marcus, this tone – ! My wound – I must beg of you to leave me! I am in no fit state to pursue this conversation, which I protest I do not understand. My doctor is expected, moreover!'

'Don't be alarmed, cousin,' said the Earl. 'I shan't try to improve this time on Pelham's handiwork. But you should remember to render up thanks in your prayers for that wound, you know.' With which sweetly-spoken valediction he went out of the room, and quietly closed the door behind him.

Mr Drelincourt might have been slightly consoled had he known that his late opponent had come off very little better at the Earl's hands.

Rule, visiting him earlier, had not much difficulty in getting the full story from Pelham, though the Viscount had tried at first to adhere to precisely the tale Mr Drelincourt told later.

However, with those steady grey eyes looking into his and that lazy voice requesting him to speak the truth, he had faltered, and ended by telling Rule just what happened. Rule listened in patently unadmiring silence, and at the end said: 'Ah – am I expected to thank you for this heroic deed, Pelham?'

The Viscount, who was in the middle of his breakfast, fortified himself with a long draught of ale, and replied airily: 'Well, I won't deny I acted rashly, but I was a trifle in my cups, you know.'

'The thought of what you might have felt yourself compelled to do had you been more than a trifle in your cups I find singularly unnerving,' remarked the Earl.

'Damn, it Marcus, do you tell me you'd have had me pass it by?' demanded Pelham.

'Oh, hardly that!' said Rule. 'But had you refrained from taking it up in public I should have been greatly in your debt.'

The Viscount carved himself a slice of beef. 'Never fear,' he said. 'I've seen to it no one will talk. I told Pom to set it about I was drunk.'

'That was indeed thoughtful of you,' said Rule dryly. 'Do you know, Pelham, I am almost annoyed with you?'

The Viscount laid down his knife and fork and said resignedly: 'Burn it if I see why you should be!'

'I have a constitutional dislike of having my hand forced,' said Rule. 'I thought we were agreed that I should be allowed to – er – manage my affairs alone, and in my own way.'

'Well, so you can,' said the Viscount. 'I ain't stopping you.'

'My dear Pelham, you have – I trust – already done your worst. Until this lamentable occurrence your sister's partiality for Lethbridge was not such as to attract any – er – undue attention.'

'It attracted that little worm's attention,' objected the Viscount.

'Do, Pelham, I beg of you, allow your brain the indulgence of a little thought,' sighed his lordship. 'You forget that Crosby is my heir. The only sustained emotion I have ever seen him display is his violent dislike of my marriage. He has made the

124

whole world privy to it. In fact, I understand he causes considerable amusement in Polite Circles. Without your ill-timed interference, my dear boy, I venture to think that his remark would have been considered mere spite.'

'Oh,' said the Viscount, rather dashed. 'I see.'

'I had hopes that you might,' said Rule.

'Well, but Marcus, so it was spite! Damned spite!'

'Certainly,' agreed Rule. 'But when the lady's brother springs up in a noble fury – you must not think I do not sympathize with you, my dear Pelham: I do, from the bottom of my heart – and takes the thing in so much earnest that he forces a quarrel on willy-nilly; and further issues a veiled challenge to the world at large – you did, did you not, Pel? Ah, yes, I was sure of it! – in case any should dare to repeat the scandal – why, then, there is food enough for speculation! By this time I imagine that there is scarcely a pair of eyes in town not fixed on Horry and Lethbridge. For which, Pelham, I have undoubtedly you to thank.'

The Viscount shook his head despondently. 'As bad as that, is it? I'm a fool, Marcus, that's what it is. Always was, you know. To tell you the truth, I was devilish set on fighting the fellow. Ought to have let him eat his words. Believe he would have.'

'I am quite sure he would,' agreed Rule. 'However, it is too late now. Don't distress yourself, Pelham: at least you have the distinction of being the only man in England to have succeeded in provoking Crosby to fight. Where did you wound him?'

'Shoulder,' said the Viscount, his mouth full of beef. 'Could have killed him half a dozen times.'

'Could you?' said Rule. 'He must be a very bad swordsman.'

'He is,' replied the Viscount with a grin.

Having visited both the principals in the late affair, the Earl dropped into White's to look at the journals. His entry into one of the rooms seemed to interrupt a low-voiced conversation which was engaging the attention of several people gathered together in one corner. The talk ceased like a snapped thread, to be resumed again almost immediately, very audibly this time.

But the Earl of Rule, giving no sign, did not really suppose that horse-flesh was the subject of the first debate.

He lunched at the club, and shortly afterwards strolled home to Grosvenor Square. My lady, he was informed upon inquiry, was in her boudoir.

This apartment, which had been decorated for Horatia in tints of blue, lay at the back of the house, up one pair of stairs. The Earl went up to it, the faintest of creases between his brows. He was checked halfway by Mr Gisborne's voice hailing him from the hall below.

'My lord,' said Mr Gisborne. 'I have been hoping you might come in.'

The Earl paused, and looked down the stairway, one hand resting on the baluster rail. 'But how charming of you, Arnold!'

Mr Gisborne, who knew his lordship, heaved a despairing sigh. 'My lord, if you would spare only a few moments to glance over some accounts I have here!'

The Earl smiled disarmingly. 'Dear Arnold, go to the devil!' he said, and went on up the stairs.

'But, sir, indeed I can't act without your authority! A bill for a perch-phaeton, from a coach-maker's! Is it to be paid?'

'My dear boy, of course pay it. Why ask me?'

'It is not one of your bills, sir,' said Mr Gisborne, a stern look about his mouth.

'I am aware,' said his lordship, slightly amused. 'One of Lord Winwood's, I believe. Settle it, my dear fellow.'

'Very well, sir. And Mr Drelincourt's little affair?'

At that the Earl, who had been absorbed in smoothing a crease from his sleeve, looked up. 'Are you inquiring after the state of my cousin's health, or what?' he asked.

Mr Gisborne looked rather puzzled. 'No, sir, I was speaking of his monetary affairs. Mr Drelincourt wrote about a week ago, stating his embarrassments, but you would not attend.'

'Do you find me a sore trial, Arnold? I am sure you must. It is time I made amends.'

'Does that mean you will look over the accounts, sir?' asked Mr Gisborne hopefully.

'No, my dear boy, it does not. But you may – ah – use your own discretion in the matter of Mr Drelincourt's embarrassments.'

Mr Gisborne gave a short laugh. 'If I were to use my own discretion, sir, Mr Drelincourt's ceaseless demands on your generosity would find their way into the fire!' he said roundly.

'Precisely,' nodded the Earl, and went on up the stairs.

The boudoir smelt of roses. There were great bowls of them in the room, red and pink and white. In the middle of this bower, curled upon a couch with her cheek on her hand, Horatia was lying, fast asleep.

The Earl shut the door soundlessly, and trod across the thick Aubusson carpet to the couch, and stood for a moment, looking down at his wife.

She made a sufficiently pretty picture, her curls, free of powder, dressed loosely in the style the French called *Grèque à boucles badines,* and one white shoulder just peeping from the lace of her négligée. A beam of sunlight, stealing through one of the windows, lay across her cheek; and seeing it, the Earl went over to the window, and drew the curtain a little way to shut it out. As he turned Horatia stirred and opened drowsy eyes. They fell on him, and widened. Horatia sat up. 'Is it you, my l-lord? I've been asleep. Did you w-want me?'

'I did,' said Rule. 'But I did not mean to wake you, Horry.'

'Oh, that d-doesn't signify!' She looked up at him rather anxiously. 'Have you come to scold me for p-playing loo last night? I w-won, you know.'

'My dear Horry, what a very unpleasant husband I must be!' said the Earl. 'Do I only seek you out to scold you?'

'No-no, of course not, but I thought it m-might be that. Is it n-nothing disagreeable?'

'I should hardly call it disagreeable,' Rule said. 'Something a little tiresome.'

'Oh, d-dear!' sighed Horatia. She shot a mischievous look at

127

him. 'You are g-going to be an unpleasant husband, sir. I know you are.'

'No,' said Rule, 'but I am afraid I am going to annoy you, Horry. My lamentable cousin has been coupling your name with Lethbridge's.'

'C-coupling my name!' echoed Horatia. 'W-well, I do think Crosby is the m-most odious little toad alive! What did he say?'

'Something very rude,' replied the Earl. 'I won't distress you by repeating it.'

'I suppose he thinks I'm in l-love with Robert,' said Horatia bluntly. 'But I'm n-not, and I don't c-care what he says!'

'Certainly not: no one cares what Crosby says. Unfortunately, however, he said it in Pelham's hearing, and Pelham most unwisely called him out.'

Horatia clapped her hands together. 'A d-duel? Oh, how f-famous!' A thought occurred to her. 'M-Marcus, Pelham isn't hurt?'

'Not in the least; it is Crosby who is hurt.'

'I am very glad to hear it,' said Horatia. 'He d-deserves to be hurt. Surely you d-did not think that would annoy me?'

He smiled. 'No. It is the sequel that I fear may annoy you. It becomes necessary for you to hold Lethbridge at arm's length. Do you understand at all, Horry?'

'No,' said Horatia flatly. 'I d-don't!'

'Then I will try to explain. You have made Lethbridge your friend – or shall I say that you have chosen to become his friend?'

'It's all the same, sir.'

'On the contrary, my dear, there is a vast difference. But however it is, you are, I believe, often in his company.'

'There is n-nothing in that, sir,' Horatia said, brows beginning to lower.

'Nothing at all,' replied his lordship placidly. 'But – you will have to forgive me for speaking plain, Horry – since Pelham has apparently considered the matter to be enough moment to fight a duel over, there are a very few people who will believe that there is nothing in it.'

Horatia flushed, but answered roundly: 'I d-don't care what people believe! You've said yourself you kn-know there's n-nothing in it, so if you don't mind I am sure no one else n-need!'

He raised his brows slightly. 'My dear Horry, I thought I had made it abundantly clear to you at the outset that I do mind.'

Horatia sniffed, and looked more mutinous than ever. He watched her for a moment, then bent, and taking her hands drew her to her feet. 'Don't frown at me, Horry,' he said whimsically. 'Will you, to oblige me, give up this friendship with Lethbridge?'

She stared up at him, hovering between two feelings. His hands slid up her arms to her shoulders. He was smiling, half in amusement, half in tenderness. 'My sweet, I know that I am quite old, and only your husband, but you and I could deal better together than this.'

The image of Caroline Massey rose up clear before her. She whisked herself away, and said, a sob in her throat: 'My l-lord, it was agreed we should not interfere with each other. You'll allow I d-don't interfere with you. Indeed, I've n-no desire to, I assure you. I won't cast R-Robert off just b-because you are afraid of what vulgar people may say.'

The smile had left his eyes. 'I see. Ah – Horry, has a husband any right to command, since he may not request?'

'If p-people talk it is all your fault!' Horatia said, disregarding this. 'If only you would be civil to R-Robert too, and – and f-friendly, no one would say a word!'

'That, I am afraid, is quite impossible,' replied the Earl dryly.

'Why?' demanded Horatia.

He seemed to deliberate. 'For a reason that has become – er – ancient history, my dear.'

'Very well, sir, and what is this reason? Do you m-mean to tell me?'

His mouth quivered responsively. 'I admit you have me there, Horry. I don't mean to tell you.'

She said stormily: 'Indeed, my lord? You won't tell me w-why, and yet you expect me to cast off R-Robert!'

'I confess it does sound a trifle arbitrary,' admitted his lordship ruefully. 'The story, you see, is not entirely mine. But even though I am unable to divulge it the reason is a sufficient one.'

'V-vastly interesting,' said Horatia. 'It is a p-pity I can't judge for myself, for I must tell you, sir, that I have no n-notion of deserting my friends only b-because a creature like your horrid c-cousin says odious things about me!'

'Then I very much fear that I shall have to take steps to enforce this particular command,' said the Earl imperturbably.

She rejoined hotly: 'You c-can't c-coerce me into obeying you, my lord!'

'What a very ugly word, my dear!' remarked the Earl. 'I am sure I have never coerced anyone.'

She felt a little baffled. 'Pray, what do you m-mean to do, sir?'

'Dear Horry, surely I told you? I mean to put an end to the intimacy between you and Robert Lethbridge.'

'W-well, you c-can't!' declared Horatia.

The Earl opened his snuff-box, and took a pinch in a leisurely fashion. 'No?' he said, politely interested.

'No!'

The Earl shut the snuff-box, and dusted his sleeve with a lace-edged handkerchief.

'W-well, have you n-nothing else to say?' demanded Horatia, goaded.

'Nothing at all, my dear,' said his lordship with unruffled good-humour.

Horatia made a sound rather like that of an infuriated kitten, and flounced out of the room.

Eleven

No lady of spirit, of course, could resist the temptation of pushing matters further, and Horatia was a lady of considerable spirit. The knowledge that the eyes of the Polite World were on her invested her behaviour with certain defiance. That anyone should dare to suppose that she, Horry Winwood, had fallen in love with Lethbridge was a ludicrous presumption to be treated only with scorn. Attracted by Lethbridge she might be, but there was a very cogent reason why she should not be in the least in love with him. The reason stood well over six foot in height, and was going to be shown, in vulgar parlance, that what was sauce for the goose could be sauce for the gander as well. And if the Earl of Rule could be roused to take action, so much the better. Horatia, her first annoyance having evaporated, was all agog to see what he would do. But he must be made to realize that his wife had no intention of sharing his favours with his mistress.

So with the laudable object of making his lordship jealous Horatia sought in her mind for some outrageous thing to do.

It did not take her long to hit upon the very thing. There was to be a ridotto held at Ranelagh, which, to tell the truth, she had given up all idea of attending, Rule having refused quite unmistakably to escort her. There had been a slight argument over the matter, but Rule had ended it by saying pleasantly: 'I don't think you would care for it, my dear. It won't be a very genteel affair, you know.'

Horatia was aware that public ridottos were looked upon by

the select as very vulgar masquerades, and she accepted the Earl's decision with a good grace. She had heard all sorts of scandalous tales of the excesses committed at such affairs, and had really no wish, beyond a certain curiosity, to be present at one.

But now that battle was joined with the Earl a different complexion was put on the matter and it seemed all at once eminently desirable that she should attend the Ranelagh ridotto, with Lethbridge, of course, as her escort. There could be no fear of scandal, since both would be masked, and the only person who should know of the prank was my Lord of Rule. And if that did not rouse him, nothing would.

The next step was to enlist Lord Lethbridge. She had feared that this might prove a little difficult (since he was so anxious not to cast a slur on her good name), but it turned out to be quite easy.

'Take you to the ridotto at Ranelagh, Horry,' he said. 'Now, why?'

'B-because I want to go, and Rule wo-can't t-take me,' said Horatia, correcting herself hurriedly.

His oddly brilliant eyes held a laugh. 'But how churlish of him!'

'N-never mind that,' said Horatia. 'W-will you take me?'

'Of course I will,' replied Lethbridge, bowing over her hand.

So five evenings later Lord Lethbridge's coach drew up in Grosvenor Square, and my Lady Rule, in full ball dress, a grey domino over her arm, and a loo-mask dangling by its strings from her fingers, came out of the house, tripped down the steps, and got into the coach. She had thoughtfully left a message with the porter for Lord Rule. 'If his lordship should inquire for me, inform him that I am gone to Ranelagh,' she said airily.

Her first view of Ranelagh made her delighted to have come, quite apart from the original object of the exploit. Thousands of golden lamps arranged in tasteful designs lit the gardens. Strains of music floated on the air; and crowds of gay dominoes thronged the gravel walks. In the various rotundas and lodges that were scattered about the ground refreshments could be had, while in the pavilion itself dancing was going forward.

Horatia, observing the scene through the slits of her mask, turned impulsively to Lethbridge, standing beside her with a scarlet domino hanging open from his shoulders, and cried: 'I am so g-glad we came! Only see how pretty! Are you not charmed with it, R-Robert?'

'In your company, yes,' he replied. 'Do you care to dance, my dear?'

'Yes, of course!' said Horatia enthusiastically.

There was nothing to shock the primmest-minded person in the demeanours of those in the ballroom, but Horatia opened her eyes a little at the sight of a scuffle for the possession of a lady's mask taking place later beside the lily-pond under the terrace. The lady fled with most ungenteel shrieks of laughter, hotly pursued by her cavalier. Horatia said nothing, but thought privately that Rule might have reason for not wishing his wife to attend public ridottos.

However, to do him justice, Lord Lethbridge steered his fair charge carefully clear of any low-bred romping, and she continued to be very well pleased with the night's entertainment. In fact, as she said over supper in one of the boxes, it was the most delightful adventure imaginable, and only wanted one thing to make it perfect. 'Good God, Horry, what have I left undone?' asked Lethbridge, in mock dismay.

She dimpled. 'Well, R-Robert, I do think it would be quite the n-nicest party I have ever been to if only we c-could play cards together!'

'Oh, rogue!' Lethbridge said softly. 'You will shock the solitary gentleman in the next box, my dear.'

Horatia paid no heed to this, beyond remarking that it was ten to one the gentleman was a stranger.

'You don't like d-dancing, Robert, you know you d-don't! And I do want to try my skill against you.'

'Too ambitious, Horry,' he teased. 'I was playing cards when

133

you were sewing samplers. And I'll wager I was playing better than you sewed.'

'L-Lizzie used to finish all my samplers for me,' admitted Horatia. 'But I p-play cards much better than I sew, I assure you. R-Robert, why won't you?'

'Do you think I would fleece so little a lamb?' he asked. 'I haven't the heart!'

She tilted her chin. 'P-perhaps I should fleece you, sir!' she said.

'Yes – if I let you,' he smiled. 'And of course I undoubtedly should.'

'L-let me win?' said Horatia indignantly. 'I am n-not a baby, sir! If I play, I play in earnest.'

'Very well,' said Lethbridge. 'I will play you – in earnest.'

She clapped her hands together, causing the man in the next box to glance round at her. 'You w-will?'

'At piquet – for a certain stake,' Lethbridge said.

'W-well, of course. I d-don't mind playing high, you know.'

'We are not going to play for guineas, my dear,' Lethbridge told her, finishing the champagne in his glass.

She frowned. 'R-Rule does not like me to stake my jewels,' she said.

'Heaven forbid! We will play higher than that.'

'G-good gracious!' exclaimed Horatia. 'For what then?'

'For a lock – one precious lock – of your hair, Horry,' said Lethbridge.

She drew back instinctively. 'That is silly,' she said. 'Besides – I c-couldn't.'

'I thought not,' he said. 'Forgive me, my dear, but you see you are not really a gamester.'

She reddened. 'I am!' she declared. 'I am! Only I c-can't play you for a lock of hair! It's stupid, and I ought not. B-besides what would you stake against it?'

He put his hand to the Mechlin cravat about his throat and drew out the curious pin he nearly always wore. It was an intaglio of the goddess Athene with her shield and owl and

134

looked to be very old. He held it in the palm of his hand for Horatia to see. 'That has come down in my family through very many years,' he said. 'I will stake it against a lock of your hair.'

'Is it an heirloom?' she inquired, touching it with the tip of her finger.

'Almost,' he said. 'It has a charming legend attached to it, and no Lethbridge would ever let it out of his possession.'

'And w-would you really stake it?' Horatia asked wonderingly.

He put it back in his cravat. 'For a lock of your hair, yes,' he answered. 'I *am* a gamester.'

'You shall n-never say that I was n-not!' Horatia said. 'I will play you for my hair! And to show I really d-do play in earnest –' she thrust her hand into her reticule searching for something – 'There!' She held up a small pair of scissors.

He laughed. 'But how fortunate, Horry!'

She put the scissors back in the reticule. 'You haven't w-won it yet, sir.'

'True,' he agreed. 'Shall we say the best of three games?'

'D-done!' said Horatia. 'P-play or pay! I have finished my supper, and I should l-like to play now.'

'With all my heart,' bowed Lethbridge, and rose, offering his arm.

She laid her hand on it, and they left the box together, wending their way across the space that lay between it and the main pavilion. Skirting a gaily chattering group, Horatia said with her pronounced stammer: 'Where shall we p-play, R-Robert? Not in that c-crowded card-room! It wouldn't be discreet.'

A tall woman in an apple-green domino turned her head quickly, and stared after Horatia, her lips just parted in surprise.

'Certainly not,' said Lethbridge. 'We shall play in the little room you liked, leading off the terrace.'

The green domino stood quite still, apparently lost either in surprise or meditation, and was only recalled to her surroundings by an apologetic voice murmuring: 'Your pardon, ma'am.'

She turned to find she was blocking the way of a large Black Domino, and stepped aside with a light word of apology.

Though there was plenty of music to be heard coming from various corners of the gardens, the fiddlers who scraped in the ballroom were temporarily silent. The pavilion was pretty well deserted, for the supper interval was not yet over. Horatia passed through the empty ballroom on Lethbridge's arm, and was just stepping out on to the moonlit terrace when someone in the act of entering almost collided with her. It was the man in the Black Domino, who must have come in from the gardens by the terrace steps. Both fell back at once, but in some inexplicable fashion the edge of Horatia's lace under-dress had got under the stranger's foot. There was a rending sound, followed by an exclamation from Horatia, and conscience-stricken apologies from the offender.

'Oh, I beg a thousand pardons, ma'am! Pray forgive me! I would not for the world – Can't think how I can have been so clumsy!'

'It does not signify, sir,' Horatia said coldly, gathering up her skirt in her hand, and walking through the long window on to the terrace.

The Black Domino stood aside for Lethbridge to follow her, and once more begging pardon, retreated into the ballroom.

'How horribly p-provoking!' Horatia said, looking at her hopelessly torn frill. 'Now I shall have to go and p-pin it up. Of course it is quite ruined.'

'Shall I call him out?' Lethbridge said. 'Faith, he deserves it! How came he to tread on your skirt at all?'

'G-goodness knows!' said Horatia. She gave a little chuckle. 'He was d-dreadfully overcome, wasn't he? Where shall I find you, R-Robert?'

'I'll await you here,' he answered.

'And then we p-play cards?'

'And then we play cards,' he concurred.

'I w-won't be above a m-moment,' Horatia promised optimistically, and vanished into the ballroom again.

Lord Lethbridge strolled towards the low parapet that ran along the edge of the terrace, and stood leaning his hands on it, and looking idly down at the lily-pond a few feet below. Little coloured lights ringed it round, and some originally minded person had designed a cluster of improbable flowers to hold tiny lamps. These floated on the still water, and had provoked a great deal of laughter and admiration earlier in the evening. Lord Lethbridge was observing them with a rather contemptuous smile twisting his lips when two hands came round his neck from behind, and jerked apart the strings that held his domino loosely together.

Startled, he tried to turn round, but the hands that in one lightning movement had ripped off his domino, closed like a flash about his throat, and tightened suffocatingly. He clawed at them, struggling violently. A drawling voice said in his ear: 'I shan't strangle you this time, Lethbridge. But I am afraid – yes, I am really afraid it will have to be that pond. I feel sure you will appreciate the necessity.'

The grip left Lord Lethbridge's throat, but before he could turn a thrust between his shoulder-blades made him lose his balance. The parapet was too low to save him; he fell over it and into the lily-pond with a splash that extinguished the lights in that cluster of artificial flowers which he had looked at so scornfully a minute before.

A quarter of an hour later the ballroom had begun to fill again, and the fiddlers had resumed their task. Horatia came out on to the terrace and found several people standing there in little groups. She hesitated, looking for the Scarlet Domino, and saw him in a moment, sitting sideways on the parapet and meditatively surveying the pond below. She went up to him. 'I w-wasn't so very long, was I?'

He turned his head, and at once stood up. 'Not at all,' he said politely. 'And now – that little room!'

She had half advanced her hand to lay it on his arm, but at that she drew back. He stretched out his own, and took hers in it. 'Is anything the matter?' he asked softly.

She seemed uncertain. 'Your v-voice sounds queer. It – it is you, isn't it?'

'But of course it is!' he said. 'I think I must have swallowed a morsel of bone at supper, and scraped my throat. Will you walk, ma'am?'

She let him draw her hand through his arm. 'Yes, b-but are you sure no one will come into the room? It would look very particular if anybody were to see me 1-lose a lock of hair to you – if I d-do lose.'

'Who is to know you?' he said, holding the heavy curtain back from a window at the end of the terrace. 'But you need not be alarmed. Once we have drawn the curtains – like that – no one will come in.'

Horatia stood by the table in the middle of the small saloon, and watched the Scarlet Domino pull the curtains together. Suddenly, in spite of all her desire to do something outrageous, she wished that she had not pledged herself to this game. It had seemed innocent enough to dance with Lethbridge, to sup with him in full eye of the public, but to be alone with him in a private room was another matter. All at once he seemed to her to have changed. She stole a look at his masked face, but the candles on the table left him in a shadow. She glanced towards the door, which very imperfectly shut off the noise of the violins. 'The d-door, R-Robert?'

'Locked,' he said. 'It leads into the ballroom. Still nervous, Horry? Did I not say you were not a real gamester?'

'N-nervous? G-gracious no!' she said, on her mettle. 'You'll find I'm not such a poor g-gamester as that, sir!' She sat down at the table, and picked up one of the piquet packs that lay on it. 'D-did you arrange everything, then?'

'Certainly,' he said, moving towards another table set against the wall. 'A glass of wine, Horry?'

'N-no, thank you,' she replied, sitting rather straight in her chair, and casting yet another glance towards the curtained window.

He came back to the card-table, slightly moved the cluster of candles on it, and sat down. He began to shuffle one of the packs.

'Tell me, Horry,' he said, 'did you come with me tonight for this, or to annoy Rule?'

She gave a jump, and then laughed. 'Oh, R-Robert, that is so very like you! You always g-guess right.'

He went on shuffling the pack. 'May I know why he is to be baited?'

'No,' she replied. 'I d-don't discuss my husband, even with you, R-Robert.'

He bowed, ironically she thought. 'A thousand pardons, my dear. He stands high in your esteem, I perceive.'

'Very high,' said Horatia. 'Shall we c-cut?'

She won the cut, and electing to deal, picked up the pack, and gave a little expert shake of her arm to throw back the heavy fall of lace at her elbow. She was far too keen a gambler to talk while she played. As soon as she touched the cards she had never a thought for anything else, but sat with a look of serious, unwavering concentration on her face, and scarcely raised her eyes from her hand.

Her opponent gathered up his cards, glanced at them, and seemed to make up his mind what to discard without the smallest hesitation. Horatia, knowing herself to be pitted against a very fine player, refused to let herself be hurried, and took time over her own discard. The retention of a knave in her hand turned out well, and enabled her to spoil the major hand's repique.

She lost the first game, but not by enough points to alarm her. Once she knew she had thrown a guard she should have kept, but for the most part she thought she had played well.

'My game,' said the Scarlet Domino. 'But I think I had the balance of the cards.'

'A little perhaps,' she said. 'Will you cut again for d-deal?'

The second game she won, in six quick hands. She had a suspicion that she had been allowed to win it, but if her opponent had played with deliberate carelessness it was never blatant enough to warrant any remark. She held her tongue therefore, and in silence watched him deal the first hand of the final game.

At the end of two hands she was sure that he had permitted

her to win the second game. The cards had run very evenly throughout, and continued to do so, but now the more experienced player was ahead on points. She felt for the first time that she was up against a gamester immeasurably more skilled than herself. He never made mistake, and the very precision of his play and judgment seemed to cast her own shortcomings into high relief. She played her cards shrewdly enough, but knew that her weakness lay in counting the odds against finding a desired card in the pick-up. Knowing him to be some forty points to the good, she began to discard with less caution, playing for a big hand.

The game had become for her a grim struggle, her opponent a masked figure of Nemesis; as she picked up her cards in the last hand her fingers quivered infinitesimally. Unless a miracle occurred there was no longer any hope of winning; the best she could expect was to avert a rubicon.

No miracle occurred. Since they were not playing for points it did not signify that she was rubiconed, yet, irrationally, when she added her score and found the total ninety-eight she could have burst into tears.

She looked up, forcing a smile. 'You win, sir. I f-fear rather l-largely. I d-didn't play well that last game. You l-let me win the second, d-didn't you?'

'Perhaps,' he said.

'I wish you had not. I d-don't care to be treated like a child, sir.'

'Content you, my dear, I had never the least notion of letting you win more than one game. I have set my mind on that curl. I claim it, ma'am.'

'Of c-course,' she said proudly. Inwardly, she wondered what Rule would say if he could see her now, and quaked at her own daring. She took the scissors out of her reticule. 'R-Robert, what are you g-going to do with it?' she asked rather shyly.

'Ah, that is my affair,' he replied.

'Yes. I kn-know. But – if anyone f-found out – horrid things would be said, and R-Rule would hear of it and I d-don't want him to, because I know I – I ought n-not to have done it!' said Horatia in a rush.

'Give me the scissors,' he said, 'and perhaps I'll tell you what I mean to do with it.'

'I c-can cut it myself,' she replied, aware of a tiny feeling of apprehensiveness.

He had risen and come round the table. 'My privilege, Horry,' he said, laughing, and took the scissors out of her hand.

She felt his fingers amongst her curls, and blushed. She remarked with would-be lightness: 'It will be a very p-powdery one, R-Robert!'

'And a charmingly scented one,' he agreed.

She heard the scissors cut through her hair, and at once got up. 'There! For g-goodness sake don't tell anyone, w-will you?' she said. She moved towards the window. 'I think it is time you took me home. It must be d-dreadfully late.'

'In a moment,' he said, coming towards her. 'You are a good loser, sweetheart.'

Before she had even a suspicion of his purpose he had her in his arms and with one deft hand nipped the mask from her face. Frightened, white with anger, she tried to break free, only to find herself held quite powerless. The hand that had untied her mask came under her chin, and forced it up; the Scarlet Domino bent and kissed her, full on her indignant mouth.

She wrenched herself away as at last he slackened his embrace. She was breathless and shaken, trembling from head to foot. 'How d-dare you?' she choked, and dashed her hand across her mouth as though to wipe away the kiss. 'Oh, how dare you *t-touch* me?' She whirled about, flew to the window, and dragging the curtain back, was gone.

The Scarlet Domino made no attempt to pursue her but stayed in the middle of the room, gently twisting a powdered curl round one finger. An odd smile hovered about his mouth; he put the curl carefully into his pocket.

A movement in the window made him look up. Lady Massey was standing there, an apple-green domino covering her gown, her mask dangling from her hand. 'That was not very well contrived, surely, Robert?' she said maliciously. 'A vastly pretty scene, but I am amazed that so clever a man as you could make such a stupid mistake. Lord, couldn't you tell the little fool was not ready for kisses? And I thinking you knew how to handle her! You'll be glad of my help yet, my lord.'

The smile had quite vanished from the Scarlet Domino's mouth, which had suddenly grown very stern. He put up a hand to the strings of his mask, and untied them. 'Shall I?' he said, in accents utterly unlike Lord Lethbridge's. 'But are you quite sure, madam, that it is not you who have made – a very great mistake?'

Twelve

*H*oratia partook of breakfast in bed some six hours later. She was too young for her troubles to deprive her of sleep, but though she had certainly slept she had had horrid dreams, and awoke not very much refreshed.

When she had fled from the little card-room at Ranelagh she had been so angry that she had forgotten that her mask was off. She had run right into Lady Massey, also maskless, and for one moment they had faced each other. Lady Massey had smiled in a way that drove the blood up into Horatia's cheeks. She had not spoken a word; and Horatia, dragging her domino closely round her, had slipped across the terrace, and down the steps into the garden.

A hackney coach had conveyed her home, and deposited her in the cold dawn in Grosvenor Square. She had half expected to find Rule sitting up for her, but to her relief there was no sign of him. She had told the tire-woman she might go to bed, and she was glad of that too. She wanted to be alone, to think over the disastrous events of the night. But when she had extricated herself from her gown, and made herself ready for bed, she was so tired that she could not think of anything, and fell asleep almost as soon as she had blown out the candle.

She awoke at about nine o'clock, and for a moment wondered why she should feel so oppressed. Then she remembered, and gave a little shudder.

She rang her silver hand-bell, and when the abigail brought in her tray of chocolate and sweet biscuits she was sitting up in bed, her curls, with the powder still clinging to them, tumbled all about her shoulders, and a deep frown on her face.

While the waiting-woman collected her scattered jewels and garments she sipped the chocolate, pondering her problem. What had seemed a mere prank twelve hours earlier had by now assumed gigantic proportions. There was first the episode of the curl. In the sane daylight Horatia was at a loss to imagine how she could ever have consented to play for such a stake. It was – yes, no use blinking facts, it was vulgar: no other word for it. And who could tell what Lethbridge might not do with it? Before that kiss she had had no fear of his discretion, but now he seemed to her monstrous, capable of boasting, even, that he had won the curl from her. As for the kiss, she supposed that she had brought that on herself; a reflection which gave her no comfort. But worst of all had been the meeting with Caroline Massey. If she had seen, and Horatia was certain that she had, the tale would be all over the town by to-morrow. And the Massey had Rule's ear. Depend upon it, if she refrained from telling anyone else she would be bound to tell him, only too glad of the opportunity to make mischief between him and his wife.

Suddenly she pushed the tray away from her. 'I'm g-going to get up!' she said.

'Yes, my lady. What gown will your ladyship wear?'

'It doesn't m-matter,' Horatia answered curtly.

An hour later she came down the stairs, and in resolute voice inquired of a footman whether the Earl was in the house.

His lordship, she was told, had that instant come in, and was with Mr Gisborne.

Horatia drew a breath, as though in preparation for a dive into deep waters, and walked across the hall to Mr Gisborne's room.

The Earl was standing by the desk with his back to the door, reading a speech Mr Gisborne had prepared for him. He had evidently been riding, for he wore top-boots, a little dusty, and buckskin breeches, with a plain but excellently cut coat of blue cloth with silver buttons. He held his whip and gloves in one hand; his hat was thrown down on a chair. 'Admirable, my dear boy, but far too long. I should forget the half of it, and the Lords would be shocked, quite shocked, you know,' he said, and gave the paper back to the secretary. 'And Arnold – do you think – a little less impassioned? Ah yes, I thought you would agree! I am never impassioned.'

Mr Gisborne was bowing to Horatia; my lord turned his head, and saw her. 'A thousand pardons, my love! I did not hear you come in,' he said.

Horatia bestowed a rather perfunctory smile on Mr Gisborne, who accustomed to the friendliest of treatment from her, instantly wondered what could be the matter. 'Are you very b-busy, sir?' she asked, raising her anxious eyes to Rule's face.

'Arnold will tell you, my dear, that I am never busy,' he replied.

'W-well, could you spare me a m-moment of your time n-now?' Horatia said.

'As many as you desire,' he said, and held open the door for her to pass out. 'Shall we go into the library, ma'am?'

'I d-don't mind where we go,' said Horatia in a small voice. 'But I want to be p-private with you.'

'My dear, this is very flattering,' he said.

'It isn't,' replied Horatia mournfully. She went into the library, and watched him shut the door. 'I want to be p-private because there is something I m-must tell you.'

The veriest hint of surprise flickered for an instant in his eyes; he looked at her for a moment, rather searchingly, she thought. Then he moved forward. 'But won't you sit down, Horry?'

She stayed where she was, her hands gripping the back of a chair. 'No, I think I'll s-stand,' she answered. 'M-Marcus, I had better tell you at once that I've done something d-dreadful!'

At that a smile quivered at the corners of his mouth. 'I'm prepared for the worst, then.'

'I assure you, it isn't f-funny,' said Horatia tragically. 'In f-fact,

I'm afraid you will be amazingly angry, and I m-must own,' she added in a rush of candour, 'I d-deserve it, even if you beat me with that whip, only I d-do hope you won't, M-Marcus.'

'I can safely promise you that I won't,' said the Earl, laying both whip and gloves down on the table. 'Come, Horry, what is the matter?'

She began to trace the pattern of the chair-back with one finger. 'Well, I – w-well, you see, I – M-Marcus, did they give you my m-message last night?' She raised her eyes fleetingly, and saw him gravely watching her. 'I desired the p-porter to tell you, if – if you asked that I was gone to Ranelagh.'

'Yes, I did get that message,' Rule answered.

'Well – w-well, I did go there. To the ridotto. And I w-went with Lord Lethbridge.'

There was a pause. 'Is that all?' Rule asked.

'No,' confessed Horatia. 'It's only the b-beginning. There's m-much worse to come.'

'Then I had better reserve my wrath,' he said. 'Go on, Horry.'

'You see, I w-went with Lord Lethbridge, and – and left the message, because – because –'

'Because you naturally wanted me to know that you had – shall we say? – thrown down the glove. I quite understand that part of it,' said Rule encouragingly.

She looked up again. 'Yes, that w-was the reason,' she admitted. 'It wasn't that I wanted very p-particularly to be with him, Rule. And I thought since everyone was to be m-masked that nobody would know, except you, so that I should just make you angry and n-not cause any scandal at all.'

'The matter is now perfectly clear,' said Rule. 'Let us proceed to Ranelagh.'

'W-well, at first it was very p-pleasant, and I liked it excessively. Then – then we had supper in one of the boxes, and I t-teased Robert to play cards with me. You must know, M-Marcus, that I wanted dreadfully to play with him, and he never would. At last he said he would, but – but not for money.' She knit her brows, puzzling over something, and suddenly said: 'Rule, d-do you think that perhaps I d-drank too much champagne?'

'I trust not, Horry.'

'Well, I c-can't account for it otherwise,' she said. 'He said he would p-play for a lock of my hair, and it's no use d-deceiving you, Rule, I agreed!' As no explosion of wrath greeted this confession she took a firm grip of the chair-back, and continued. 'And I l-let him take me to a p-private room – in fact, I wanted it to be p-private – and we played p-piquet, and – and I lost. And I m-must say,' she added, 'though he is the most odious m-man I ever met he is a very, very fine card-p-player.'

'I believe he is,' said the Earl. 'I need not ask, of course, whether you paid your stake.'

'I had to. It was a d-debt of honour, you see. I let him cut one of my c-curls off, and – and he's got it n-now.'

'Forgive me, my dear, but have you told me this because you wish me to get that curl back for you?' inquired his lordship.

'No, no!' Horatia replied impatiently. 'You c-can't get it back; I lost it in fair play. Something much, m-much worse happened then – though it w-wasn't the worst of all. He – he caught hold of me, and took my m-mask off, and – kissed me! And Rule, the m-most dreadful thing! I f-forgot about my mask, and I ran away, and – and Lady Massey was just outside the w-window, and she saw me, and I know she had been w-watching all the time! So you see, I've m-made a vulgar scandal, and I thought the only thing I could do was to t-tell you at once, because even if you are furious with me, you ought to know, and I couldn't b-bear anyone else to tell you!'

The Earl did not seem to be furious. He listened calmly to the whole of this hurried speech, and at the end of it walked forward across the space that separated them, and to Horatia's astonishment took her hand in his and raised it to his lips. 'My compliments, Horry,' he said. 'You have surprised me.' He released her hand, and went towards the desk that stood in the window. Taking a key from his pocket he unlocked one of the drawers and pulled it open. Horatia blinked at him, utterly at a loss. He came back to her, and held out his hand. In the palm of it lay a powdered curl.

Horatia gave a gasp, staring at it. Then she looked up, quite dumbfounded. 'M-mine?' she stammered.

'Yours, my dear.'

'But I – but – how did you c-come by it?'

He gave a little laugh. 'I won it.'

'Won it?' she repeated, uncomprehending. 'How *c-could* you? Who – Rule, whom did you win it from?'

'Why, from you, Horry. Whom else could I have won it from?'

She clutched his wrist. 'Rule, it – it was not *you*?' she squeaked.

'But of course it was, Horry. Did you think I would let you lose to Lethbridge?'

'Oh!' cried Horatia on a sob. 'Oh, I am so th-thankful!' She let go of his wrist. 'But I d-don't understand. How did you know? Where were you?'

'In the next box to yours.'

'The m-man in the black d-domino? Then – then it was you who trod on my g-gown?'

'You see, I had to contrive that you should be out of the way for a few moments,' he apologized.

'Yes, of course,' nodded Horatia, quite appreciating this. 'It was very c-clever of you, I think. And when I c-came back and thought your voice odd – *that* was you?'

'It was. I flatter myself I imitated Lethbridge's manner rather well. I admit that the noise those fiddles made helped me.'

She was frowning again. 'Yes, b-but I don't understand quite. D-did Robert exchange d-dominoes with you?'

A laugh lurked in his eyes. 'It was not precisely an exchange. I – er – took his, and hid my own under a chair.'

Horatia was regarding him keenly. 'D-didn't he mind?'

'Now I come to think of it,' said the Earl pensively, 'I am afraid I forgot to ask him.'

She came a little nearer. 'Marcus, did you m-make him give it to you?'

'No,' replied the Earl. 'I – er – took it.'

'T-took it? But why did he let you?'

'He really had no choice in the matter,' said his lordship.

She drew a long breath. 'You m-mean you took it by f-force? And didn't he do anything? What became of him?'

'I imagine that he went home,' said the Earl calmly.

'W-went home! Well, I n-never heard of anything so poor-spirited!' exclaimed Horatia, with disgust.

'He could hardly do anything else,' said the Earl. 'Perhaps I ought to explain that the gentleman had the – er – misfortune to fall into the lily-pond.'

Horatia's lips parted. 'Rule, d-did you push him in?' she asked breathlessly.

'You see I had to dispose of him somehow,' said his lordship. 'He was really quite *de trop*, and the lily-pond so conveniently situated.'

Horatia gave up all attempt to preserve her gravity, and went off into a peal of laughter. 'Oh, R-Rule, how famous! I w-wish I had seen it!' A thought occurred to her; she said quickly: 'He w-won't call you out, will he?'

'Alas, I fear there is no likelihood of that,' Rule replied. 'You see, Horry, you are my wife – a circumstance that makes Lethbridge's position a little awkward.'

She was not satisfied. 'R-Rule, suppose he tries to do you a m-mischief?' she said anxiously.

'I hardly think he would succeed,' said Rule, unconcerned.

'W-well, I don't know, but I wish you will take care, Marcus.'

'I promise you you need have no fear for me, my dear.'

She looked a trifle uncertain, but allowed the matter to drop. She said rather gruffly: 'And perhaps you will tell Lady M-Massey that it was you all the time?'

His mouth hardened. 'Lady Massey,' he said deliberately, 'need not trouble you – in any way, Horry.'

She said with difficulty: 'I think I would rather you told her, sir. She – she looked at me in a way that – in a way that –'

'It will not be necessary for me to tell Lady Massey anything,' said Rule. 'She will not, I think, mention what happened last night.'

She glanced up at him, puzzled. 'Did she know then that it was you?'

He smiled rather grimly. 'She did indeed know it,' he replied.

'Oh!' Horatia digested this. 'Were you going to t-tell me all this if I hadn't told you?' she asked.

'To be frank with you, Horry, no: I was not,' Rule answered. 'You will have to forgive my stupidity. I did not think that you would tell me.'

'W-well, I don't think I should have told you if Lady M-Massey hadn't seen me,' said Horatia candidly. 'And I d-don't suppose Robert would have explained it, because it m-makes him look quite ridiculous. And I w-wouldn't have spoken to him again. Now I see, of course, that he did not behave so very b-badly after all, though I must say I d-don't think he should have proposed that stake, do you?'

'Most certainly I do not.'

'No. Well, I won't have him for a friend, Rule!' said Horatia handsomely. 'You won't m-mind if I am civil to him, will you?'

'Not at all,' Rule replied. 'I am civil to him myself.'

'I d-don't call it civil to push a person into a p-pond,' objected Horatia. She caught sight of the clock. 'Oh, I said I would d-drive out with Louisa! Only look at the time!' She prepared to depart. 'There is one thing that makes me very c-cross,' she said, frowning at him. 'It was odious of you to l-let me win the second game!'

He laughed, and caught her hands, pulling her towards him. 'Horry, shall we consign Louisa to the devil?' he suggested.

'N-no, I must go,' Horatia answered, suddenly shy. 'B-besides, she hasn't seen my landaulet!'

The landaulet, the possession of which was enough to set any lady in the forefront of fashion, was glitteringly bright and new, having only just come from the coach-maker. Lady Louisa duly admired it, pronounced it to be extremely comfortable, and was so obliging as to say that she had not in the least minded being kept waiting over half an hour. Since she had shopping to do in

Bond Street the coachman was instructed to drive there first, and the two ladies leaned back against the cushions and embarked on a discussion concerning the proper kind of ribbons to wear with a ball dress of green Italian taffeta for which Lady Louisa had just purchased two ells of stuff. By the time the rival merits of ribbons *à l'instant, à l'attention, au soupir de Vénus,* and a great many others had been fully weighed, the carriage drew up outside a fashionable milliner's, and the ladies went in to select a branch of artificial flowers which Lady Louisa hoped to make bearable a hat she had bought two days ago, and quite detested already.

It was naturally impossible for Horatia to visit a milliner without purchasing something on her own account, so when the flowers had been selected, she tried on a number of hats, and bought finally an enormous confection composed chiefly of stiff muslin in Trianon grey, which was labelled, not without reason, '*Grandes Prétentions*'. There was a *collet monté* gauze scarf in the same detectable shade of grey, so she bought that as well. A cap *à la glaneuse* caught her eye as she was about to leave the shop, but she decided not to add that to her purchases, Lady Louisa having had the presence of mind to declare that it made her look rather prim.

Horatia was just a little nervous of her sister-in-law, whom she suspected of disapproving of her, but Lady Louisa was behaving quite delightfully, and had not suggested by so much as a look that she thought it extravagant of Horry to buy that hat. She had even said that it was ravishing, so when they stepped into the landaulet again Horatia was feeling more friendly towards Louisa than she ever remembered to have felt before.

This was precisely what Lady Louisa wanted. As the carriage moved forward she pointed her furled sunshade at the coachman's back, and said: 'My dear, how much does he hear of what one says?'

'Oh, n-nothing!' Horatia assured her. 'He is very d-deaf, you know. D-didn't you notice how I have to shout at him?'

'I fear it would take me an age to grow used to an open carriage,' sighed Lady Louisa. 'But if he is really deaf – my dear,

there was something I wanted to say to you. That is – no, I don't
want to say it at all, but I think I ought to, for I know Rule never
would.'

Horatia's smile faded. 'Indeed?' she said.

'I detest people who interfere,' said her ladyship hastily, 'but I
do feel you have a right to know why you shouldn't admit Lord
Lethbridge to your friendship.'

'I am aware, L-Louisa,' said Horatia stiffly. 'His r-reputation –'

'It isn't that, my love. Only he, and Rule, and I know, and
Rule won't tell you because he'd never give me away bless him!'

Horatia turned, round-eyed. 'G-give you away, Louisa?'

Lady Louisa sank her voice to a confidential murmur, and
started bravely to tell her sister-in-law just what had happened in
a mad spring-tide seven years ago.

Thirteen

At about the same moment that Lady Louisa was engaged laying bare her past history for Horatia's inspection, Lord Lethbridge was being admitted into a house in Hertford Street. Declining the footman's escort he walked up the stairs to the saloon overlooking the street, where Lady Massey was impatiently awaiting him.

'Well, my dear,' he said, closing the door behind him. 'I am flattered of course, but why am I summoned so urgently?'

Lady Massey was staring out of the window but she wheeled about. 'You had my billet?'

He raised his brows: 'If I had not, Caroline, I should not be here now,' he said. 'It is not my practice to pay morning calls.' He put up his glass and critically surveyed her through it. 'Allow me to tell you, my cherished one, that you are looking something less than your usual incomparable self. Now what can be amiss?'

She took a step towards him. 'Robert, what happened at Ranelagh last night,' she shot at him.

His thin fingers tightened perceptibly about the shaft of his quizzing glass, his eyes, narrowed to mere slits, stared across at her. 'At Ranelagh . . .' he repeated. 'Well?'

'Oh, I was there!' she replied. 'I heard you speak to that little fool. You went into the pavilion. What happened then?'

He had let his glass fall and drawn a snuff-box from his pocket. He tapped it with one finger and opened it. 'And pray what is that to you, Caroline?' he asked.

'Someone said a Scarlet Domino had gone into the smallest

card-room. I saw no one there. I went out on to the terrace. I saw – you, as I thought – cut one of the bride's curls off – oh, that doesn't signify now! She ran out and I went in.' She stopped, pressing her handkerchief to her lips. 'My God, it was Rule!' she said.

Lord Lethbridge took a pinch of snuff, shook away the residue, and raised the pinch first to one nostril, then to the other. 'How very disconcerting for you, my love!' he said blandly. 'I'm sure you betrayed yourself.'

She shuddered. 'I thought it was you. I said – it makes no odds what I said. Then he took off his mask. I was near to swooning.'

Lord Lethbridge shut the snuff-box and dusted his ruffles. 'Very entertaining, Caroline. And I hope it will be a lesson to you not to interfere in my affairs. How I wish I had seen you!'

She reddened angrily, and moved towards a chair. 'You were always spiteful, Robert. But you were at Ranelagh last night, and you wore that scarlet domino. I tell you I saw no other there!'

'There was no other,' replied Lethbridge coolly. He smiled, not very pleasantly. 'What an instructive evening our dear Rule must have spent! And what a fool you are, Caroline! Pray, what did you say to him?'

'It's no matter,' she said sharply. 'Perhaps you lent him your domino? It would be so like you!'

'Now there you are wrong,' he replied with great affability. 'It would not be in the least like me. That domino was wrested from me.'

Her lips curled. 'You permitted it? You let him take your place with the girl? That is not very probable!'

'I had no choice in the matter,' he said. 'I was eliminated in the neatest possible way. Yes, I said "eliminated," Caroline.'

'You take it very calmly!' she remarked.

'Naturally,' he replied. 'Did you suppose I should gnash my teeth?'

She plucked at the folds of her gown. 'Well, are you satisfied? Do you mean to be done with the bride? Is it all over?'

'As far as you are concerned, my dear, I should imagine that it is certainly all over,' he said reflectively. 'Not, of course, that I was privileged to witness your meeting with Rule. But I can guess. I am quite acute, you know.'

She abandoned the sarcastic attitude she had adopted, and stretched out her hand. 'Oh, Robert, can you not see that I am upset?'

'Easily,' he answered. 'So are my plans upset, but I don't permit that to put me in a taking.'

She looked at him, wondering. He had an alert air, his eyes were bright and smiling. No, he was not one to give way to unprofitable emotion. 'What are you going to do?' she asked. 'If Rule means to stop the girl –'

He snapped his fingers. 'I said my plans were upset. I believe it to be quite true.'

'You don't seem to care,' she remarked.

'There are always more plans to be made,' he said. 'Not for you,' he added kindly. 'You may as well make up your mind to that. I am really distressed for you, my dear. Rule must have been so useful.' He eyed her for a moment, and his smile broadened. 'Oh, did you love him, Caroline? That was unwise of you.'

She got up. 'You're abominable, Robert,' she said. 'I must see him. I must make him see me.'

'Do, by all means,' Lethbridge said cordially. 'I wish you may plague him to death; he would dislike that. But you won't get him back, my poor dear. Very well do I know Rule. Would you like to see him humbled? I promise you you shall.'

She walked away to the window. 'No,' she said indifferently.

'Odd!' he commented. 'I assure you, with me it has become quite an obsession.' He came towards her. 'You are not very good company today, Caroline. I shall take my leave of you. Do make Rule a scene and then I will come to see you again, and you shall tell me all about it.' He picked up her hand and kissed it. '*Au revoir*, my love!' he said sweetly, and went out humming a little tune under his breath.

He was on his way home to Half-Moon Street when my Lady

Rule's landaulet turned a corner of the road and came at a smart pace towards him. Horatia, seated alone now, saw him at once, and seemed undecided. Lethbridge swept off his hat and stood waiting for the carriage to draw up.

Something in that calm assumption that she would order her coachman to stop appealed to Horatia. She gave the necessary command and the landaulet came to a standstill beside Lethbridge.

One look at her was enough to assure Lethbridge that she knew just what had happened at Ranelagh. The grey eyes held a gleam of amusement. It annoyed him but he would not let that appear.

'Alas, the jealous husband came off with the honours!' he said.

'He w-was clever, wasn't he?' Horatia agreed.

'But inspired!' Lethbridge said. 'My damp fate was particularly apt. Make him my compliments, I beg of you. I was certainly caught napping.'

She thought that he was taking his humiliating defeat very well, and replied a little more warmly: 'We were b-both caught napping, and p-perhaps it was as well, sir.'

'I blame myself,' he said meditatively. 'Yet I don't know how I could have guessed . . . If I had but been aware of Caroline Massey's presence I might have been more on my guard.'

The arrow struck home as he knew it would. Horatia sat up very straight. 'Lady Massey?'

'Oh, did you not see her! No, I suppose not. It seems that she and Rule laid their heads together to plan our undoing. We must admit they succeeded admirably.'

'It's n-not t-true!' Horatia stammered.

'But –' He broke off artistically, and bowed. 'Why, of course not, ma'am!'

She stared fiercely at him. 'Why did you say that?'

'My dear, I beg a thousand pardons! Don't give it another thought! Depend upon it, it was no such thing.'

'Who told you?' she demanded.

'No one told me,' he said soothingly. 'I merely thought that the fair lady knew a vast deal of what happened last night. But I am sure I was wrong.'

'You w-were wrong!' she said. 'I shall ask R-Rule!'

He smiled. 'An excellent notion, ma'am, if it will set your mind at rest.'

She said rather pathetically: 'You do think he will say it was n-nonsense, don't you?'

'I am quite sure he will,' said Lethbridge, laughing, and stood back to allow the coachman to drive on.

He flattered himself he was an adept at shooting tiny poisonous shafts; certainly that one had gone home. While she assured herself it was a lie Horatia could not help remembering, first Lady Massey's cruel little smile, and second, Rule's own words: *She did indeed know.* And of course now Lethbridge had put her in mind of it she realized that whether the tale was true or not Rule would be bound to deny it. She did not believe it, no, but she could not help thinking about it. She could not rid herself of the idea that as a rival to the beautiful Lady Massey she stood no chance of success. Crosby Drelincourt had been the first to tell her in his oblique fashion that Lady Massey was Rule's mistress, but it was to Theresa Maulfrey that she was indebted for further information. Mrs Maulfrey had never liked her young cousin very much, but she had made a determined attempt to cultivate her friendship as soon as she became a Countess. Unfortunately, Horatia had no more liking for Theresa than Theresa had for her, and perfectly understood the meaning of that lady's sudden amiability. As Charlotte had so shrewdly guessed, Mrs Maulfrey had tried to patronize Horatia and when the gay Countess showed plainly that she stood in no need of patronage she had found herself quite unable to resist the temptation of saying a great many spiteful things. On the subject of Rule and his loves she spoke as a woman of the world, and as such carried weight. Horatia was left with the impression that Rule had been for years the Massey's slave. And, as Mrs Maulfrey so sapiently remarked, a man did not change his mode of life for a chit in her teens. Mrs Maulfrey spoke of him admiringly as an accomplished lover:

Horatia had no notion of swelling the ranks of his conquests. She supposed – for gentlemen were known to be strange in these matters – that he would be quite capable of making love to his wife in the interval between dalliance with widows and opera-dancers. However, since she had married him on the tacit understanding that he might amuse himself as he pleased, she could hardly object now.

So the Earl of Rule, setting out to woo his young wife, found her polite, always gay, but extremely elusive. She treated him in the friendliest way possible – rather, he thought ruefully, as she might treat an indulgent father.

Lady Louisa, considering that the state of affairs was unsatisfactory, took him roundly to task. 'Don't tell me!' she said. 'You're in a fair way to doting on that child! Lord, I'm out of all patience with you! Why don't you make her love you? You seem to be able to do it with any other misguided female, though why I don't know!'

'Ah!' said the Earl. 'But then you are only my sister, Louisa.'

'And don't try to turn it off!' said Lady Louisa wrathfully. 'Make love to the girl! Gracious heaven, why *isn't* she in love with you?'

'Because,' said the Earl slowly, 'I am too old for her.'

'Stuff and fiddle!' snapped her ladyship.

When the Earl went down to Meering a week later he suggested that Horatia should accompany him. Perhaps if Lady Massey had not chosen the previous evening to throw herself in his way Horatia might have wished for nothing better. But Rule and she had gone to Vauxhall Gardens with a snug party of their own contriving, and Lady Massey had gone there also.

It had all been mighty pleasant until after supper. There was music and dancing and everything had been very gay, the supper excellent and the Earl an ideal husband and host. And then it had all gone awry, for when she had tripped off with Mr Dashwood, and Pelham, and Miss Lloyd to look at the cascade, Rule too had left the box and wandered over to greet some friends. Horatia had seen him strolling down one of the paths with Sir Harry Topham, a racing crony. Twenty minutes later she had seen him again, but not with Sir Harry. He was in the Lover's Walk (which made it worse) and standing very close to him and looking up at him in the most melting way was Lady Massey. Even as Horatia caught sight of them the Massey put up her hands to Rule's shoulders.

Horatia had whisked round and declared her intention of walking down quite another path. Miss Lloyd and Pelham had fallen behind; probably Mr Dashwood had not observed the Earl. She had him away from the fatal spot in a trice so that she did not see her husband remove Lady Massey's hands from his shoulders.

No one could have been in greater spirits than my Lady Rule for the rest of that horrid evening. Several people remarked on it, and Mr Dashwood thought her more entrancing than ever.

But when Rule visited her room next morning and sat down on the edge of her bed while she drank her chocolate he found her in a wayward mood. Go to Meering? Oh, no, she could not! Why, she had a hundred engagements and it would be dreadfully dull in the country.

'That is not very complimentary of you,' Rule said, half smiling.

'Well, but Rule, you are only g-going for a week, I daresay, and think how tiresome to pack for such a short stay! Of c-course I shall come with you after the Newmarket m-meeting, if we d-don't go to Bath.'

'I would very much rather you come with me now, Horry.'

'Very w-well,' Horatia said, in the voice of a martyr. 'If you say I m-must, I will.'

He got up. 'Heaven forbid, my dear!'

'R-Rule, if you feel cross about it, please tell me! I d-don't want to be a b-bad wife.'

'Do I look cross?' he inquired.

'N-no, but I never can tell what you think by l-looking at you,' said Horatia candidly.

He laughed. 'Poor Horry, it must be very difficult for you.

Stay in town, my dear. You are probably quite right. Arnold will make me attend to business at Meering.' He put a finger under her chin, and tilted it up. 'Don't game all my fortune away while I am gone, will you?' he said teasingly.

'No, of c-course not. I will be very g-good. And you need not be afraid that I shall encourage Lord Lethbridge, for Louisa told me all about him and I quite see that I m-mustn't know him.'

'I am not afraid of that,' he answered, and bent and kissed her.

Fourteen

So the Earl of Rule went away to Meering accompanied only by Mr Gisborne, while his wife stayed in London and tried to convince herself that she did not miss him at all. If she was not successful in this, at least nobody could have suspected it from her demeanour. Since the big house in Grosvenor Square seemed unbearably empty without his lordship Horatia spent as much of her time as she could away from it. No one meeting her at all the card-parties, routs, drums, and picnics that she attended could have supposed her to be pining most unfashionably for her own husband. In fact, her sister Charlotte said severely that her frivolity was excessively unbecoming.

Lord Lethbridge she had no difficulty in keeping at arm's length. They naturally met at a great many parties, but his lordship, finding Horatia was civil but very formal, seemed to accept with equanimity his relegation to the ranks of her merest acquaintance and made no attempt to win her over again. Horatia put him out of her life without much regret. Glamour might still have clung to a rakehell who abducted noble damsels, but no glamour remained about a man who had been pushed into a pond in full ball-dress. Horatia, sorry only that she never had played cards with him, discarded him without a pang, and proceeded to forget about him.

She was succeeding admirably when he forced himself on her notice again in a manner as unexpected as it was outrageous.

A charming entertainment was held at Richmond House,

with dancing and fireworks. Never was there so elegantly contrived a party. The gardens were brightly illuminated, supper spread in the apartments, and the fireworks let off from a platform of barges anchored in the river to the admiration of the guests and all the unbidden spectators who crowded every near-by house. At midnight a shower of rain came, but since by that time all the fireworks had been finished, it could not be thought to signify, and the guests retired to the ballroom for the dancing.

Horatia left the party early. It had been pretty to see the fireworks, but she found that she did not care to dance. For this a new pair of diamond-embroidered shoes was partly respon-sible. They pinched her abominably, and nothing, she discovered, could so effectually ruin one's enjoyment as an uncomfortable shoe. Her coach was called for shortly after twelve, and resisting all the entreaties of Mr Dashwood, she departed.

She decided she must have attended too many balls, for certainly she had found this one almost tedious. It was really very difficult to dance and chatter gaily when one was all the time wondering what a large, sleepily smiling gentleman was doing miles away in Berkshire. It was apt to make one *distraite,* and to give one a headache. She leaned back in the corner of the coach and closed her eyes. Rule was not coming back for a week. What if one were to take him by surprise, and drive down to Meering the very next day? No, of course one could not do any such thing . . . she would send these shoes back to the makers, and let them make her another pair. The coiffeur too – really, he had dressed her head abominably; there were dozens of pins sticking into her scalp, and the wretch should have known that the Quésaco style did not become her at all. All those heavy plumes bunched up made her look forty if she was a day. And as for the new Serkis rouge Miss Lloyd had induced her to use, it was the horridest stuff in the world, and so she would tell Miss Lloyd the very next time she saw her.

The coach drew up and she opened her eyes with a start. It was raining quite fast now, and the footman was holding an umbrella to protect his mistress's finery. The rain seemed to have extinguished the flambeaux that always burned in iron brackets at the foot of the steps leading up to the front door. It was quite dark, the clouds obscuring what had been a fine moon.

Horatia drew her cloak, an affair of white taffeta with a collar of puffed muslin, tightly round her, and holding her skirts up in one hand, stepped down on to the wet pavement. The footman held the umbrella well over her, and she sped quickly up the steps to the open door.

In her hurry she was over the threshold before she realized her mistake. She gave a gasp and stared round her. She was standing in a narrow hall-way, not in her own house, nor any like it, and the lackey, even now in the act of shutting the door, was no servant of Rule's.

She turned quickly. 'There is a m-mistake,' she said. 'Open the d-door, please!'

A step sounded behind her; she looked over her shoulder and saw Lord Lethbridge.

'A thousand welcomes, my lady!' Lethbridge said, and flung open the door of the saloon. 'Pray enter!'

She stood perfectly still, dawning anger struggling with the bewilderment in her face. 'I don't understand!' she said. 'What does this m-mean, sir?'

'Why, I will tell you, ma'am, but pray come in!' Lethbridge said.

She was aware of the silent lackey behind her; one could not make a scene before servants. After a moment's hesitation she walked forward, and into the saloon.

It was lit by a great many candles, and at one end of the room a table was laid with a cold supper. Horatia frowned. 'If you are giving a p-party, sir, I assure you I was not invited, and d-don't mean to stay,' she announced.

'It is not a party,' he replied, shutting the door. 'It's for you and me, my dear.'

'You must be mad!' said Horatia, gazing at him in perplexity. 'Of c-course I would never c-come to supper with you alone! If

163

you asked me, I vow I never knew of it, and I c-can't imagine why my coachman set me down here.'

'I didn't ask you, Horry. I planned it as a little surprise for you.'

'Then it was a great piece of impertinence!' said Horatia. 'I suppose you b-bribed my coachman? Well, you may escort me out to the coach again, sir, at once!'

He laughed. 'Your coach, my dear, has gone, and your coachman and groom are lying under a table in a tavern off Whitehall. My own men conveyed you here. Now, do you not agree that I planned it very neatly?'

Wrath blazed in Horatia's eyes. 'I think it was m-monstrous of you!' she said. 'Do you m-mean to tell me you had the audacity to overpower my servants?'

'Oh, no!' he answered lightly. 'That would have been unnecessarily violent. While you were at Richmond House, my love, what more natural than that the honest fellows should refresh themselves at the nearest tavern?'

'I d-don't believe it!' snapped Horatia. 'You d-don't know much of Rule if you think he keeps a coachman who gets d-drunk! You m-must have had him set upon, and I shall send for a c-constable in the morning and tell him! Then perhaps you will be sorry!'

'I expect I should be,' agreed Lethbridge. 'But do you think the constable would believe that one tankard of beer apiece could have so disastrous effect on your servants? For you see, I didn't have them overpowered quite as you think.'

'D-drugged!' Horatia cried hotly.

'Precisely,' smiled his lordship. 'Do, I beg of you, let me take your cloak!'

'No!' said Horatia. 'I w-won't! You are quite out of your senses, and if you have not the civility to summon me a chair, I will w-walk home!'

'I wish you would try and understand, Horry,' he said. 'You will not leave my house tonight.'

'N-not leave your house – oh, you *are* m-mad!' Horatia said with conviction.

'Then be mad with me, love,' Lethbridge said, and put his hand on her cloak to remove it.

'D-don't call me "love"!' choked Horatia. 'Why – why you are trying to ruin me!'

'That's as you choose, my dear,' he said. 'I'm ready – yes, I'm ready to run away with you, or you may return home in the morning and tell what tale you please.'

'You m-make a habit of running away with f-females, do you not?' said Horatia.

His brows contracted, but only for a moment. 'So you have that story, have you? Let us say that I make a habit of running away with the females of your family.'

'I,' said Horatia, 'am a W-Winwood, which you will find makes a vast d-difference. You can't force me to elope with you.'

'I shan't try,' he replied coolly. 'Yet I believe we might deal extremely together, you and I. There's something about you, Horry, which is infinitely alluring. I could make you love me you know.'

'N-now I know what is the m-matter with you!' exclaimed Horatia, suddenly enlightened. 'You're drunk!'

'Devil a bit,' answered his lordship. 'Come, give me your cloak!' He twitched it from her as he spoke, and threw it aside, and stood for a moment looking at her through half shut eyes. 'No, you're not beautiful,' he said softly, 'but – damnably seductive, my pretty!'

Horatia took a step backward. 'D-don't come near me!'

'Not come near you!' he repeated. 'Horry, you little fool!'

She tried to dodge away from him, but he caught her, and pulled her roughly into his arms. There was a wild struggle; she got one hand free and dealt him a ringing slap; then he had both her arms clamped to her sides, and kissed her suffocatingly. She managed to jerk her head away, and brought one sharp heel down full on his instep. She felt him flinch, and twisted herself free, hearing the lace at her corsage rip in his clutching fingers. The next moment the table was between them, and Lethbridge was nursing his bruised foot and laughing. 'Gad, you little spitfire!' he said. 'I never dreamed you would show such spirit! Damme, I believe I shan't let you go back to that dull husband of yours after all. Oh, don't scowl so, sweetheart, I'm not going to chase you round the room. Sit down.'

She was by now really frightened, for it seemed to her as though he must be out of his senses. She kept a wary eye on his movements, and decided that the only thing to do was to pretend to humour him. Trying to speak quite steadily, she said: 'If you sit down, so will I.'

'Behold me!' Lethbridge replied, flinging himself into a chair.

Horatia nodded, and followed his example. 'P-please try and be sensible, my l-lord,' she requested. 'It isn't the least use telling me that you are fallen in l-love with me, because I d-don't believe it. Why did you bring me here?'

'To steal your virtue,' he answered flippantly. 'You see, I am quite frank with you.'

'W-well, I can be frank too,' retorted Horatia, her eyes gleaming. 'And if you think you are g-going to ravish m-me, you quite mistake the m-matter! I'm much nearer the door than you are.'

'True, but it is locked, and the key' – he patted his pocket – 'is here!'

'Oh!' said Horatia. 'So you don't even play f-fair!'

'Not in love,' he replied.

'I wish,' said Horatia forcefully, 'you would stop talking about l-love. It makes me feel sick.'

'My dear,' he said, 'I assure you I am falling deeper in love with you every moment.'

She curled her lip. 'Stuff!' she snorted. 'If you l-loved me the l-least little bit, you wouldn't do this to me. And if you did ravish me you would be p-put into prison, if Rule d-didn't kill you first, which I daresay he would do.'

'Ah!' said Lethbridge. 'No doubt I should be put into prison – if you had the courage to tell the world of this night's work. It would be worth it. Oh, it would be worth it, only to know that Rule's damned pride was in the dust!'

Her eyes narrowed; she leaned a little forward, her hands clenched in her lap. 'So that is it!' she said. 'F-fustian, my lord! It would d-do very well at Drury Lane, I d-daresay, but in life, n-no!'

'We can but try,' said Lethbridge. The mockery had vanished, leaving his face very harsh, the mouth set in grim lines, the eyes staring straight ahead.

'I can't imagine how ever I c-could have wanted you for a friend,' said Horatia, meditatively. 'You are d-dreadfully poor-spirited, I think. C-couldn't you find a way of revenge except through a woman?'

'None so exquisitely complete,' Lethbridge answered, unmoved. His gaze travelled to her face. 'But when I look at you, Horry, why, I forget revenge, and desire you for yourself alone.'

'You c-can't imagine how flattered I am,' said Horatia politely.

He burst out laughing. 'You adorable rogue, I believe a man might keep you a twelvemonth and not be tired of you!' He got up. 'Come, Horry, throw in your lot with mine! You were made for something better than to be tied to a man who don't care a rap for you. Come away with me, and I'll teach you what love can be!'

'And then Rule can divorce m-me, and of c-course you'll m-marry me?' suggested Horatia.

'I might even do that,' he concurred. He walked over to the table and picked up one of the bottles that stood on it. 'Let us drink to – the future!' he said.

'Very w-well, sir,' Horatia answered in a voice of deceptive mildness. She had risen when he did, and taken a step towards the empty fireplace. Now, as he stood with his back to her, she bent swiftly and picked up the heavy brass poker that lay there.

Lethbridge was filling the second glass. 'We will go to Italy, if you like,' he said.

'Italy?' said Horatia, tiptoeing forward.

'Why not?'

'B-because I wouldn't go to the end of the street with you!' flashed Horatia, and struck with all her might.

The poker fell with a rather sickening thud. Half horrified, half triumphant, Horatia watched Lethbridge sway a moment, and crash to the ground. The wine-bottle, slipping from his nerveless fingers, rolled over the carpet spilling its contents in a dark ruby flood.

Horatia caught her underlip between her teeth, and went down on her knees beside the limp form, and thrust her hand into the pocket he had patted so confidently. She found the key, and pulled it out. Lethbridge was lying alarmingly still; she wondered whether she had killed him, and shot a frightened look towards the door. No sound disturbed the silence; she realized with a sigh of thankfulness that the servants must have gone to bed, and got up. There was no blood on the poker, and none that she could see on Lethbridge's head, though his wig, gaping up from his forehead, might conceal that. She put the poker back in the grate, caught up her cloak and sped over to the door. Her hand shook so that she could scarcely fit the key into the lock, but she managed it at last, and the next moment was out in the hall, tugging at the bolts of the front door. They scraped noisily, and she cast a quick nervous glance behind her. She got the door open, and wrapping her cloak round her fled down the steps into the street.

There were large puddles in the road, and heavy clouds threatening to obscure the moon, but for the moment it had stopped raining. The road was eerily quiet; blank, shuttered windows on either side, and a little draughty wind sneaking up to whip Horatia's skirts about her ankles.

She set off, almost running in the direction of Curzon Street. She had never in her life been out alone on foot at this hour, and she prayed fervently that she would not meet anyone. She had nearly reached the corner of the street when, to her dismay, she heard voices. She checked, trying to see who these late wayfarers might be. There were two of them, and their progress seemed a little uncertain. Then one of them spoke in a quite unmistakable if slightly thick voice. 'I'll tell you what I'll do,' it said. 'I'll lay you a pony you're wrong!'

Horatia gave a tiny shriek of relief and hurled herself forward, straight into the arms of the astonished roysterer, who reeled under the impact. 'P-Pel!' she sobbed. 'Oh, P-Pel, take me home!'

The Viscount steadied himself by grasping at the railings. He blinked at his sister in a bemused fashion, and suddenly made a discovery. 'Burn it, it's you, Horry!' he said. 'Well, well, well! Do you know my sister, Pom? This is my sister, Lady Rule. Sir Roland Pommeroy, Horry – friend o' mine.'

Sir Roland achieved a beautiful leg. 'Your la'ship's most obedient!' he said.

'P-Pel, will you take me home?' begged Horatia, clasping his wrist.

'Permit me, ma'am!' said Sir Roland, gallantly presenting his arm. 'Should be honoured!'

'Wait a minute,' commanded the Viscount, who was frowning portentously. 'What's the time?'

'I d-don't know, but it m-must be dreadfully late!' said Horatia.

'Not a second after two!' Sir Roland said. 'Can't be after two. We left Monty's at half-past one, didn't we? Very well, then, call it two o'clock.'

'It's more than that,' pronounced the Viscount, 'and if it's more than that, what's bothering me is, what the devil are you doing here, Horry?'

'Pel, Pel!' besought his friend. 'Remember – ladies present!'

'That's what I say,' nodded the Viscount. 'Ladies don't walk about at two in the morning. Where are we?'

Sir Roland thought. 'Half-Moon Street,' he said positively.

'Very well, then,' said the Viscount, 'tell me this: what's my sister doing in Half-Moon Street at two in the morning?'

Horatia, who had listened impatiently to this interchange, gave his wrist a shake. 'Oh, don't stand there talking, P-Pel. I couldn't help it, indeed I couldn't! And I'm dreadfully afraid I've killed Lord Lethbridge!'

'What?'

'K-killed Lord Lethbridge,' shuddered Horatia.

'Nonsense!' said the Viscount.

'It isn't nonsense! I hit him with a p-poker as hard as I could, and he f-fell and lay quite still.'

'Where did you hit him?' demanded the Viscount.

'On the head,' said Horatia.

The Viscount looked at Sir Roland. 'D'you suppose she killed him, Pom?'

'Might have,' said Sir Roland judicially.

'Lay you five to one she didn't,' offered the Viscount.

'Done!' said Sir Roland.

'Tell you what,' said the Viscount suddenly. 'I'm going to see.'

Horatia caught him by the skirts of his coat. 'No, you sh-shan't! You've got to take me home.'

'Oh, very well,' replied the Viscount, relinquishing his purpose. 'But you've no business to go killing people with a poker at two in the morning. It ain't genteel.'

Sir Roland came unexpectedly to Horatia's support. 'Don't see that,' he said. 'Why shouldn't she hit Lethbridge with a poker? You don't like him. I don't like him.'

'No,' said the Viscount, acknowledging the truth of this statement. 'But I wouldn't hit him with a poker. Never heard of such a thing.'

'No more have I,' admitted Sir Roland. 'But I tell you what I think, Pel: it's a good thing.'

'You think that?' said the Viscount.

'I do,' maintained Sir Roland doggedly.

'Well, we'd better go home,' said the Viscount, making another of his sudden decisions.

'Th-thank goodness!' said Horatia, quite exasperated. She took her brother's arm, and turned him in the right direction. 'This way, you stupid, horrid c-creature!'

But the Viscount at that moment caught sight of her elaborate coiffure, with its bunch of nodding plumes, and stopped short. 'I knew there was something mighty queer about you, Horry,' he said. 'What have you done to your hair?'

'N-nothing, it's only a Quésaco. D-do hurry, Pel!'

Sir Roland, interested, bent his head. 'I beg pardon, ma'am, what did you say it was?'

'I s-said it was a Quésaco,' replied Horatia, between tears and laughter. 'And that's Provençal signifying "What does it mean?"'

'Well, what does it mean?' asked the Viscount reasonably.

'Oh, P-Pel, I don't know! Do, do, take me home!'

The Viscount permitted himself to be drawn onward. They traversed Curzon Street without mishap, and Sir Roland remarked that it was a fine night. Neither the Viscount nor his sister paid any heed to this. The Viscount who had been thinking, said: 'I don't say it ain't a good thing if you've killed Lethbridge, but what I can't make out is what brought you here at this time of night?'

Horatia, feeling that in his present condition it was useless to attempt to explain to him, replied: 'I went to the p-party at Richmond House.'

'And was it agreeable, ma'am?' inquired Sir Roland politely.

'Yes, th-thank you.'

'But Richmond House ain't in Half-Moon Street,' the Viscount pointed out.

'She walked home,' explained Sir Roland. 'We were walking home, weren't we? Very well, then. She walked home. Passed Lethbridge's house. Went in. Hit him on the head with the poker. Came out. Met us in the street. There you are. Plain as a pikestaff.'

'Well, I don't know,' said the Viscount. 'Seems queer to me.'

Sir Roland drew nearer to Horatia. 'Deeply regret!' he whispered hoarsely. 'Poor Pel not quite himself.'

'For m-mercy's sake, do hurry!' replied Horatia crossly.

By this time they had reached Grosvenor Square, and it had begun to rain again. The Viscount said abruptly: 'Did you say it was a fine night?'

'I may have,' said Sir Roland cautiously.

'Well, I think it's raining,' announced the Viscount.

'It is raining, and my f-feathers will be ruined!' said Horatia. 'Oh, now what is it Pel?'

The Viscount had stopped. 'Forgotten something,' he said. 'Meant to go and see whether that fellow Lethbridge was dead.'

'P-Pel, it doesn't matter, really it d-doesn't!'

'Yes it does, I've got a bet on it,' replied the Viscount, and plunged off in the direction of Half-Moon Street.

Sir Roland shook his head. 'He shouldn't have gone off like that,' he said severely. 'Lady on his arm – walks off, not a word of apology. Very cool, very cool indeed. Take my arm, ma'am!'

'Thank g-goodness we're there!' said Horatia, hurrying him along.

At the foot of the steps of her own house, she stopped and looked Sir Roland over dubiously. 'I shall have to explain it all to you, I suppose. C-come and see me to-morrow. I mean today. Please remember to c-come! And if I've really k-killed Lord Lethbridge, don't, don't say anything about it!'

'Certainly not,' said Sir Roland. 'Not a word.'

Horatia prepared to ascend the steps. 'And you will go after P-Pelham and take him home, won't you?'

'With the greatest pleasure on earth, ma'am,' said Sir Roland, with a profound bow. 'Happy to be of service!'

Well, at least he doesn't seem to be as drunk as Pelham, thought Horatia, as the sleepy porter opened the door to her knock. And if only I can make him understand how it all happened, and Pelham doesn't do anything foolish, perhaps Rule need never know anything about this.

Slightly cheered by this reflection, she went up the stairs to her bedroom, where a lamp was burning. Picking up a taper, she lit the candles on her dressing-table, and sat down before the mirror, quite worn out. The plumes in her hair were draggled and limp; her corsage was torn. She put her hand to it mechanically, and suddenly her eyes widened in horror. She had been wearing some of the Drelincourt jewels – a set of pearls and diamonds, ear-rings, brooch and bracelets. The ear-rings were there, the bracelets still on her wrists, but the brooch had gone.

Her mind flew back to her struggle in Lethbridge's arms, when her lace had been torn. She stared at her own image in the glass. Under the Serkis rouge she had turned deathly pale. Her face puckered; she burst into tears.

Fifteen

*N*othing intervening to cause the Viscount to swerve from his purpose, he pursued a somewhat erratic course back to Half-Moon Street. Finding the door of Lethbridge's house open, as Horatia had left it, he walked in without ceremony. The door into the saloon was also ajar, and lights shone. The Viscount put his head into the room and looked round.

Lord Lethbridge was seated in a chair by the table, holding his head in his hands. An empty bottle of wine lay on the floor, and a Catogan wig, slightly dishevelled. Hearing a footfall his lordship looked up and stared blankly across at the Viscount.

The Viscount stepped into the room. 'Came to see if you was dead,' he said. 'Laid Pom odds you weren't.'

Lethbridge passed his hand across his eyes. 'I'm not,' he replied in a faint voice.

'No. I'm sorry,' said the Viscount simply. He wandered over to the table and sat down. 'Horry said she killed you, Pom said So she might, I said No. Nonsense.'

Lethbridge, still holding a hand to his aching head, tried to pull himself together. 'Did you?' he said. His eyes ran over his self-invited guest. 'I see. Let me assure you once more that I am very much alive.'

'Well, I wish you'd put your wig on,' complained the Viscount. 'What I want to know is why did Horry hit you on the head with the poker?'

Lethbridge gingerly felt his bruised scalp. 'With a poker was it? Pray ask her, though I doubt if she will tell you.'

'You shouldn't keep the front door open,' said the Viscount. 'What's to stop people coming in and hitting you over the head? It's preposterous.'

'I wish you would go home,' said Lethbridge wearily.

The Viscount surveyed the supper-table with a knowing eye. 'Card-party?' he inquired.

'No.'

At that moment the voice of Sir Roland Pommeroy was heard, calling to his friend. He too put his head round the door, and, perceiving the Viscount, came in. 'You're to come home,' he said briefly. 'Gave my word to my lady I'd take you home.'

The Viscount pointed a finger at his unwilling host. 'He ain't dead, Pom. Told you he wouldn't be.'

Sir Roland turned to look closely at Lethbridge. 'No, he ain't dead,' he admitted with some reluctance. 'Nothing for it but to go home.'

'Blister it, that's a tame way to end the night,' protested the Viscount. 'Play you a game of piquet.'

'Not in this house,' said Lethbridge, picking up his wig and putting it cautiously on his head again.

'Why not in this house?' demanded the Viscount.

The question was destined to remain unanswered. Yet a third visitor had arrived.

'My dear Lethbridge, pray forgive me, but this odious rain! Not a chair to be had, positively not a chair nor a hackney! And your door standing wide I stepped in to shelter. I trust I don't intrude?' said Mr Drelincourt, peeping into the room.

'Oh, not in the least!' replied Lethbridge ironically. 'By all means come in! I rather think that I have no need to introduce Lord Winwood and Sir Roland Pommeroy to you?'

Mr Drelincourt recoiled perceptibly, but tried to compose his sharp features into an expression of indifference. 'Oh, in that case – I had no notion you was entertaining, my lord – you must forgive me!'

'I had no notion of it either,' said Lethbridge. 'Perhaps you would care to play piquet with Winwood?'

'Really, you must hold me excused!' replied Mr Drelincourt, edging towards the door.

The Viscount, who had been regarding him fixedly, nudged Sir Roland. 'There's that fellow Drelincourt,' he said.

Sir Roland nodded. 'Yes, that's Drelincourt,' he corroborated. 'I don't know why, but I don't like him, Pel. Never did. Let's go.'

'Not at all,' said the Viscount with dignity. 'Who asked him to come in? Tell me that! 'Pon my soul, it's a nice thing, so it is, if a fellow can come poking his nose into a private card-party. I'll tell you what I'll do: I'll pull it for him.'

Mr Drelincourt, thoroughly alarmed, cast an imploring glance at Lethbridge, who merely looked saturnine. Sir Roland, however, restrained his friend. 'You can't do that, Pel. Just remembered you fought the fellow. Should have pulled his nose first. Can't do it now.' He looked round the room with a frown. ''Nother thing!' he said. 'It was Monty's card-party, wasn't it? Well, this ain't Monty's house. Knew there was something wrong!'

The Viscount sat up, and addressed himself to Lord Lethbridge with some severity. 'Is this a card-party or is it not?' he demanded.

'It is not,' replied Lethbridge.

The Viscount rose and groped for his hat. 'You should have said so before,' he said. 'If it ain't a card-party, what the devil is it?'

'I've no idea,' said Lethbridge. 'It has been puzzling me for some time.'

'If a man gives a party, he ought to know what kind of party it is,' argued the Viscount. 'If you don't know, how are we to know? It might be a damned soirée, in which case we wouldn't have come. Let's go home, Pom.'

He took Sir Roland's arm and walked with him to the door. There Sir Roland bethought himself of something, and turned back. 'Very pleasant evening, my lord,' he said formally, and bowed, and went out in the Viscount's wake.

176

Mr Drelincourt waited until the two bottle-companions were well out of earshot, and gave a mirthless titter. 'I did not know you was so friendly with Winwood,' he said. 'I do trust I have not broken up your party? But the rain, you know! Not a chair to be had.'

'Rid yourself of the notion that any of you are here by my invitation,' said Lethbridge unpleasantly, and moved across to the table.

Something had caught Mr Drelincourt's eye. He bent, and picked up from under the corner of the Persian rug a ring-brooch of diamonds and pearls of antique design. His jaw dropped; he shot a quick, acute glance at Lethbridge, who was tossing off a glass of wine. The next moment the brooch was in his pocket, and as Lethbridge turned he said airily: 'I beg a thousand pardons! I daresay the rain will have stopped. You must permit me to take my leave.'

'With pleasure,' said Lethbridge.

Mr Drelincourt's eye ran over the supper-table laid for two; he wondered where Lethbridge had hidden his fair visitor. 'Don't, I implore you, put yourself to the trouble of coming to the door!'

'I wish to assure myself that it is shut,' said Lethbridge grimly, and ushered him out.

Some hours later the Viscount awoke to a new but considerably advanced day, with the most imperfect recollections of the night's happenings. He remembered enough, however, to cause him, as soon as he had swallowed some strong coffee, to fling off the bedclothes and spring up, shouting for his valet.

He was sitting before the dressing-table in his shirt-sleeves, arranging his lace cravat, when word was brought to him that Sir Roland Pommeroy was below and desired a word with him.

'Show him up,' said the Viscount briefly, sticking a pin in the cravat. He picked up his solitaire, a narrow band of black ribbon, and was engaged in clipping this round his neck when Sir Roland walked in.

The Viscount looked up and met his friend's eyes in the

mirror. Sir Roland was looking very solemn; he shook his head slightly, and heaved a sigh.

'Don't need you any longer, Corney,' said the Viscount, dismissing his valet.

The door closed discreetly behind the man. The Viscount swung round in his chair, and leaned his arms along the back of it. 'How drunk was I last night?' he demanded.

Sir Roland looked more lugubrious than ever. 'Pretty drunk, Pel. You wanted to pull that fellow Drelincourt's nose.'

'That don't prove I was drunk,' said the Viscount impatiently. 'But I can't get it out of my head that my sister Rule had something to do with it. Did she or did she not say she hit Lethbridge over the head with a poker?'

'A poker, was it?' exclaimed Sir Roland. 'Could not for the life of me remember what it was she said she hit him with! That was it! Then you went off to see if he was dead.' The Viscount cursed softly. 'And I took her la'ship home.' He frowned. 'And what's more, she said I was to wait on her this morning!'

'It's the devil of a business,' muttered the Viscount. 'What in God's name was she doing in the fellow's house?'

Sir Roland coughed. 'Naturally – needn't tell you – can rely on me, Pel. Awkward affair – mum's the word.'

The Viscount nodded. 'Mighty good of you, Pom. I'll have to see my sister first thing. You'd best come with me.'

He got up and reached for his waistcoat. Someone scratched on the door, and upon being told to come in, the valet entered with a sealed letter on a salver. The Viscount picked it up and broke the seal.

The note was from Horatia, and was evidently written in great agitation. *Dear Pel: The most Dredful thing has happened. Please come at once. I am quite Distracted. Horry.*

'Waiting for an answer?' the Viscount asked curtly.

'No, my lord.'

'Then send a message to the stables, will you, and tell Jackson to bring the phaeton round.'

Sir Roland, who had watched with concern the reading of the

note, thought he had rarely seen his friend turn so pale, and coughed a second time. 'Pel, dear old boy – must remind you – she hit him with the poker. Laid him out, you know.'

'Yes,' said the Viscount, looking a trifle less grim. 'So she did. Help me into my coat, Pom. We'll drive round to Grosvenor Square now.'

When, twenty minutes later, the phaeton drew up outside Rule's house, Sir Roland said that perhaps it would be better if he did not come in, so the Viscount entered the house alone, and was shown at once to one of the smaller saloons. Here he found his sister, looking the picture of despair.

She greeted him without recrimination. 'Oh, P-Pel, I'm so glad you've come! I am quite undone, and you must help me!'

The Viscount laid down his hat and gloves, and said sternly: 'Now, Horry, what happened last night? Don't put yourself in a taking: just tell me!'

'Of c-course I'm going to tell you!' said Horatia. 'I w-went to Richmond House to the b-ball and the fireworks.'

'Never mind about the fireworks,' interrupted the Viscount. 'You weren't at Richmond House, nor anywhere near it, when I met you.'

'No, I was in Half-Moon Street,' said Horatia innocently.

'You went to Lethbridge's house?'

At the note of accusation in her brother's voice, Horatia flung up her head. 'Yes, I did, but if you think I w-went there of my own choice you are quite odious!' Her lip trembled. 'Though w-why you should believe that I didn't, I can't imagine, for it's the stupidest tale you ever heard, and I know it d-doesn't sound true.'

'Well, what is the tale?' he asked, drawing up a chair.

She dabbed at her eyes with the corner of her handkerchief. 'You see, my shoes p-pinched me, and I left the b-ball early, and it was raining. My c-coach was called, and I suppose I never looked at the footman – indeed, why should I?'

'What the devil has the footman to do with it?' demanded the Viscount.

'Everything,' said Horatia. 'He w-wasn't the right one.'

'I don't see what odds that makes.'

'I m-mean he wasn't one of our servants at all. The c-coachman wasn't either. They were L-Lord Lethbridge's.'

'What?' ejaculated the Viscount, his brow growing black as thunder.

Horatia nodded. 'Yes, and they drove me to his house. And I w-went in before I realized.'

The Viscount was moved to expostulate: 'Lord, you must have known it wasn't your house!'

'I tell you I didn't! I know it sounds stupid, but it was raining, and the f-footman held the umbrella so that I c-couldn't see m-much and I was inside b-before I knew.'

'Did Lethbridge open the door?'

'N-no, the porter did.'

'Then why the devil didn't you walk out again?'

'I know I should have,' confessed Horatia, 'but then Lord Lethbridge came out of the s-saloon, and asked me to step in. And, P-Pel, I didn't understand; I thought it was a m-mistake, and I d-didn't want to make a scene before the p-porter, so I went in. Only n-now I see how foolish it was of me, because if Rule comes to hear of it, and m-makes inquiries, the servants will say I went in w-willingly and so I did!'

'Rule mustn't hear of this,' said the Viscount grimly.

'No, of c-course he mustn't, and that's why I sent for you.'

'Horry, what happened in the saloon? Come, let me hear the whole of it!'

'It was d-dreadful! He said he w-was going to ravish me, and oh, Pel, it was just to revenge himself on R-Rule! So I p-pretended I might run away with him, and as soon as he turned his back, I hit him with the p-poker and escaped.'

The Viscount drew a sigh of relief. 'That's all, Horry?'

'No, it isn't all,' said Horatia desperately. 'My g-gown was torn when he k-kissed me, and though I d-didn't know till I got home, my brooch fell out, and, P-Pel, he's got it now!'

'Make yourself easy,' said the Viscount, getting up. 'He won't have it long.'

Catching sight of his face, which wore a starkly murderous expression, Horatia cried out: 'What are you going to do?'

'Do?' said the Viscount, with a short, ugly laugh. 'Cut the dog's heart out!'

Horatia sprung up suddenly. 'P-Pel, you can't! For g-goodness' sake don't fight him! You know he's m-much better than you are, and only think of the scandal! P-Pel, you'll ruin me if you do! You can't do it!'

The Viscount checked in bitter disgust. 'You're right,' he said. 'I can't. Fiend seize it, there must be some way of forcing a quarrel on him without bringing you into it!'

'If you fight him everyone will say it was about m-me, because after you f-fought Crosby people t-talked, and I did silly things – oh, you mustn't, P-Pel. It's b-bad enough with Sir Roland knowing –'

'Pom!' exclaimed the Viscount. 'We'll have him in! He might have a notion how I can manage it.'

'Have him in? W-why, where is he?'

'Outside with the phaeton. You needn't mind him, Horry; he's devilish discreet.'

'W-well, if you think he could help us, he can c-come in,' said Horatia dubiously. 'But p-please explain it all to him, first, P-Pel, for he must be thinking the most d-dreadful things about me.'

Accordingly, when the Viscount returned presently to the saloon with Sir Roland, that worthy had been put in possession of all the facts. He bowed over Horatia's hand, and embarked on a somewhat involved apology for his inebriety the night before. The Viscount cut him short. 'Never mind about that!' he adjured him. 'Can I call Lethbridge out?'

Sir Roland devoted deep thought to this, and after a long pause pronounced the verdict. 'No,' he said.

'I m-must say, you've got m-much more sense than I thought,' said Horatia approvingly.

'Do you mean to tell me,' demanded the Viscount, 'that I'm to sit by while that dog kidnaps my sister, and do nothing? No, damme, I won't!'

'Devilish hard on you, Pel,' agreed Sir Roland sympathetically. 'But it won't do, you know. Called Drelincourt out. Deal of talk over that. Call Lethbridge out – fatal!'

The Viscount smote the table with his fist. 'Hang you, Pom, do you realize what the fellow did?' he cried.

'Very painful affair,' said Sir Roland. 'Bad *ton*. Must hush it up.'

The Viscount seemed to be bereft of words.

'Hush it up now,' said Sir Roland. 'Talk dies down – say three months. Pick a quarrel with him then.'

The Viscount brightened. 'Ay, so I could. That solves it.'

'S-solves it? It doesn't!' declared Horatia. 'I m-must get my brooch back. If Rule m-misses it, it will all come out.'

'Nonsense!' said her brother. 'Say you dropped it in the street.'

'It's no good saying that! I tell you Lethbridge means m-mischief. He may wear it, just to m-make Rule suspicious.'

Sir Roland was shocked. 'Bad blood!' he said. 'Never did like the fellow.'

'What sort of brooch is it?' asked the Viscount. 'Would Rule be likely to recognize it?'

'Yes, of c-course he would! It's part of a set, and it's very old – fifteenth century, I think.'

'In that case,' decided his lordship, 'we've got to get it back. I'd best go and see Lethbridge at once – though how I'll keep my hands off him I don't know. Burn it, a pretty fool I look, calling on him last night!'

Sir Roland was once more plunged in thought. 'Won't do,' he said at last. 'If you go asking for a brooch, Lethbridge is bound to guess it's my lady's. I'll go.'

Horatia looked at him with admiration. 'Yes, that would be m-much better,' she said. 'You are very helpful, I think.'

Sir Roland blushed, and prepared to set forth on his mission. 'Beg you won't give it a thought, ma'am. Affair of delicacy – tact required – a mere nothing!'

'Tact!' said the Viscount. 'Tact for a hound like Lethbridge!

My God, it makes me sick, so it does! You'd better take the phaeton; I'll wait for you here.'

Sir Roland once more bowed over Horatia's hand. 'Shall hope to put the brooch in your hands within half an hour, ma'am,' he said, and departed.

Left alone with his sister, the Viscount began to pace about the room, growling something under his breath whenever he happened to think of Lethbridge's iniquity. Presently he stopped short. 'Horry, you'll have to tell Rule. Damme, he's a right to know!'

'I c-can't tell him!' Horatia answered with suppressed passion. 'Not again!'

'Again?' said his lordship. 'What do you mean?'

Horatia hung her head, and recounted haltingly the story of the ridotto at Ranelagh. The Viscount was delighted with at least one part of the story, and slapped his leg with glee.

'Yes, b-but I didn't know it was Rule, and so I had to confess it all to him next d-day and I won't – I won't make another c-confession! I said I w-wouldn't see anything of Lethbridge while he was away and I can't, I c-can't tell him about this!'

'I don't see it,' said the Viscount. 'Plenty to bear you out. Coachman – what happened to him, by the way?'

'D-drugged,' she replied.

'All the better,' said his lordship. 'If the coach came back to the stables without him, obviously you're telling the truth.'

'But it didn't! He was too clever,' said Horatia bitterly. 'I had the c-coachman in this morning. He thinks it was the b-bad beer, and the coach was taken back to the tavern. So I said I had been forced to get a link-boy to summon me a hackney. And I d-didn't think it was quite fair to send him off when I knew he and the footman had been d-drugged, so I said this time I wouldn't tell Rule.'

'That's bad,' said the Viscount, frowning. 'Still, Pom and I know you hit Lethbridge on the head, and got away.'

'It's no good,' she said mournfully. 'Of c-course you would be bound to stand by me, and that's what Rule would think.'

'But hang it, Horry, why should he?'

'Well, I – well, I w-wasn't very nice to him b-before he went away, and he wanted me to g-go with him and I wouldn't, and d-don't you see, P-Pel, it looks as if I p-planned it all, and hadn't really given up Lethbridge at all? And I l-left that horrid b-ball early, to make it worse!'

'It don't look well, certainly,' admitted the Viscount. 'Have you quarrelled with Rule?'

'No. N-not quarrelled. Only – No.'

'You'd best tell me, and be done with it,' said his lordship severely. 'I suppose you've been up to your tricks again. I warned you he wouldn't stand for 'em.'

'It isn't that at all!' flamed Horatia. 'Only I f-found out that he had planned the R-Ranelagh affair with that odious Lady M-Massey.'

The Viscount stared at her. 'You're raving!' he said calmly.

'I'm not. She was there, and she knew!'

'Who told you he planned it with her?'

'W-well, no one precisely, but Lethbridge thought so, and of course I realized –'

'Lethbridge!' interrupted the Viscount with scorn. 'Upon my word, you're a damned little fool, Horry! Lord don't be so simple! A man don't plot with his mistress against his wife. Never heard such a pack of nonsense!'

Horatia sat up. 'P-Pel, do you really think so?' she asked wistfully. 'B-but I can't help remembering that he said *she d-did indeed know* it was he all the t-time.'

The Viscount regarded her with frank contempt. 'Well if he said that it proves she wasn't in it – if it needs proof, which it don't. Lord, Horry, I put it to you, would he be likely to say that if she'd had a finger in the pie? What's more, it explains why the Massey's gone off to Bath so suddenly. Depend on it, if she found out it was he in the scarlet domino they had some sort of a scene, and Rule's not the man to stand that. Wondered what happened to make her go off in such a devil of a hurry. Here, what the deuce – ?' For Horatia, with a sudden squeak of joy, had flung herself into his arms.

'Don't do that,' said the Viscount testily, disengaging himself.

'Oh, P-Pel, I never thought of that!' sighed Horatia.

'You're a little fool,' said the Viscount.

'Yes, I see I am,' she confessed. 'B-but if he has b-broken with that woman, it makes me more than ever decided not to tell him about l-last night.'

The Viscount thought this over. 'I must say it's a devilish queer story,' he said. 'Daresay you're right. If we can get that brooch back you're safe enough. If Pom don't succeed –' His lip tightened, and he nodded darkly.

Sir Roland, meanwhile, had arrived in Half-Moon Street, and was fortunate enough to find Lord Lethbridge at home.

Lethbridge received him in a gorgeous flowered dressing-gown. He did not look to be much the worse for the blow he had received, and he greeted Sir Roland with suave amiability. 'Pray sit down, Pommeroy,' he said. 'To what do I owe this unexpected honour?'

Sir Roland accepted the chair, and proceeded to display his tact. 'Most unfortunate thing,' he said. 'Last night – not quite myself, you know – lost a brooch. Must have dropped out of my cravat.'

'Oh?' said Lethbridge, looking at him rather hard. 'A pin, in fact?'

'Not a pin, no. A brooch. Family jewels – sometimes wear it – don't care to lose it. So I came round to see if I dropped it here.'

'I see. And what is it like, this brooch?'

'Ring-brooch; inner circle pearls and openwork bosses, outer row pearls and diamonds,' said Sir Roland glibly.

'Indeed? A lady's ornament, one would almost infer.'

'Belonged to my great-aunt,' said Sir Roland, extricating himself from that predicament with masterly skill.

'Ah, no doubt you value it highly then,' remarked his lordship sympathetically.

'Just so,' said Sir Roland. 'Sentiment, you know. Should be glad to put my hand on it again.'

'I regret infinitely that I am unable to help you. May I suggest that you look for it in Montacute's house? I think you said you spent the evening there?'

'I didn't lose it there,' replied Sir Roland firmly. 'Naturally went there first.'

Lethbridge shrugged. 'How very unfortunate! I fear you must have dropped it in the street.'

'Not in the street, no. Remember having it on just before I came here.'

'Dear me!' said Lethbridge. 'What makes you remember so particularly?'

Sir Roland took a moment to think this out. 'Remember it because Pel said: "That's a queer tie-pin, Pom." And I said: "Belonged to my great-aunt." Then we came here. Must have had it on then.'

'It would certainly seem so. But perhaps you lost it after you left my house. Or do you remember that Winwood then said: "Where's your tie-pin?" '

'That's it,' said Sir Roland, grateful for the assistance. 'Pel said: "Why, what's become of your tie-pin, Pom?" Didn't come back – time getting on, you know. Knew it would be safe here!'

Lethbridge shook his head. 'I fear your recollection is not very clear, Pommeroy. I have not got your brooch.'

There was nothing for Sir Roland to do after that but to take his leave. Lord Lethbridge escorted him out into the hall, and sweetly bade him farewell. 'And do pray advise me if you succeed in finding the brooch,' he said with great civility. He watched his crestfallen visitor go off down the steps, and transferred his gaze to the porter's face. 'Send Moxton to me,' he said, and went back into the saloon.

In a few moments his butler appeared. 'My lord?'

'When this room was swept this morning, was a brooch found?' asked Lethbridge.

The lids descended discreetly over the butler's eyes. 'I have not heard of it, my lord.'

'Make inquiries.'

'Yes, my lord.'

While the butler was out of the room, Lethbridge stood looking out of the window, slightly frowning. When Moxton came back he turned. 'Well?'

'No, my lord.'

The frown lingered. 'Very well,' Lethbridge said.

The butler bowed. 'Yes, my lord. Your lordship's luncheon is served.'

Lethbridge went into the dining-room, still attired in his dressing-gown, still wearing a thoughtful, puzzled look on his face.

He sat for some time over his meal, absently sipping his port. He was not, as he had told Caroline Massey, the man to gnash his teeth over his own discomfiture, but the miscarriage of last night's plans had annoyed him. That little vixen wanted taming. The affair had become tinged, in his mind, with a sporting element. Horatia had won the first encounter; it became a matter of supreme importance to force a second one, which she would not win. The brooch seemed to present him with the opportunity he lacked – if only he could lay his hand on it.

His mind went back; his acute memory re-created for him the sound of ripping lace. He raised his glass to his lips, savouring the port. Ah, yes, undoubtedly the brooch had been lost then. No doubt a distinctive trinket, possibly part of the Drelincourt jewels. He smiled a little, picturing Horatia's dismay. It could be turned into a shrewd weapon, that ring-brooch – wielded in the right hands.

The brooch was not in his house, unless his servants were lying. He did not, for more than a fleeting moment, suspect any of them of theft. They had been with him some years; probably knew that he was an ill master to cheat.

The image of Mr Drelincourt's face flashed across his mind. He set down his glass. Crosby. Such a sharp-eyed fellow, Crosby. But had he had the opportunity to pick up a brooch from the floor unseen? He went over his movements during that brief visit. Crosby's arrival: no chance then. The departure of Winwood and Pommeroy. Had he taken them to the door? No. Still no chance for Crosby. Some talk he had had with him, not very much, for his head had been aching furiously, and then what? His fingers closed again around the stem of his glass, and instantly he remembered drinking a glass of wine to steady himself. Yes, certainly a chance for Crosby then. He had tossed off the wine, and turned. Now, had Crosby had one hand in his pocket? The picture lived again; he could see Crosby standing behind a chair, looking at him, withdrawing his hand from his pocket.

Really, it was quite amusing. There was no proof, of course, not a shadow of proof, but perhaps a visit to Crosby might be not unfruitful. Yes, one might hazard a guess that the brooch was an heirloom. Crosby – an astute fellow: quite needle-sharp – would recognize a Drelincourt heirloom. Decidedly a visit to Crosby was likely to repay one for one's trouble. Crosby, no doubt, was hatching a little plan to make mischief between Rule and his bride. Well, he would spare Crosby the pains. There should be mischief enough, but more mischief than the mere displaying of a brooch.

He got up from the table, and went in a leisurely fashion up the stairs, still revolving these delectable thoughts in his head. What a surprise for dear Crosby to receive a call from my Lord Lethbridge! He rang his hand-bell for his valet, and discarding his dressing-gown, sat down before the mirror to complete his elaborate toilet.

On his way, an hour later, to Mr Drelincourt's lodging, he looked in at White's but was told upon inquiry that Mr Drelincourt had not been into the Club that day. He went on towards Jermyn Street, twirling his ebony cane.

Mr Drelincourt lived in a house owned by a retired gentleman's gentleman, who himself opened the door to his lordship. He said that Mr Drelincourt was gone out.

'Perhaps,' said his lordship, 'you can give me his direction.'

Oh, yes, that could easily be done. Mr Drelincourt was gone out of town, and had taken a small cloak-bag with him.

'Out of town, eh?' said his lordship, his eyes narrowing. He drew a guinea from his pocket, and began to juggle gently with it. 'I wonder, can you tell me where, out of town?'

'Yes, my lord. To Meering,' replied Mr Bridges. 'Mr Drelincourt desired me to hire a post-chaise for him, and set off at two o'clock. If your lordship had come twenty minutes ago, you'd have caught him.'

Lethbridge dropped the guinea into his hand. 'I may still catch him,' he said, and ran lightly down the steps of the house.

Hailing a hackney, he had himself driven back to Half-Moon Street. His household found itself goaded into sudden activity; a footman was sent off to the stables to order my lord's light post-chaise and four to be brought round immediately, and my lord went upstairs, calling to his valet to bestir himself, and lay out a travelling dress. In twenty minutes his lordship, now clad in a coat of brown cloth, with his sword at his side, and top-boots on his feet, came out of the house again, gave his postilions certain pithy instructions, and climbed up into the chaise, a light carriage very like a sedan, slung on whip springs over very high wheels. As the equipage rounded the corner into Piccadilly, heading westwards, his lordship leaned back at his ease, calm in the knowledge that no hired post-chaise and four could hope to reach Meering, even with an hour's start, before being overtaken by him.

Sixteen

*M*r Drelincourt, as it happened, had no idea that Lord Lethbridge could be on his heels.

Not dreaming that anybody, least of all my Lord Lethbridge, had discovered his theft of the brooch, he saw no need to make haste down to Meering, and put off starting on his journey until after luncheon. Mr Drelincourt, though lavish in dress and some matters, was very careful how he spent money on small items. The hiring of a chaise to carry him thirty-three miles into the country cost him a pang, and to pay, on top of that, possibly as much as four or five shillings for lunch at an inn would have seemed to him a gross extravagance. By lunching at his lodgings he would not be put to the necessity of baiting on the road at all, for he thought he would arrive at Meering in time to dine with his cousin. He would put up for the night there, and if Rule did not offer him one of his own carriages for his return it would be a shabby piece of behaviour, and one which he did not at all anticipate, for Rule, to do him justice, was not mean, and must be well aware that the charges for a post-chaise would be lightened if it made the return journey empty.

It was in a pleasurable frame of mind that Mr Drelincourt set forward upon his journey. The day was fine, quite ideal for a drive into the country, and after he had let down the window in the door in front of him to order the postilions not to ride at such a rattling pace, he had nothing to do but to lean back and admire the scenery or indulge his imagination in agreeable reflection.

It was not to be supposed that there was any portion of the

Drelincourt inheritance unknown to Mr Drelincourt. He had recognized the brooch in a flash, and could have recited unerringly the different pieces which comprised that particular set of jewels. When he had stooped so quickly to pick it up he had had no very clear idea in his head of what he meant to do with it, but a night's repose had brought him excellent counsel. He had no doubt at all that Horatia had been concealed somewhere in Lethbridge's house; the brooch proved that to his satisfaction, and ought to prove it to Rule's satisfaction also. He had always thought Horatia a jade; for his part he was not in the least surprised (though shocked) to discover that she had taken advantage of Rule's absence to spend the night in her lover's arms. Rule, who was always too stupidly sleepy to see what was going on under his nose, would probably be greatly surprised, and even more shocked than his cousin, whose obvious and not too painful duty it was to appraise him of his wife's loose conduct at once. There could be only one course open to his lordship then, and Mr Drelincourt was inclined to think that after so disastrous a venture into matrimony, he would hardly risk another.

Altogether the world seemed a better place to Mr Drelincourt this mild September day than it had seemed for several months.

Not in the general way a keen student of Nature, he was moved today to admire the russet tints in the trees, and to approve from the well-sprung chaise the bursts of fine country through which he passed.

Meering being situated near Twyford, in the county of Berkshire, the road to it led out of town by way of Knightsbridge and Hammersmith to Turnham Green and Hounslow, where at the George Inn the chaise stopped to change horses. The two postilions, who had formed the poorest opinion of Mr Drelincourt from the moment of his commanding them not to drive too fast, were disgusted by his conduct at the George, for instead of getting down to drink a glass of Nantes brandy, and allowing them time also to refresh themselves, he sat tight in the chaise, and never gave the ostler so much as a groat.

The second stage was Slough, ten miles farther on. The chaise set forward again, drawing out of Hounslow on to the heath, a tract of wild land so ill-famed that for several unpleasant minutes Mr Drelincourt sat wishing that he had gone to the expense of hiring a guard to accompany the chaise. Nothing untoward happened, however, and he was soon being driven over Cranford Bridge in the direction of Longford.

At Slough Mr Drelincourt got down to stretch his legs, while the horses were changed. The landlord, who had come bustling out of the Crown Inn as a good landlord should on the approach of a gentleman's chaise, allowed the jolly smile to fade from his face at the sight of Mr Drelincourt, and abated a little of his welcoming civility. Mr Drelincourt was well known upon this road, and no favourite with honest landlords. Since he was my Lord of Rule's relative, Mr Copper went through the form of suggesting refreshment, but upon this being refused, he went back to his inn, remarking to his wife that the one thing in life that beat him was how a genial, open-handed gentleman like his lordship came to have such a mean worm as Mr Drelincourt for his cousin.

After Slough, the road ran by way of Salt Hill to Maidenhead. A mile further on, at Maidenhead Thicket, it branched off from the Worcester way, and took the Bath Road to Hare Hatch and Twyford.

The chaise had passed through Maidenhead, and was bowling along at a respectable pace towards the Thicket, when one of the postilions became aware of a second chaise some way behind. A bend in the road enabled him to get a glimpse of it. He said over his shoulder to the other postilion: 'Lordy, that'll be the Quality, sure enough! Springing his horses, he is. No good racing him with our precious Missy squawking at the back of us.'

The lad riding one of the wheelers understood him to refer to Mr Drelincourt, and agreed, though regretfully, that they had better draw into the side and let the Quality go by.

The thunder of hooves galloping in the rear soon penetrated

to Mr Drelincourt's ears and caused him to rap with his cane on the window, and upon the postilion's looking over his shoulder, to signal to him to draw in to the side of the road. Mr Drelincourt had had experience of good-for-nothing lads who raced their horses against other chaises, and he disapproved strongly of this pastime.

The second chaise rapidly overhauled the first and swung past in a little cloud of dust struck up by the galloping hooves. Mr Drelincourt had the briefest view of it but caught sight of the flash of a crest on one of the panels. He felt much annoyed with the unknown traveller for driving at such a pace, and was uneasily hoping that his postilions were able to control their own horses (which showed signs of wishing to dash off after the other chaise) when he saw that the other chaise was pulling up ahead of them. That seemed very strange to him, for there was no apparent reason to account for it. It seemed stranger still when the horses wheeled and backed, and wheeled again, till the chaise lay right across the road, effectively barring the way.

Mr Drelincourt's postilions, also observing this manœuvre, supposed the other chaise to have overshot its objective, and to be about to turn round again. They reined their horses to a walk. But the crested chaise remained across the road, and they were forced to come to a standstill.

Mr Drelincourt, considerably astonished, sat forward to see more closely, and called to his postilions: 'What is it? Why don't they go on? Is it an accident?'

Then he saw Lord Lethbridge spring down from the other chaise, and he shrank back in his seat, his heart jumping with fright.

Lethbridge walked up to Mr Drelincourt's equipage, and that shivering gentleman pulled himself together with an effort. It would not do for him to cower in the corner, so he leaned forward and let down the window. 'Is it you, indeed, my lord?' he said in a high voice. 'I could scarce believe my eyes! What can have brought you out of town?'

'Why, you, Crosby, you!' said his lordship mockingly. 'Pray

step down out of that chaise. I should like to have a little talk with you.'

Mr Drelincourt clung to the window frame and gave an unnatural laugh. 'Oh, your pleasantries, my lord! I am on my way to Meering, you know, to my cousin's. I – I think it is already five o'clock, and he dines at five.'

'Crosby, come down!' said Lethbridge, with such an alarming glitter in his eyes that Mr Drelincourt was quite cowed, and began to fumble with the catch of the door. He climbed down carefully, under the grinning stare of his postilions. 'I vow I can't imagine what you was wanting to say to me,' he said. 'And I am late, you know. I ought to be on my way.'

His arm was taken in an ungentle grip. 'Walk with me a little way, Crosby,' said his lordship. 'Do you not find these country roads quite charming? I am sure you do. And so you are bound for Meering? Was not that a rather sudden decision, Crosby?'

'Sudden?' stammered Mr Drelincourt, wincing at the pressure of his lordship's fingers above his elbow. 'Oh, not at all, my lord, not in the least! I told Rule I might come down. I have had it in mind some days, I assure you.'

'It has nothing to do, of course, with a certain brooch?' purred Lethbridge.

'A b-brooch? I don't understand you, my lord!'

'A ring-brooch of pearls and diamonds, picked up in my house last night,' said his lordship.

Mr Drelincourt's knees shook. 'I protest, sir, I – I am at a loss! I –'

'Crosby, give me that brooch,' said Lethbridge menacingly.

Mr Drelincourt made an attempt to pull his arm away. 'My lord, I don't understand your tone! I tell you frankly, I don't like it. I don't take your meaning.'

'Crosby,' said his lordship, 'you will give me that brooch, or I will take you by the scruff of your neck and shake you like the rat you are!'

'Sir!' said Mr Drelincourt, his teeth chattering together, 'this is monstrous! Monstrous!'

'It is indeed monstrous,' agreed his lordship. 'You are a thief, Mr Crosby Drelincourt.'

Mr Drelincourt flushed scarlet. 'It was not your brooch, sir!'

'Or yours!' swiftly replied Lethbridge. 'Hand it over!'

'I – I have called a man out for less!' blustered Crosby.

'That's your humour, is it?' said Lethbridge. 'It's not my practice to fight with thieves; I use a cane instead. But I might make an exception in your case.'

To Mr Drelincourt's horror, he thrust forward his sword hilt and patted it. That unfortunate gentleman licked his lips and said quaveringly: 'I shall not fight you, sir. The brooch is more mine than yours!'

'Hand it over!' said Lethbridge.

Mr Drelincourt hesitated, read a look in his lordship's face there was no mistaking, and slowly inserted his finger and thumb into his waistcoat pocket. The next moment the brooch lay in Lethbridge's hand.

'Thank you, Crosby,' he said, in a way that made Mr Drelincourt long for the courage to hit him. 'I thought I should be able to persuade you. You may now resume your journey to Meering – if you think it still worthwhile. If you don't – you may join me at the Sun in Maidenhead, where I propose to dine and sleep. I almost feel I owe you a dinner for spoiling your game so unkindly.' He turned, leaving Mr Drelincourt speechless with indignation, and walked back to his chaise, which had by this time drawn up to the side of the road, facing towards London again. He climbed lightly into it and drove off, airily waving his hand to Mr Drelincourt, still standing in the dusty road.

Mr Drelincourt gazed after him, rage seething up in him. Spoiled his game, had he? There might be two words to that! He hurried back to his own chaise, saw the looks of rich enjoyment on the postilions' faces, and swore at them to drive on.

It was only six miles to Meering from the Thicket, but by the time the chaise turned in at the Lodge gates it was close on six o'clock. The house was situated a mile from the gates, in the middle of a very pretty park, but Mr Drelincourt was in no mood to admire the fine oaks, and rolling stretches of turf, and sat in a fret of impatience while his tired horses drew him up the long avenue to the house.

He found his cousin and Mr Gisborne lingering over their port in the dining-room, which apartment was lit by candles. It might be broad daylight outside, but my lord had a constitutional dislike of dining by day, and excluded it by having the heavy curtains drawn across the windows.

Both he and Mr Gisborne were in riding-dress. My lord was lounging in a high-backed chair at the head of the table, one leg, encased in a dusty top-boot, thrown negligently over the arm. He looked up as the footman opened the door to admit Mr Drelincourt, and for a moment sat perfectly still, the look of good humour fading from his face. Then he picked up his quizzing-glass with some deliberation, and surveyed his cousin through it. 'Dear me!' he said. 'Now why?'

This was not a very promising start, but his anger had chased from Mr Drelincourt's mind all memory of his last meeting with the Earl, and he was undaunted. 'Cousin,' he said, his words tripping over one another. 'I am here on a matter of grave moment. I must beg a word with you alone!'

'I imagine it must indeed be of grave moment to induce you to come over thirty miles in pursuit of me,' said his lordship.

Mr Gisborne got up. 'I will leave you, sir.' He bowed slightly to Mr Drelincourt, who paid not the slightest heed to him, and went out.

Mr Drelincourt pulled a chair out from under the table and sat down. 'I regret extremely, Rule, but you must prepare yourself for most unpleasant tidings. If I did not consider it my duty to apprise you of what I have discovered, I should shrink from the task!'

The Earl did not seem to be alarmed. He still sat at his ease, one hand lying on the table, the fingers crooked round the stem of his wine-glass, his calm gaze resting on Mr Drelincourt's face. 'This self-immolation on the altar of duty is something new to me,' he remarked. 'I daresay my nerves will prove strong enough to enable me to hear your tidings with – I trust – tolerable equanimity.'

'I trust so, Rule, I do indeed trust so!' said Mr Drelincourt, his eyes snapping. 'You are pleased to sneer at my notion of duty –'

'I hesitate to interrupt you, Crosby, but you may have noticed that I never sneer.'

'Very well, cousin, very well! Be that as it may, you will allow that I have my share of family pride.'

'Certainly, if you tell me so,' replied the Earl gently.

Mr Drelincourt flushed. 'I do tell you so! Our name – our honour, mean as much to me as to you, I believe! It is on that score that I am here now.'

'If you have come all this way to inform me that the catch-polls are after you, Crosby, it is only fair to tell you that you are wasting your time.'

'Very humorous, my lord!' cried Mr Drelincourt. 'My errand, however, concerns you more nearly than that! Last night – I should rather say this morning, for it was long past two by my watch – I had occasion to visit my Lord Lethbridge.'

'That is, of course, interesting,' said the Earl. 'It seems an odd hour for visiting, but I have sometimes thought, Crosby, that you are an odd creature.'

Mr Drelincourt's bosom swelled. 'There is nothing very odd, I think, in sheltering from the rain!' he said. 'I was upon my way to my lodging from South Audley Street, and chanced to turn down Half-Moon Street. I was caught in a shower of rain, but observing the door of my Lord Lethbridge's house to stand – inadvertently, I am persuaded – ajar, I stepped in. I found his lordship in a dishevelled condition in the front saloon, where a vastly elegant supper was spread, covers, my lord, being laid for two.'

'You shock me infinitely,' said the Earl, and leaning a little forward, picked up the decanter and refilled his glass.

Mr Drelincourt uttered a shrill laugh. 'You may well say so! His lordship seemed put out at seeing me, remarkably put out!'

'That,' said the Earl, 'I can easily understand. But pray continue, Crosby.'

'Cousin,' said Mr Drelincourt earnestly, 'I desire you to believe that it is with the most profound reluctance that I do so. While I was with Lord Lethbridge, my attention was attracted by something that lay upon the floor, partly concealed by a rug. Something, Rule, that sparkled. Something –'

'Crosby,' said his lordship wearily, 'your eloquence is no doubt very fine, but I must ask you to bear in mind that I have been in the saddle most of the day, and spare me any more of it. I am not really very curious to know, but you seem anxious to tell me: what was it that attracted your attention?'

Mr Drelincourt swallowed his annoyance. 'A brooch, my lord! A lady's corsage brooch!'

'No wonder that Lord Lethbridge was not pleased to see you,' remarked Rule.

'No wonder, indeed!' said Mr Drelincourt. 'Somewhere in the house a lady was concealed at that very moment. Unseen, cousin, I picked up the brooch and slipped it into my pocket.'

The Earl raised his brows. 'I think I said that you were an odd creature, Crosby.'

'It may appear so, but I had a good reason for my action. Had it not been for the fact that Lord Lethbridge pursued me on my journey here, and by force wrested the brooch from me, I should lay it before you now. For that brooch is very well known both to you and me. A ring-brooch, cousin, composed of pearls and diamonds in two circles!'

The Earl never took his eyes from Mr Drelincourt's; it may have been a trick of the shadows thrown by the candles on the tables, but his face looked unusually grim. He swung his leg down from the arm of the chair leisurely, but still leaned back at his ease. 'Yes, Crosby, a ring-brooch of pearls and diamonds?'

'Precisely, cousin! A brooch I recognized at once. A brooch that belongs to the fifteenth-century set which you gave to your –'

He got no further. In one swift movement the Earl was up, and had seized Mr Drelincourt by the throat, dragging him out of his chair, and half across the corner of the table that separated them. Mr Drelincourt's terrified eyes goggled up into blazing grey ones. He clawed ineffectively at my lord's hands. Speech was choked out of him. He was shaken to and fro till the teeth rattled in his head. There was a roaring in his ears, but he heard my lord's voice quite distinctly. 'You lying, mischief-making little cur!' it said. 'I have been too easy with you. You dare to bring me your foul lies about my wife, and you think that I may believe them! By God, I am of a mind to kill you now!'

A moment more the crushing grip held, then my lord flung his cousin away from him, and brushed his hands together in a gesture infinitely contemptuous.

Mr Drelincourt reeled back, grasping and clutching at the air, and fell with a crash on to the floor, and stayed there, cowering away like a whipped mongrel.

The Earl looked down at him for a moment, a smile quite unlike any Mr Drelincourt had ever seen curling his fine mouth. Then he leaned back against the table, half sitting on it, supported by his hands, and said: 'Get up, my friend. You are not yet dead.'

Mr Drelincourt picked himself up and tried mechanically to straighten his wig. His throat felt mangled, and his legs were shaking so that he could hardly stand. He staggered to a chair and sank into it.

'You said, I think, that Lord Lethbridge took this famous brooch from you? Where?'

Mr Drelincourt managed to say, though hoarsely: 'Maidenhead.'

'I trust he will return it to its rightful owner. You realize, do you, Crosby, that your genius for recognizing my property is sometimes at fault?'

Mr Drelincourt muttered: 'I thought it was – I – I may have been mistaken.'

'You were mistaken,' said his lordship.

'Yes, I – yes, I was mistaken. I beg pardon, I am sure. I am very sorry, cousin.'

'You will be still more sorry, Crosby, if one word of this passes your lips again. Do I make myself plain?'

'Yes, yes, indeed, I – I thought it my duty, no more, to – to tell you.'

'Since the day I married Horatia Winwood,' said his lordship levelly, 'you have tried to make mischief between us. Failing, you were fool enough to trump up this extremely stupid story. You bring me no proof – ah, I am forgetting! Lord Lethbridge took your proof forcibly from you, did he not? That was most convenient of him.'

'But I – but he did!' said Mr Drelincourt desperately.

'I am sorry to hurt your feelings,' said the Earl, 'but I do not believe you. It may console you to know that had you been able to lay that brooch before me I still should not have believed ill of my wife. I am no Othello, Crosby. I think you should have known that.' He stretched out his hand for the bell, and rang it. Upon the entrance of a footman, he said briefly: 'Mr Drelincourt's chaise.'

Mr Drelincourt heard this order with dismay. He said miserably: 'But, my lord, I have not dined, and the horses are spent. I – I did not dream you would serve me so!'

'No?' said the Earl. 'The Red Lion at Twyford will no doubt supply you with supper and a change of horses. Be thankful that you are leaving my house with a whole skin.'

Mr Drelincourt shrank, and said no more. In a short time the footman came back to say that the chaise was at the door. Mr Drelincourt stole a furtive glance at the Earl's unrelenting face, and got up. 'I'll – I'll bid you good night, Rule,' he said, trying to collect the fragments of his dignity.

The Earl nodded, and in silence watched him go out in the wake of the footman. He heard the chaise drive past the curtained windows presently, and once more rang the bell. When the footman came back he said, absently studying his finger-nails: 'I want my racing curricle, please.'

'Yes, my lord!' said the footman, startled. 'Er – now, my lord?'

'At once,' replied the Earl with the greatest placidity. He got up from the table and walked unhurriedly out of the room.

Ten minutes later the curricle was at the door, and Mr Gisborne, descending the stairs, was astonished to see his lordship on the point of leaving the house, his hat on his head, and his small sword at his side. 'You're going out, sir?' he asked.

'As you see, Arnold,' replied the Earl.

'I hope, sir – nothing amiss?'

'Nothing at all, dear boy,' said his lordship.

Outside a groom was clinging to the heads of two magnificent greys, and endeavouring to control their capricious movements.

The Earl's eye ran over them. 'Fresh, eh?'

'Begging your lordship's pardon, I'd say they were a couple of devils.'

The Earl laughed, and climbed into the curricle, and gathered up the reins in one gloved hand. 'Let them go.'

The groom sprang to one side, and the greys plunged forward.

The groom watched the curricle flash round a bend in the avenue and sighed. 'If I could handle them like that –' he said, and wandered back to the stables, sadly shaking his head.

Seventeen

he Sun at Maidenhead was a very popular posting inn, its appointments and kitchens being alike excellent.

Lord Lethbridge sat down to dinner in one of the private rooms, a pleasant apartment, panelled with old oak, and was served with a duck, a quarter of mutton with pickled mushrooms, a crayfish, and a quince jelly. The landlord, who knew him, found him to be in an unusually mellow mood, and wondered what devilry he had been engaged on. The reflective smile that hovered over his lordship's thin lips meant devilry of some sort, of that he was quite certain. For once in his life the noble guest found no fault with the food set before him, and was even moved to bestow a word of praise on the burgundy.

My Lord Lethbridge was feeling almost benign. To have outwitted Mr Drelincourt so neatly pleased him more than the recovery of the brooch. He smiled to think of Crosby travelling disconsolately back to London. The notion that Crosby could be fool enough to carry an empty tale to his cousin never occurred to him; he himself was not one to lose his head, and although he had a poor opinion of Mr Drelincourt's intelligence, such heights of folly were quite beyond his comprehension.

There was plenty of company at the Sun that evening, but whoever else was kept waiting for his dinner, the landlord saw to it that Lethbridge was served instantly. When the covers were withdrawn, and only the wine left on the table, he came himself to ask whether my lord required anything else, and closed the shutters with his own hand. He set more candles on the table, assured his lordship the he would find his sheets well aired, and bowed himself out. He had just told one of the abigails to be sure not to forget to take a warming-pan up presently, when his wife called to him from the doorway: 'Cattermole, here's my lord driven up!'

'My lord,' in Maidenhead, could mean only one person, and Mr Cattermole sped forth at once to welcome this honoured guest. He opened his eyes rather at the sight the racing curricle, but shouted to an ostler to come to the horses' heads, and himself hurried up all bows and smiles.

The Earl leaned over to speak to him. 'Good evening, Cattermole. Can you tell me if Lord Lethbridge's chaise changed horses here rather more than an hour ago?'

'Lord Lethbridge, my lord? Why, his lordship is putting up here for the night!' said Cattermole.

'How very fortunate!' said the Earl, and climbed down from the curricle, flexing the fingers of his left hand. 'And where shall I find his lordship?'

'In the oak parlour, my lord, just finished his dinner. I will escort your lordship.'

'No, you need not do that,' replied the Earl, walking in the inn. 'I know my way.' At the foot of the shallow stairs he paused, and said softly over his shoulder: 'By the way Cattermole, my business with his lordship is private. I feel sure I can rely on you to see that we are not disturbed.'

Mr Cattermole shot him a quick, shrewd glance. There was going to be trouble, was there? Not good for the house, no, not good for the house, but still worse for it to offend my Lord Rule. He bowed, his face a plump, discreet mask. 'Certainly, my lord,' he said, and drew back.

Lord Lethbridge was still sitting over his wine, still meditating over the events of the day, when he heard the door open. He looked up, and stiffened. For a moment they faced one another, Lethbridge rigid in his chair, the Earl standing silent in the doorway, looking across at him. Lethbridge read that look in an instant. He got up. 'So Crosby did visit you?' he said. He put his hand in his pocket and drew out the brooch. 'Is that what you came for, my lord?'

The Earl shut the door, and turned the key in the lock. 'That is what I came for,' he said. 'That, and one other thing, Lethbridge.'

'My blood, for instance?' Lethbridge gave a little laugh. 'You will have to fight for both.'

The Earl moved forward. 'That should afford us both gratification. You have a charming taste in revenge, but you have failed, Lethbridge.'

'Failed?' said Lethbridge, and looked significantly at the brooch in his hand.

'If your object was to drag my name in the mud, why, certainly!' said Rule. 'My wife remains my wife. Presently you shall tell me by what means you forced her to enter your house.'

Lethbridge raised his brows. 'And what makes you so sure that I had any need to employ force, my lord?'

'Merely my knowledge of her,' replied the Earl. 'You have a vast deal of explaining to do, you see.'

'I don't boast of my conquests, Rule,' Lethbridge said softly, and saw the Earl's hand clench involuntarily. 'I shall explain nothing.'

'That we shall see,' said Rule. He pushed the table down to one end of the room, against the wall, and blew out the candles on it, leaving only the pendent chandelier in the centre of the room to light them.

Lethbridge thrust the chairs back, picking up his sword from one of them, and drawing it from the scabbard. 'My God, how I have waited for this,' he said suddenly. 'I am glad Crosby went to you.' He put the sword down again, and began to take off his coat.

The Earl made no reply, but set about his own preparations, pulling off his top-boots, unbuckling his sword-belt, rolling up his deeply ruffled shirt-sleeves.

They faced one another under the soft candlelight, two big men in whom rage, long concealed, burned with a steady strength too great to admit of vain flusterings. Neither seemed to be aware of the strangeness of the scene, here in the upper parlour of an inn, with below them, penetrating faintly to the quiet room, the hum of voices in the coffee-room. With deliberation they set the stage, with deliberation snuffed a candle that was guttering, and divested themselves of coats and boots. Yet in this quiet preparation was something deadly, too deadly to find relief in a noisy brawl.

The swords flashed in a brief salute, and engaged with a scrape of steel on steel. Each man was an experienced swordsman, but this was no affair of the fencing-master's art, with its punctilious niceties, but a grim fight, dangerous in its hard swiftness. For each antagonist the world slid back. Nothing had reality but the other man's blade, feinting, thrusting, parrying. Their eyes were on each other's; the sound of their stockinged feet shifting on the boards was a soft thud; their breathing came quick and hard.

Lethbridge lunged forward on his right foot, delivering a lightning thrust in tierce, his arm high, the muscles standing out on it ribbed and hard. Rule caught forte on forte; the foible glanced along his arm, leaving a long red slash, and the blades disengaged.

Neither checked; this was no quarrel to be decided by a single hit. The blood dripped slowly from Rule's forearm to the floor. Lethbridge leaped back on both feet and dropped his point. 'Tie it!' he said curtly. 'I've no mind to slip in your blood.'

Rule pulled a handkerchief from his breeches pocket, and twisted it round the cut, and dragged the knot tight with his teeth.

'On guard!'

The fight went on, relentless and untiring. Lethbridge attempted a flanconnade, opposing his left hand. His point barely grazed Rule's side; the Earl countered in a flash. There was a scuffle of blades, and Lethbridge recovered his guard, panting a little.

It was he who was delivering the attack all the time, employing every wile known to his art to lure Rule into giving an opening. Time after time he tried to break through the guard; time after time his blade was caught in a swift parry, and turned aside. He was beginning to flag; the sweat was rolling in great drops off his forehead; he dared not use his left hand to dash it from his eyes lest in that second's blindness Rule should thrust home. He thrust rather wildly in carte; the Earl parried it half-circle, and before Lethbridge could recover, sprang in, and seized the blade below the hilt. His own point touched the floor. 'Wipe the sweat from your eyes!'

Lethbridge's lips writhed in a queer, bitter smile. – 'So – you are – quits?'

The Earl did not answer; he released the sword, and waited. Lethbridge passed his handkerchief across his brow and threw it aside.

'On guard!'

A change came; the Earl was beginning at last to press the attack. Hard driven, Lethbridge parried his blade again and again, steadily losing strength. Knowing himself to be nearly done, he attempted a *botte coupée*, feinting in high carte and thrusting in low tierce. His blade met nothing but the opposition of Rule's and the fight went on.

He heard the Earl speak, breathlessly, but very clearly. 'Why did my wife enter your house?'

He had no struggle left to waste in attack; he could only parry mechanically, his arm aching from shoulder to wrist.

'Why did my wife enter your house?'

He parried too late; the Earl's point flashed under his guard, checked, and withdrew. He realized that he had been spared, would be spared again, and yet again, until Rule had his answer. He grinned savagely. His words came on his heaving breaths: 'Kidnapped – her.'

The swords rang together, disengaged. 'And then?'

He set his teeth; his guard wavered; he recovered miraculously; the hilt felt slippery in his wet grasp.

'And then?'

'I do not – boast – of my – conquests!' he panted, and put forth the last remnant of his strength to beat back the attack he knew would end the bout.

His sword scraped on Rule's; his heart felt as though it would burst; his throat was parched; the ache in his arm had become a dull agony; a mist was gathering before his eyes. The years rolled back suddenly; he gasped out: 'Marcus – for God's sake – end it!'

He saw the thrust coming, a straight lunge in high carte aimed for the heart; he made one last parry too late to stop the thrust, but in time to deflect it slightly. Rule's point sliding over his blade, entered deep into his shoulder. His own dropped; he stood swaying for an instant, and fell, the blood staining his shirt bright scarlet.

Rule wiped the sweat from his face; his hand was shaking a little. He looked down at Lethbridge, lying in a crumpled heap at his feet, sobbing for breath, the blood on his shirt soaking through, and forming a pool on the oak boards. Suddenly he flung his sword aside and strode to the table, and swept the bottle and the glass off it. He caught up the cloth and tore it with his strong teeth, and ripped it from end to end. The next moment he was on his knees beside Lethbridge, feeling for the wound. The hazel eyes opened, considering him. 'I believe – I shan't die – this time – either!' Lethbridge whispered mockingly.

The Earl had laid bare the wound, and was staunching the blood. 'No, I don't think you will,' he said. 'But it's deep.' He tore another strip from the cloth and made it into a pad, and bound it tightly round the shoulder. He got up and fetched Lethbridge's coat from a chair, and rolling it up placed it under his head. 'I'll get a doctor,' he said briefly, and went out, and from the head of the stairs shouted for the landlord.

Stout Cattermole appeared so promptly that it seemed as though he must have been waiting for that call. He stood with his hands on the banister, looking anxiously up at the Earl, his brow puckered, his lips close-folded.

'Send one of your lads for a doctor,' said Rule, 'and bring up a bottle of cognac.'

The landlord nodded and turned away. 'And Cattermole!' said his lordship. 'Bring it yourself.'

At that the landlord smiled rather sourly. 'Be sure, my lord.'

Rule went back into the oak parlour. Lethbridge was lying where he had left him, with his eyes closed. He looked very white; one of his hands lay limply on the floor beside him, the fingers curling upwards. Rule stood looking down at him, frowning. Lethbridge did not move.

Cattermole came in with a bottle and glasses. He put these down on the table, casting a worried appraising glance at the still figure on the floor. He muttered: 'Not dead, my lord?'

'No.' The Earl picked up the bottle, and poured some brandy into one of the glasses.

'Thank God for it! You do me no good by this, my lord.'

'I don't think you'll suffer,' replied the Earl, calmly, and returned to Lethbridge and knelt again.

'Lethbridge, drink this!' he said, slightly raising him.

Lethbridge opened his eyes; they were blank with exhaustion, but grew keener as he swallowed the cognac. He raised them to Rule's face a moment, made an odd little grimace, and looked beyond Rule at Cattermole, bending over him. 'What the devil do you want?' he said unpleasantly.

The landlord drew down the corners of his mouth. 'No, he's not dead,' he remarked under his breath. 'I'll be within call, my lord.'

He went out and shut the door behind him.

The blood had soaked through the pad; the Earl tightened the bandage and stood up again. Picking up the sword he wiped it carefully, and put it back into the scabbard.

Lethbridge lay watching him with a look of cynical amusement on his face. 'Why mar what you have made?' he inquired. 'I was under the impression that you wished to kill me.'

The Earl glanced down at him. 'If I let you die, the consequences to myself might prove a trifle difficult to avoid,' he replied.

Lethbridge grinned. 'That is more in my manner than in

yours,' he said. He raised himself on his elbow and tried to sit up.

'You had better lie still,' said the Earl, slightly frowning.

'Oh, no!' gasped Lethbridge. 'The position is – altogether – too lowly. Add to your humanity by assisting me to that chair.'

The Earl bent over him, and hoisted him up; he sank into the chair panting a little, and pressing his hand to his shoulder. A grey shade had crept into his face; he whispered: 'Give me the brandy – quite a deal to say to you.'

The Earl had already poured it out, and now held the glass to Lethbridge's lips. Lethbridge took it unsteadily in his own hands, saying with a snap: 'Damn you, I'm not helpless!' He drank it at a gulp, and lay back recovering his strength. The Earl began to unroll his sleeve. Presently Lethbridge spoke again.

'Sent for a doctor, did you? How magnanimous! Well, he'll be here any moment. I suppose. Let's be done with this. Your wife took no harm of me.' He saw the grey eyes lift quickly, and gave a faint laugh. 'Oh, make no mistake! I am all the villain you think me. She saved herself.'

'You interest me,' said Rule, moving towards a chair, and sitting down on the arm of it. 'I have always thought her a lady of infinite resource.'

'Resource,' murmured Lethbridge. 'Yes, decidedly. She used a poker.'

The Earl's lips twitched. 'I see. Your recollection of the subsequent events is no doubt a little – shall we say – imperfect?'

A laugh shook Lethbridge; he winced and pressed his hand to his shoulder again. 'I believe she thought she had killed me. Tell her the only grudge I bear her is for having left my front door open.'

'Ah, yes!' said Rule. 'The arrival of Crosby.'

Lethbridge had shut his eyes, but he opened them again at that. 'Is that all you know? I suppose Crosby did not tell you that he found Winwood and Pommeroy with me?'

'He did not,' said Rule. 'Perhaps he thought it irrelevant, or perhaps – who knows? – he considered it might spoil the effect of his story. I am sorry if it fatigues you, but I fear I must request

209

you to tell me a little more. What, for instance, brought Winwood to your house?'

'Oh, the intelligence that I had been slain – with a poker.'

Rule drew a breath. 'You dismay me,' he said. 'I hardly dare to ask – what then?'

'Be at ease. He took my recovery in good part. You may pour me some more brandy. Yes, in quite good part. He even offered me a game of piquet.'

'Ah,' said Rule. 'Now I begin to understand. Is it too much to hope that Pommeroy was in the same condition?'

'I did not descry much difference. They were both induced to take their leave on the discovery that I was not – as they had apparently thought – giving a card-party.' He took his replenished glass and drained it. 'My relief was only equalled by Crosby's. Crosby then pocketed the brooch. This morning I sustained a second visit from Pommeroy. He came to get it back. The humour of that should appeal to you. I had not known till then of the brooch's existence. The rest I imagine you know. If Crosby had not been fool enough to carry his tale to you – there would be a hand still to play.' He put his empty glass down and drew the brooch from the pocket of his breeches. 'Take it. It is not worth while. Don't cheat yourself with the notion that you behold me repentant. Revenge – your wife called it fustian. I don't know. But had we met – thus' – he nodded to where his sword lay – 'years ago – who shall say?' He moved, trying to ease his shoulder; he was frowning. 'Experience – leads me to admit – you may have been right to stop Louisa marrying me. I have none of the husbandly virtues. Is she happy with her country squire? I am sure she is; at best women are – dull creatures.' His face contracted with pain. He said irritably: 'Wipe my sword and sheath it. I shall use it again, believe me.' He watched Rule in silence for a moment, and as the sword slid back into the scabbard, he sighed. 'Do you remember fencing with me at Angelo's?'

'I remember,' Rule answered, half smiling. 'We were always very even-matched.'

'You have improved. Where's that damned leech? I've not the slightest desire to oblige you by dying.'

'Do you know, Robert, it would really not oblige me?'

Lethbridge looked up at him, the mockery back in his eyes. 'Memory is a damnably intrusive thing, eh? I shan't die.' His head sank a little on his chest; he lifted it with an effort, and leaned it against the upholstered chair-back. 'You'll admit it was clever of me to win Horry's friendship. I told her, by the way, that Caroline was in your Ranelagh plot.'

Rule said gently: 'You had always a poisonous tongue, Robert.'

'Oh, always,' Lethbridge agreed.

He heard the opening of the door and turned his head. 'At last! Pray take that look off your face, my good man; I suppose you have seen a sword-wound before.'

The doctor set down his bag on the table. 'I have seen many, sir,' he answered primly. His eye alighted on the brandy bottle. 'Cognac? That is not a remedy. I wish you may not end this night in a high fever.' He looked at the bloodstained bandage and sniffed. 'H'm! Some bleeding. Landlord, send up two of your lads to carry his lordship to his room. Pray sit still, sir. I shall not inspect your hurt till I have you in bed.'

Lethbridge gave a wry smile. 'I could not wish you a deadlier fate than to be in my shoes now, Marcus.' He held out his left hand. 'I've done with you. You arouse the worst in me, you know. Your cut will heal quicker than mine, for which I am sorry. It was a good fight – I don't remember a better. Hatred lends a spice, doesn't it? If you want to add to your damned goodness, send word to my fool of a valet to join me here.'

Rule took his hand and gripped it. 'The only thing that ever made you tolerable, my dear Robert, was your impudence. I shall be in town to-morrow. I'll send him down to you. Good night.'

Half an hour later he strolled into the library at Meering, where Mr Gisborne sat reading a newspaper, and stretched himself on the couch with a long sigh of content.

Mr Gisborne looked at him sideways, wondering. The Earl had clasped his hands behind his head, and where the lace ruffle fell back from his right wrist the corner of a bloodstained handkerchief showed. The lazy eyelids lifted. 'Dear Arnold, I am afraid you will be disappointed in me again. I hardly dare tell you but we are going back to London to-morrow.'

Mr Gisborne met those twinkling eyes and bowed slightly. 'Very well, sir,' he said.

'You are – yes, positively you are – a prince of secretaries, Arnold,' said his lordship. 'And you are quite right, of course. How do you contrive to be so acute?'

Mr Gisborne smiled. 'There's a handkerchief round your forearm, sir,' he pointed out.

The Earl drew the arm from behind his head and regarded it pensively. 'That,' he said, 'was a piece of sheer carelessness. I must be growing old.' With which he closed his eyes and relapsed into a state of agreeable coma.

Eighteen

ir Roland Pommeroy, returning empty-handed from his mission, found Horatia and her brother playing piquet together in the saloon. For once Horatia's mind was not wholly concentrated on her cards, for no sooner was Sir Roland ushered in than she threw down her hand and turned eagerly towards him. 'Have you g-got it?'

'Here, are you going to play this game, or not?' said the Viscount, more single-minded than his sister.

'No, of c-course not. Sir Roland, did he give it to you?'

Sir Roland waited carefully until the door was shut behind the footman and coughed. 'Must warn you, ma'am — greatest caution needed before the servants. Affair to be hushed up — won't do if it gets about.'

'Never mind about that,' said the Viscount impatiently. 'Never had a servant yet who did not know all my secrets. Have you got the brooch?'

'No,' replied Sir Roland. 'Deeply regret, ma'am, but Lord Lethbridge denies all knowledge.'

'B-but I know it's there!' insisted Horatia. 'You d-didn't tell him it was mine, d-did you?'

'Certainly not, ma'am. Thought it all out on my way. Told him the brooch belonged to my great-aunt.'

The Viscount, who had been absently shuffling the pack, put the cards down at this. 'Told him it belonged to your great-aunt?' he repeated. 'Burn it, even if the fellow was knocked out, you'll never get him to believe your great-aunt came tottering into his house at two in the morning! 'Tain't reasonable. What's more, if he did believe it, you oughtn't to set a tale like that going about your great-aunt.'

'My great-aunt is dead,' said Sir Roland with some severity.

'Well, that makes it worse,' said the Viscount. 'You can't expect a man like Lethbridge to listen to ghost stories.'

'Nothing to do with ghosts!' replied Sir Roland, nettled. 'You're not yourself, Pel. Told him it was a bequest.'

'B-but it's a lady's brooch!' said Horatia. 'He c-can't have believed you!'

'Oh, your pardon, ma'am, but indeed! Plausible story – told easily – nothing simpler. Unfortunately, not in his lordship's possession. Consider, ma'am – agitation of the moment – brooch fell out in the street. Possible, you know, quite possible. Daresay you don't recollect perfectly, but depend upon it that's what happened.'

'I do recollect p-perfectly!' said Horatia. '*I* w-wasn't drunk!'

Sir Roland was so much abashed at this that he relapsed into a blushful silence. It was left to the Viscount to expostulate. 'Now, that'll do Horry, that'll do! Who said you were? Pom didn't mean anything of the kind, did you, Pom?'

'N-no, but you were, b-both of you!' said Horatia.

'Never mind about that,' replied the Viscount hastily. 'Nothing to do with the point. Pom may be right, though I don't say he is. But if you did drop it in the street, there's no more to be done. We can't go all the way to Half-Moon Street hunting in the gutters.'

Horatia clasped his wrist. 'P-Pel,' she said earnestly, 'I d-did drop it in Lethbridge's house. He tore my lace and it was p-pinned to it. It has a very stiff catch and c-couldn't fall out just for n-no reason.'

'Well, if that's so,' said the Viscount, 'I'll have to go and see Lethbridge myself. Ten to one it was all that talk about Pom's great-aunt that made him suspicious.'

This plan did not commend itself to either of his hearers. Sir Roland was unable to believe that where tact had failed the

Viscount's crude methods were likely to succeed, and Horatia was terrified lest her hot-headed brother should attempt to recover the brooch at the sword's point. A lively discussion was only interrupted by the entrance of the butler announcing luncheon.

Both the visitors partook of this meal with Horatia, the Viscount needing no persuasion, and Sir Roland very little. While the servants were in the room the subject of the brooch had necessarily to be abandoned, but no sooner were the covers withdrawn than Horatia took it up again just where it had been dropped, and said: 'D-don't you see, Pel, if you go to Lethbridge now that Sir Roland has already been, he m-must suspect the truth?'

'If you ask me,' replied the Viscount, 'he knew all along. Great-aunt! Well, I've a better notion than that.'

'P-Pel, I do wish you wouldn't!' said Horatia worriedly. 'You know what you are! You fought Crosby, and there was a scandal. I know you'll d-do the same with Lethbridge if you see him.'

'No, I shan't,' answered the Viscount. 'He's a better swordsman than I am, but he ain't a better shot.'

Sir Roland gaped at him. 'Mustn't make this a shooting affair, Pel. Sister's reputation! Monstrous delicate matter.'

He broke off, for the door had opened.

'Captain Heron!' announced the footman.

There was a moment's amazed silence. Captain Heron walked in, and pausing on the threshold, glanced smilingly round. 'Well, Horry, don't look at me as though you thought I was a ghost!' he said.

'Ghosts!' exclaimed the Viscount. 'We've had enough of them. What brings you to town, Edward?'

Horatia had sprung up out of her chair. 'Edward! Oh, have you brought L-Lizzie?'

Captain Heron shook his head. 'No, I'm sorry, my dear, but Elizabeth is still in Bath. I am only in town for a few days.'

Horatia embraced him warmly. 'Well, n-never mind: I am

so very g-glad to see you, Edward. Oh, do you know Sir Roland P-Pommeroy?'

'I believe I have not that pleasure,' said Captain Heron, exchanging bows with Sir Roland. 'Is Rule from home, Horry?'

'Yes, thank g-goodness!' she answered. 'Oh, I d-don't mean that, but I am in a d-dreadful fix, you see. Have you had luncheon?'

'I lunched in South Street. What has happened?'

'Painful affair,' said Sir Roland. 'Best say nothing, ma'am.'

'Oh, Edward is perfectly safe! Why, he's my brother-in-law. P-Pel, don't you think perhaps Edward could help us?'

'No, I don't,' said the Viscount bluntly. 'We don't want any help. I'll get the brooch back for you.'

Horatia clasped Captain Heron's arm. 'Edward, p-please tell Pelham he m-mustn't fight Lord L-Lethbridge! It would be fatal!'

'Fight Lord Lethbridge?' repeated Captain Heron. 'It sounds a most unwise thing to do. Why should he?'

'We can't explain all that now,' said the Viscount. 'Who said I was going to fight him?'

'You d-did! You said he w-wasn't a better shot than you are.'

'Well, he ain't. All I've got to do is to put a pistol to the fellow's head, and tell him to hand over the brooch.'

Horatia released Captain Heron's arm. 'I m-must say that is a very clever plan, P-Pel!' she approved.

Captain Heron looked from one to the other, half laughing, half startled. 'But you're all very murderous!' he expostulated. 'I wish you would tell me what has happened.'

'Oh, it's nothing,' said the Viscount. 'That fellow Lethbridge got Horry into his house last night, and she dropped a brooch there.'

'Yes, and he wants to c-compromise me,' nodded Horatia. 'So you see, he won't give the brooch up. It's all d-dreadfully provoking.'

The Viscount got up. 'I'll get it back for you,' he said. 'And we won't have any damned tact about it.'

'I'll come with you, Pel,' said the crestfallen Sir Roland.

'You can come home with me while I get pistols,' replied the Viscount severely, 'but I won't have you going with me to Half-Moon Street, mind.'

He went out, accompanied by his friend. Horatia sighed. 'I d-do hope he'll get it this time. Come into the library, Edward, and tell me all about L-Lizzie. Why didn't she c-come with you?'

Captain Heron opened the door for her to pass out into the hall. 'It was not considered advisable,' he said, 'but I am charged with messages for you.'

'N-not advisable? Why not?' asked Horatia, looking over her shoulder.

Captain Heron waited until they had reached the library before he answered. 'You see, Horry, I am happy to tell you that Lizzie is in a delicate situation just now.'

'Happy to tell me?' echoed Horatia. 'Oh! Oh, I see! How famous, Edward! Why, I shall be an aunt! Rule shall take me to B-Bath directly after the Newmarket M-meeting. That is, if he d-doesn't divorce me,' she added gloomily.

'Good God, Horry, it's not as bad as that?' cried Heron, aghast.

'N-no, it isn't, but if I d-don't get my brooch back, I daresay he will. I am a b-bad wife, Edward. I see it now.'

Captain Heron took his seat beside her on the sopha, and possessed himself of her hand. 'Poor Horry!' he said gently. 'Will you tell me all about it, right from the start?'

The story that was haltingly told him was rather involved, but he unravelled it after a time, and gave it as his opinion that there would be no divorce. 'But I think one thing, Horry,' he said. 'You should tell Rule.'

'I c-can't, and I won't,' said Horatia vehemently. 'Who ever heard such a story?'

'It is an odd story,' he admitted. 'But I think he would believe you.'

'N-not after all the stupid things I've done. And if he d-did he would have to c-call Lethbridge out, or something, and that

217

would m-make a scandal, and he'd n-never forgive me for having b-been the cause of it.'

Captain Heron held his peace. He reflected that there might well be more behind the story. He was not very well acquainted with Rule, but he remembered that Elizabeth had perceived the inflexibility about the Earl's mouth, and had owned to some misgivings. Captain Heron had great faith in his wife's judgment. It did not seem to him, from what Horatia unconsciously told him, that the pair were living in that perfect state of conjugal happiness which he and his fair Lizzie enjoyed. If there was already a slight coldness between them (which, since Horatia had declined going to Meering, there seemed to be) it was perhaps an ill moment to choose for the recounting of this improbable adventure. At the same time Captain Heron was not inclined to place much reliance on his brother-in-law's powers of persuasion. He patted Horatia's hand, and assured her it would all come right, but inwardly he was not very hopeful. However, he felt that he owed a great debt of gratitude to her for having given him his Lizzie, and it was with real sincerity that he offered to help her in any way that he could.

'I knew you w-would, Edward,' said Horatia, rather tremulously. 'But perhaps P-Pel will get it, and then everything will be all right.'

It was a long time before the Viscount, still accompanied by the faithful Sir Roland, returned to Grosvenor Square, and Horatia had begun to fret, picturing some hideous scene of combat, convinced that the Viscount's lifeless body would at any moment be borne in. When at last he walked in, she almost hurled herself on his chest. 'Oh, P-Pel, I made sure you were d-dead!' she cried.

'Dead? Why the deuce should I be dead?' said the Viscount, removing his elegant cloth coat from her clutch. 'No, I haven't got the brooch. The fellow wasn't in, blister him!'

'Not in? Then what are we to d-do?'

'Call again,' replied the Viscount grimly.

But the Viscount's second call, made shortly before dinner, proved as fruitless as the first. 'It's my belief he's keeping out of my way,' he said. 'Well, I'll catch him in the morning before he has a chance to go out. And if that damned porter tells me he's out then, I'll force my way in and see for myself.'

'Then I think I had better accompany you,' decided Captain Heron. 'If you try to break into another man's house there's likely to be trouble.'

'Just what I said myself,' nodded Sir Roland, still in attendance. 'Better all go. Call for you at your lodging, Pel.'

'Devilish good of you, Pom,' said the Viscount. 'Say nine o'clock.'

'Nine o'clock,' agreed Sir Roland. 'Nothing for it but to go to bed betimes.'

Captain Heron was the first to arrive at the Viscount's lodgings in Pall Mall next morning. He found the Viscount fully dressed, and busy with the loading of one of his silver-mounted pistols.

'There's a sweet little pistol for you,' said the Viscount, stopping the hammer at half-cock. 'Blew the pips out of a playing card with it once. Cheston laid me ten to one against. Why, you couldn't miss with this pistol! At least,' he added naïvely, 'I daresay you might, but I couldn't.'

Captain Heron grinned at this aspersion cast on his marksmanship, and sat down on the edge of the table, watching the Viscount pour in his powder. 'Well, all I beg of you is, don't blow Lethbridge's head off, Pelham!'

'Might have to wing him,' said the Viscount, picking up a piece of soft kid from the table and placing his ball in it. 'I won't kill him, though, damme, I'll be hard put to it not to!' He lifted the gun, and with his thumb over the touch-hole gently rammed down the ball. 'There you are. Where's Pom? Might have known he'd over-sleep.' He slipped the pistol into his pocket, and stood up. 'Y'know, Edward, this is the devil of a business,' he said seriously. 'No knowing how Rule would take it if it came to his ears. Rely on you to help me.'

'Of course I'm going to help you,' replied Captain Heron. 'If Lethbridge has the brooch, we'll get it.'

Sir Roland appearing at this moment, they picked up their hats, and set off for Half-Moon Street. The porter who opened the door to them once more denied his master.

'Not in, eh?' said the Viscount. 'Well, I think I'll step in and take a look.'

'But he's not in, my lord!' insisted the porter, holding the door. 'He went out yesterday in his chaise, and is not back yet.'

'Don't believe him, Pel,' counselled Sir Roland in the rear.

'But sir, indeed my lord is not in! There is another – well, a person, sir, asking for him besides yourself.'

Captain Heron set his sound shoulder to the door, and thrust it back.

'That's mighty interesting,' he said. 'We will step upstairs to be quite sure that his lordship has not come in unbeknown. In with you Pel!'

The porter found himself driven firmly backwards, and raised a shout for help. A burly individual in a frieze greatcoat and a dirty neck-cloth, who was sitting on a chair in the narrow hall, looked on grinning but offered no assistance. The butler came puffing up the stairs, but paused when he saw the company. He bowed to the Viscount, and said severely: 'His lordship is from home, my lord.'

'Perhaps you didn't look under the bed,' said the Viscount.

A hoarse laugh from the man in the frieze coat greeted this sally. 'Ah, you've hit it, your honour. He's a peevy cull, and so I allus said.'

'Eh?' said Sir Roland, regarding him through his eye-glass. 'Who's this fellow, Pel?'

'How the devil should I know?' demanded the Viscount. 'Now you stay where you are, what-ever-your-name is. I'm going up to have a little talk with his lordship.'

The butler placed himself at the foot of the stairs. 'Sir, his lordship is not in the house!' He saw the Viscount draw the pistol from his pocket, and gasped: 'My lord!'

'Stand out of my way, or you might get hurt,' said the Viscount.

The butler retreated. 'I assure your lordship – I – I don't understand, my lord! My master is gone into the country!'

The Viscount gave a snort, and ran up the stairs. He came back in a very few moments. 'True enough. He's not there.'

'Loped off!' ejaculated the burly man. 'Damn my blood if I ever deal with a flash cull again!' With which cryptic remark he drove his fist into his hat, and sat glowering.

The Viscount looked at him with interest. 'What do you want with him, hey? Who are you?'

'That's my business,' retorted the burly man. 'Twenty rum guineas, that's what I wants, and that's what I'll get if I stays here till tomorrow.'

Captain Heron spoke, addressing himself to the butler. 'Our business with his lordship is urgent – can you inform us of his direction?'

'His lordship,' said the butler stiffly, 'left no word, sir. Indeed, I wish that I were aware of his destination, for this – this person, sir, insists upon staying until his return, though I have warned him I shall send for a constable.'

'You don't dare send for no harman,' said the burly man scornfully. 'I knows what I know, ah, and I knows who'll sleep in Rumbo if I splits.'

Sir Roland, who had been listening intently to this speech, shook his head. 'Y'know, I don't follow what he says at all,' he remarked. 'Rumbo? Never heard of the place.'

'The likes of you calls it Newgate,' explained the burly man. 'I calls it Rumbo. See?'

The Viscount looked at him frowningly. 'I've a notion I've met you before,' he said. 'I don't know your face, but damme, I do know your voice!'

'Might have been masked,' suggested Sir Roland helpfully.

'Lord, Pom, don't be such a – Wait a bit, though! Masked?' The Viscount slapped his leg. 'That's given it to me! Blister it, you're the rogue that tried to hold me up on Shooter's Hill once!'

The burly man, who had changed colour, slid towards the door, muttering: 'No, I never did so! It's a lie!'

'Lord, I don't bear you any malice,' said the Viscount cheerfully. 'You got nothing from me.'

'A highwayman, is he?' said Sir Roland with interest. 'Devilish queer company Lethbridge keeps! Devilish queer!'

'H'm!' remarked Captain Heron, surveying the burly man with scant approval. 'I can guess what your business is with his lordship, my man.'

'Can you?' said Sir Roland. 'Well, what is it?'

'Use your wits,' said Captain Heron unkindly. 'I should like very much to give him up to the Watch, but I suppose we can't.' He turned to the butler. 'I want you to cast your mind back. The night before last a brooch was lost in this house. Do you recall finding it?'

The butler seemed pleased to be able to answer at least one question. 'No, sir, I don't. There wasn't a brooch found in this house. His lordship asked me particularly whether it had been picked up, just after that gentleman called yesterday.' He nodded towards Sir Roland.

'What's that?' ejaculated the Viscount. 'Did you say *after* he called?'

'I did, my lord. His lordship sent for me not more than a minute or so after the gentleman had left the house.'

Captain Heron grasped the Viscount's arm restrainingly. 'Thank you,' he said. 'Come Pelham, there's no more to be done here.'

He drew the unwilling Viscount towards the door, which the porter opened with alacrity.

The three conspirators descended the steps, and set off slowly towards Piccadilly.

'Dropped in the street,' said Sir Roland. 'Said so all along.'

'It begins to look like it,' agreed Captain Heron. 'Yet Horry is certain the brooch was lost in that house. I imagine the butler was speaking the truth. Could anyone else have found the brooch?'

The Viscount stopped short. 'Drelincourt!' he said. 'By the lord Harry, that little viper, that toad, that –'

'Are you talking of that Macaroni cousin of Rule's?' asked Captain Heron. 'What had he to do with it?'

Sir Roland, who had been staring at the Viscount, suddenly shook him by the hand. 'You've got it, Pel. You've got it,' he said. 'Lay you odds he took the brooch.'

'Of course he took it! Didn't we leave him with Lethbridge? By God, I'll wring his damned scraggy neck!' said the Viscount wrathfully, and plunged off at a great rate towards Piccadilly.

The other two hurried after him.

'Was Drelincourt there that night?' asked Captain Heron of Sir Roland.

'Came in because it was raining,' explained Sir Roland. 'Pel wanted to pull his nose. Daresay he will now.'

Captain Heron caught up with the Viscount. 'Pelham, go easy!' he said. 'If he hasn't got it and you accuse him, you'll only work a deal of harm. Why should he have taken the brooch?'

'To make mischief! Don't I know him!' replied the Viscount. 'If he's gone off with it to Rule already, we're finished.'

'That's so,' nodded Sir Roland. 'Yes, that's so, Pel. No getting away from it. Better finish Drelincourt too. Nothing else to do.'

'Pelham, you young madman, give me that pistol of yours!' commanded Captain Heron.

The Viscount shook him off, and strode on. Sir Roland plucked at the Captain's sleeve. 'Better let Pel deal with the fellow,' he said confidentially. 'Devilish fine shot, you know.'

'Good God, you're as mad as he is,' groaned Captain Heron. 'We mustn't let this come to a fight, man!'

Sir Roland pursed his lips. 'I don't see why not,' he said judicially. 'Trifle irregular, but there's two of us to see fair play. Do you know Drelincourt?'

'No, but –'

223

'Ah, that accounts for it!' nodded Sir Roland. 'If you knew him, you'd agree. Fellow ought to be killed. Thought so for a long time.'

Captain Heron gave it up in despair.

Nineteen

*M*r Crosby Drelincourt had been much too shaken by his experiences to think of dinner when he left Meering. All he desired was to reach his own lodgings. He drove from Meering to Twyford, where he changed horses, and went to the grievous expense of hiring an armed guard to protect him from highwaymen. The journey home seemed to him interminable, but the chaise set him down in Jermyn Street not long after ten o'clock, by which time he had recovered a little from his adventures, and had begun to feel the pangs of hunger. Unfortunately, since he had not been expected to return that night, no supper had been provided, and he was forced to go out to an ordinary, so that he might just as well, he reflected bitterly, have dined on the road after all.

He slept late next morning, and was sitting down to breakfast in his dressing-gown when he heard a thundering on the front door, followed in a few moments by the sound of voices. He dropped his knife, listening. One voice was raised insistently, and Mr Drelincourt knew that voice. He turned quickly to his valet, who had just set the coffee-pot down before him: 'I'm not at home!' he said. 'Quick, don't let them come up!'

The valet said obtusely: 'Beg pardon, sir?'

Mr Drelincourt thrust him towards the door. 'Tell them I'm away, you fool! Stop them coming up! I'm not well; I can't see any one!'

'Very good, sir,' said the valet, hiding a smile.

Mr Drelincourt sank back into his chair, nervously wiping his face with his napkin. He heard the valet go downstairs to parley with the visitors. Then, to his horror, he heard someone come up, three steps at a time.

The door was rudely burst open. Viscount Winwood stood on the threshold. 'Away, are you?' he said. 'Now why are you so anxious not to see me, eh?'

Mr Drelincourt rose, gripping the edge of the table. 'Really, my lord, if – if a man may not be private when he chooses!' He perceived the face of Sir Roland Pommeroy peering over the Viscount's shoulder, and licked his lips. 'Pray – pray what's the meaning of this intrusion, sir?' he demanded weakly.

The Viscount advanced into the room, and sat down without ceremony on the corner of the table, one hand in his capacious coat-pocket. Behind him Sir Roland propped his shoulders against the wall, and began dispassionately to pick his teeth. Captain Heron ranged alongside the Viscount, ready to intervene at need.

Mr Drelincourt looked from one to the other with the deepest misgiving. 'I can't conceive what – what should bring you here, gentlemen!' he said.

The Viscount's angelic blue eyes were fixed on his face. 'What took you out of town yesterday, Drelincourt?' he inquired.

'I – I –'

'I have it from your man below that you went away in a chaise and four, and came home late – too late to be disturbed now. Where did you go?'

'I fail – I fail entirely to see how my movements should concern you, my lord!'

Sir Roland withdrew the toothpick from his mouth. 'Don't want to tell us,' he remarked. 'Black, very black!'

'Well, he's going to tell us,' said the Viscount, and got up.

Mr Drelincourt took a backward step. 'My lord! I – I protest! I don't understand you! I went into the country on private business – purely private business, I assure you!'

'Private, was it?' said the Viscount, advancing towards him. 'It wasn't on business connected with jewellery, I take it?'

Mr Drelincourt turned ashen-pale. 'No, no!' he gasped.

The Viscount whipped the pistol from his pocket, and levelled it. 'You lie, you little viper!' he said through his teeth. 'Stand still!'

Mr Drelincourt stood rooted to the floor, his fascinated gaze on the pistol. Sir Roland was moved to protest. 'Not out of hand, Pel, not out of hand! Must do the thing decently!'

The Viscount paid no heed. 'You picked up a ring-brooch in Lethbridge's house the other night, didn't you?'

'I don't know what you mean!' chattered Mr Drelincourt. 'A brooch? I know nothing about it, nothing!'

The Viscount pressed the muzzle of his pistol into the pit of Mr Drelincourt's stomach. 'There's a mighty light trigger on this pistol of mine,' he said. 'It only needs a touch to send it off. Don't move. I know you took that brooch. What did you do with it?'

Mr Drelincourt was silent, breathing rather fast. Sir Roland replaced his toothpick carefully in its gold case, and pocketed it. He strolled forward, and tucked his fingers into the back of Mr Drelincourt's neck-cloth, and twisted it scientifically. 'Take the pistol away, Pel. Going to choke it out of him.'

Mr Drelincourt, his throat already bruised from his cousin's crushing grip, gave a strangled shriek. 'Yes, I took it! I didn't know how it came to be there – indeed, I had no notion!'

'You carried it to Rule? Answer!' snarled the Viscount.

'No, no, I didn't. I swear I didn't!'

Captain Heron, watching him closely, nodded. 'Don't choke him, Pommeroy, I think he's speaking the truth.'

'If you didn't take it to Rule, where is it?'

'I haven't got it!' gasped Mr Drelincourt, his eyes on the Viscount's pistol.

'Can't expect us to believe that,' said Sir Roland, impersonally. 'Went off to Meering with it, didn't you?'

'Yes, I did, but I never gave it to Rule. Lord Lethbridge has it!'

Sir Roland was so surprised that he released him. 'Damned if I can make head or tail of this!' he said. 'How the deuce did he come by it?'

'He – he overtook me, and wrested the brooch from me. I couldn't stop him. I swear I'm telling the truth!'

'There, that's what all your talk of great-aunts brought about, Pom!' said the Viscount bitterly.

'It's a good thing,' said Sir Roland. 'Now we know who has got the brooch. Makes it simple. Find Lethbridge – get the brooch – whole affair settled.'

The Viscount turned to Mr Drelincourt. 'Where is Lethbridge?'

Mr Drelincourt said sullenly: 'I don't know. He said he should sleep the night in Maidenhead.'

The Viscount was thinking fast. 'Maidenhead? That's a matter of twenty-six or seven miles. Call it a three-hour run. We'll get him.' He slipped the pistol back into his pocket. 'Nothing more to be done here. As for you –' he rounded on Mr Drelincourt, who shrank perceptibly, '– the next time you cross my path will be the last. Come on, Pom; come, Edward.'

When they were once more in the street Captain Heron began to shake with silent laughter.

'What the devil's the matter with you?' said the Viscount, pausing to frown at him.

Captain Heron grasped the railing. 'His face!' he choked. 'You breaking in in the middle of his breakfast – oh lord!'

'Ha!' said Sir Roland. 'Middle of his breakfast, was he? Dashed amusing!'

Suddenly the humour of the situation dawned upon the Viscount. He went off into a crack of laughter. Mr Drelincourt, peering from between the curtains of his room, was infuriated by the sight of his three visitors doubled up with mirth on the pavement.

Captain Heron let go the railings at last. 'Where now?' he asked faintly.

'White's,' decided the Viscount. 'Won't be anyone there at this hour. We must think this one out.'

'I'm not a member, you know,' said Captain Heron.

'What's that matter? Pom ain't either. I am, though,' replied the Viscount, and led the way up the street.

They found the coffee-room in the club deserted, and took possession of it. The Viscount stretched himself in a chair, and thrust his hands into his breeches pockets.

'Say Lethbridge started from Maidenhead at ten,' he mused. 'He'll arrive about one. Maybe earlier. Drives fast horses.'

Sir Roland was inclined to cavil at this. 'Wouldn't start at ten, Pel. Too early.'

'What's to keep him?' asked the Viscount. 'Nothing to do in Maidenhead that I ever heard of.'

'There's a bed, ain't there? Do you ever get up before nine? Lay you odds he don't either. Call it eleven.'

'Does it signify?' inquired Captain Heron, adjusting his sash.

'Signify? Of course it signifies!' replied the Viscount. 'We've got to intercept the fellow. Does he take his luncheon on the road, Pom?'

'Takes his lunch at Longford – King's Head,' said Sir Roland.

'Or Colnbrook,' said the Viscount. 'They do you a very good dish of mutton and broiled mushrooms at the George.'

'No, no, Pel,' said Sir Roland gently. 'You're thinking of the Pigeons at Brentford.'

The Viscount devoted some thought to this, and came to the conclusion that his friend was right. 'Well, then, call it Longford. Lunches at noon. Won't get to London before two.'

'I wouldn't say that, Pel,' objected Sir Roland.

'Damme, you must give the fellow time to sit a bit over his wine!'

'Not at Longford,' said Sir Roland simply. 'He won't sit over his wine at the King's Head.'

'Well, if it's like that, he won't take his luncheon there,' said the Viscount. 'That puts us out.'

Captain Heron sat up. 'Stop talking about his luncheon!' he begged. 'He'll eat it somewhere, and that's all that concerns us. How are you going to intercept him?'

229

The Viscount let his chin sink into his cravat, and pondered deeply.

'Short of holding him up, you can't do it,' said Captain Heron. 'You can only wait for him at his house.'

The Viscount jerked himself in his chair. 'You've hit it, Edward! That's a devilish good idea of yours! We'll do it.'

'What, wait for him in Half-Moon Street? I don't say it's a good idea, but –'

'Lord no!' interrupted the Viscount. 'No sense in that, We'll hold him up.'

'Good God, that wasn't my idea!' said Captain Heron, alarmed.

'Of course it was your idea; you thought of it, didn't you? And one thing I will say, Edward, I never expected it of you. Always thought you too devilish respectable.'

'You were right,' said Captain Heron firmly. 'I am as respectable as can be. I won't be a party to any hold-up.'

'Why not? No harm in it. Shan't hurt the fellow – much.'

'Pelham, will you have some sense? Consider my uniform!'

Sir Roland, who had been pensively sucking the end of his cane, raised his head. 'Got a notion,' he said. 'Go home and change it. Can't hold a man up in regimentals. Wouldn't be reasonable to expect it of him, Pel.'

'Lord, you don't suppose we'll any of us do it dressed like this, do you? We want greatcoats and masks.'

'I've got a roquelaure,' said Sir Roland helpfully. 'Had it made for me last month by Grogan. Meant to show it to you, Pel. Pretty shade of grey – silver buttons, but I don't know about the lining. Grogan was all for a Carmelite silk, but I'm not sure I care for it, not at all sure.'

'Well, you can't hold up a chaise in a silk-lined roquelaure. We've got to have frieze coats and mufflers.'

Sir Roland shook his head. 'Can't be done, Pel. You got a frieze coat, Heron?'

'No, thank God, I haven't!' said Captain Heron.

'Nor have I,' said the Viscount, springing up. 'And that's why we must get hold of that fellow we left at Lethbridge's. Come along! We've no time to waste.'

Sir Roland rose, and said admiringly: 'Dashed if I should ever have thought of that. It's you who have the head, Pel, not a doubt of it.'

'Pelham, do you realize that in all probability it was that ruffian that kidnapped your sister?' demanded Captain Heron.

'Do you think so? Yes, by God, I believe you're right! Said he was waiting for twenty guineas, didn't he? Well, if Lethbridge can hire him so can we,' declared the Viscount, and strode out.

Captain Heron caught him up in the street. 'Pelham, it's all very well, but we can't do a hare-brained thing like that! If we're caught I'm like to be broke.'

'Well, it always beat me why you ever wanted to go into the Army,' said the Viscount. 'But if you want to rat, Pom and I can do it without you!'

Sir Roland, shocked, said: 'Pel, dear old boy, Pel! Think what you're saying! Heron ain't ratting. Only said he'd be broke if we was caught. Mustn't jump down a man's throat just because he makes a remark.'

'If it were for anyone but Horry, I would rat,' said Captain Heron. 'Why in thunder don't you wait for Lethbridge to come home, Pelham? If three of us can't get the brooch away from him without masquerading as highwaymen –'

'Because this is a better way!' said the Viscount. 'Great thing is to avoid scandal. If I put a pistol to the fellow's head, and he calls me out, where are we then? Worse off than ever! Affair's bound to come to Rule's ears, and if you think he won't suspect Horry's in it, you don't know him. This way, we'll have the brooch without a breath of scandal, and no one the wiser. Now, are you with me, or not, Edward?'

'Yes, I'm with you,' said Captain Heron. 'There is something in what you say, if it doesn't go awry!'

'It can't go awry, man – unless that rogue's left Lethbridge's house.'

'Can't have done that,' said Sir Roland. 'Said he was going to stay there till he had his twenty guineas. Lethbridge not back – can't have had 'em. Must be there still.'

Sir Roland proved to be right. When they arrived once more in Half-Moon Street, the burly man was still seated in the hall. The porter, as soon as he saw who it was on the doorstep, made a spirited attempt to slam the door. This was frustrated by Sir Roland, who hurled himself against it with great presence of mind, and nearly knocked the breath out of the porter by jamming him between the door and the wall. When he had extricated himself he found all three gentlemen inside the hall again, and groaned. However, as soon as it was explained to him that they only wanted to take away the burly man, he brightened considerably, and even permitted them to hail that worthy into the saloon for a little private conversation.

The burly man, confronted by the Viscount's pistol, flung up his hands. 'Don't you go for to let off that pop, your honour!' he said huskily. 'I ha'n't done you a mite o' harm!'

'Not a mite,' agreed the Viscount. 'What's more, I won't do you any harm if you behave yourself. What's your name? Come on, man, I've got to call you something, haven't I?'

'You call me Ned. Ned Hawkins,' replied the burly man. 'It ain't the name, but it's one I got a fancy for. Edward Hawkins, that's me, at your service, gen'lemen.'

'We don't want another Edward,' objected Sir Roland. 'Heron's name's Edward, and we shall only get 'em mixed up.'

'Well, I don't mind being Frederick – to oblige the company,' conceded Mr Hawkins.

'Hawkins will do,' replied the Viscount. 'You're on the High Toby, aren't you?'

'Me?' exclaimed Mr Hawkins virtuously. 'Cross me heart if –'

'That'll do,' interrupted the Viscount. 'Blew the hat off your head on Shooter's Hill six months ago. Now I've got a piece of work for you to do. What do you say to twenty guineas, eh?'

Mr Hawkins recoiled. 'Dang me if ever I works with a flash cull again, that's what I says!'

232

The Viscount lifted his pistol. 'Then I'll hold you, while my friend there goes for a constable.'

'You dassn't!' grinned Mr Hawkins. 'You get me put in the Whit, and I takes his peevy lordship with me – ah, and how'll you like that?'

'Pretty well,' said the Viscount. 'He's no friend of mine. Friend of yours?'

Mr Hawkins spat comprehensively. Sir Roland, his sense of propriety offended, interposed. 'Here, I say, Pel, can't have the fellow spitting all over another man's house. Bad *ton*, dear boy. Devilish bad!'

'Don't do that again!' ordered the Viscount. 'What's the use of it? Diddled you out of your money, hasn't he?'

'Ay, loped off,' growled Mr Hawkins. 'A boman prig, he is! When I gets my hands on him –'

'I can help you to do that,' said the Viscount. 'What do you say to holding him up? – for twenty guineas?'

Mr Hawkins looked suspiciously from one to the other. 'What's the lay?' he demanded.

'He's got something I want,' said the Viscount briefly. 'Make up your mind! The Watch, or twenty guineas?'

Mr Hawkins caressed his stubby chin. 'Who's in it? All of you coves?' he inquired.

'All of us. We're going to hold up his chaise.'

'What, in them toges?' said Mr Hawkins, indicating the Viscount's gold-laced coat.

'Of course not, you fool!' answered the Viscount impatiently. 'That's what we want you for. We must have three greatcoats like your own, and masks.'

A broad grin spread over Mr Hawkins's countenance. 'Damn my blood, but I like your spirit!' he announced. 'I'll do it! Where is this cull?'

'On the Bath Road, heading for London.'

'That'll mean the Heath, that will,' nodded Mr Hawkins. 'When's it for?'

'Any time after noon. Can't say precisely.'

Mr Hawkins pulled down his mouth. 'Dang me if I like it, then. I like to work when the tattler's up, see?'

'If there's one thing we don't want it's any tattlers,' replied the Viscount firmly.

'Lord love your honour, ain't you ever heard on the moon?'

'The moon! By the time that's up our man will be safe in this house. This is daylight or nothing.'

Mr Hawkins sighed. 'Just as you say, your honour. And you wants a set of toges and shaps? Bring your own nags?'

'Own horses, own pistols,' agreed the Viscount.

'You'll have to mount me, then, Pelham,' put it Captain Heron.

'Mount you with pleasure, my dear fellow.'

'Own pops?' said Mr Hawkins. 'Us bridle culls don't use them little pops all over wedge, your honour.'

The Viscount glanced down at his pistol. 'What's wrong with it? Devilish good pistol. Gave a hundred guineas for the pair.'

Mr Hawkins pointed a grimy finger at the silver mountings. 'All that wedge. That's what's wrong with it.'

'Oh, very well,' said the Viscount. 'But I like my own pistols, you know. Now where do we get these coats and mufflers?'

'You know the Half-Way House?' said Mr Hawkins 'That's where I'll be. There's a flash ken thereabouts where I keeps my nag. I'll be off there now, and when you comes, why dang me if I don't have the toges and tyes ready for you!'

'And how do I know you will be there?' said the Viscount.

'Because I wants twenty guineas,' replied Mr Hawkins logically. 'And because I wants to get my hands on that boman prig. That's how.'

234

Twenty

An hour later three gentlemen might have been observed riding soberly out to Knightsbridge. Captain Heron, bestriding a raking chestnut from the Viscount's stables, had changed his scarlet regimentals and his powdered wig for a plain suit of buff, and a brown tie-wig. He had found time, before joining the Viscount at his lodging, to call in Grosvenor Square again, where he had found Horatia in a fever of anxiety. When she learned of the new development in the affair, she first expressed herself as extremely dissatisfied that no one had killed the wretched Mr Drelincourt, and it was some few minutes before Captain Heron could induce her to speak of anything but that gentleman's manifold iniquities. When her indignation had abated somewhat he laid the Viscount's plan before her. This met with her instant approval. It was the cleverest notion she had ever heard of, and of course it could not fail.

Captain Heron warned her to keep her own counsel, and went off to Pall Mall.

He had not much expectation of finding Mr Hawkins either at the Halfway House or anywhere else, but it was obviously no use saying so to the optimistic Viscount. By this time his brother-in-law was in fine fettle, so that whether Mr Hawkins kept his appointment or not, it seemed probable that the plan would be carried out.

About a quarter of a mile before the Halfway House was reached, a solitary rider, walking his horse, came into view. As they drew closer he looked over his shoulder, and Captain Heron was forced to admit that he had misjudged their new acquaintance.

Mr Hawkins greeted him jovially. 'Dang me if you wasn't speaking the truth!' he exclaimed. His eyes ran over the Viscount's mare approvingly. 'That's a nice bit of horse-flesh, that is,' he nodded. 'But tricksy – tricksy, I'll lay my life. You come along o' me to the boozing ken I telled you of.'

'Got those coats?' asked the Viscount.

'Ay, all's bowman, your honour.'

The ale-house which Mr Hawkins had made his head-quarters lay some little distance off the main road. It was an unsavoury haunt, and from the look of the company in the tap-room seemed to be frequented largely by ruffians of Mr Hawkins' calling. As a preliminary to the adventure the Viscount called for four bumpers of brandy, for which he paid with a guinea tossed on to the counter.

'Don't throw guineas about, you young fool!' said Captain Heron in a low voice. 'You'll have your pocket picked if you're not more careful.'

'Ay, the Capting's in the right of it,' said Mr Hawkins, overhearing. 'I'm a bridle cull, I am – never went on the dublay yet, no, and never will, but there's a couple of files got their winkers on you. We gets all sorts here – locks, files, common prigs, and foot-scamperers. Now, my bullies, drain your clanks! I got your toges up the dancers.'

Sir Roland plucked at the Captain's sleeve. 'You know, Heron,' he whispered confidentially, 'this brandy – not at all the thing! Hope it don't get into poor Pel's head – very wild in his cups – oh, very wild! Must keep him away from any dancers.'

'I don't think he meant "dancers",' soothed Captain Heron. 'I fancy that's a cant word.'

'Oh, that's it, is it,' said Sir Roland, relieved. 'It's a pity he don't speak English. Don't follow him at all, you know.'

Mr Hawkins' dancers proved to be a flight of rickety stairs, up which he led them to a malodorous bedroom. Sir Roland recoiled on the threshold, raising his scented handkerchief to his nose. 'Pel – no, really Pel!' he said faintly.

'Smells a bit of onions,' remarked the Viscount. He picked up a battered tricorne from a chair, and casting aside his rakish chapeau *à la Valaque*, clapped it over his fair, unpowdered locks. He surveyed the effect in the cracked mirror, and chuckled. 'How d'you like it, Pom?'

Sir Roland shook his head. 'It ain't a hat, Pel. You couldn't call it a hat.'

Mr Hawkins gave a guffaw. 'It's a rare shap, that one. Better nor yours.'

He handed the Viscount a muffler, and showed him how to tie it to conceal every vestige of his lace cravat. The Viscount's shining top-boots made him purse his lips. 'You could see your face in them stampers,' he said. 'Hows'ever, it can't be helped.' He watched Sir Roland struggle into a large triple-caped overcoat, and handed him a hat more battered than the Viscount's. He eyed Sir Roland's elegant gauntlets disparagingly. 'Properly speaking, you don't want no famstrings,' he said. 'But I dunno. Maybe best keep them white dabblers o' yours covered. Now, you gen'lemen, stow these here masks away till I gives the word to put 'em on. Not till we gets to the Heath that won't be.'

Captain Heron pulled his muffler tight and jammed his beaver well over his eyes. 'Well, at all events, Pelham, I defy my own wife to recognize me in these clothes,' he remarked. 'I could only wish that the coat were not so tight round the chest. Are we ready?'

Mr Hawkins was pulling a wooden case from under the bed. This he opened, and displayed three horse pistols. 'I got two myself, but I couldn't come by no more,' he said.

The Viscount lifted one of these weapons, and grimaced. 'Clumsy. You can have it, Pom. I brought my own.'

'Not them little pops all over wedge?' asked Mr Hawkins, frowning.

'Lord, no! Horse pistols like your own. You'd best leave the shooting to me, Pom. No knowing what will happen if you let that barker off.'

'That gun,' said Mr Hawkins, offended, 'belonged to Gentleman Joe, him as went to the Nubbing Cheat a twelve-month back. Ah, and a rare buzz he was!'

'Fellow who robbed the French Mail about a year ago?' inquired the Viscount. 'Hanged him, didn't they?'

'That's what I said,' replied Mr Hawkins.

'Well, I don't care for his taste in pistols,' said the Viscount, handing the weapon over to Sir Roland. 'Let's be going.'

They trooped down the wooden stairs again, and out into the yard, where a couple of seedy-looking men were walking the horses up and down. These Mr Hawkins sent about their business. The Viscount tossed them a couple of silver pieces, and went to see that his pistols were still safe in the saddle holsters. Mr Hawkins told him he need not be anxious. 'Couple o' my own lads, they are,' he said, hoisting himself on to the back of a big brown gelding.

The Viscount swung lightly into the saddle, glancing over the brown horse's points. 'Where did you steal that nag?' he asked.

Mr Hawkins grinned, and laid a finger to the side of his nose.

Sir Roland, whose horse, apparently having as poor an opinion of the hostelry as his master, was sidling and fidgeting in a fret to be off, ranged alongside the Viscount and said: 'Pel, we can't ride down the high road in these clothes! Damme, I won't do it!'

'High road?' said Mr Hawkins. 'Lord love you, it ain't high roads for us, my bully! You follow me.'

The way Mr Hawkins chose was unknown to his companions, and seemed very tortuous. He skirted every village, took a wide detour round Hounslow and led them eventually on to the Heath shortly after one. Ten minutes' canter brought the main Bath Road into sight.

'You want to lie up where no one won't see you,' advised Mr Hawkins. 'There's a bit of a hill I knows of, with some bushes atop. Know the look of our man's rabler?'

'Do I know the look of his what?' said the Viscount.

'His rabler – his coach is what I mean!'

'Well, I do wish you'd say what you mean,' said the Viscount severely. 'He's driving a chaise-and-four, that's all I know.'

'Don't you know his horses?' asked Captain Heron.

'I know the pair he drives in his curricle, but that don't help us. We'll stop the first chaise we see, and if it ain't him, we'll stop the next.'

'That's it,' agreed Sir Roland, dubiously eyeing his mask. 'Daresay we'll need some practice. Look here, Pel, I don't at all like this mask. There's too much of it.'

'For my part,' said Captain Heron with an irrepressible laugh, 'I'm thanking God for mine!'

'Well, if I put it on it'll hang down all over my face,' objected Sir Roland. 'Shan't be able to breathe.'

They had come by this time to the hillock Mr Hawkins had mentioned. The bushes which grew on its slope afforded excellent protection, and it commanded a long view of the road, from which it was set back at a distance of about fifty yards. Reaching the top of it, they dismounted, and sat down to await their prey.

'I don't know if it has occurred to you, Pelham,' said Captain Heron, removing his hat, and throwing it down on the grass beside him, 'but if we stop many chaises before we chance on the one we're after, our first victims are likely to have plenty of time to inform against us in Hounslow.' He looked across the Viscount's sprawling person to Mr Hawkins. 'Ever had that happen to you, my friend?'

Mr Hawkins, who was chewing a blade of grass, grinned. 'Ah, I've had it happen. No scout-cull ain't snabbled me yet.'

'Burn it, man, how many chaises do you expect to see?' said the Viscount.

'Well, it's the main Bath Road,' Captain Heron pointed out.

Sir Roland removed his mask, which he had been trying on, to say: 'Bath season not begun yet.'

Captain Heron stretched himself full-length on the springy

turf, and clasped his hands lightly over his eyes to protect them from the sun. 'You're fond of betting, Pelham,' he said lazily. 'I'll lay you ten to one in guineas that something goes wrong with this precious scheme of yours –'

'Done!' said the Viscount promptly. 'But it was your scheme, not mine.'

'Something coming!' announced Sir Roland suddenly.

Captain Heron sat up, and groped for his hat.

'That's no post-chaise,' said their guide and mentor still chewing his blade of grass. He glanced up at the sun calculating the time. 'Likely it's the Oxford stage.'

In a few moments the vehicle came into sight round a bend in the road, some way off. It was a great lumbering coach, drawn by six horses, and piled high with baggage. Beside the coachman sat an armed guard, and all over the roof such passengers who could only afford to pay half their fare perched and clung precariously.

'Don't touch stage rablers myself,' remarked Mr Hawkins, watching the coach lurch and sway over the bumps in the road. 'Nothing to be had but a rum fam or two, or a thin truss.'

The coach laboured ponderously on, and was presently lost to sight. The noise of the plodding hooves was borne back in the still air for long after it had gone, growing fainter and fainter until at last it died.

A solitary horseman bearing westwards passed next. Mr Hawkins sniffed at him, and shook his head. 'Small game,' he said scornfully.

Silence, except for the trill of a lark somewhere overhead, again fell over the Heath. Captain Heron dozed peacefully; the Viscount took snuff. The sound of a coach travelling fast broke the stillness after perhaps twenty minutes had elapsed. The Viscount nudged Captain Heron sharply, and picked up his mask. Mr Hawkins cocked his head on one side, listening. 'Six horses there,' he pronounced. 'Hear 'em?'

The Viscount had risen, and put his mare's bridle over her head. He paused. 'Six?'

'Ay, outriders, I dessay. Might be the Mail.' He looked his three companions over. 'Four on us – what do you say, my bullies?'

'Good God, no!' replied the Viscount. 'Can't rob the Mail!'

Mr Hawkins sighed. 'It's a rare chance,' he said wistfully. 'Ah, what did I tell you? Bristol Mail, that is.'

The Mail had swept round the bend, accompanied by two outriders. The horses, nearing the end of the stage, were sweating, and one of the leaders showed signs of lameness.

A wagon, going at a snail's pace along the white road, was the only other thing that relieved the monotony during the next quarter of an hour. Mr Hawkins remarked that he knew a cove who got a tidy living prigging the goods off tumblers, but he himself despised so debased a calling.

Sir Roland yawned. 'We've seen one stage, one mail, man riding a roan cob, and a wagon. I call it devilish dull, Pel. Poor sport! Heron, did you think to bring a pack of cards?'

'No,' answered Captain Heron sleepily.

'No, no more did I,' said Sir Roland, and relapsed into silence.

Presently Mr Hawkins put his hand to his ear. 'Ah,' he said deeply, 'that sounds more like it! You want to get your masks on, gen'lemen. There's a chaise coming.'

'Don't believe it,' said Sir Roland gloomily, but he put his mask on and got into the saddle.

The Viscount fixed his own mask, and once more crushed the hat on to his head. 'Lord, Pom, if you could see yourself!' he said.

Sir Roland, who was engaged in blowing the curtain of his mask away from his mouth, paused to say: 'I can see you, Pel. That's enough. More than enough.'

Mr Hawkins mounted the brown gelding. 'Now, my bullies all, take it easy. We ride down on 'em, see? You wants to be careful how you looses off them pops. I'm a peaceable cove, and we don't want no killing.' He nodded at the Viscount. 'You're handy with your pop; you and me'll do the shooting, and mind it's over their nobs!'

The Viscount drew one of his pistols from the holster.

'Wonder how the mare will take it?' he said cheerfully. 'Steady, Firefly! Steady, lass!'

A post-chaise drawn by four trotting horses came round the bend. Mr Hawkins snatched at the Viscount's bridle. 'Easy, easy!' he begged. 'Give 'em time to come alongside! No sense in letting 'em see us yet. You wait on me.'

The post-chaise came on. 'Nice pair of wheelers,' commented Sir Roland. 'Good holders.'

'Capting, you'll cover them postilions, see?' ordered Mr Hawkins.

'If we don't move soon, there'll be no postilions to cover!' snapped the Viscount. 'Come on, man!'

The post-chaise was almost abreast of them. Mr Hawkins released the Viscount's bridle. 'At 'em, then!' he said, and drove his heels into his horse.

'Yoiks! Forrard away!' halloed Sir Roland, and thundered down the slope, waving his pistol.

'Pom, don't you let that barker off!' shouted the Viscount, abreast of him, and levelling his own slenderer weapon. Rising in his stirrups, he pulled the trigger, and saw one of the postilions duck as the shot whistled over his head. The mare shied violently and tried to bolt. He held her head on her course, and came down like a thunderbolt across the road. 'Stand and deliver! – steady, lass!'

The postilions had dragged their frightened horses to a standstill. Captain Heron pressed up closer, covering them with his pistol. Sir Roland, a connoisseur of horse-flesh, had allowed his attention to be diverted by the two wheelers, and was studying them closely.

The Viscount and Mr Hawkins had ridden up to the chaise. The window was let down with a bang, and an old gentleman with a red face pushed his head and shoulders out, and extending his arm fired a small pistol at the Viscount. 'Dastardly rogues! Cut-throat robbers! Drive on, you cowardly rascals!' he spluttered.

The shot sang past the Viscount's ear; the mare reared up in alarm, and was steadied again. 'Hi, mind what you're about, sir!' said his lordship indignantly. 'You devilish near got me in the head!'

Mr Hawkins on the other side of the chaise, thrust his pistol into the old gentleman's face. 'Drop your pops!' he growled. 'And step out, d'you see? Come on, out with you!' He let the reins fall on his horse's neck, and leaned sideways in the saddle, and wrenched open the door of the chaise. 'A rare gager, you are! Hand over your truss! Ah, and that pretty lobb o' yourn!'

The Viscount said quickly: 'Draw off, you fool! Wrong man!'

'Lordy, he's good enough for me!' replied Mr Hawkins, wresting a snuff-box from the old gentleman's grasp. 'A nice little lobb, this! Come on now, where's your truss?'

'I'll have the Watch on you!' raved his victim. 'Damnable! Broad daylight! Take that, you thief!' With which he dashed his hat at Mr Hawkins' pistol, and diving back into the coach seized a long ebony cane.

'Lord, he'll have an apoplexy,' said the Viscount, and rode round the chaise to Mr Hawkins' side. 'Give me that snuff-box,' he ordered briefly. 'Edward! Here, Edward! Take the fool away! We've got the wrong man.' He dodged a blow aimed at his head with the ebony cane, tossed the snuff-box into the chaise, and reined back. 'Let 'em go, Pom!' he called.

Sir Roland came round to him. 'Wrong man, is it? Tell you what, Pel – as nice a pair of wheelers as I've seen. Just what I've been looking for. Think he'd sell?'

The old gentleman, still perched on the step of the chaise, shook his fist at them. 'Murderous dogs!' he raved. 'You'll find I'm a match for you, you rogues! Don't like the look of this little cane of mine, eh? I'll break the head of the first man to come a step nearer! Robbers and cowards! White-livered scoundrels! Drive on, you damned shivering fools! Ride 'em down!'

Captain Heron, in charge of the baffled Mr Hawkins, said in a voice that shook with suppressed mirth: 'For God's sake come away! He'll burst a blood-vessel at this rate.'

'Wait a bit,' said Sir Roland. He swept off his abominable

beaver, and bowed over his horse's withers. 'Haven't the honour of knowing your name, sir, but you've a very pretty pair of wheelers there. Looking for just such a pair.'

The old gentleman gave a scream of rage. 'Insolence! Steal my horses, would you? Postilion! I command you, drive on!'

'No, no! Assure you nothing of the sort!' protested Sir Roland.

Captain Heron bore down upon him, and seizing his bridle, dragged him away. 'Come away,' he said, 'you'll ruin us all, you young madman!'

Sir Roland allowed himself to be led off. 'A pity,' he said, shaking his head. 'Great pity. Never saw such a queer-tempered fellow.'

The Viscount, who was speaking a few pithy words to Mr Hawkins, turned his head. 'How the devil should he know you wanted to buy his horses? Besides, we haven't time to buy horses. We'd better get back to our ambush. Mare stood the firing pretty well, didn't you, sweetheart?'

Captain Heron watched the chaise rolling away up the road. 'He'll lay information in Hounslow, Pelham, you mark my words.'

'Let him,' said the Viscount. 'He won't get the Watch out against us. Why, we didn't take a thing!'

'Not a thing,' muttered Mr Hawkins sulkily. 'And him with his strong-box under the seat! Dang me if I ever works with flash culls again!'

'Don't keep on saying that,' said the Viscount. 'You can take what you like from the right man, but you don't rob anyone else while you're with me!'

They rode on up the slope, and once more dismounted. 'Well, if I'm broke for this, I think I'll take to the – what-do-you call it? Bridle-lay. I'd no notion it was so easy,' said Captain Heron.

'Yes, but I don't like the clothes,' said the Viscount. 'Devilish hot!'

Sir Roland sighed. 'Beautiful wheelers!' he murmured sadly.

The afternoon wore on. Another wagon lumbered past, three more horsemen, and one stage.

'Can't have missed the fellow, can we?' fretted the Viscount.

'All we missed was our luncheon,' replied Captain Heron. He pulled his watch out. 'It's on three already, and I dine in South Street at five.'

'Dining with my mother, are you?' said the Viscount. 'Well, the cook's damned bad, Edward, and so I warn you. Couldn't stand it myself. One reason why I live in lodgings. What's that, Hawkins? Heard something?'

'There's a chaise coming up the road,' said Mr Hawkins. 'And I hope it's the right one,' he added bitterly.

When it came into sight, a smart, shining affair, slung on very high swan's-neck springs, the Viscount said: 'That's more like it! Now then, Pom, we've got him!'

The manœuvre that had succeeded so well with the first chaise, succeeded again. The postilions, alarmed to find no less than four ruffians descending upon them, drew up in a hurry. Captain Heron once more covered them with his pistol, and the Viscount dashed up to the chaise, shouting in as gruff a voice as he could assume: 'Stand and deliver there! Come on, out of that!'

There were two gentlemen in the chaise. The younger of them started forward, levelling a small pistol. The other laid a hand on his wrist. 'Don't fire, my dear boy,' he said placidly. 'I would really rather that you did not.'

The Viscount's pistol hand dropped. He uttered a smothered exclamation.

'Wrong again!' growled Mr Hawkins disgustedly.

The Earl of Rule stepped unhurriedly down on to the road. His placid gaze rested on the Viscount's mare. 'Dear me!' he said. 'And – er – what do you want me to deliver, Pelham?'

Twenty-one

Not long after four o'clock a furious knocking was heard on the door of the Earl of Rule's town house. Horatia, who was on her way upstairs to change her gown, stopped and turned pale. When the porter opened the door and she saw Sir Roland Pommeroy on the doorstep without his hat, she gave a shriek, and sped down the stairs again. 'Good G-God, what has happened?' she cried.

Sir Roland, who seemed much out of breath, bowed punctiliously. 'Apologize unseemly haste, ma'am! Must beg a word in private!'

'Yes, yes, of course!' said Horatia, and dragged him into the library. 'Someone's k-killed? Oh, n-not Pelham? Not P-Pelham?'

'No, ma'am, upon my honour! Nothing of that sort. Most unfortunate chance! Pel desired me to apprise you instantly. Rode home post-haste – left my horse nearest stables – ran round to wait on you. Not a moment to lose!'

'Well, w-what is it?' demanded Horatia. 'You found L-Lethbridge?'

'Not Lethbridge, ma'am, Rule!' said Sir Roland, and flicking his handkerchief from his sleeve, dabbed at his heated brow.

'Rule?' exclaimed Horatia in accents of the profoundest dismay.

'No less, ma'am. Very awkward situation.'

'You – you d-didn't hold Rule up?' she gasped.

Sir Roland nodded. 'Very, very awkward,' he said.

'Did he re-recognize you?'

'Deeply regret, ma'am – recognized Pel's mare.'

Horatia wrung her hands. 'Oh, was ever anything so unlucky? What d-did he say? What d-did he think? What in the world b-brings him home so soon?'

'Beg you won't distress yourself, ma'am. Pel carried it off. Presence of mind, you know – mighty clever fellow, Pel!'

'B-but I don't see how he could carry it off!' said Horatia.

'Assure your ladyship, nothing simpler. Told him it was a wager.'

'D-did he believe it?' asked Horatia, round-eyed.

'Certainly!' said Sir Roland. 'Told him we mistook his chaise for another's. Plausible story – why not? But Pel thought you should be warned he was on his way.'

'Oh, yes, indeed!' she said. 'But L-Lethbridge?' My b-brooch?'

Sir Roland tucked his handkerchief away again. 'Can't make the fellow out,' he replied. 'Ought to be home by now, instead of which – no sign of him. Pel and Heron are waiting on with Hawkins. Have to carry a message to Lady Winwood. Heron – very good sort of a man indeed – can't dine in South Street now. Must try to stop Lethbridge, you see. Beg you won't let it distress you. Assure you – brooch shall be recovered. Rule suspects nothing – nothing at all, ma'am!'

Horatia trembled. 'I d-don't feel as though I can p-possibly face him!' she said.

Sir Roland, uneasily aware that she was on the brink of tears, retreated towards the door. 'Not the slightest cause for alarm, ma'am. Think I should be going, however. Won't do for him to find me here.'

'No,' agreed Horatia forlornly. 'No, I s-suppose it won't.'

When Sir Roland had bowed himself out she went slowly upstairs again, and to her bed-chamber, where her abigail was waiting to dress her. She had promised to join her sister-in-law at Drury Lane Theatre after dinner, and a grande toilette in satin of that extremely fashionable colour called Stifled Sigh was laid out over a chair. The abigail, pouncing on her to untie her laces, informed her that M. Frédin (pupil of that celebrated academician in coiffures, M. Léonard of Paris) had already arrived, and was in the powder-closet. Horatia said 'Oh!' in a flat voice, and stepping out of her polonaise, listlessly permitted the satin underdress to be slipped over her head. She was put into her powdering-gown next, and then was delivered into the hands of M. Frédin.

This artist, failing to perceive his client's low spirits, was full of enthusiastic suggestions for a coiffure that should ravish all who beheld it. My lady has not cared for the Quésaco? Ah, no, by example! a little too sophisticated! My lady would prefer her hair dressed in Foaming Torrents – a charming mode! Or – my lady being *petite* – perhaps the Butterfly would better please the eye.

'I d-don't care,' said my lady.

M. Frédin, extracting pins with swift dexterity, shaking out rolled curls, combing away a tangle, was disappointed, but redoubled his efforts. My lady, without doubt, desired something new, something *épatante*. One could not consider the Hedgehog, therefore, but my lady would be transported by the Mad Dog. A mode of the most distinguished: he would not suggest the Sportsman in a Bush; that was for Ladies past their first blush; but the Royal Bird was always a favourite; or, if my lady was in a pensive mood, the Milksop.

'Oh, d-dress it *à l'urgence*!' said Horatia impatiently. 'I'm l-late!'

M. Frédin was chagrined, but he was too wise in the knowledge of ladies' whims to expostulate. His deft fingers went busily to work, and in an astonishingly short space of time Horatia emerged from the closet, her head a mass of artlessly tumbled curls, dashed over with powder *à la Maréchale*, violet-scented.

She sat down at her dressing-table, and picked up the rouge-pot. It would never do for Rule to see her looking so pale. Oh, if it was not that odious Serkis rouge that made her look a hag! Take it away at once!

She had just laid down the haresfoot and taken the patch-box out of the abigail's hand when someone scratched on the door. She started, and cast a scared look over her shoulder. The door opened and the Earl came in.

'Oh!' said Horatia faintly. She remembered that she must show surprise, and added: 'G-good gracious, my l-lord, is – is it indeed you?'

The Earl had changed his travelling dress for an evening toilet of puce velvet, with a flowered waistcoat and satin small clothes. He came across the room to Horatia's side, and bent to kiss her hand. 'None other, my dear. Am I – now don't spare me – am I perhaps *de trop*?'

'No, of c-course not,' replied Horatia uncertainly. She felt a trifle breathless. At sight of him her heart had given the oddest leap. If the abigail had not been there – if she had not lost her brooch – ! But the abigail, tiresome creature, was there, bobbing a curtsy, and Lethbridge had her brooch, and of course she could not fling herself into Rule's arms and burst into tears on his chest. She forced herself to smile. 'No, of c-course not,' she repeated. 'I am prodigiously g-glad to see you. But what brings you b-back so soon, sir?'

'You, Horry,' he answered, smiling down at her.

She blushed and opened the patch-box. Her thoughts jostled one another in her head. He must have broken with the Massey. He was beginning to love her at last. If he found out about Lethbridge and the brooch it would all be spoiled. She was the most deceitful wretch alive.

'Ah, but I beg you will let me show *my* skill,' said his lordship, removing the patch-box from her hand. He selected a tiny round of black taffeta, and gently turned Horatia's head towards him. 'Which shall it be?' he said. 'The Equivocal? I think not. The Gallant? No, not that. It shall be – ' He pressed the patch at the corner of her mouth. 'The Kissing, Horry!' he said, and bent quickly and kissed her on the lips.

Her hand flew up, touched his cheek, and fell again. Deceitful, odious wretch that she was! She drew back, trying to laugh. 'My l-lord, we are not alone! And I – I m-must dress, you know, for I p-promised to g-go with Louisa and Sir Humphrey to the p-play at Drury Lane.'

He straightened. 'Shall I send a message to Louisa, or shall I go with you to this play?' he inquired.

'Oh – oh, I m-mustn't disappoint her, sir!' said Horatia in a hurry. It would never do to be alone with him a whole evening. She might blurt out the whole story, and then – if he believed her – he must think her the most tiresome wife, for ever in a scrape.

'Then we will go together,' said his lordship. 'I'll await you downstairs, my love.'

Twenty minutes later they faced one another across the dining table. 'I trust,' said his lordship, carving the duck, 'that you were tolerably well amused while I was away, my dear?'

Tolerably well amused? Good heavens! 'Oh, yes, sir – t-tolerably well,' replied Horatia politely.

'The Richmond House ball – were you not going to that?'

Horatia gave an involuntary shudder. 'Yes, I – went to that.'

'Are you cold, Horry?'

'C-cold? No, sir, n-not at all.'

'I thought you shivered,' said his lordship.

'N-no,' said Horatia. 'Oh, no! The – the Richmond House b-ball. It was vastly pretty, with fireworks, you know. Only my shoes p-pinched me, so I d-didn't enjoy myself m-much. They were new ones, too, with diamonds sewn on them, and I was so c-cross I should have sent them back to the m-makers only that they were ruined by the wet.'

'Ruined by the wet?' repeated the Earl.

Horatia's fork clattered on her plate. That was what came of trying to make conversation! She had known how it would be; of course she would make a slip! 'Oh, yes!' she said breathlessly. 'I f-forgot to tell you! The b-ball was spoiled by rain. Wasn't it a pity? I – I got my feet wet.'

'That certainly was a pity,' agreed Rule. 'And what did you do yesterday?'

'Yesterday?' said Horatia. 'Oh, I – I d-didn't do anything yesterday.'

There was a laugh in his eyes. 'My dear Horry, I never thought to hear such a confession from you,' he said.

'No, I – I did not feel very w-well, so I – I – so I stayed at home.'

'Then I suppose you haven't yet seen Edward,' remarked the Earl.

Horatia, who was sipping her claret, choked. 'Good gracious, yes! Now, however c-could I have come to forget that? Only f-fancy, Rule, Edward is in town!' She was aware that she was sinking deeper into the quagmire, and tried to recover her false step. 'B-but how did you know he was here?' she asked.

The Earl waited while the footman removed his plate, and set another in its place. 'I have seen him,' he replied.

'Oh – oh, have you? W-where?'

'On Hounslow Heath,' replied the Earl, putting up his glass to survey a pupton of cherries which was being offered to him. 'No, I think not . . . . Yes, on Hounslow Heath, Horry. A most unexpected rencontre.'

'It m-must have been. I – I wonder w-what he was doing there?'

'He was holding me up,' said the Earl calmly.

'Oh, w-was he?' Horatia swallowed a cherry stone inadvertently and coughed. 'How – how very odd of him!'

'Very imprudent of him,' said the Earl.

'Yes, v-very. P-perhaps he was doing it for a w-wager,' suggested Horatia, mindful of Sir Roland's words.

'I believe he was.' Across the table the Earl's eyes met hers. 'Pelham and his friend Pommeroy were also of the party. I fear I was not the victim they expected.'

'W-weren't you? No, of c-course you weren't! I mean – d-don't you think it is t-time we started for the p-play, sir?'

Rule got up. 'Certainly, my dear.' He picked up her taffeta cloak and put it round her shoulders. 'May I be permitted to venture a suggestion?' he said gently.

She glanced nervously at him. 'Why, y-yes, sir! What is it?'

'You should not wear rubies with that particular shade of satin, my dear. The pearl set would better become it.'

There was an awful silence; Horatia's throat felt parched suddenly; her heart was thumping violently. ' It – it is too l-late to change them n-now!' she managed to say.

'Very well,' Rule said, and opened the door for her to pass out.

All the way to Drury Lane Horatia kept up a flow of conversation. What she found to talk about she could never afterwards remember, but talk she did, until the coach drew up at the theatre, and she was safe from a *tête-à-tête* for three hours.

Coming home there was of course the play to be discussed, and the acting, and Lady Louisa's new gown, and these topics left no room for more dangerous ones. Pleading fatigue, Horatia went early to bed, and lay for a long time wondering what Pelham had done, and what she should do if Pelham had failed.

She awoke next morning heavy-eyed and despondent. Her chocolate was brought in on a tray with her letters. She sipped it, and with her free hand turned over the billets in the hope of seeing the Viscount's sprawling handwriting. But there was no letter from him, only a sheaf of invitations and bills.

Setting down her cup she began to open these missives. Yes, just as she had thought. A rout-party; a card-party; she did not care if she never touched a card again; a picnic to Boxhill: never! of course it would rain; a concert at Ranelagh: well, she only hoped she would never be obliged to go to that odious place any more! . . . Good God, could one have spent three hundred and seventy-five guineas at a mantua-maker's? And what was this? Five plumes at fifty louis apiece! Well, that was really too provoking, when they had been bought for that abominable Quésaco coiffure which had not become her at all.

She broke the seal of another letter, and spread open the single sheet of plain, gilt-edged paper. The words, clearly written in a copper-plate hand, fairly jumped at her.

'If the Lady who lost a ring-brooch of pearls and diamonds in Half-Moon

Street on the night of the Richmond House Ball will come alone to the Grecian Temple at the end of the Long Walk at Vauxhall Gardens at midnight precisely on the twenty-eighth day of September, the brooch shall be restored to her by the Person in whose possession it now is.'

There was no direction, no signature; the handwriting was obviously disguised. Horatia stared at it for one incredulous minute and then, with a smothered shriek, thrust her chocolate tray into the abigail's hands and cast off the bed-clothes. 'Quick, I m-must get up at once!' she said. 'Lay me out a w-walking dress, and a hat, and my g-gloves! Oh, and run d-downstairs and tell someone to order the l-landaulet – no, not, the l-landaulet! my town-coach, to c-come round in half an hour. And take all these l-letters away, and oh, d-do p-please hurry!'

For once she wasted no time over her toilet, and half an hour later ran down the stairs, her sunshade caught under her arm, her gloves only half on. There was no sign of Rule, and after casting a wary glance in the direction of the library door, she sped past it and was out in the street before anyone could have time to observe her flight.

The coach was waiting, and directing the coachman to drive to Lord Winwood's lodging in Pall Mall, Horatia climbed in and sank back against the cushions with a sigh of relief at having succeeded in leaving the house without encountering Rule.

The Viscount was at breakfast when his sister was announced, and looked up with a frown. 'Lord, Horry, what the devil brings you at this hour? You shouldn't have come; if Rule knows you've dashed off at daybreak it's enough to make him suspect something's amiss.'

Horatia thrust a trembling hand into her reticule and extracted a crumpled sheet of gilt-edged paper. 'Th-that's what brings me!' she said. 'Read it!'

The Viscount took the letter and smoothed it out. 'Well, sit down, there's a good girl. Have some breakfast . . . Here, what's this?'

'P-Pel, can it be L-Lethbridge?' she asked.

The Viscount turned the letter over, as though seeking

enlightenment on the back of it. 'Dashed if I know!' he said. 'Looks to me like a trap.'

'B-but why should it be? Do you think p-perhaps he is sorry?'

'No, I don't,' said his lordship frankly. 'I'd say at a guess that the fellow's trying to get his hands on you. End of the Long Walk? Ay, I know that Temple. Devilish draughty it is, too. And it's near one of the gates. Tell you what, Horry: I'll lay you a pony he means to abduct you.'

Horatia clasped her hands. 'But, P-Pel, I must go! I must try and g-get the brooch b-back!'

'So you shall,' said the Viscount briskly. 'We'll see some sport now!' He gave back the letter and took a long drink of ale. 'Now you listen to me, Horry!' he ordered. 'We'll all go to Vauxhall to-night – you and I and Pom, and Edward too if he likes. At midnight you'll go to that temple, and the rest of us will lie hid in the shrubbery there. We shall see who goes in, never fear. If it's Lethbridge, we've got him. If it's another – though, mind you, it looks to me like Lethbridge – you've only to give a squawk and we'll hear you. We shall have that damned brooch by to-morrow, Horry!'

Horatia nodded. 'Yes, that's a very clever plan, P-Pel. And I'll tell Rule that I am g-going with you, and he w-won't mind that at all. D-didn't Lethbridge c-come to town yesterday?'

The Viscount scowled. 'Can't have done. Edward and that fellow Hawkins and I stayed till past nine on that cursed Heath, and never saw a sign of him. You know we stopped Rule's chaise?'

'Yes, of c-course. Sir Roland told me and Rule did too.'

'Gave me a devilish queer turn when I saw who it was,' confessed the Viscount. 'He's quick, is Rule. Must own he's quick, Horry. Recognized my mare the instant he clapped eyes on her.'

'B-but he didn't suspect, P-Pel? You're sure he d-didn't suspect?' she cried anxiously.

'Lord, no! How should he?' said the Viscount. He glanced at the clock. 'I'd best get hold of Pom, and as for you, you go home, Horry.'

Arrived once more in Grosvenor Square, Horatia discarded her hat and her gloves and went in search of Rule. She found him in the library, reading the *Morning Chronicle*. He rose at her entrance and held out his hand. 'Well, my love? You're up betimes.'

Horatia put her hand in his. 'It was such a f-fine morning,' she explained. 'And I am to d-drive in the park with M-mama.'

'I see,' he said. He lifted her fingers to his lips. 'Is not to-day the twenty-eighth, Horry?'

'Yes. Yes, it is,' she replied.

'Then will you come with me to the ball at Almack's rooms?' suggested Rule.

Consternation spread over her face. 'Oh – oh, how d-delightful that would be!' she said. 'Only I c-can't! I've promised to go to Vauxhall with P-Pel.'

'I have always found,' remarked his lordship pensively, 'that most of one's engagements were only made to be broken.'

'I can't break this one,' Horatia said with real regret.

'Is it so important? You will make me jealous, Horry of Pelham.'

'It's very, very important!' she said earnestly. 'That is to say, I m-mean – Well, P-Pel wants me to be there particularly, you see!'

The Earl was playing with her fingers. 'Do you think Pel would permit me to make one of this expedition?' he said.

'Oh, no, I am quite sure he w-wouldn't like that at all!' said Horatia, appalled. 'At least – I d-don't mean that, of course, but – but he is to present some people to me, and they are strangers, you see, and I daresay you would not c-care for them.'

'But I have a reputation for being the most friendly of mortals,' said the Earl plaintively. He let go her hand and turned to arrange his cravat in the mirror. 'Don't distress yourself on my account, my dear. If I don't care for these strangers I promise I will dissemble.'

Horatia gazed at him in complete dismay. 'I d-don't think you would enjoy it, M-Marcus. Really, I do not.'

He bowed slightly. 'At your side, Horry, I could enjoy anything,' he said. 'And now, my dear, if you will excuse me, I will go and attend to all the affairs which my poor Arnold wants me to deal with.'

Horatia watched him go out of the room, and straightway sat herself down at the desk in the window and scribbled a frantic note to her brother.

This missive, brought by hand, reached the Viscount's lodging just as he came back to it from his visit to Sir Roland. He read it, swore under his breath, and dashed off an answer.

'The devil fly away with Rule,' he wrote. *'I'll set Pom on to draw him off.'*

When this brief note was delivered to her Horatia read it rather doubtfully. Her experience of Sir Roland's tact was not such as to lead her to place very much reliance on his handling of an awkward situation. However, she herself had said all she dared to dissuade Rule from accompanying her to Vauxhall, and Sir Roland could hardly be less successful.

The Earl was still closeted with Mr Gisborne when a lackey came in to announce that Sir Roland Pommeroy desired to speak with him. He looked up from the paper he was about to sign, and Mr Gisborne, who happened to be watching him, was surprised to see a gleam of amusement in his eyes. The information that Sir Roland had called did not seem to warrant that particular gleam. 'Very well,' said his lordship. 'Tell Sir Roland that I will be with him immediately . . . Alas, Arnold, something always interrupts us, does it not? I am quite desolated, believe me, but I shall have to go.'

'Desolated, sir?' said Mr Gisborne, cocking an eyebrow. 'If you will permit me to say so, I thought that you looked rather pleased.'

'But that was not because the interruption drags me from your side, my dear boy,' said his lordship, putting down his quill and rising. 'I am enjoying myself this morning.'

Mr Gisborne wondered why.

Sir Roland Pommeroy had been shown into one of the

saloons, and was standing by the window when the Earl came in. From the movement of his lips it might have been supposed that he was silently rehearsing a speech.

'Good morning, Pommeroy,' said the Earl, closing the door. 'This is an unexpected pleasure.'

Sir Roland turned and came forward. ''Morning, Rule, Beautiful day! Trust you reached home safely yesterday? Extremely distressed I should have mistaken your chaise for – er – for the other one.'

'Not at all,' replied his lordship with great civility. 'There was not the slightest need for you to put yourself to the trouble of calling, my dear fellow.'

Sir Roland tugged at his cravat. 'To tell you the truth – didn't come on that score,' he confessed. 'Felt sure you would understand how it was.'

'Quite right,' said the Earl, opening his snuff-box. 'I did understand.'

Sir Roland helped himself to a pinch and sniffed it up one nostril. 'Very good blend. I always have my own put up by my man in the Haymarket. Always use the same, you know. Plain Spanish.'

'Ah, indeed?' said the Earl. 'This is blended for me by Jacobs, in the Strand.'

Sir Roland perceived that he was being led into a discussion that had nothing whatsoever to do with his mission, and firmly abandoned it. 'Reason I called,' he said, 'was quite different. Hoping very much you will join a little card-party – my house – this evening.'

'Why, this is very kind of you,' said Rule, with the faintest inflexion of surprise in his pleasant voice.

This was not lost on Sir Roland, who, thrust out by the Viscount to 'draw off' his lordship, had protested feebly: 'Deuce take it, Pel, I hardly know the man! Years older than I am! Can't ask him to my house like that!' He sought once more to loosen his cravat, and said: 'Aware – devilish short notice – trust you'll forgive – very difficult to find a fourth. Last moment, you understand. Game of whisk.'

'Nothing,' said the Earl, 'would please me more than to be able to oblige you, my dear Pommeroy. Unfortunately, however –'

Sir Roland threw up his hand. 'Now don't say you cannot come! Pray do not! Can't play whisk with only three people, my lord. Most awkward situation!'

'I am sure it must be,' agreed his lordship sympathetically. 'And I expect you have tried everyone else.'

'Oh, everyone!' said Sir Roland. 'Can't find a fourth at all. Do beg of your lordship not to fail me!'

'I am extremely sorry,' said the Earl, shaking his head. 'But I fear I must decline your – er – very flattering invitation. You see, I have promised to join a party at Vauxhall Gardens with my wife.'

'Feel sure her ladyship would excuse you – almost bound to rain – very dull evening!' said Sir Roland feverishly. 'Apprehend it is Pel's party – not your taste at all, sir. Very queer people, Pel's friends. Wouldn't like them, I assure you.'

The Earl's lips twitched. 'You quite decide me, my dear Pommeroy. If they are like that I think I would rather be at her ladyship's side.'

'Oh, they are not!' said Sir Roland hastily. 'Oh, dear me, no, nothing of that sort! Very respectable people, but dull, you know – a set of company you would not like. Much better play whisk at my house.'

'Do you really think so?' The Earl appeared to meditate. 'I am, of course, very fond of whisk.'

Sir Roland breathed a sigh of relief. 'Knew I could count on you! Beg you will dine first – five o'clock.'

'Who are your other guests?' inquired his lordship.

'Well, to tell you the truth – not quite sure yet,' said Sir Roland confidentially. 'Bound to find someone glad of a game. Have it all fixed by five o'clock.'

'You tempt me very much,' said the Earl. 'And yet – no, I fear I must not yield. Some other evening, perhaps. You'll take a glass of madeira with me before you go?'

The crestfallen Sir Roland shook his head. 'Thank you, no – must get back to – that is to say, must get to Boodle's. Might find a fourth there, you understand. No chance of persuading your lordship?'

'I regret infinitely, but none,' Rule answered. 'I must – I positively must accompany my wife.'

Sir Roland went sadly back to Pall Mall, where he found the Viscount kicking his heels impatiently. 'No good, Pel,' he said. 'Did what I could – no moving him.'

'The devil fly away with the fellow!' said the Viscount wrathfully. 'What in thunder ails him? Here we have the whole affair planned out as snug as you please, and he must needs ruin all by taking it into his head to join my party! Damme, I won't have him in my party!'

Sir Roland rubbed his chin thoughtfully with the knob of his cane. 'Trouble is, Pel, you haven't got a party,' he said.

The Viscount, who had cast himself into a chair, said irritably: 'What the hell does that matter?'

'Does matter,' insisted Sir Roland. 'Here's Rule joining you to-night, and I told him he wouldn't like the party – said they were queer people – hoping to put him off, you know – and if you don't arrange a party – well, you see what I mean, Pel?'

'Well, if that don't beat all!' said the Viscount indignantly. 'It ain't enough for me to waste the whole day planning this damned affair, I have to get a party together as well just to fall in with your silly tale! Burn it we don't want a party! Where am I to find a lot of queer people? Tell me that!'

'Meant it for the best, Pel,' said Sir Roland placatingly. 'Meant it for the best! Must be any number of queer people in town – know there are – Club's full of them.'

'But they ain't friends of mine!' replied the Viscount. 'You can't go round the club asking a lot of queer-looking strangers to come to Vauxhall with you. Besides, what should we do with them when we got 'em there?'

'Give them supper,' said Sir Roland. 'While they have supper we slip off – get the brooch – come back – ten to one no one notices.'

'Well, I won't do it!' said the Viscount flatly. 'We'll have to think of some way to keep Rule off.'

Ten minutes later Captain Heron walked in to find both gentlemen plunged in profound thought, the Viscount propping his chin in his hands, Sir Roland sucking the head of his cane. Captain Heron looked from one to the other, and said: 'I came to see what you mean to do next. You've heard nothing of Lethbridge, I suppose?'

The Viscount lifted his head. 'By God, I have it!' he exclaimed. 'You shall draw Rule off!'

'I shall do what?' asked Captain Heron, startled.

'I don't see how,' objected Sir Roland.

'Lord, Pom, nothing easier! Private affairs to discuss. Rule can't refuse.'

Captain Heron laid his hat and gloves down on the table. 'Pelham, do you mind explaining? Why has Rule to be drawn off?'

'Why, because of – oh, you don't know, do you? You see, Horry's had a letter from someone offering to give her back the brooch if she'll meet him in the temple at the end of the Long Walk at Vauxhall to-night. Looks like Lethbridge to me – must be Lethbridge. Well, I had it all fixed that she and I and Pom here and you should go to Vauxhall, and while she went to the temple we'd stand guard.'

'That seems a good idea,' nodded Captain Heron. 'But it's surely odd of –'

'Of course it's a good plan! It's a devilish good plan. But what must that plaguy fellow Rule do but take it into his head to come too! As soon as I heard that I sent Pom off to invite him to a card-party at his house.'

Sir Roland sighed. 'Pressed him as much as I could. No use. Bent on going to Vauxhall.'

'But how the deuce am I to stop him?' asked Captain Heron.

'You're the very man!' said the Viscount. 'All you have to do is to go off to Grosvenor Square now and tell Rule you've matters of importance to discuss with him. If he asks you to discuss 'em at once, you say you can't. Business to attend to. Only time you can spare is this evening. That's reasonable enough: Rule knows you're only in town for a day or two. Burn it, he can't refuse!'

'Yes, but, Pelham, I haven't anything of importance to discuss with him!' protested Captain Heron.

'Lord, you can think of something, can't you?' said the Viscount. 'It don't signify what you talk about as long as you keep him away from Vauxhall. Family affairs – money – anything!'

'I'm damned if I will!' said Captain Heron. 'After all Rule's done for me I can't and I won't tell him that I want to talk about money!'

'Well, don't tell him so. Just say you must have a private word with him to-night. He ain't the man to ask you what it's about, and dash it, Edward, you must be able to talk about something when it comes to the point!'

'Of course you must,' corroborated Sir Roland. 'Nothing simpler. You've been at this War in America, haven't you? Well, tell him about that. Tell him about that battle you was in – forgotten its name.'

'But I can't beg Rule to give me an evening alone with him, and then sit telling him stories he don't want to hear about the war!'

'I wouldn't say that,' temporized Sir Roland. 'You don't know he doesn't want to hear them. Any number of people take a deal of interest in this war. I don't myself, but that ain't to say Rule doesn't.'

'You don't seem to understand,' said Captain Heron wearily. 'You expect me to make Rule believe I've urgent business to discuss with him –'

The Viscount interposed. 'It's you who don't understand,' he said. 'All we care about is keeping Rule away from Vauxhall to-night. If we don't do it the game's up. It don't matter a ha'porth how you keep him away so long as you do keep him away.'

Captain Heron hesitated. 'I know that. I'd do it if only I could think of anything reasonable to discuss with him.'

'You'll think of it, never fear,' said the Viscount encouragingly. 'Why, you've got the whole afternoon before you. Now you go round to Grosvenor Square at once, there's a good fellow.'

'I wish to God I'd put off my visit to town till next week!' groaned Captain Heron, reluctantly picking up his hat again.

The Earl of Rule was just about to go in to luncheon when his second visitor was announced. 'Captain Heron?' he said. 'Oh, by all means show him in!' He waited, standing before the empty fireplace until the Captain came in. 'Well, Heron?' he said, holding out his hand. 'You come just in time to bear me company over luncheon.'

Captain Heron blushed in spite of himself. 'I'm afraid I can't stay, sir. I'm due in Whitehall almost immediately. I came – you know my time is limited – I came to ask you whether it would be convenient – in short, whether I might wait on you this evening for – for a talk of a confidential nature.'

The Earl's amused glance rested on him thoughtfully. 'I suppose it must be to-night?' he said.

'Well, sir – if you could arrange – I hardly know how I may manage to-morrow,' said Captain Heron, acutely uncomfortable.

There was a slight pause. 'Then naturally I am quite at your service,' replied his lordship.

262

Twenty-two

The Viscount, resplendent in maroon velvet, with a fall of Dresden lace at his throat, and his hair thickly powdered and curled in pigeon's wings over the ears, came at his sister's urgent request to dine in Grosvenor Square before taking her on to Vauxhall. His presence protected her from *a tête-à-tête* and if Rule was minded to ask any more awkward questions he, she considered, was better able to answer them than she was.

The Earl, however, behaved with great consideration and conversed affably on most unexceptionable topics. The only bad moment he gave them was when he promised to follow them to Vauxhall if Captain Heron did not detain him at home too long.

'But we've no need to worry over that,' said the Viscount as he got into his coach beside Horatia. 'Edward's pledged himself to keep Rule in check till midnight, and by that time we shall have laid hands on that trumpery brooch of yours at last.'

'It isn't a trumpery b-brooch!' said Horatia. 'It's an heirloom!'

'It may be an heirloom,' replied the Viscount, 'but it's caused more trouble than any heirloom was ever worth, and I've come to hate the very mention of it.'

The coach set them down by the waterside, where the Viscount hired a boat to take them the rest of the way. They had three hours to while away before midnight and neither of them was in the mood for dancing. Sir Roland Pommeroy met them at the entrance to the gardens and was very punctilious in handing Horatia out of the boat on to the landing-stage, warning her against wetting her silk-shod foot on a damp patch, and proffering his arm with a great air. As he escorted her down one of the walks towards the centre of the gardens he begged her not to be nervous. 'Assure your la'ship Pel and I shall be on the watch!' he said.

'I'm not n-nervous,' replied Horatia, 'I w-want very much to see Lord Lethbridge, for I have a great desire to tell him just what I think of him!' Her dark eyes smouldered. 'If it weren't for the scandal,' she announced, 'I d-declare I wish he would abduct me, I would make him sorry he d-dared!'

A glance at her fierce frown almost persuaded Sir Roland that she would.

When they arrived at the pavilion they found that in addition to the dancing and the other amusements provided for the entertainment of the company, an oratorio was being performed in the concert hall. Since neither the Viscount nor his sister wished to dance, Sir Roland suggested that they should sit for a while and listen to this. He himself had no great opinion of music, but the only distraction likely to find favour with the Viscount or Horatia was gaming, and he wisely dissuaded them from entering the card-room, on the score that once they had sat down to pharaoh or loo they would entirely forget the real object of their expedition.

Horatia fell in with this suggestion readily enough: diversions were all alike to her until the ring-brooch was in her possession again. The Viscount said that he supposed it could not be more tedious than walking about the gardens or sitting in one of the boxes with nothing to do but to watch the other people passing by. Accordingly they made their way to the concert hall and went in. A play-bill handed them at the door advertised that the oratorio was *Susanna*, by Handel, a circumstance that nearly made the Viscount turn back at once. If he had known it was a piece by that fellow Handel, nothing would have induced him to come within earshot of it, much less to have paid half a guinea for a ticket. He had once been obliged by his Mama to accompany her to a performance of *Judas Maccabeus*. Of course he had not had the remotest notion what it would be like or not even filial duty would have dragged him to it, but he did know now and he was damned if he would stand it a second time.

A dowager in an enormous turban who was seated at the end of the row said 'Hush!' in accents so severe that the Viscount subsided meekly into his chair and whispered to Sir Roland: 'Must try and get out of this, Pom!' However, even his audacity failed before the ordeal of squeezing past the knees of so many musical devotees again, and after glancing wildly to right and left he resigned himself to slumber. The hardness of his chair and the noise the performers made rendered sleep impossible, and he sat in increasing indignation until at long last the oratorio came to an end.

'W-well, I think perhaps I d-don't care very much for Handel either,' remarked Horatia, as they filed out of the hall. 'Though now I c-come to think of it, I believe M-mama said that *Susanna* was not a very good oratorio. Some of the singing was p-pretty, wasn't it?'

'Never heard such a din in my life!' said the Viscount. 'Let's go and bespeak some supper.'

Green goose and burgundy partaken of in one of the boxes did much to restore his equanimity, and he had just told Horatia that they might as well stay where they were in comfort until midnight, when Sir Roland, who had been studying the throng through his quizzing-glass, suddenly said: 'Ain't that Miss Winwood, Pel?'

The Viscount nearly choked over his wine. 'Good God, where?'

Horatia set down her glass of ratafia. 'Ch-Charlotte?' she gasped.

'Over there – blue sacque – pink ribbons,' said Sir Roland, pointing.

'I c-can't see, but it sounds very l-like,' said Horatia pessimistically. 'She will wear blue and it d-doesn't become her in the least.'

By this time the Viscount had perceived his elder sister, and gave a groan. 'Ay, it's Charlotte sure enough. Lord, she's with Theresa Maulfrey!'

Horatia caught up her cloak and her reticule and retired to the back of the box. 'If Theresa sees us she'll c-come and join us, and we shall n-never shake her off!' she said agitatedly. 'P-Pel, do come away!'

The Viscount consulted his watch. 'Eleven o'clock. What the deuce do we do now?'

'We shall have to w-walk about the gardens,' decided Horatia. 'D-dodge them, you know.'

Apparently Mrs Maulfrey's guests were also seized by an inclination to wander about the gardens. No less than five times did the two parties almost converge and the Viscount whisk his sister round to hurry off down a different path, and when the conspirators at last found a secluded seat in the Lover's Walk the Viscount sank down upon it quite exhausted and declared that his sister might in the future lose every jewel in the Drelincourt collection before he would stir a finger to help her to recover them.

Sir Roland always gallant, protested. 'Pel, dear old boy, Pel!' he said reprovingly. 'Assure your la'ship – pleasure to be of assistance!'

'You can't say it's a pleasure to dodge round shrubberies and corners for the best part of an hour!' objected the Viscount. 'Not but what if we can but lay hands on Lethbridge I don't say it won't have been worth it.'

'What are you g-going to do with him?' inquired Horatia with interest.

'Never you mind!' replied the Viscount darkly, and exchanged a glance with Sir Roland. 'What do you make the time, Pom?'

Sir Roland consulted his watch. 'All but ten minutes to the hour, Pel.'

'Well, we'd best be moving,' said the Viscount, getting up.

Sir Roland laid a hand on his arm. 'Just thought of something,' he said. 'Suppose we find someone else in the temple?'

'Not at midnight,' replied the Viscount, having considered the matter. 'Everyone's at supper. Lethbridge must have thought of that. Are you ready, Horry? You ain't scared?'

'Of c-course I'm not scared!' said Horatia scornfully.

'Well, don't forget what you've to do,' said the Viscount. 'We'll leave you at the bottom of the Long Walk. Won't do to escort you any further. Fellow might be watching. All you have to do –'

'D-don't tell me all over again, P-Pel!' begged Horatia. 'You and Sir R-Roland will go to the temple the other way and hide and I am to g-go slowly up the Long Walk. And I'm not in the least afraid, except of meeting Charlotte.'

Several secluded paths led to the little temple at the end of the Long Walk, and since it was conveniently surrounded by flowering shrubs the Viscount and Sir Roland had no difficulty in concealing themselves hard by it. Sir Roland, indeed, was unfortunate enough to scratch himself on a particularly thorny rose-bush, but as there was no one within earshot at the moment this did not signify.

Meanwhile Horatia trod up the Long Walk, keeping a wary eye cocked for any sign of her sister. The Viscount had been right in supposing that most of the company would be at supper; Horatia met few people on the way. One or two couples were strolling down the Walk; near the lower end a party of young ladies were ogling in a very ill-bred manner every gentleman who passed; but towards the upper end the Walk grew more and more deserted. Encountering at first one or two stares from young bucks, Horatia felt rather conspicuous in being quite unattended, but her alarming frown stood her in good stead, and a rakish gentleman in puce satin who had taken a step in her direction retreated hastily.

The Walk was lit by coloured lamps, but a fine moon riding high in the sky made these almost superfluous, though pretty. At the end of the Walk Horatia could see the little temple, incongruously festooned with lanterns. She wondered where her faithful swains were lying in ambush and what Captain Heron was talking about in Grosvenor Square.

A few shallow steps led up to the temple. Feeling in spite of her brave words just a trifle apprehensive, Horatia paused at the foot of them and glanced nervously around. She thought that she had caught the sound of footsteps.

She was right. Someone was approaching down one of the smaller paths that led to the temple.

She drew her cloak closer about her shoulders, hesitated a moment, and then setting her lips firmly ran up the steps and into the temple.

The footsteps came nearer and she heard them on the steps and resolutely faced the pillared archway, secure in the knowledge that Pelham was within hail.

She was prepared for Lethbridge, or for a masked form, or even for a hired ruffian, but none of these sinister apparitions met her bemused gaze. It was the Earl of Rule who stood on the threshold.

'R-Rule!' she stammered. 'Oh, d-dear, whatever shall – I – I mean how you s-startled me! I was waiting for P-Pelham, I n-never expected to see you!'

The Earl came across the marble floor to her side. 'You see, I was able to – er – escape from Edward,' he said.

Outside, Sir Roland Pommeroy whispered aghast: 'Pel – Pel, dear fellow – did you see?'

'See?' hissed the Viscount. 'Of course I saw! Now what's to be done? The devil seize that fool Heron!'

Inside, Horatia said with a hollow little laugh: 'How – how d-delightful that you c-could come after all! Have – have you had s-supper?'

'No,' replied his lordship. 'I didn't come for supper, you know. I came to find you.'

Horatia forced a smile. 'That was very p-pretty of you, sir. But – but you should take some s-supper. Do pray g-go and bespeak a b-box and I will w-wait for P-Pel and bring him to join you.'

The Earl looked down at her whimsically. 'My dear, you are very anxious to be rid of me, are you not?'

Horatia's eyes lifted quickly to his, brimful of sudden tears. 'N-no, I am not! Only I – oh, I c-can't explain!' she said wretchedly.

'Horry,' said his lordship, gathering her hands into his, 'once I thought you trusted me.'

'I do – oh, I do!' cried Horatia. 'Only I've been such a bad wife, and I did m-mean not to get into a scrape while you were away, and though it w-wasn't my fault it n-never would have happened if I hadn't d-disobeyed you and l-let Lethbridge be a f-friend of mine, and even if you b-believe me, which I d-don't see how you can, because it's such an impossible story, you w-won't ever forgive me for having m-made another d-dreadful scandal!'

The Earl retained his hold on her hands. 'But, Horry, what have I done that you should think me such a bugbear?'

'You aren't a bugbear!' she said vehemently. 'But I know you'll w-wish you'd never m-married me when you hear what a scrape I am in!'

'It would have to be a very bad scrape to make me wish that,' said his lordship.

'W-well, it is,' replied Horatia candidly. 'And it's all in such a m-muddle I don't know how to explain it.' She cast an anxious glance towards the archway. 'I d-daresay you are wondering why I am in this place all by m-myself. Well –'

'Not at all,' said Rule. 'I know why you are here.'

She blinked at him. 'B-but you can't know!'

'But I do,' said Rule gently. 'You came to meet me.'

'No, I d-didn't,' said Horatia. 'In fact, I c-can't imagine how you knew I was here.'

His eyes were alight with amusement. 'Can't you, Horry?'

'N-no, unless –' her brows snapped together. 'Oh, surely Edward c-can't have b-betrayed me?' she exclaimed.

'Certainly not,' said his lordship. 'Edward made a most – really, a most praiseworthy – attempt to keep me at home. Indeed, I believe that if I had not taken him into my confidence he would have barred me into my own house.' He slipped his hand into his pocket and drew it out again. 'I came, Horry, to keep an assignation with a lady, and to restore to her – that.'

The ring-brooch lay in the palm of his hand. Horatia gave a choked cry. 'M-Marcus!' Her startled eyes flew to his and saw them smiling down at her. 'Then you – but how? Where did you f-find it?'

'In Lord Lethbridge's possession,' replied Rule.

'Then – then you know? You knew all the t-time? But how c-could you have? Who t-told you?'

'Crosby told me,' said the Earl. 'I am afraid I was rather rough with him, but I didn't think it would be good for him to know how deeply I was indebted to him.'

'Crosby!' said Horatia, her eyes kindling. 'Well, I don't care if he is your cousin, Rule, I think he is the m-most odious toad alive and I hope you strangled him!'

'I did,' said the Earl.

'I am very glad to hear it,' said Horatia warmly. 'And if it was he who t-told you, you c-can't possibly know the t-truth, because for one th-thing he wasn't there and d-doesn't know anything about it, and for another I am perfectly certain he made up some horrid t-tale just to put you against me!'

'That would be a task quite beyond Crosby's power,' said the Earl, pinning the brooch into her lace. 'I learned the true story from Lethbridge. But it did not need his or any man's word, Horry, to convince me that only force could have induced you to enter Lethbridge's house that night.'

'Oh, R-Rule!' Horatia quavered, two large tears rolling down her cheeks.

The Earl's hands went out to her, but a footstep outside made him turn. The Viscount came in, fluent words on his lips. 'Beg pardon to have kept you waiting, Horry, but Lady Louisa – Well, by all that's fortunate!' He executed a well-feigned start. 'Rule! Never thought to see you here tonight! What a lucky chance!'

The Earl sighed. 'Go on, Pelham. I feel sure you have some urgent message for me which will take me to the other end of the gardens.'

'Oh, no, not as far as that!' the Viscount assured him. 'Only to the boxes. Met Lady Louisa – looking for you all over, Marcus. She wants to see you very particularly.'

'What I chiefly admire in you, Pelham, is your resourcefulness,' said his lordship.

'Pel, it doesn't m-matter any longer!' said Horatia, drying her eyes. 'M-Marcus knew the whole time, and it was he who had the b-brooch, and wrote me that letter, and there's nothing to worry about any m-more!'

The Viscount stared at the brooch, then at Rule, opened his mouth, shut it again and swallowed violently. 'Do you mean to tell me,' he demanded, 'that Pom and I have been moving heaven and earth to get that damned brooch back when all the time you had it in your pocket? No, damme, that's too much!'

'You see, when you held me up on Hounslow Heath I found myself quite unable to resist the temptation – an over-mastering one, believe me, Pelham – of – er – leading you on a little,' apologized his lordship. 'You will have to try to forgive me, my dear boy.'

'Forgive you?' said the Viscount indignantly. 'Do you realize that I haven't had a spare moment since that brooch was lost? We've even had to drag a highwayman into it, not to mention poor old Pom's great-aunt!'

'Really!' said Rule, interested. 'I had the pleasure of meeting the highwayman, of course, but I was not aware that Pommeroy's great-aunt also had a hand in the affair.'

'She hadn't, she's dead,' said the Viscount shortly. A thought occurred to him. 'Where's Lethbridge?' he asked.

'Lethbridge,' said his lordship, 'is at Maidenhead. But I do not think you need concern yourself with him.'

'Need I not?' said the Viscount. 'Well, I've a strong notion I shall be on my way to Maidenhead in the morning.'

'You will, of course, do just as you please, my dear boy,' said Rule amiably, 'but I should perhaps warn you that you will not find his lordship in a fit condition to receive you.'

The Viscount cocked a knowing eyebrow. 'Ha, like that, is it? Well, that's something. Pom will be glad to know. I'll call him in.'

'Pray don't put yourself to the trouble!' besought his lordship. 'I do not wish to seem uncivil, Pelham, but I am constrained to tell you that I find you – shall we say a trifle *de trop*?'

The Viscount looked from Rule to Horatia. 'I take you,' he said. 'You want to be alone. Well, I think I'll be off then.' He nodded at Rule. 'If you take any advice, Marcus, you'll keep an eye on that chit,' he said severely, and walked out.

Left alone with her husband, Horatia stole a glance at him under her lashes. He was looking gravely down at her. She said, the stammer very pronounced: 'Rule, I truly w-will try to be the s-sort of wife you w-wanted, and not m-make any m-more scandals or get into any scrapes.'

'You are the sort of wife I wanted,' he answered.

'Am-am I?' faltered Horatia, lifting her eyes to his face.

He came up to her. 'Horry,' he said, 'once you told me that I was rather old, but in spite of that we married one another. Will you tell me now, my dearest – was I too old?'

'You're not old at all,' said Horatia, her face puckering. 'You are j -just the right age for – for a husband, only I was young and stupid and I thought – I thought –'

He raised her hand to his lips. 'I know, Horry,' he said. 'When I married you there was another woman in my life. She is not there now, my darling, and in my heart she never had a place.'

'Oh, M-Marcus, put m-me there!' Horatia said on a sob.

'You are there,' he answered, and caught her up in his arms and kissed her, not gently at all, but ruthlessly, crushing all the breath out of her body.

'Oh!' gasped Horatia. 'Oh, I n-never knew you could k-kiss like that!'

'But I can, you see,' said his lordship. 'And – I am sorry if you do not like it, Horry – I am going to do it again.'

'But I d-do like it!' said Horatia. 'I l-like it very m-much!'

AVAILABLE IN ARROW BY GEORGETTE HEYER

arrow books

ALSO AVAILABLE IN ARROW

Georgette Heyer:
Biography of a Bestseller

Jennifer Kloester

**The ground-breaking biography of one of Britain's
best-loved and best-selling novelists.**

Georgette Heyer remains an enduring international bestseller,
read and loved by four generations of readers and extolled by
today's bestselling authors. Despite her enormous popularity she
never gave an interview or appeared in public. Georgette Heyer
wrote her first novel, *The Black Moth*, when she was seventeen in
order to amuse her convalescent brother. It was published in
1921 to instant success and it has never been out of print.

A phenomenon even in her own lifetime, to this day she is the
undisputed queen of regency romance.

During ten years of research into Georgette Heyer's life and writing,
Jennifer Kloester had unlimited access to Heyer's notebooks and
private papers and the Heyer family records, and exclusive access
to several untapped archives of Heyer's early letters.

arrow books

ALSO AVAILABLE IN ARROW

Georgette Heyer's Regency World

Jennifer Kloester

A unique and beautifully illustrated companion to Georgette Heyer's Regency Novels

A bestselling novelist since 1921, Georgette Heyer is known across the world for her historical romances set in Regency England. Millions of readers love the period for its fashion, famous people and events, and its elegant and often outrageous mayfly upper-class. It was Georgette Heyer who created the Regency genre of historical fiction in the 1930s and 40s with books such as *Regency Buck* and *Friday's Child*. Since then, in many minds, Georgette Heyer and the Regency have become synonymous.

Not a dry history book, but the ultimate, definitive guide to Georgette Heyer's world: her heroines, her villains and dashing heroes, the shops, clubs and towns they frequented, the parties and seasons they celebrated, how they ate, drank, dressed, socialised, voted, shopped and drove. An utterly delightful and fun read for any Heyer fan.

'An invaluable guide to the world of the *bon ton*. No lover of Georgette Heyer's novels should be without it.'
Katie Fforde

arrow books

A Blunt Instrument

Ernest Fletcher, a man liked and respected. So when he is found bludgeoned to death, no one can imagine who would want him dead. Enter Superintendent Hannasyde, who slowly uncovers the real Fletcher, anything but a gentleman, and a man with many enemies. But the case takes a gruesome twist when another body is found . . .

Behold, Here's Poison

Gregory Matthews, patriarch of the Poplars is found dead. Imperious Aunt Harriet blames it on the roast duck he ate, but a post-mortem determines it's a case of murder by poison. Suspicion falls immediately on his quarrelsome family, and it is up to Hannasyde to sift through their secrets and lies before the killer strikes again.

Death in the Stocks

When the body of Andrew Vereker is found locked in the stocks on the village green, Hannasyde soon realises that this may be his toughest case yet. Vereker was not a popular man, his corrupt family are uncooperative, and the suspects are many.

They Found Him Dead

The morning after his sixtieth birthday party, Silas Kane is found dead at the foot of a cliff. The coroner rules death by misadventure, but when Kane's nephew and heir is found murdered, a new and sinister case develops for Hannasyde to investigate.

arrow books

ALSO AVAILABLE IN ARROW BY GEORGETTE HEYER

Cotillion

The three great-nephews of cantankerous Mr Penicuik know better than to ignore his summons, especially when it concerns the bestowal of his fortune. The wily old gentleman has hatched an outrageous plan for his stepdaughter's future and his own amusement: his fortune will be Kitty's dowry. But while the beaux are scrambling for her hand, Kitty counters with her own inventive, if daring, scheme: a sham engagement that should help keep wedlock at bay.

Venetia

In all her twenty-five years, lovely Venetia Lanyon has never been further than Harrogate, nor enjoyed the attentions of any but her two wearisomely persistent suitors. Then, in one extraordinary encounter, she finds herself involved with her neighbour, a libertine whose way of life has scandalised the North Riding for years.

Devil's Cub

The excesses of the young Marquis of Vidal are even wilder than his father's before him. But when the reckless duellist and gamester – the Devil's Cub – is forced to leave the country, Mary Challoner discovers his wicked plans to abduct her sister. And only by daring to impersonate her, can Mary save her sibling from certain ruin.

arrow books

The Reluctant Widow

Stepping into the wrong carriage at a Sussex village, Elinor Rochdale is swept up in a thrilling and dangerous adventure. Overnight the would-be governess becomes mistress of a ruined estate and partner in a secret conspiracy to save a family's name. By midnight she is a bride, by dawn a widow.

Arabella

Impetuosity is Arabella's only fault. An enchanting debutante and the eldest daughter of a country parson, she should know better than to allow herself to be provoked by Mr Beaumaris, the most eligible Nonpareil of the day.

Sylvester

Endowed with rank, wealth and elegance, Sylvester, Duke of Salford, has decided to travel to Wiltshire to discover if the Hon Phoebe Marlow will meet his exacting requirements for a bride. If he doesn't expect to meet a tongue-tied stripling in need of both manners and conduct, he is even more intrigued when his visit causes Phoebe to flee her home. They meet again on the road to London, where her carriage has come to grief in the snow. Yet Phoebe, already caught in one *imbroglio*, now knows she soon could be well deep in another.

arrow books

The Foundling

The shy, young Duke of Sale has never known his parents. Instead, he has endured twenty-four years of rigorous mollycoddling from his uncle and valet. But when the Duke hears of Belinda, the beautiful foundling who appears to be blackmailing his cousin, he absconds with glee. No sooner has he entered this new and dangerous world than he is plunged into a frenzy of intrigue, kidnap and adventure.

Charity Girl

When Fate and a chivalrous impulse combine to saddle Viscount Desford with a friendless, homeless waif named Cherry Steane, who else should he turn to in such a scrape but his old childhood playmate, Henrietta Silverdale?

Lady of Quality

Independent and spirited, Miss Annis Wychwood gives little thought to finding herself a suitable husband, thus dashing the dreams of many hopeful suitors. When she becomes embroiled in the affairs of the runaway heiress Lucilla, though, she encounters the beautiful fugitive's guardian – as rakish and uncivil a rogue she has ever met. Although, chafing a bit at the restrictions of Regency society in Bath, Annis does have to admit that Oliver Carleton, at least, is never boring.

arrow books

Sprig Muslin

Finding so young and pretty a girl as Amanda wandering unattended, Sir Gareth Ludlow knows it is his duty as a man of honour to restore her to her family. But it is to prove no easy task for the Corinthian. His captive in spring muslin has more than her rapturous good looks and bandboxes to aid her – she is also possessed of a runaway imagination.

The Black Moth

The disgraced Earl of Wyncham left England seven years ago, sacrificing his honour for that of his brother when he was accused of cheating at cards. Not long after his return, he encounters an old adversary, just in time to dispute at the point of his sword, the attempted abduction of a society beauty. But foiled once, the 'Black Moth' has no intention of failing again.

The Corinthian

The only question, which hangs over the life of Sir Richard Wyndham, notable whip, dandy and Corinthian, is one of marriage. On the eve of making the most momentous decision of his life, he is on his way home, when he chances upon a beautiful young fugitive climbing out of a window by means of knotted sheets.

arrow books

A Civil Contract

Adam Deveril, the new Viscount Lynton and a hero at Salamanca, returns from the Peninsular War to find his family on the brink of ruin and the broad acres of his ancestral home mortgaged to the hilt. It is Lord Oversley, father of Adam's first love, who tactfully introduces him to Mr Jonathan Chawleigh, a City man of apparently unlimited wealth with no social ambitions for himself, but with his eyes firmly fixed on a suitable match for his one and only daughter.

Bath Tangle

The Earl of Spenborough has always been noted for his eccentricity. Leaving a widow younger than his own daughter was one thing. Leaving his fortune to the trusteeship of the Marquis of Rotherham – the one man the same daughter had jilted – was quite another.

Black Sheep

Charming and wise in the ways of the world, Bath society-belle Abigail Wendover has tried hard to detach her spirited niece Fanny from a plausible fortune-hunter. Her efforts become vastly more complicated with the arrival of Miles Calverleigh. The black sheep of his family, a cynical devil-may-care with a scandalous past – why, that would be a connection more shocking even than Fanny's unwise liaison with his nephew.

arrow books

April Lady

When the new Lady Cardross begins to fill her days with fashion and frivolity, the Earl has to wonder whether she did really only marry him for his money, as his family so helpfully suggests. And now Nell doesn't dare tell him the truth. What with the concern over his wife's heart and pocket, sorting out her brother's scrapes and trying to prevent his own half sister from eloping, it is no wonder that the much-tried Earl almost misses the opportunity to smooth the path of true love in his marriage.

The Nonesuch

Sir Waldo Hawkridge – wealthy, handsome, eligible, illustrious, and known as The Nonesuch for his athletic prowess – believes he is past the age of falling love. But when he comes north to inspect his unusual inheritance at Broom Hall in the West Riding, his arrival leads to the most entertaining of ramifications.

False Colours

The Honourable Christopher Fancot, on leave from the diplomatic service in the summer of 1817, is startled to find his entrancing but incorrigibly extravagant mother on the brink of financial and social ruin – and more than alarmed to find that his twin brother has disappeared without trace. The unfortunate Kit is forced into an outrageous masquerade by the tangled affairs of his wayward family. But in the face of Evelyn's continued absence, Kit's ingenuity is stretched to the limit.

arrow books

An Infamous Army

In 1815, beneath the aegis of the Army of Occupation, Brussels is the gayest town in Europe. And the widow Lady Barbara Childe, as outrageous as she is beautiful, is at the centre of all that is fashionable and light-hearted. When she meets Charles Audley, handsome aide-de-camp to the great Duke of Wellington himself, her *joie de vivre* knows no bounds – until the eve of the fateful Battle of Waterloo.

The Unknown Ajax

Miles from anywhere, Darracott Place is presided over by irascible and short-tempered Lord Darracott. The recent drowning of his eldest son has done nothing to improve his temper. For now he must send for the unknown offspring of the uncle whom the family are never permitted to mention. Yet none of the beleaguered family are prepared for the arrival of the weaver's brat and heir apparent.

Cousin Kate

Kate Malvern, rescued from penury by her aunt Minerva, hardly knows what to expect at Staplewood – the grand household is so very different from a life spent following the drum in the Peninsula. But surely, other households are more homelike? When Kate begins to suspect the shocking reason for Minerva's generosity, she has no one to confide in but cousin Philip – who appears to have taken an instant dislike to her.